Awake
(Are We)?

Part 3
Judgment

Awake (Are We)?

Part 3
Judgment

Story by
Marty Connor

Written by
Marty Connor and Rosie J. May

Edited by
King Bad Dog

Strategic Book Publishing and Rights Co.

Strategic Book Publishing and Rights Co.
12620 FM 1960, Suite A4-507
Houston, TX 77065
www.sbpra.com

ISBN: 978-1-61204-816-1

Design: Dedicated Book Services, Inc. (www.netdbs.com)

I would like to once again dedicate the Awake Saga to my grandparents:

Joan Coble

Reginald Coble

Eva O'Connor

Fredrick O'Connor

May they all continue to rest in peace?

Contents

1

In the Beginning

"Three, two, one, here I come, ready or not!" announced Connor as he uncovered his eyes. "And remember, no cheating. I expect all of you to stick to the Wake World rules and not use your dream energy to blend into your surroundings. That wouldn't be fair on some of you, including me."

A tittering of glee from the hidden children echoed around the forest as Connor slowly and deliberately wandered through the trees.

"I can hear you," he cooed childishly as he walked.

It had been eleven years since the victory of the Great War against the Shadow Night Lord, and even now, all these years later, the armies of Sublin were still scouring their lands for the final remnants of the last few remaining Exsoms unable to return to their previous lives.

Despite their short time in Sublin, Connor and Will had easily settled into their new roles but of late, with little to occupy the Dream Lord's time, he and Will had been spending many hours playing with the nearby children and telling them stories of battles and victories.

"Hmm," joked Connor as he looked around a tree stump. "I wonder where you're hiding." Again he pretended to look around, deliberately overlooking a hidden child. "Nope, then maybe here?" he added as he teleported himself to a clearing a few metres away.

Once again the children giggled from their hiding places as Connor tried extremely hard not to find them, so as to continue with their game. A sense of juvenile fun emitted a carefree atmosphere around the Dream Lord, and only when he reached the Lantan tree did a strange disturbance alert him that something had upset the balance of normality. Instinctively he moved away from the concealed children. If there was a danger nearby, he did not want them involved.

Closing his eyes and focussing on the disorder, Connor tried to ascertain the unidentified sensation and its intentions, but nothing untoward entered his mind. So, fully satisfied that all was as it should be with the world, he opened them again.

"Hello?" he asked casually as he glanced around but as he looked, he noticed that his surroundings had now taken on a different image.

The glorious suns above him no longer pierced their warmth through the trees and the once bright, blue sky had been transformed to a dark, murky orange.

"Hello?" he echoed again as a cold breezed chilled up and down his spine. "Will? Children?" But there was no response.

Not even the giveaway laughter from their hiding places. Everyone had vanished.

"Ha, ha, ha very fun," he commented in an attempt to lift his own spirits. "You've got me, great joke. Just come out to where I can see you and I'll teleport you all home for lunch."

Still nothing moved, just an eerie silence numbing his ears. Not even a friendly breeze glancing lightly upon the succulent leaves ruffled the forest. Connor was completely alone.

"Where are you guys?" he muttered, more to himself than in expectation of a reply.

His heightened senses had already warned him to expect a response of some type but not one he could ever imagine. As if right on cue, a piercing screech ripped through the air and battered his ears. In a crude attempt to protect himself from the noise, he clapped his hands over them, but the clamour still managed to infiltrate his meagre defences.

"What the hell?" he thought to himself as his gaze was drawn upwards towards a blanket of blackness as it crept across the skies.

A pang of dread slithered into his mind as he recalled the last time this anomaly took place. It was during his last meeting with the Dark Shadow Lord.

"How can this be? Volnar was lost between worlds," he said aloud but there was no one there to acknowledge his statement, making him feel even more isolated as he continued to be mesmerised with an eerie fascination by the sky show.

The blackened cumulus had formed a dark hole and as the portal ripped open through the Sublin atmosphere, it released a screech of tortured souls. His sensitive hearing, deafened by the decibels of sound, caused Connor to drop to his knees in an attempt to protect himself again but nothing he did could escape such a resonance. Instead, his only defence was to watch and learn and try and conjure up a plan to shield himself from danger, should it be required.

In horror and macabre interest, he continued to watch as the portal spewed out a number of black silhouettes that floated silently earthward but landed with a stable thud as they touched the ground, not too far from his position. With the cadavers now deployed, the shrieking stopped and just as quickly as it had appeared, the portal closed and evaporated once more, into the darkness.

Connor looked around again and saw how his kingdom had changed once more. No longer did it project a colourful and vibrant environment, nor did the birds sing happily in the trees. It had plummeted, yet again, into the depth of darkness and despair, so reminiscent of his former adversary's time.

Dreading what was about to follow, his thoughts were suddenly broken by the sound of heavy footsteps pulsating against the solid ground and if Connor was not mistaken, which he very rarely was, they were heading in his direction. His options at this time were limited, apart from the obvious one of teleportation. This he quickly dismissed. With little understanding of the new surroundings, it would be foolhardy to jettison away, and so he decided that standing his ground to fight the new foe was the only solution left to him. Deliberately he took a deep breath and braced himself to his full height in preparation for a battle.

"Come on then," he said aloud. "So you think you can take me?" he bragged.

If there was one thing that could be said about Connor, it would be his immovable confidence in his own abilities but standing alone in the unrecognisable woods he felt somewhat vulnerable by this new arrival to his world and hoped that the skills of the Dream Lord would be sufficient to see him through.

Each second that passed, caused the darkness to evaporate from the skies, leaving an orange hew to shine upon the petrified kingdom and expose the two-by-two formation of what could only be assumed was the enemy. At first the visuals were not clear and Connor could only presume their identity. By his estimation, they were probably about eight feet in height, maybe more. It was merely an assessment, for the closer they advanced, the easier it was to see the hunched up profile of the silhouettes, giving a false impression of size. The really scary thing though was even when they were no more than a few feet away, Connor was still none the wiser as to their origins.

"What are you?" he asked but again not really expecting an answer.

The apparitions before him were nothing he had ever encountered before and in all his years of living in Sublin. he had come across some very strange things. These creatures were two-legged reptilian in visuals, supporting a toughened, leather, scaly skin protected by even stronger-looking armour. With their eight-foot height and their cold, black, beady eyes, it was safe to assume they were not beings of Sublin but more like throwbacks to the Jurassic age.

"What do want?" demanded Connor. "Why are you here?"

The creatures did not respond. Instead, two of them removed knives from each leg and took on a fighting pose.

"Is that the best you can do?" asked the Dream Lord, who was beginning to feel a little more confident after seeing their primitive weapons.

Again they did not speak but reacted by emitting a low growl from the back of their throats.

"Look," interrupted Connor, not intimidated by their show of aggression but still doing his level best to avoid a confrontation. "I'm not sure what business you think you have here but it is not with me or this world, so I suggest you just leave, peacefully."

Without warning, one of the creatures suddenly lashed out its tongue in a whip-like action, catching Connor on the side of his face before retrieving it again. As pain seared through the wound, the Dream Lord touched the wound. Blood was seeping from the laceration and it was of no surprise to him now why they only needed to carry additional knives. Their weapons of birth were the serrated tongues, sharper than a Samurai sword and used like the deadly "cat of nine tails." Definitely now in fear of his life, Connor took a few steps back in the hope he had moved out of range but as the other four creatures took on a similar stance, he figured this wasn't the case.

"Hey," said Connor as calmly as he could, "perhaps I was a little hasty. If it means that much to you guys, you can stay. Let's hang out together, take a walk, and chat about what it is you want."

The lizards took in a deep breath and Connor, pre-warned from their previous action, knew that another attack was on its way as two more tongues were spat in his direction. Quickly he threw an energy shield around himself but to his dismay, it did nothing for his defence, as the tongues penetrated the protection and caught Connor on his leg and arm.

"Now this could be a problem," he stated as the weapons retracted and he noticed the remaining creatures prepare for another attack.

Through speed of thought, Connor racked his brains for a solution but then suddenly heard a voice from behind.

"Drop to the ground Lord Connor, now!"

Without hesitation or checking out the command, Connor did as he was instructed, just in time to avoid the six, razor-sharp attack. Briefly he lifted his head to take a quick look, only to be shouted down again by the voice of his salvation.

"Please, my lord, for your own safety, stay down!"

Connor, well aware of the danger he was in, accepted any help being offered and immediately obeyed as he heard footsteps pass him by. Curious about his rescuer, he sneaked a quick look and although he was pretty sure he had never seen the being before, he felt a sense of familiarity about him.

The lizards attacked again and to avoid any inhospitable tongues, the being somersaulted into the air and away from danger. As he returned to earth, Connor caught a glimpse of his face.

"It cannot be," Connor muttered to himself as the warrior pulled out his glowing cinxi swords.

With the white heat of his arms running down through his weapons, he severed and cauterised the tongue one of the lizards. Howls of agony emitted from the drooling mouth as the injured figure fell to the floor next to Connor.

"Run back, my lord," advised the figure as the other lizards rushed forward and picked up their wounded soldier. With him safely out of the way, the remaining warriors intended to continue the fight.

Connor did as he was instructed. He scrambled to his feet and backed away from their attackers tripping over some vegetation in his way. Promptly he lost his footing and found himself once more hitting terra firma. Almost immediately though this time, two strong hands gripped him under the arms and dragged him up.

"Come, my Lord Connor, we must prepare to defend ourselves," said a second figure.

"Do you have him?" asked the first being.

"I do," was the response.

"Back, deeper into the woods," ordered the first warrior as he ran to join Connor and his new associate. "It will be far easier to isolate them there."

The three of them quickly retreated into the safety of the forest and within seconds they had found a safe hiding place as an excellent lookout point.

"How badly are you hurt, my lord?" said one of his rescuers

"I'm fine," explained Connor, somewhat agitated by the unexpected encounter. "What are those things and what's happening to Sublin?"

"My lord," apologised one of the men, "there is little time and even less for explanations but on your bidding I will keep it brief. Those creatures are known as the Razars. They are one of the inhabitant races of a hell dimension. We cannot be certain which one, for hell has many proportions of evil. The one thing we are sure of, though, is that the one you once knew as the Night Lord has procured their services.

"That is not possible!" exclaimed Connor. "My father and I banished him with the help of the Tukurak Knife to the limbo between worlds. There was no way he could have broken through."

"Indeed, my lord. That should be true," said the being, "unless he had help."

At that moment, the orange sky opened out her wings, scattering rays of light between the trees. It was only then did Connor get a proper look at his two new friends.

"This is impossible" he muttered. "Durban? How can this be?"

"It is me, my lord," replied Durban, "and you are very much still in Sublin."

"But you are . . ." began Connor.

"Dead, my lord," interrupted Durban. "I know I am, but a far greater danger has come to light and acting on instinct, I refused to let them pass judgment on me so I could choose my own ultimate resting place. My journey was not to relax in peace but be here with you once more, where I am needed the most."

"Forgive me, Connor, my lord," said the other being, "but we do not have time for further explanations. The Razars will be quickly upon us."

"Wait!" ordered Connor as he moved to leave. "Are you not Fortis?"

"Yes, my lord," Fortis replied. "Kustos was my salvation and rescued me from one of the hell dimensions. I was on my way to the Judgment Halls when I met up with Durban. He told me of the battles and pains of my beloved Sublin, and I felt an urgency to help in any way I could. Like him, I too have put my judgment on hold in further hope to save the ones I love and redeem the pain and suffering I cast upon them. The atmosphere of the Judgment World is buzzing. Something is going to happen. What, how, or when, none of us can possibly know but the one sure thing, is that you, my lord and Master Will are somehow involved."

Connor wanted to know more and was about to ask when he caught the stubborn look so often seen upon Kustos' face.

"Please, my lord" continued Fortis with some urgency, "forgive me for my impatience but we must make ready. The Razars will soon be upon us." And just as he had finished talking, a large tree trunk crashed inches from their feet.

"They're here," echoed Connor.

"Get ready, Durban, my lord," ordered Fortis. "These things will not stop until we kill them, or, alternatively, they kill us."

"Oh, that's a comforting thought," joked Connor, quickly getting back into the swing of defending himself in a fight. "Just how are we expected to do that?"

Fortis took the lead and as he stood his ground, his arms burst into flame in readiness.

"Ready?" he shouted back at Connor and Durban.

"I have a question," said Connor anxiously, "for those of us that cannot charge our arms with fire. Do you have any tips on how we can take these things down?"

"They do have a weakness, my lord," explained Durban. "Their armour, if you look, does have a certain amount of vulnerability. It exposes their knees and elbows and is joined at the base of their backs. If you can get close enough to them, you can slice the arteries on their knee and elbow joints, which, trust me, will stop them immediately from fighting."

"That shouldn't be too hard," replied Connor. "I'm sure I'm quick enough to dodge their tongues."

"That might be so, my lord," continued Durban, "but as you have probably already noticed, your Dream Energy is useless against the Razars. It does not have the unique essence required to penetrate the creatures of a hell dimension, or that is what I am led to believe."

"Then I'll have to use plan B." Connor grinned.

"Plan B, my lord?" asked Durban.

"Yes." Connor smiled. "Just do your best not to get killed."

Durban smiled to himself as he remembered the bravery of the young Dream Lord and knew then that he had made the right choice in forestalling his destiny. His presence in this latest adventure was yet another epic for the survival of the three worlds, or so he thought, and with the new skills he had learned in the Judgment World, it was his intention to see that Connor took that pathway.

Menacingly, the Razor troop stood their ground, each waiting their turn to fight. The first assailant spat out his tongue, and it shot past Fortis, directly towards Connor. Aware of the danger, the Dream Lord was about to sidestep it but Durban issued his own command.

"Stay fast, my lord," he ordered as he threw his arms into the air and created a shield of liquid metal around them.

The projectile, skimming the shiny surface, veered off towards Fortis who instinctively swung his cinxi swords to defer the lethal weapon. His hope was that he somehow managed to slice it from its owner, but the Razar's reaction was far too quick as the tongue was recalled efficiently back into its mouth. Silently the creature smiled to itself with malevolent pleasure as it conjured up the next plan of action. Fortis was not about to give him another chance to bombard them with the serrated weapon and ran towards the warrior, heating his body as he moved. By the time he reached his opponent, his legs were burning white, and a single kick toward his adversary was sufficient to melt through the armour and burn into the ribcage, destroying the bone structure as it passed through.

Horror briefly swept across the Razar's face as the reality of its
fate infiltrated through its mind. Darkness glazed over its thoughts
before extinguishing its evil life force.

Fortis, aware of the danger he was now in, quickly regained
balance as he sensed a breeze of movement whip past his face,
and he threw himself to the ground. Evidently the Razars were not
happy about losing a colleague and were now directing their rag-
ing anger unanimously upon him. Rolling as fast as he could along
the ground, Fortis attempted to keep moving. His only hope was
their inability to get a clear target, but unfortunately, the plan was
not successful as he found himself about to get stabbed through
the chest by an oncoming tongue. In defeat, Fortis closed his eyes
and was surprised that no pain followed. Slowly he opened them
again, and there beside him were Connor and Durban.

"How can this be?" Fortis asked.

"Guess my dream energy has some uses against these things."
Connor smiled.

"But you teleported, my lord," said a confused Fortis. "Durban
never mentioned that."

"I dare say there's quite a few things Durban hasn't told you,
none of which he considers that important," replied the Dream
Lord.

There was no time for further conversation about the unique
skills that Connor had acquired as another attack of the deadly
tongues flickered dangerously in their direction. Again, Durban
threw up the liquid, metal shield, and the three tongues bounced
uselessly away.

"How do you do that?" queried Connor, hoping that it was
something he could claim for himself as another method of
defence.

"It has taken many patient years, my lord," replied Durban,
"but it was worth the effort. I have learned to manipulate objects

by using the iron in my blood. It is conducted into liquid metal, which enables me to generate the shapes. Once I am satisfied with the creation, it can be cooled to harden as our protection, a very useful trick with these creatures."

No sooner had he finished his explanation than the shield around them dissipated and dissolved back into his body. Connor was impressed by Durban's skill and wondered how long it would take him to control such elements. Immediately would have been his choice, as three Razars began menacingly edging their way towards him but with only the powers of Sublin, he decided to check out exactly what he could use in his own defence. At first, he charged his arms and fired a stream of electricity directly at an oncoming Razar. Unfortunately, his attack was unsuccessful as the creature stood his ground and absorbed the power like a flower soaking up the sun's rays on its open petals.

"Hmm," mused Connor, "I guess I can strike that one off the list."

With the Razar preoccupied with the electrical charge, Connor turned his attentions to Fortis and Durban. Both were engrossed in arm-to-arm combat with two of the Razars. Totally focussed on their own survival, neither one of them noticed the imminent rear attack. Durban unfortunately was the member of the duo about to be outnumbered from both sides and Connor racked his brains to provide some support.

"I need to be able to fight Fortis," exclaimed Connor, already understanding his own vulnerabilities.

"I agree," replied Fortis. "Catch." And with that he threw Connor what looked like a pair of gloves.

Reactively he caught them and slipped them over his hands. They were, in fact, like a half glove. No fingers to hold the clothing in place but still slipped directly over them and rested across the top of the hand. From each of the gloves protruded a metal shard, sharpened to the intensity of a Razar tongue. Quickly, Connor tightened the strap around each wrist and flexed his fingers in preparation, just as he sensed a rush of air whisk past his face. Immediately he responded to the challenge and turned just in time to catch a glimpse of a Razar about to make a second attack. Instinctively, like the warrior he had become, Connor dropped to the ground and with adept agility, rolled towards the waiting creature. Concluding this action, he ended up facing his attacker on bended knee with arms outstretched. His newly acquired weapons sliced easily through the kneecaps of Razar and immediately they began to spew a putrid, greenish, brown, sticky liquid. Surprised by such an assault, the monster fell to the ground but as he did so, he managed to spit out a final attack. Connor, prepared for a reluctant submission, rolled again but this time to the side, the same direction as the Razar. On his return to his knees, he stabbed forward and caught the creature in both eyes, blinding him in an instant. The Razar knew it had lost and aware of its ebbing life force, submitted quietly to the ground as it waited to die.

Confident that his enemy was no longer a threat, Connor turned his attention once more towards his friends. Durban was in the worst situation as the Razar behind him was almost close enough to attack. Connor knew he would not be able to reach them in time and instead shouted a warning.

"Durban! Shield!" he yelled.

Without hesitation, Durban engulfed himself in his metallic defence, just in time to feel the vibration of a heavy thud as a serrated tongue crashed into its parameter. The force made such an impact that the old captain of the guard stumbled to the ground.

"Keep the shield up," instructed Connor as he ran towards Durban.

One of the Razars licked its lips as he watched the Dream Lord run towards him and mused over what fate he could inflict upon the young lord. Confusion though quickly covered his face when the image he saw before him no longer filled the space and instead of victory being his, he felt a sudden, sharp pain in his arms and legs. Turning around to face his aggressor, he saw patches of blood soaking the ground. The Razar knew this essence was undoubtedly his and as he looked a second time, he saw Connor standing before him with a sticky substance dripping from the hand knives. A strangled gurgle of unintelligible sound emitted from the creature's mouth, as if asking what magic Connor had used.

"Ever heard of teleportation, my friend?" said Connor as he stared into the dying eyes. "No? Well, I guess that was to my advantage then."

Convinced that the Razar was no longer a threat, Connor once more turned his attention to Durban but before he had an opportunity to ask about his welfare, he noticed the old soldier throw his shield out once more but this time to protect Fortis. The timing was impeccable as a tongue crashed against the hardened pod.

"We must regroup," ordered Durban.

The others agreed and avoiding attacks from the remaining three Razars, they huddled together behind Durban's shield.

One creature managed to creep to the left of the group but Fortis, aware of its closeness, decided an opportunity for its destruction had shown itself. Leaning down towards his boot, the prince retrieved a small knife. It was the last resort in case a situation like this ever arose, a weapon to be used if faced with a final judgment from the evils that haunted them now. Carefully, so as not to affect the others, he charged up his arms as the white heat of fire ran down to the tip of the knife.

"When I ask for the shield to be dropped for a second, Durban, please do not question me," said Fortis.

Durban nodded his acknowledgment as Connor looked on with curiosity. They had an obvious understanding of one another and it reminded him very much of his own relationship with Will.

"Steady . . . steady," Fortis warned. "Now, Durban, now!"

Immediately obeying the order, Durban lowered the shield and in a split second, Fortis aimed and threw his knife. In a slightly longer second, Durban reraised the shield. Together the three of them watched as the knife flew through the air. The impact of the throw and sizzling heat from his energy cut clean through the Razar's neck, severing the head cleanly from the body. The headless corpse stood its ground for a moment before limply collapsing into a heap.

"Nice move," applauded Connor.

"You also, can I say, are fighting well, my Lord Connor. Better than I would have given you credit for under such circumstances," replied Fortis.

"A wise warrior once told me to take advantage of the opportune moments and not force a victory just for the glory. That way you will stay alive a lot longer," said Connor with a smile.

"A very wise warrior indeed," agreed Fortis. "Who was this man?"

"Not was, but is," replied Connor. "The warrior is Kustos."

Fortis smiled with pride. His younger brother had grown into a wise and honourable king, just as their father had hoped.

"This is no time to remember old friends," reprimanded Durban. "We are doing well but there are still two Razars to dispose of. We must focus if we are to complete this mission."

"You are right, my friend," replied Fortis as they began to back away towards the woods.

"Wait a minute," interrupted Connor. "I think I've a way of taking them both down together."

Durban and Fortis looked at one another briefly. Fortis had not experienced Connor's hair brained schemes before and was slightly nervous at such a suggestion. Durban however nodded his approval and smiled at Fortis to reassure him of Connor's intentions. Having watched the Dream Lord fight at the battle of the Great Waterfall Kingdom, he understood that although some of his methods were unorthodox, he was an unusually skilled warrior.

"Have you two ever combined your strengths together?" asked Connor.

"My lord," said Durban, "I do not follow this plan of thinking."

"It is alright." Fortis smiled. "I think I do." And he quickly began to charge up his arms. "When I give the word, Durban, I want you to create as many metal spikes as you can and throw them towards the Razars," he added.

Durban did as he was instructed and dropping their metal shelter, he quickly recreated a number of large spikes. As they sped away towards the Razars, Fortis raised his arms and threw intense heat over the projectiles, forcing them to consume the energy as they hit their mark. Several weapons pinned a Razar against a tree as the spikes melted from the heat and began dissolving the armour and flesh of its victim. Pain surged through the creature's brain as its evil essence of life evaporated into a pool of sticky liquid on the ground.

The second soldier tried to run away but the spears homed in on the metal armour and forced themselves through into the flesh. Just like its companion, the Razar liquefied into a mass of gloop.

"I hope that's the last of them," said Connor as they walked over to the gooey remains. "They certainly make a mess when they die."

"I would never have thought of combining our forces," exclaimed Fortis. "That was a brilliant idea, my lord."

"Nah, not so much," replied Connor who was embarrassed by such adoration. "It was nothing . . . really."

After the demise of their final victims, Durban recalled his metal spears and absorbed them back into his body. The heat from Fortis' energy had passed, and all that remained was a number of lifeless bodies.

"Where can I get me some of that?" asked Connor as he watched the liquid disappear within Durban.

"I cannot answer that, my lord," replied Durban.

"Just kidding." The Dream Lord smiled. "It seems I still have much to learn about the skills of Sublin."

"Sublin I think you know, my lord," Durban assured him, "but now the Judgment World is what you must understand."

"Not for a very long time, I hope," Connor replied.

Fortis was checking that all the Razars were dead by kicking them violently where they lay.

"It seems this time that we have lived to tell the tale." Fortis grinned as he returned to the duo.

"But what does it mean?" asked Connor. "Why did they come and what do they want?"

"They wanted you, my lord," explained Fortis, "but this is merely a taste of the trouble we will be facing in the Judgment World. A battle is ensuing, and only you can finish it once and for all. Perhaps with a little help from us, of course."

"I can't go there," stated Connor, "I thought you had to pass over via the pathway to the Judgment World. Unless I'm mistaken, I appear very much alive in Sublin, or at least I did before you guys turned up. Besides there's another thing, my dream energy, as you've told me, is useless in that world anyway so what help can I give you?"

"In its present form, I agree, it is useless," continued Durban, "but your energy will evolve in the Judgment World. It will become the purest form of yourself, your very essence, your soul energy."

"And how am I supposed to get there? Commit suicide?" asked Connor.

"No, no, my lord," Durban quickly assured him. "You must go and see Oakhanogan. He holds all the answers on how you can pass over to the Judgment World."

Connor was not totally convinced. He wanted to understand more and was just about to ask them how they managed to escape in the first place when a serrated tongue headed straight for his heart. The weapon was too close to react and so Connor closed his eyes and prayed for a miracle.

At first he felt or heard nothing but then the sound of his name echoed in his ears and he forced himself to open his eyes.

"Connor . . . Connor?" he heard Will say. "What the hell is going on? You're creeping me out."

Cautiously Connor looked around.

"Where's Durban and Fortis?" he asked. "The Razars were here." And he pointed to the ground where they had left the defeated warriors but nothing out of the ordinary was there.

The two suns once more shone upon the lush grasses, painting the woodlands and skies in the glory of its iridescent beauty for as far as the eye could see.

"I think we need to talk, Will," he whispered to his friend. "Children, my little friends," he announced to the still hidden children, "I am sorry but Will and I must attend to urgent matters. Please stay and play together, and I will send someone with a picnic."

Will looked at Connor, knowing that his friend was not prone to the dramatic and wondered what had unsettled him but before he had a chance to ask, Connor had grabbed his wrist and teleported them both back to the throne room.

2

So What's the Plan?

"What happened to you?" asked Will, once they were alone.

"I'm not sure," replied Connor as he picked up a goblet and sipped the cold, refreshing liquid. "I was hoping you could tell me that."

"All I know is that you suddenly stopped what you were doing and froze just like a statue," said Will. "At first I thought you were messing about but then the colour from your face drained away and I feared that some sort of hex had been cast upon you. What happened? Where did you go?"

"I don't think I went anywhere," explained the Dream Lord. "From what I can remember, I was there in the forest, only everything had changed. The sky was no longer bright, and darkness had once more shrouded the world, just as it did in the times of the Shadow Night Lord. At first, I thought I was dreaming but when a portal from a hell dimension spewed out these revolting creatures called Razars, I knew then it was no hallucination."

"Come on, Connor," interrupted Will, "you know how overactive your mind can be sometimes."

"I don't want to take your nightmares lightly," smiled Connor, "but this is me we're talking about and tell me when you can ever remember me having a nightmare in this world—or even you having one for that matter."

"So if it wasn't your overactive imagination," asked Will, "then what was it?"

"The easiest explanation I guess," surmised Connor, "is perhaps I was drawn into some type of portal that enabled me to interact with the Judgment World."

"But how can that be? You expect me to believe you were in the Judgment World?" queried Will, who had no idea what Connor was attempting to describe.

"After all we've seen and done, you still doubt your own eyes? I tell you I was in the Judgment World," Connor assured his friend.

"But how can you be so certain?" asked Will. "It's not as if you know what it's like."

"Because I met Durban and Fortis—that's how I know," was the response.

"Wasn't that Kustos' brother?" said Will.

"Yes he was . . . is," Connor corrected, "and as we both know, they took the pathway to the Judgment World eleven years ago."

"Then, if you think this is a portal, how come you spoke with them? Surely they would have passed over at least a decade ago?" asked Will who was still confused by Connor's latest adventure.

"I was puzzled by that as well at first but it was definitely them," said his friend emphatically. "They told me they had refused sentence, for fear of what would happen to the Judgment World if they left it to fend for itself. It's him, Will. He's broken through."

"Him, who?" asked Will and then the implications dawned on him. "Oh lord, no," he replied as he sat down.

Many memories came flooding through his mind of the Dark Lord and not one of them he found comforting.

"How do you know all of this?" he suddenly asked.

"Durban and Fortis must have created some sub reality and somehow managed to tune into my dream energy," said Connor, "but they were not the first to contact me. Before their arrival, I watched another enemy appear through the portal, a creature known as the Razar, just the type of monster that the Dark Lord would take great delight in recruiting. They are tough, Will, far harder to defeat than the Exsoms."

"But surely your power can take them out," stated Will.

"If only that were true," replied the Dream Lord. "Most of my power was useless against them. It was only my teleportation that got us out of trouble."

"You mean Durban and Fortis?" asked Will.

"Yes," came the reply. "They turned up when I became outnumbered. Without them, I doubt I'd be here to tell you the tale."

"Are you really sure this wasn't a dream?" queried Will again but even as he asked the question, he knew exactly what the answer would be.

"This was no dream. You know that's impossible in Sublin," responded Connor, "and the more I think about it, the more I'm convinced that something really bad IS going to happen . . . again. Durban and Fortis need our help. They told me that someone from the Judgment World had pulled him through."

"And by HIM, you mean Volnar?" grimaced Will.

"Yes, the Dark Lord. My uncle," agreed his friend. "Durban and Fortis also told me that beings with that type of power, who can manipulate the realms of limbo, could only have resided in the Judgment Halls. Can't you see what's happening here? The Dark Wars are beginning all over again, only this time with the assistance of a more potent ally. This is our fault so we have to take on this fight, Will," said Connor as he sat down next to his friend. "We have to find a way into the Judgment World and ensure that Volnar is destroyed once and for all. It was my mistake that left him in limbo, so it must be my responsibility to ensure he doesn't take over the Judgment World and use it for his own evil means."

"Okay," replied Will. "I can see your point and let's say for argument sake that what you've experienced is true. Durban and Fortis are still in the Judgment World and asked for your help. How are we expected to join them, without exactly killing ourselves that is? You know judgment would be passed on to us as soon as we step foot in the place."

"You doubt me?" said Connor as he watched Will squirming uncomfortably in his seat. "How can you disbelieve when you accepted so much of this strange world in the early days? Has your comfortable life made you forget? If that's the case, then maybe this is one fight I should take on alone."

"Have you heard yourself lately?" Will chuckled.

"What?" asked Connor.

"We're alone you know, so no need for heroics." His friend laughed. "Besides you've got to be kidding me if you think you can leave me out of this one," he exclaimed as he jumped to his feet and strutted backwards and forwards in front of his friend. "How dare you even consider leaving me behind? I'm supposed to be the Dream Warrior, you know. We're a team, remember? It's not that I don't believe you, for as you said, we've experienced more than our share of the unusual. I just don't understand how we're expected to get to the Judgment World, that's all."

"Well, that's a relief." Connor smiled. "For a minute there I really thought you were going to make me do this alone."

"As if you could survive without me," joked his friend.

Connor laughed again and felt comfort in the fact that despite how bizarre his story was, Will still had the faith to follow him on some wild adventure.

"We have to visit Oakhanogan," he told Will. "Durban told me that he is the oldest and wisest seer in Sublin and will be able to show us the pathway of the Judgment World."

"So teleport us there already and let's get started," said Will.

"I don't think I can," confessed Connor. "It's been many years since we entered that forest and to be honest I didn't really take a lot of notice of where it was at the time. It didn't seem that important and what with the trees continually hiding our way, I could never be confident of getting us to the right place."

"Then don't," said Will, "just take us somewhere close. How about the field we arrived in? Surely, you haven't forgotten that. I know I haven't."

"How could I forget the milestone of our existence," replied Connor. "It was the turning pointing of our destiny. One that I know I couldn't have taken without your help."

"Then it's agreed." Will grinned, feeling somewhat exuberant about this latest adventure, despite its seriousness. "Things were getting a little routine around here anyway. Some excitement once every eleven years is hardly taxing of my position as your Dream Warrior, now is it? I might as well earn the wages you're paying me."

"But I don't pay you," said Connor.

"In that case," replied Will, "then I'll just have to stick with you until you put your hand in your pocket and reimburse me for back pay."

"So I take it by your remarks that we do this, then?" asked Connor.

"You're my friend, Connor and where you go, I follow," came the response.

Connor breathed a sigh of relief. As much he knew he could take the journey alone, he much preferred the company of his life-long friend.

"Thank you," he said with a smile. "I was hoping you'd say that." And with that, he took Will's arm and swiftly transported them to the fields outside of Oakhanogan's forest.

Within seconds they were staring over the grasslands of a familiar sight. This was where they had their first encounter with the

Metalmares and made the transformation from two normal young men into absolute warriors.

"Wow!" exclaimed Will as he looked around. "It's just as I remembered it from all those years ago. Though, I must admit, the grass could do with a good mowing."

That was an understatement, as the lush meadow grasses had grown taller than either Connor or Will and standing on their toes, they could almost make out the parameters of the forest, someway in the distance.

"I think I can see the forest over there," said Connor, pointing in the direction he sensed it should be.

"Hang on and I'll check," replied his friend.

Slowly Will began to walk forward and as he did so, he gradually lifted from the ground so that his head was about a foot above the seven-foot grass. Over the years, he had perfected the use of his gravity power and found its usefulness an asset in his everyday life.

"Yep," he agreed, "you're right. The edge of the forest is about half a mile in front of us."

Gently Will descended to the ground and the two friends wandered off in the general direction. Bee-like creatures flittered silently amongst the tall stems and only the soothing hum from crickets and grasshopper like creatures broke the silence. In essence, this was the personification of harmony and yet to think that a disruption in its reality could once more threaten its existence was more than Connor was prepared to contemplate. His duty as the Dream Lord of Sublin was to ensure the safety of every realm under his mantle and if that meant once more taking up arms against his old enemy, then so be it.

As they reached the forest edge, they found the tree that almost saved their lives from the Metalmares was still standing. The broken branch that had once exposed their identity was lying on the ground, enriched with brightly coloured fungi taking advantage of the still succulent sap.

"Was it really all those years ago that we fell into Sublin?" asked Will.

"Hmm . . . yes it was," mused Connor as he shuffled his foot through the leaf-littered floor. "I sometimes find it hard to believe myself. It seems like only yesterday."

"Do you ever think about the Wake World and what our lives could have been like had we not come here?" asked Will as he looked around again.

"Sometimes but not so much now," replied Connor. "Somehow the future there doesn't seem so important anymore. I know it's our history and all that and I'll never forget it but life is what you make of it, wherever you are. If we were back in the Wake World, we'd probably be doing nine-to-six jobs, having a bit of fun here and there when we could afford it and just existing, like everyone else. Had we not experienced the wonders of Sublin, it wouldn't have mattered but since we have, I wouldn't want to be anywhere else. This is my home now and my life and with the exclusion of avoiding death on a massive scale, I've enjoyed every minute of it. It's been nothing but one long fantasy, only for real."

"I have to agree with you there." Will nodded. "Our life has been the type of adventure novels have been written about. For me, I couldn't have asked for anything more. I'm only glad that I've experienced it with you. Otherwise you might accuse me of dreaming again."

"No. Our adventures have been no dream," Connor assured him.

"I can agree with that," replied Will, "but still think there's something funny about all this."

"And that would be what?" queried Connor.

Will was about to air his thoughts and then thought better of it so decided to change the subject and hope Connor had not noticed.

"Do you actually know the way to Oakhanogan?" he asked his friend.

"Well . . . ," mused Connor as he stroked his chin in thought, "I don't think I do. It was Kustos who led us to him last time and as we were both shell-shocked by our experiences with the Metal-mares, I didn't really take a lot of notice of our route. I guess this is going to be lot harder than I first thought."

Together the two of them stared into the depths of the forest, trying to recognise any single landmark that might jolt their memory but nothing came to them. It all looked the same. For all they knew, this could have easily been any other forest of Sublin. Only when the leaves began to sway backwards and forwards when there was no wind to caress the foliage did Connor believe that help was at hand. The movement became more urgent and as the two warriors watched, a pathway began to show itself.

"I think they want us to follow," suggested Will as he stepped towards the opening. "Why aren't I surprised that the forest will take us to Oakhanogan?"

"Because we're familiar to it," replied Connor as he joined him. "The forest has protected us in the past and now it'll lead us once more towards our destination. It knows we've important business with Oakhanogan that cannot wait."

Will laughed.

"What's the matter with you?" asked Connor.

"Have you heard yourself talk recently?" Will replied. "You're beginning to sound more like Kustos than he does."

"I take that as an insult," said Connor indignantly. "I've been giving Kustos lessons on the Wake World language."

"Well, all I can say is that I think Kustos has been rubbing off on you," Will said with a smile as he laughed again.

"Get away with you," chuckled Connor as he pushed his friend forward. "I'm your boss, remember?"

"However could I forget that, sir." And Will bowed sarcastically.

⚜ ⚜ ⚜

For several hours the two of them wandered aimlessly through the forest, following the pathway shown to them by the moving tress but as they reached closer towards its heart, the pace of the exposed route quickened.

"Something's wrong," Connor told Will as he sensed panic within each branch and leaf. "Oakhanogan is in danger."

"How can you know that?" asked Will.

"I don't know," replied Connor. "I can feel it." And to confirm his suspicions, a tortured screech resounded throughout the compacted trees.

"Oakhanogan," whispered Connor as he slowly peered through a small gap that had appeared before them.

As they focussed on the clearing, what little light that managed to pierce through the thickened flora exposed two unfamiliar figures.

"What are they?" whispered Will as he watched. "I've never seen anything like that before. Are they Razars?"

"No," replied Connor. "These aren't the creatures I encountered earlier. I've no idea who or what they are but one thing is for sure . . . they're not of Sublin."

As they continued to watch for a moment, the two creatures unrelentingly carried on with what they were doing, oblivious of the onlookers only metres away. Their noticeable task from what Connor could decipher was to cut down the Great Lord Oakhanogan. Wanting to take a closer look, he took a step forward and as he did so, the bracken snapped and crackled beneath his feet, echoing around the quiet forest. The slight disturbance unnerved

the creatures and for a moment they stopped what they were doing to investigate. Cautiously one of them moved forward, leaving
him only metres from where Connor and Will were hiding. This
gave the Dream Lord an opportunity to see what they were up
against and what he saw, he did not like that much.

On first viewing, it looked almost human but as Connor perused the figure more closely, he could see this was not the case.
Its skin was pale, grey in colour and looked far too big for its
body, as it hung in large wrinkles at every possible point of expo-
sure. The face held no distinctive features, apart from the fact it
had no eyes and Connor wondered to himself how the creatures
managed to see their way around. Perhaps the pointed ears on the
hairless head acted as some sort of sonar but that was only sup-
position, as opposed to fact. Their attire was also not unusual and
the wasted tunic over black trousers and boots could have been
purchased in any one of his realms, which in turn offered very
little indication of their identity.

"Boy," whispered Will, "they certainly are ugly looking but I
reckon we can take them. Look, they don't even have eyes." With
that he pushed his way into the clearing.

"Will, no!" shouted Connor as he tried to stop his friend but
the warning fell upon deaf ears as Will continued to confront the
new enemy.

Once in the clearing, Will ran silently towards one of the creatures, rising into the air with each step. When he was fully satisfied he was directly above the life form, he drew up the pressure
from his created gravity and thrust it upon the being below. Oakhanogan's attacker, oblivious of the assault, continued to cut away
eagerly at the old sage. Against any foe of Sublin, this gravity
offence would have crushed anything in its path but as the atmo-
spheric ball fell to the ground, it slid off the creature's framework
to merely create a ditch around it. Will followed and found himself within fighting distance of the unknown assailant.

Taken aback by the surprising reaction of his power, he turned to face the enemy, just in time to receive a blow that sent him flying backwards past Connor into a tree. Despite the unexpected attack, Will still had the foresight to control sufficient gravity and create padding around himself, preventing a fatal injury. Instead, he thumped into the tree trunk and ended up in a heap, sprawled across the complex rooting system.

"What the hell was that?" asked Will as he scrambled to his feet, rubbing his shoulders.

"You okay?" Connor asked with concern from his hiding place.

"I'll live," was the response.

Satisfied that Will was still able to back him up in a fight, Connor forced himself through the trees protecting him from detection and started to walk towards the creature. By this time, it had put down its saw and was making its way slowly towards Will. Seeing the immediate danger, Connor quickly charged up his electrical energy and threw it in the direction of the two life forms. As previously experienced with Will, the dream power recoiled harmlessly off them and bounced back towards Connor. Nonchalantly he absorbed the approaching force back into his own body but was knocked slightly backwards.

"A little too much power," Connor admitted to himself as he stepped forward again in preparation of another shot.

"Connor," Will shouted across the clearing, "see if you can direct the force to Oakhanogan's trunk and try and seal the damaged area."

"Good idea," replied Connor as he once more summoned up his electrical charge and released it in the direction of the tree.

The moment the energy touched the trunk it began to melt the injured area and harden like a protective film, sealing the precious life force of Oakhanogan within.

"We must defend Oakhanogan at all cost," Connor told his friend as Will joined him by his side. "He's the key to our mission."

"But how?" asked Will. "Our powers appear ineffective on these beings. What are they?"

"I've no idea what they are," replied Connor, "but I had the same problem with my weapons being ineffective against the Razars, and they were supposed to have come from a hell dimension. Now these things aren't Razars, but if I was a betting man, I'd also assume their natural habitat is from another dimension. Despite their haggard skin, lack of vision, and the look of an ancient man, they're nimble and pick up on our every motion. I've no idea how it's done, but what species they are is unimportant."

"Well, that's not very comforting," scoffed Will as he rushed towards them.

Frantically he kicked and lashed out, but despite the fact that he managed to lay a couple of blows on them, very few made any real impact as they ducked and dived out of the way.

"They're too quick for me," Will muttered to himself before calling to Connor. "A little help would be nice!"

Connor was taking a moment to watch their adversaries and could not believe how comfortable they were in the surroundings, considering they had no obvious vision. Another sense must have been providing them with the information, one that was not obvious to the human eye. Quickly he racked his brains to create an attack plan, but as Will appeared in need of assistance, he dared not take a minute longer to find an answer. Aware now that his electrical power and Will's gravity energy were useless, he thought perhaps arm-to-arm combat might be a better ploy, and so gearing himself up to use his speed kicks and punches, he rushed into the fight. For a while his plan actually worked—that was until one of the creatures caught him squarely in the chest and knocked him to the ground. Momentarily immobilised, the strange warrior then stuck his foot on Connor's chest plate, pinning him to the undergrowth. As the weight increased upon his body, so did the indent on the ground beneath him. It was fortunate that the softness of the earth was surrendering under the weight, that way at least Connor was not being crushed to death.

Will was having little success as well, as the second creature grabbed him by the neck and lifted him from the ground. Connor managed a quick glance to see his friend's situation. In fact it was pretty dire—he was gasping for air as the hand tightened around his throat. Connor continued to watch in helpless fascination. The creature, suitably satisfied with its victim, opened its mouth. The mandibles expanded to the complete width of Will's head and as it leaned over, it inhaled a deep breath. Will yelled in pain and wriggled powerlessly, as he felt the essence of his life force being sucked from his body. Like blood from a donor, he began to weaken as the energies were dragged from him. Connor looked up at his own captor as it laughed.

"You're . . . next," it sneered in a deep, rasping whisper.

Connor and Will had been overpowered, and a tear rolled down the Dream Lord's face as he watched his friend slowing dying. When all looked futile, out of nowhere, two blue energy pulses whizzed from behind a tree and hit the creature torturing Will. Surprised by the attack, he dropped his prey, allowing Will to quickly regain some composure in order to summon up as much gravity energy as he could in the time permitted. Satisfied of its power, he threw it in the direction of the already stricken creature but this time with greater effect. The pressure of the energy blast was more than it could contain, and the sound of crushing bones, one by one, reverberated around the clearing. Within seconds, it lay motionless on the ground. Its final action was the gapping of its oversized mouth. As it dropped opened, Will released another scream as his stolen energy homed back to its owner and rejoined the collective.

The second being appeared unmoved by such an attack as it held its pose over Connor. It did however sway its head menacingly from side to side as if trying to sense its counterpart.

"So you are vulnerable then?" said Connor, who had already worked out the weakness of the creature.

Will turned towards the direction from where the lifesaving pulses had appeared and was delighted to see Kustos and Jasmine standing there ready for further action.

"How did you find us?" asked Will.

"We will explain everything later," replied Kustos, "but right now I think Master Connor needs our help."

The three of them took a step closer to Connor but the crushing weight on his chest warned him the frontal attack was not going to work.

"Back away from me," ordered Connor as he stared hard into Will's face.

For a moment Will held the gaze and then nodded his acknowledgement of the plan.

"Can you get inside his mind, Jasmine?" he asked turning to her. "Tell him we've run away."

Jasmine smiled her own understanding of the situation and took a step forward. Closing her eyes, she focussed on the being's mind as she congratulated herself with the success of her efforts. The life form, convinced by her suggestion of their evacuation, removed his foot from Connor and knelt over him.

"It's worked." And Will smiled.

"But to what purpose?" asked Kustos. "Connor is still in danger."

"Only slightly," added Will. "We do have a plan, but for it to work that creature needs to think it's safe so that it can endeavour to steal Connor's essence of life. It appears their only vulnerability is when they are preoccupied with stealing your life force."

For a second time the huge mandibles dislocated at the jaw and extended to the size of Connor's head. Its hand was now around the Dream Lord's neck, pulling him from the ground, making it easier to feast upon his soul.

"We need it to feed on Connor," said Jasmine, "so you two can do whatever it was you did last time to kill it?"

"Well, that's the idea." Will answered.

"But how did you know that was the plan?" asked Kustos.

"Connor and I have learned to communicate through thought," responded Will. "It happened by chance when playing with the children and since then we've perfected it to an art form."

The creature by this time was beginning to feed, and Connor squirmed in pain as his essence was dragged from his body. Then, just as before, Kustos fired one of his blue bolts, forcing it to release its prey. The Dream Lord fell to the ground as Will once more called upon his gravity ball. When happy with its level of strength, he cast it towards the warrior. The creature's death was equally as quick as its companion's, and its mouth once more dropped opened, releasing what little essence it had managed to procure from Connor. He yelled out in pain as the life force pushed its way back into his soul.

"That was interesting," Jasmine mused as she freed her hold over the creature.

Connor scrambled to his feet and took a deep breath to refresh the staleness in his lungs.

"Am I glad to see you, old friend." He smiled, patting Kustos on the shoulder. "As usual your timing is impeccable. How did you know we were here?"

"We followed you, Lord Connor," replied Jasmine as she curtseyed before him.

Connor laughed and hugged her.

"I'll never like that." He smiled as he let her go. "Nor would I ever expect it of anyone of Sublin."

"You are looking well, Connor," Jasmine added, "or should I say, did up until a few hours ago."

"What made you follow us?" Will asked, still shaken by the encounter.

"Kustos and I were travelling through the woods when we overheard the children mention that Connor was acting strange. Well, . . . stranger than normal that is—" Jasmine continued.

"And you know what women are like," interrupted Kustos, "if they think you are in need of their services."

Jasmine hit Kustos playfully on the arm and tried to hide her embarrassment at the implication.

"That is not true," she said emphatically. "You were just as curious as me."

"It is true, Connor," Kustos admitted. "I was interested. By the tone of the children, they were worried over your actions, so they must have been unusually out of the normal for you. Anyway, we followed you back to the throne room, admittedly a little slower in arriving without the added bonus of your teleportation and heard you talking about Oakhanogan."

"So why didn't we know you were there?" asked Will.

"I must apologise," said Jasmine. "I did not think you were ready to divulge your secret and mind altering your thoughts into believing you were alone was the only way we could get close to you."

"Why did you think I had a secret?" Connor asked her.

"Because your thoughts were unclear to me, Connor," she replied, "jumbled in a protective way. It is not my normal habit to read your mind but the aura you were emitting was one of grave concern."

For a moment Connor showed little reaction and then a broad smile filled his face once more.

"Well, I'm glad you did listen in to our conversation and follow us to the forest. Without your help, both Will and I would have been lost and for reality in its present form, that would not be a good thing."

Kustos kicked one of the creatures lying still on the ground.

"What were these things?" he asked.

"Whatever they were," interrupted Jasmine, "was not of this world. When I looked into their minds all I could hear was noise and confusion, the sounds of thousands of painful cries from all walks of life. It was the most awful thing I have ever listened in to." And tears filled her big, brown eyes as she remembered the pain. "It was the sound of tortured souls, neither dead nor alive but . . . trapped."

Kustos put his arm around his wife to comfort her as she continued.

"Only once they were dead did the agonising sobbing cease and a sense of peace and freedom hovered through the air," she added.

"You're right in assuming the existence of these things is alien to our world," said Connor, "and it's for that reason alone Will and I are here to speak with Oakhanogan, but for you, I can't even hazard a guess why you're so far from your home."

Kustos was about to reply when the stillness of the forest was invaded by a strong breeze.

"I suggest we all hold on to something!" shouted Connor above the noise.

Kustos and Jasmine smiled at one another as they grabbed the nearest tree. Connor and Will quickly did the same as the breeze began to draw its strength to full power. The inert bodies of the creatures were lifted helplessly into the air like rag dolls until they finally hit the massive trunk of Oakhanogan and split into pieces.

After several minutes of lashing wind, Oakhanogan eventually awoke, and the attack of the elements subsided, leaving the gentle rustling of leaves as the forest breeze caressed their palms once more. Suddenly, the huge tree trunk before them creaked and the features of a face began to appear, line by line, until finally the full image of the ancient tree was complete.

"Lord Connor," Oakhanogan said in its whispering voice, "I am indebted to you for my life. Without your timely visit and energy, I would have seen my last days in this wonderful world."

"I must curse myself for delaying too long," replied Connor. "Had we been earlier, no pain would have been inflicted upon you."

"Pain is what tells you that you are alive." And the old tree smiled.

Jasmine wiped a tear from her eye as she stared at the ancient legend. All her life she had heard tales of the great Oakhanogan and that privileged few would ever stand in his presence, but here she was before the oldest living being in Sublin.

"My great, wise, old friend," said Will, "your knowledge is vast and infinite. Tell us what those creatures were and why they trying to destroy you."

The tree moved his eyes to look at Will.

"Ahh, Master William." It smiled. "You have come a long way since our last meeting. You look more like a man who belongs here now."

"Thank you, my lord." Will bowed in an attempt to show his appreciation of the compliment.

"Those creatures," continued Oakhanogan, "were once the Oracle of Judgment. Their roles—to discuss with the higher Oracles what verdict should be passed . . . a simple task for simple minds.

Over time, one or two of them became curious and found that rather than passing judgment and sending the souls to a final resting place, they had a better use for them . . . consumption of their energies. Just like the Dream Stealers that you defeated. Over time, the power of these souls became addictive to them, and their only way of survival was to feed upon soul after soul. For this reason they were named the Soul Crunchers and banished from the Judgment Halls, whilst at the same time condemned to walk the Judgment World alone and survive in any way they could.

"One day, quite by chance, these monsters found a master. One who promised them a war and as many souls as they could find. In return for his leadership, they would become his minions."

"Don't tell me, I think I already know the answer to this one," interrupted Connor. "This new leader of theirs is Volnar, isn't it?"

For a moment no one spoke as the silence deafened their ears.

"So it is still not over?" said Jasmine in disbelief.

Oakhanogan did not reply, instead Connor offered what little explanation he understood.

"So Durban and Fortis were right, Oakhanogan?" he said and turned to Kustos to explain. "Your brother and Durban have not yet passed on from the Judgment World," he told him.

"I cannot believe that," exclaimed Kustos. "I set him free to follow the path."

"And in a way, Kustos, he did." Connor smiled. "When he arrived at the Judgment World, your absolution gave him an insight to his destiny, and he knew then that he had a greater purpose to fulfil than taking the path of judgment. He found Durban, and together they remained hidden."

"That is impossible," interrupted Kustos.

"Not so strange, Lord Kustos," interrupted the ancient sage. "Lord Connor speaks the truth. It is correct that someone pulled Volnar into the world against his will. His name is Armon. When

Armon realised what he had done, he ran from the Judgment Halls and found Fortis and Durban. Together they joined their soul energy to send out a message to contact Lord Connor, which dragged him into the sub realm between Sublin and the Judgment World. That way they could ask for help."

For a moment Oakhanogan stopped as if waiting for any questions, but as none were offered, he continued with the explanation.

"Unfortunately," he added, "they had not realised how quickly Volnar had increased in strength, and he tapped into the distress call and sent some of his new army after Lord Connor."

"What? The Soul Crunchers we have just defeated?" asked Jasmine.

"No, my lady," answered Oakhanogan.

"No, Jasmine," Connor reiterated. "It was the Razars that Fortis, Durban, and I were forced to defend ourselves against. They have lizard-like tongues as sharp as the blade of Kustos' sword that they use in a whip-like fashion and, their armour is more solid than that of the Sanies Bug."

"So I take it because you are here, they were defeated," interrupted Jasmine again.

"Yes but only by using our combined skills and the weakest spots in their armour," replied Connor.

"But how do you know about this, Lord Oakhanogan?" Will asked the old tree.

"I am privy to all knowledge, young William," he answered, "as I am the link between Sublin and the Judgment World. What I did not foresee was the Soul Crunchers also breaking through the portal."

"So that was why they were trying to destroy you?" mused Connor. "So you couldn't warn us of coming events?"

The old tree said nothing for the moment but instead took pleasure in the soft breezes rustling through his leaves.

"Do you remember, young masters," he finally said, "when we first met all those years ago, I told you it was safe. I was not referring to your pathway of the time, although it suited my purpose for you to believe so, but to the portal within me that links to the Judgment World. I have been its receptacle for thousands of years. It is protected by the Guardians of the portal, who will not permit just anyone to pass. You, Master Connor and William are not yet ready for this accolade but if you wish to finish this fight you must learn to handle the skills that will evolve once you cross over."

"By cross over, I assume you mean there's no way back?" asked Will.

"That is not exactly true," replied Oakhanogan. "It is not that there is no return . . . just that no one has ever attempted it before."

"So what do we need to do?" asked Connor, who was really trying not to focus on the fact this might be the last time he stood on the ground of the place he had come to love as his own.

"If you are ready to take on this fight," continued Oakhanogan, "you must go to the Untouched Forest, the home of the Hallucium, unseen by any man. There you must reacquaint yourselves with Lord Thisabow. He will advise you what must be done."

"Can we go as well?" asked Kustos.

"No, Lord Kustos," replied the tree, "only Lord Connor and Master William are permitted to take the tests. If you are both successful and Lord Thisabow is in an amiable mood, then maybe he will let your friends join you in this fight. Now go, my lords, and see how much you have learned in Sublin. Once you have completed the tasks return to me and I will help you pass through the portal."

Kustos and Jasmine were about to protest but before either of them had an opportunity to speak, Oakhanogan asked Connor to step forward.

The large, droopy eyes of the ancient tree stared caringly into Connor's face. The Dream Lord stared back and the bulky gnarled branches groaned and creaked as they engulfed him within their protection, hiding him from the rest of his friends. As he looked around the open space, there standing beside him was Oakhanogan, tall and strong, just as he would have been in his youth.

"Lord Connor," Connor heard him say but saw no movement from his mouth, "you have learned much and survived all hurdles placed in front of you. For this I am proud of you, as if you were one of my own, but the pathway that you are about to undertake is far more dangerous than anything you have ever encountered before. When you meet with Lord Thisabow, show him the courage that you have bestowed upon the rest of us. A time will come when your heart will feel like giving up. Do not be swayed by weakness and remember that hope can always pull you through. You will be asked to act upon faith more than fact and to teleport to places you have never seen before. Trust in your own instincts and search deep within your soul. There you will find the answers to permit you to travel to infinite places, not just within this world . . . but in the next. Many will never know the sacrifices you have made for this world but my memory is long and will never forget what you have done for us."

Connor had so many questions, but before he had an opportunity to ask them, the branches silently retracted themselves and he found himself once more back with his friends, surrounded by the flora of Sublin. Oakhanogan was no longer present and all that remained was for him and Will to find the Untouched Forest. He turned to face his friends to say his final farewells but before he could speak, Jasmine caught his eye. She looked at him, serene and calm, with an expression of understanding as if she too had experienced his vision.

"I have heard the wisdom of Oakhanogan," he heard her say in his head. "It seems it is not enough the dangers we have all been through together and I fear there are still many more left for us to face. As spoken by Oakhanogan, I too will never forget all you have done for the people of Sublin and what you are about to face for the survival of the Judgment World. This time though the burden of our fate does not rest with you alone. Do not shut us out. Both Kustos and I have sworn to serve you, and we will lay down our lives to be by your side."

Connor smiled and although the mission bestowed upon him by Oakhanogan daunted him, he felt some comfort knowing that his trusted friends would be there to help. Acknowledgement of Jasmine's declaration was offered by a simple nod of the head, and he hoped the slight action was unnoticed by anyone else. For him to be at one with her mind was his own private sanctuary.

"What was that all about?" asked Will, turning to Jasmine for an explanation.

"Oakhanogan was giving me instructions on what we must learn to take this forward," replied Connor. "I'm to teleport us to the Untouched Forest. There we shall meet with the Halluciums who will present us with a task to prove our worth in the Judgment World."

"Are you able to transport yourself to a place you have never visited before?" asked Kustos.

"Since being in Sublin, Kustos," replied Connor, "I'd say anything is possible."

"In that case, Lord Connor," said the Lord of the Waterfall Kingdom, "my faith is in your abilities. Go to the Untouched Forest and find Lord Thisabow. Do what must be done and return for us."

"Does this mean you want to help?" asked Connor, hoping that Kustos would not desert him now.

"Without a second thought, old friend," he quickly replied. "This is an opportunity for me to fight one last time by my brother's side—"

"And where Kustos goes, so do I," interrupted Jasmine as she slipped her tiny hand in his.

Kustos was about to stop her but looking at the beautiful and determined vision before him, he knew his efforts would be futile.

"Besides," she added, "I might not be a physical warrior but my mental abilities have increased dramatically. I can be of great use in such a place as the Judgment World."

"In Sublin, Jasmine, I would say that was true," said Connor, "but this is going to be different."

"In what way?" asked Will, Kustos and Jasmine together.

"In the way that we can't rely upon our powers," Connor told them.

Will and Kustos remained unfazed but Jasmine let out a quiet, "Oh."

"That's not to say we are powerless," continued the Dream Lord, "Just that they take on different forms, some of which might not be of use. As well as that, we don't have the numbers for a full frontal attack and you can bet that Volnar has a whole army of fighters. This time we must slip in unnoticed. Once in the Judgment World, we must treat it as a covert operation."

"A what?" queried Kustos.

"A secret mission," Will advised him.

"That is not an honourable way to fight," replied Kustos.

"Nor was the way Volnar tried to take over Sublin, . . . but he did it anyway," Connor pointed out.

Kustos nodded confirmation of the devious methods Volnar attempted in an effort to take over Sublin and smiled.

"Then a covert operation it is," he agreed sternly.

"Great," continued Connor. "What we'll need to do once in the Judgment World is find a backdoor into the Hall of Justice. I'd bet a month's pay that's where Volnar's hiding out. Hopefully, he'll not expect us and with the element of surprise, we could take him."

"One disadvantage to your plan," pointed out Kustos. "We do not know the Judgment World or some of the races of people that do not wish to be reviewed. How will we recognize who we can trust?"

"We'll find your brother and Durban," Connor told him, "they'll know. They've found allies in this world that we can rely on."

"And how do we fight?" asked the lord of the Waterfall Kingdom.

"We must quickly learn what powers can be of use. In this world they evolve and what we once thought was to our benefit could cause an opposite effect. The only known useful aspect of this world is arm-to-arm combat, although it'll be difficult to determine the weakness of an enemy. Basically, the way I see it . . . is that this is a one-way trip with no return."

Kustos looked at Jasmine before speaking.

"So you are telling us that, we might not be able to use our powers, we will be greatly outnumbered and anyone we fight might be indestructible?" asked Jasmine.

Connor nodded.

"Oh . . . and that it is a one-way mission?" Kustos added.

"That's about the size of it," replied Connor.

"Then all I can say," said Kustos with a grin, "in the words of the Great Dream Lord Connor . . . sounds like our kind of fight."

Connor laughed at Kustos' imitation of his colloquialism.

"If you're sure about this," he finally added.

"Just one small problem," interrupted Will, "that neither of you have thought about."

The others looked at Will and waited.

"You guys are the main rulers of this world. You can't all leave, in case something happens here. Who would defend the realms if this was all a plot to get you out of the way?"

"I can see your point," agreed Connor, "but in my case Sublin spent many years without a Dream Lord, so I doubt if a few months will make a lot of difference. For Kustos and Jasmine though, it could be a problem."

"Not at all," Jasmine quickly replied, "although my parents are old, they still have the abilities of people half their age. They will look after the Waterfall Kingdom until our return and believe me . . . we will return."

Her voice was so determined, it was almost as if she had glimpsed the future and Connor, Will and Kustos took comfort in her words.

"So it's agreed then," said Connor. "I'll teleport us first to the edge of Mallusion where Will and I will take our leave of you. We shall then go to the Untouched Forest while you both wait for our return."

Accepting the challenges that lay ahead, they gathered around Connor. Slowly he closed his eyes and imagined the forest parameter of Jasmine's beloved home. Instantly they vanished.

"So this is it for the time being?" said Kustos as they reappeared at the edge of the Forest of Mallusion.

"I guess so," agreed Connor who really hated goodbyes, especially when he did not know whether or not he was ever going to come back.

"Remember, Connor," smile Jasmine, "I will be with you always. So do not think you can leave us behind."

"As if I dare," smiled Connor as he stared intensely into Jasmine's eyes and was suddenly lost.

She bounced her thoughts around his mind and he understood immediately how fond she was of him. He had never been able to bring himself to defy her in any way, despite the dangers it might lead to.

"Take care, my friends," he finally added. "Enjoy your time together and prepare for our return."

After several handshakes and hugs, Kustos and Jasmine turned away and within minutes, they had vanished deep into the forest.

3

The Untouched Forest

"Time to go then?" said Connor when he noticed they were finally alone. "Are you ready?"

"I suppose so," Will replied with trepidation in his voice. "Are you sure you can do this?"

"Not really," Connor said, "but there's only one way to find out."

And with that he grasped Will's shoulder, picked one of the flashing lights he saw around him and finally closed his eyes. Instantly they vanished.

"Did it work?" asked Will seconds later, not daring to open his eyes.

"I don't know," replied Connor. "I haven't had the nerve to look, but it can't be all that bad, because we both appear to be okay. Let's open on the count of three," he suggested. "One—"

"Two, three," interrupted Will quickly as he opened his eyes.

Surprised by the seven-foot grasses that marred his vision, he mumbled a bemused response. "I recognise this place," he added. "We're in the Yarra fields."

"Okay, okay, so I didn't get it right first time," Connor responded somewhat disappointed by his efforts. "This time . . . I promise."

"It's no big deal." Will laughed. "We're still in one piece aren't we? You'll just have to give it another go, that's all."

Again Connor closed his eyes and once more they disappeared from view.

"How about now?" he asked, not daring to open them again.

"Nope, sorry," replied Will. "We're on the borders of the Waterfall Kingdom this time. Let's try the best of three, shall we?"

"We could be pinging around like this for hours," Connor pointed out to his friend. "I see so many places when I teleport. It's just too difficult to pick one I don't know."

"I think that's the problem," suggested Will. "You're trying too hard. You should clear your mind and allow the empty space to fill naturally with images that it feels you want to see, not the ones you already know of."

"You could be right," Connor admitted, now with a little more confidence in his voice. "I'm sometimes prone to over analysing things and it obviously doesn't help here. Close your eyes, let's try again."

"You over analyse? Did I hear correctly?" joked Will. "What's happened to Connor? Who is this impostor?"

"Very funny," laughed Connor as his friend's comments broke his self-imposed tension. "Seriously, just close your eyes."

Will did as he was told and immediately they vanished. This time though he was positive that Connor had mastered the new skill and on arrival both opened their eyes.

"Are we there yet?" asked Will as he looked around at the unfamiliar landscape.

"Well, I don't recognise this place. Do you?" replied Connor.

Will shook his head as he looked around.

"So we agree this could be the Untouched Forest then?" queried the Dream Lord.

"But shouldn't a forest have trees?" Will pointed out as the lush grass glistened and swayed in the sunshine.

"It does," answered Connor, excitedly pointing in the distance, "over there. That has to be the Untouched Forest."

"Well, it certainly lives up to its name, that's for sure," commented Will as he stared at the mass of vegetation. "I doubt if anyone has been here for years."

As they moved closer to the forest edge, they noticed how inhospitable it appeared. Not at all as they expected. Each tree stood proudly side by side, barely allowing an inch of light to penetrate inside, let alone a gap wide enough for any living being to pass through. Every branch over centuries of plentiful sunshine had intertwined with its brothers and sisters, building an impassable barrier of bark and leaves.

"Yep," said Connor as he stared at the wall of plant life, "this has to be it."

"So you did it," said Will excitedly. "You really did it. With just a little more practice you'll be able to teleport anywhere, which I guess in the scheme of things to come, is what you'll have to do but still, it's great it worked. Aren't you pleased?"

"I guess I am," answered Connor, who for the moment had not considered his great achievement. "It felt strange not having a picture in my mind. Normally when we teleport, I have all these pictures and lights around me and I can choose where to go. This time, all I had was darkness, with a single thought in my mind. It felt kinda weird but at the same time a real buzz."

"It just sounds so wicked," replied his friend who was completely blown away by Connor's latest addition to his skills. "It

means that with time you'll improve and be able to teleport anywhere. How cool is that?"

"I guess it is," agreed Connor who was preoccupied with how
they were going to get into the Untouched Forest, more than how
they had actually got there. "Hmm!" he mused. "This could be a
problem though."

"There must be a way in," suggested Will as he perused the
area with his friend. "How else would the Hallucium manage to
leave?"

"They don't exactly need to walk anywhere, do they?" answered Connor. "They just sort of appear and disappear when it
suits them."

"Maybe so," said Will, "but Oakhanogan wouldn't have sent us
here if there was no way of getting into the forest, now would he?"

"Perhaps this is part of the test," stated Connor as he began
wandering along the parameter of the forest in an attempt to find
a way in.

"Maybe . . ." mused his friend, "or maybe they just want to be
left alone. Do you remember when we met Lord Thisabow? He
seemed nice enough and I can't bring myself to think he lives in
this dingy, old place, lost to the world. This must just be a barrier
of trees . . . a living wall."

"I agree with you there," replied Connor. "There's a reason
we're here now and all we have to do is find out what it is."

"Didn't Lord Thisabow say something about reporting to a
higher life form?" asked Will, trying to recall their conversation
eleven years earlier.

"I believe he did," agreed the Dream Lord.

"Then perhaps that's why their realm is so protected," surmised
his friend. "They don't actually belong here and if that's the case,
they might not take too kindly to us visiting."

"Well, looking at this forest, I don't see us visiting anywhere unless we can find a way in," replied Connor.

"Any chance of teleporting?" asked Will.

"No way, not this time," answered his friend. "There appears to be some kind of magic creating an invisible barrier around the forest, a safeguard to keep out unwelcome guests. That has to be the answer otherwise I'm certain Volnar would have undoubtedly found his way here long ago."

"Good point," agreed Will, "and as we don't have any magical skills that can get us in, I guess this is as far as we go, then?"

"I'm not so sure," surmised Connor. "Oakhanogan would not have sent us here if he thought we'd fail at the first hurdle. There must be a hidden entrance somewhere. All we have to do . . . is find it."

"Well, if there is," said Will, "damned if I can see it. It could be anywhere around the parameter."

"It could be, but I doubt it," replied Connor. "My power would not have brought us to this area if there was no way in. I'm convinced of that. All we have to do is look around a bit until we find it."

"Well, I'm glad you're oozing with confidence," moaned Will, "because I'm not."

"Am I not the Dream Lord?" smiled Connor. "Can I not do amazing things? Finding the entrance will be just another demonstration of my incredible skill."

"Okay then, boss," said Will, "so get us inside then?"

"I will, just wait and see," laughed Connor as he started to look around the lower levels of the trees. "How about that tree trunk?" And he pointed to a fallen tree resting at a thirty-degree angle.

"As if it would be that easy," Will scoffed as he bent to the ground and looked through the end of the trunk. "I don't believe it," he muttered. "It's hollow and if I'm not mistaken, just wide enough for us to crawl through."

"And you didn't believe me," scoffed Connor.

Will raised an eyebrow in disbelief and was about to say something when he thought better of it. For whatever reason, Connor had found the entrance to the Untouched Forest and no real explanation was going to tell him how it was done.

The trunk, although hollow and on first reflection their way in, did not appear to be big enough for them to squeeze into and for a moment the two men stood staring at it, weighing up their options.

"Basically . . . it's this or nothing," stated Will.

"I'm inclined to agree with you there, my friend," replied Connor.

"So! Do we take a little bit of that faith of yours and give it a go?" asked Will.

"I think so," replied his friend, convinced this was the entrance he was supposed to find. "I can't explain it, Will, but I actually think this is our way in, put here for just the two of us to find."

"Some more of that magic?" asked Will.

"Yes!" came the response. "Put aside for us alone. Come on, follow me." And Connor got down on the ground and started to pull himself slowly through the hollow tunnel. "That's odd!" he shouted back. "There seems to be more room in here than I thought."

Connor was right, for as soon as Will also began to pull himself through, he sensed the rim began to retract to accommodate his frame, making the journey far less claustrophobic than either of them had anticipated.

"Well, that was easier than I expected," Connor announced as he pulled himself finally through to the other side and tumbled out into the open.

As he got to his feet, he took the time to survey their surroundings in case of danger but the vision that faced him allayed all his

fears. From the image of the outside of the forest, he had conjured up pictures of closeted, darkened shadows and mystery but
instead he was met with brilliance and colourful illuminations that
made him blink at the splendour. The forest was abundant with
exotic flowers of every hue, providing the sweetest perfumes to
ever fill their noses and yet at the same time inciting the gentle
buzz of insects as they flittered from one flower to the next, collecting their daily rations. In front of them ran a river, reflecting
the silvery rays as they bounced from the open skies whilst rip-
pling carelessly over the colourful stony bed. Fish of every creed
and size swam happily along the current as they dodged playfully
in and out of the swaying, reeds.

"Wow!" echoed Connor. "This is beautiful. I always wondered
why Sublin had two suns, and now I know the answer. The second
one is dedicated solely to this place."

Will bent down and scooped up a handful of water.

"This water is fantastic," he told Connor. "The best I've ever
tasted."

"I guess you can understand now why the Halluciums wanted
to be left alone," surmised the Dream Lord. "If I had a place like
this, I wouldn't want intruders to destroy it either."

"So now we've made it this far, which way do we go now?"
asked Will.

"No idea," replied Connor, "but we've got here by guess work
so I suppose the rest of the journey shouldn't be any different. How
about following the river? It looks as though it's running into the
forest. That way we'll either find Lord Thisabow, or he'll find us."

"Sounds like a plan to me," answered his friend, who promptly
started walking along the riverbank.

Connor took one last look around them and followed. For several hours they travelled in silence as they took in the scenery
and relaxed from the fragrances floating through the air. At that

moment in time, there was no purpose to their life, just the enjoyment of their surroundings.

Suddenly, out of the blue, Connor broke the silence.

"Did you hear that?" he said as he stopped to listen again.

"Hear what?" asked Will.

"The sound of laughter, I heard the sound of laughter," he reiterated. "There it is again."

Will strained his ears, but all he could hear was the river, burbling blissfully along.

"I don't hear anything," he replied. "I know you have oversensitive hearing, but all this peace and quiet must be playing tricks with your senses."

"I'm telling you," replied his friend emphatically, "I definitely heard someone laughing."

Will was again about to defy Connor's super hearing when he also heard a sound, but instead of the chuckles of happy laughter, it was a whoosh as if something was coming towards them. He turned and faced the direction of the sound, just in time to see tiny arrows appear out of nowhere. Instinctively he pushed his arms forward in a breaststroke action and as he did so dismissed the weapons away with his gravity energy.

"Where did they come from?" asked Connor stupidly.

"Out of nowhere," was the sarcastic reply and on that response, another barrage of arrows materialised.

Again Will threw his arms skyward, forcing the arrows to lift over their heads.

"Wait! Stop!" implored Connor but before he had time to announce himself, a further fifty or so arrows flew towards them.

Will was outnumbered but Connor had another plan as he pushed his friend to the ground and quickly threw an energy field around them. One by one the lethal weapons bounced into the shield and dropped ineffectively to the ground, enabling the pair to remain unharmed.

"Stop, stop!" they suddenly heard a voice scream as Connor lowered the shield. "There are only two people I know that have this type of dream energy. All of you must hold your fire."

Curiously, Connor and Will looked around and although they could hear the footsteps of several pairs of feet, they still saw nothing. Then suddenly, right beside them, they heard a voice.

"Lord Connor, Master William, my apologies. I did not expect to see you here. I cannot believe it is you."

"Believe it, young friend. For it is true," replied the Dream Lord. "We mean you no harm. Lord Oakhanogan has sent us to meet with Lord Thisabow."

Connor heard no interruption to his explanation and so he continued with the complete story of their mission.

"A new threat has arisen in the Judgment World that could ultimately destroy all the three worlds. The Shadow Night Lord has been freed and is continuing his evil work, causing devastation of Judgment. The only chance of defence is for Will and me to go there and destroy the Dark Lord once and for all. I've been told that Lord Thisabow is the key for us to cross over."

"Please, you must help us," begged Will.

"It has been so long, William," said a voice as Will felt something wrap around his leg. As he looked down, he watched the image of a small creature appear.

"Vanisheo!" exclaimed Will in delight. "Is it really you?"

"Yes, Master William," said the Hallucium. "I am so happy to see you again. If you follow us, I will take you to my father."

"Us?" queried Connor, and as he watched, he saw a number of Halluciums appear, all pointing and chatting at the same time.

"I must apologise for my friend's behaviour," said Vanisheo.

"Friends?" queried Connor and with that even more of the Hallucium appeared, all talking and pointing at the same time.

"Hello," said Connor to the crowd.

They all stopped what they were doing and in unison replied, "Greetings Lord Connor, Dream Lord of Sublin, and Master Will, Dream Warrior to the Lord."

"You have made quite a stir amongst my friends, Lord Connor, Master William," said Vanisheo. "Many stories have they heard about the adventures of the Dream Lord and his warrior. To see you standing in the Untouched Forest is like seeing a walking legend."

"Well, I wouldn't go that far," replied Connor, somewhat embarrassed by the awe bestowed upon them by the tiny beings. "Our adventures wouldn't have been successful without the help of our friends, as you well know dear Vanisheo and I am hopeful that the assistance of your father will bring about a new adventure."

"Father, yes, yes," he quickly burbled. "Please follow me. I will take you to him." And with that, he grabbed Will's hand and started to drag him along the riverbank.

Connor followed and was quickly surrounded by a number of Hallucium all pushing and shoving to get closer to the Dream Lord. If this was anywhere else, Connor could easily have mistaken the sight of the excitable, little beings for a school outing.

For what seemed like hours, Vanisheo chattered away eagerly to Will, oblivious of the rest of the company. Connor tried to listen to the conversation but every now and then he found himself drifting off to the task that lay ahead. He wondered about Fortis and Durban and whether or not they had been successful in continuing to elude the Judgment Halls. He also pondered on the challenges he and Will expected to face and wondered if either of them would ever return from the Judgment World. Still deep in thought, his focus was suddenly broken by an announcement.

"We are here," said Vanisheo as he stopped by Will's side, still tightly holding his hand.

Connor looked and saw in front of him a huge clearing in the forest. It was lined with row upon row of tiny wooden houses. Streets were buzzing as Halluciums went about their daily chores and children played hide and seek amongst the cluster of tiny streets. It was a hive of activity, and Connor felt comforted by the normality of the sight. Away in the distance, built on a hillock overlooking the complete town, was a large colonial building. White wooden shutters, opened to let in the air, were dotted aside every window, and wooden green roof tiles protected it from the sun. This was the home of Lord Thisabow, ruler of the Untouched Forest.

He hated segregation from his people as he found it more acceptable to understand his followers and he hoped by living on a more level plane, he appeared approachable to his subjects. For this reason, he was highly revered by all and feared by none.

In order to seek audience with Lord Thisabow, Connor and Will had to walk through the tiny streets and were amused by the commotion they were causing among the Halluciums. Some of them had never seen a human before and others were just curious to catch a glimpse of the fabled Dream Lord and his Warrior. Neither group appeared disappointed as they rushed forward merely to brush pass them. This continued for some time until, just as Connor and Will had experienced in the past, the crowd of followers faded into their background and disappeared. The only indication of their presence was the chatter of voices and shouts of goodbye off in the distance behind them.

Finally they came to the end of the street and as they made their way through the large marketplace they saw the open gates of the big, white house before them. Standing at the gates stood two guards protecting the entranceway. They were slightly larger than the other Halluciums they had seen and were dressed in military uniform.

"Do not be perturbed by them," advised Vanisheo. "It is only for show. They have not once stopped anyone entering the gates."

"Halt! Who goes there?" asked one of the guards.

"It is me, Vanisheo," announced the young prince. "I have brought Master Will and Lord Connor to see my father. Their presence is of great importance."

The two guards eyed Will and Connor up and down and then nodded their approval.

"You may enter," announced one of them.

Connor nodded in acknowledgment and slowly wandered through, followed closely by his friend and the Halluicum.

"We must hurry," urged Vanisheo as he trotted off. "Father does not like it if I am late."

Connor could sense that the Hallucium was nervous about their visit and to alleviate his fears, he gently jostled Will to follow. As they were just about to enter through the front door, they heard a voice drifting through the air.

"Please follow me around the back," it said.

Connor found it somewhat amusing that he was asked to follow something he could not see, but as he watched, a shape began to materialise before them.

"It is good to see you again, Lord Thisabow," greeted Connor. "We must apologise for this intrusion."

"Apology accepted," replied the lord as he turned his back on them and walked off.

Connor quickly chased after him trying to explain their visit, while Will and Vanisheo dawdled some distance behind.

"We have been sent here," Connor told Lord Thisabow, "by the Great Lord Oakhanogan. He's advised us, that with your knowledge and assistance we may find passage to the Judgment World."

"And why should you want to go there before your calling?" asked Lord Thisabow.

"Volnar, the Shadow Night Lord, has been set free," explained Connor, "and it's my place to put things right."

"And do you take this mission readily?" asked the Hallucium, "or has this challenge been thrust upon you with resentment?"

"There's no resentment in my heart, Lord Thisabow," replied Connor. "I am the Dream Lord of Sublin and it's my responsibility to protect my people through every pathway that they take. With danger lurking in the Judgment World, I'm powerless to protect my subjects. I must go there in order to change this."

"I am glad you have accountability." The old lord smiled. "It will make your task much easier to accept, but I must warn you, I am afraid time is not on your side. A window of opportunity has presented itself from the Higher Powers, and we must make haste to take advantage of it. Vanisheo?"

"Yes, Father," replied the prince.

"You must say goodbye to your friends for now," said his father, "but do not be sad. Rest assured you will see Master William and Lord Connor again very soon."

"But, Father, I can help," protested Vanisheo.

"Not this time, my son," smiled Lord Thisabow. "This time, Master William must face the challenges without you."

Vanisheo looked at his father and knew no amount of pleading was going to change his mind, so throwing his little arms around Will's legs once more, he hugged them tightly before melting away.

"His heart is good," said the Lord proudly, "and his love for you Master William is an attachment I have never seen in a Hallucium before, but he is my son, and I love him despite his odd failings."

"Lord Thisabow?" asked Connor. "What did you mean when you mentioned the Higher Powers? Are they the overall seers of the three worlds?"

"Some say yes, and some say no," replied Lord Thisabow. "It is not our right to ask questions but merely one to serve—"

"It's okay," interrupted Will. "You don't have to tell us if you don't want to. Just one thing though?"

"Yes, Master William?" he replied.

"What do we have to do?" asked Will.

"We must leave the Untouched Forest and head for the ocean behind my kingdom," explained Lord Thisabow. "The Higher Power has given you and Connor a chance to learn about the evolution of your energy but in order to do this, you must pass a test set for you. Only then can you inherit the markings of the traveller, the key that will open your mind and pass you over to the Judgment World."

Suddenly, without warning, Lord Thisabow stopped.

"I need you to hold on to me," he said. "This is going to feel a little strange, but where we must go is some distance away and it is imperative you rest during our journey. By sharing my aura you will get that repose and arrive refreshed and ready to take on the world."

Connor and Will did not argue. Instead they each took hold of a tiny, bony hand and waited. Instantly they blacked out and when they reawakened, found themselves on the shores of the ocean, rejuvenated by a peaceful rest.

"What happened?" asked Connor as he sat up and looked around. "Do you have the skill of teleportation?"

"Yes . . . and no, Lord Connor," replied the Hallucium. "The quickest way to reach these shores is to melt out of reality and back again. For a moment you disappeared from your reality and ceased to exist. A dangerous concept for if you never returned, everything you have affected since arriving in Sublin would never have happened, and who knows what state the world would be in then. It does however have its advantages, for when you re-enter the existence, it is like the rebirth of your energy."

"Wow! That's mind blowing," said Connor. "To think that one mistake and all of history could be changed."

"A skill then not to be taken lightly, I think you would agree," said Lord Thisabow with a smile.

"Without a doubt," agreed Connor. "What I don't understand though, is why Vanisheo didn't use it to rescue Will in the hospital, when he was born?"

"The simple answer to that," smiled Lord Thisabow, "is that I am, even all those years ago, the only one strong enough to control the skill. It was my power that created the car crash to pull you through into Sublin. My intention at the time was that the transference would go unnoticed—"

"Well, it did . . . sort of," interrupted Will. "At least you gave us a head start,"

"Not quite the plan, I have to admit," said the Hallucium, "but the best that could be done under the circumstances." For a moment he thought, as if assessing whether or not to divulge further information, then, when satisfied with his decision, he continued. "When my time ends here," he said, "this skill will not be lost. It will be passed on to Vanisheo and over time to his sons and theirs. As long as there is a Hallucium, so will this gift be preserved."

"Well, hopefully that's a long way off," said Will who was finding the sound of gentle waves caressing the orange sands suppressing the urgency of their mission.

"But enough of this idle chit chat," Thisabow suddenly announced. "It is time." And turning towards the shimmering waters, they saw a small boat suddenly materialise. "You must take this boat and head towards the dark clouds," he instructed them as he pointed towards the distance. "Do not fear them. They are your passageway to another sub reality. Similar to the one Fortis and Durban took you into, Lord Connor. There you will face the test of travellers."

"But what weapons can we use?" asked Connor.

"In this reality you are blessed with two. Your own dream energy and the soul energy you have seen your friends use," replied the Hallucium.

"How did you know about Fortis and Durban?" queried Will.

"It is my place and duty," said Lord Thisabow, "to know all that transpires within the worlds. The tiniest of incidents must be reported back. What appears insignificant to you and I could be the changing of our existence."

Both Will and Connor wanted to know more but Lord Thisabow became agitated and urged them to begin.

"Please, Lord Connor, Master Will. You must set sail, now," he said. "The sands of time are slipping away."

"But how will we return?" asked Will.

"I shall wait here, as is my instruction," answered Lord Thisabow.

"And so shall I," came another voice from behind them.

The three of them quickly spun around and there materialising into view was the familiar figure of Vanisheo.

"Do you never listen to me, my son?" scolded his father.

"Most of the time . . . if it suits me," said Vanisheo.

"Reprimands must wait until later," replied Lord Thisabow. "My lord and master, you must leave . . . now."

Not wanting to incur the wrath of the old Hallucium Lord, Connor and Will did as they were instructed. Pushing the boat out into the ocean, they jumped into it and began rowing towards the dark clouds. As they looked back to the shoreline, they saw the two tiny figures start to disappear into the distance. Shivers ran down their spines at the prospect of this unknown adventure and they looked at one another for comfort.

"Are you ready for this?" Connor asked Will.

"A bit late now if I wasn't," replied his friend. "There's no going back. Never was or will be, for us anyway. Haven't you got it yet?"

"Got what?" asked Connor.

"You're the Dream Lord and me the Dream Warrior," stated Will. "We're never going to have an easy life."

"And why not?" asked his friend again. "Hadn't we paid our dues by rescuing Sublin the first time?"

"Yes, we did," was the reply, "but you know yourself it was never going to end there. With power comes responsibility. At some point your services would be called upon again. It just goes with the territory."

"So wise for one so young," Connor said laughingly as he punched his friend in the arm. "I just sort of hoped we'd already done the 'til the death thing,' that was all."

"No, you don't, not really," interrupted Will. "This is who we are and what we do."

Connor thought about things for a moment and then smiled—the type of smile that Will had learned over the years meant business. The Dream Lord had now embraced this latest task with the zeal of a true leader and Will, as usual, had accepted it for what it was—another expectation of their calling.

In unison the two of them pulled on the oars and headed towards the unknown.

4

The Dual Tasks

As they sailed forward towards the dark clouds, the wind began to whip across the gentle, undulating ocean, causing the white horses to flair their nostrils and conjure up the waves.

"The wind's too strong for us!" shouted Will over the sounds of crashing water as they were jostled from side to side in the tiny boat. "We'll be drowned."

"We must trust Lord Thisabow!" Connor shouted back. "He wouldn't deliberately send us to our death. It's in his interest as well that we pass the test."

The storm by this time had reached a pinnacle, as they reached the eye of the dark clouds. How their boat had not been crushed amongst the violent waves was luck in itself and all Connor and Will could do was to hold onto the vessel and pray.

"Do you think this is the test?" yelled Will above the noise.

"It can't be," replied Connor. "We don't have control over these elements."

No sooner had Connor spoken than a huge wave engulfed them and the boat and drew it into its waters. A strong gust of wind then caught the craft and dragged it from the watery grasp as it catapulted the two warriors and their mode of travel into the air. In desperation they held on for all their life was worth. Their only hope of a safe landing was resting on the contours of land that had suddenly appeared before them. Without thinking, Will released the grip of one hand and, using his gravity energy, reduced the speed of the dropping boat as it headed towards the ground.

"Hold on!" he shouted as the boat crashed onto the surface, throwing them clear. "Are you okay?" asked Will as he got to his feet.

"I think so," replied Connor as he dusted the orange sand from his clothes.

Satisfied that neither of them was injured, they allowed a minute or two to look around and see exactly where they were.

"Wow!" exclaimed Connor, merely for something to say. "Where are we?"

They looked out into the distance and could see a mantle of dark clouds surrounding the island and protecting it from prying eyes.

"Guess that's why we couldn't see this place," surmised Connor. "The clouds must act as a screen but I don't see the reason behind it. What's the point of protecting an empty island?"

"Err, Connor," interrupted Will, "perhaps to hide that?" And he pointed to a building that had suddenly materialised before them.

Connor turned around and found himself face to face with an enormous stone tower that stretched skywards for as far as the eye could see. It was round in shape and had one door and no windows.

"How did we miss this?" he asked. "Has this always been here?"

"I don't think so," replied his friend. "I'm sure we would've noticed something this large. Besides. by its sheer size, it probably should have been seen from the Island of Kusp. I know it sounds weird but if I was a betting man, I'd say it just appeared."

"Hmm, spooky," replied Connor as he headed towards the door. "Nothing odd about something suddenly appearing, especially in Sublin. It happens all the time, doesn't it?"

For a moment he studied the solid structure and was just about to lift the heavily engraved doorknocker when the door slowly began to open, filling the silent air with the squeaking of its old rusted hinges. Wood ground upon the solid floor as the door eventually stopped, leaving a gap just large enough for the two of them to squeeze through. Connor took the lead and manoeuvred himself through the entrance. Will followed quickly for fear of being left behind.

"Hello?" Connor shouted once inside.

His voiced echoed eerily as it bounced around the circular structure, but no response came. Flamed torches spaced evenly along the walls offered the only illumination there was, as they flickered gently in the breeze that had now managed to force itself in behind the two men. For a moment the pair stood still and took in their surroundings. Within the building, identical to the tower was another circular structure, reaching to the sky. Just like its counterpart, there was a single stone door and no windows.

"Didn't go much for imaginative design then?" stated Connor. "I guess that has to be the way in." And he pointed to the second door.

"You're definitely one to state the obvious, aren't you?" laughed Will nervously.

Together they approached the door, and as they did so, a whisper drifted on the air.

"Are you ready to learn?" it asked.

Sensing another presence, Connor and Will turned around, and there before them stood a figure. Its clothing was that of any inhabitant of Sublin. A dark, long robe supported by a hood covered any features of the being, apart from the distinctive burn of its green eyes as they reflected the glow of the dim, lit flames.

"As ready as we'll ever be," replied Will.

"Good, good," was the eager response, before pausing for a moment to take a breath. "Ahead of you are but two tests, one for each of you. They are not designed to trick you but to push you into learning the kind of power you can call upon. Only when the Higher Powers are satisfied with the understanding of the manifestation will the tests come to an end, and you will earn their markings. These will be your licence to pass through the Judgment World. A second benefit also comes of this accolade. Each will be permitted an ally to assist you on your journey and a single guide to show you the path."

Connor wanted to understand more before taking on his test but the figure was not open to interrogation and quickly carried on.

"Please step forward," it instructed, "and make your way into the tower. There you shall begin."

When it had finished, a long, thin, bony hand appeared from its robe and pointed to the stone entranceway of the second tower. Just the same as the first door, it slowly began to open.

"What more must we know?" asked Connor as he turned back to the apparition but to his surprise, it had vanished.

Once more they were completely alone.

"After you." Connor bowed as he urged his friend forward. "I am your Lord," said the Dream Lord, pulling rank, "and request you take the lead."

Will laughed again, nervous at their stupidity.

"Okay, if you insist," he answered.

Cautiously he stepped forward and then through the doorway. Connor followed closely behind. Once the two of them were inside, the door quickly shut, leaving them in almost total darkness. Only a shaft of light from an opening at the very top of the tower added a subtle glow.

Will looked quickly around and then decided on their strategy.

"Well, I guess we have to go up," he suggested. "Any ideas how we do that?"

"Shall we try a spot of teleportation?" asked Connor, and with that he closed his eyes and tried to clear his mind, allowing images to appear but unlike in the past, when a simple thought was all it took, this time he was unable to conjure up a vision. It was as if he had forgotten how.

For a moment or two he continued to try and then convinced nothing was going to happen, he reopened his eyes.

"What's the matter?" asked Will.

"I . . . I can't do it," replied Connor. "I know it sounds stupid but I can't remember how."

"This is no time for practical jokes," scolded Will. "We could be here forever otherwise."

"Does this look like the face of a comedian?" asked Connor seriously. "I'm telling you, I can't remember how to do it. This must be part of the test. We have to find another way."

"Okay, okay," soothed his friend. "Not to worry. I'm sure there must be a way around this. We'll just have to think of something else that's all." And with that he shouted towards the ceiling, "Hello! Is there anyone there? Can we have a clue to help us get started? I mean, I thought time was not on our side and all that."

There came no response, just a faint pounding as Connor and Will's hearts thumped rapidly in their chests.

"Listen!" ordered Connor. "I hear something."

"So do I," agreed Will, "but what is it?"

"It sounds like water," suggested Connor, "but that can't be right."

But sure enough it was. All of sudden, part of the wall by their feet broke away and water rapidly started to trickle through.

"Hmmm," said Connor somewhat concerned. "Are you thinking what I'm thinking?"

"That this place is going to fill up with water, and we are going to drown?" replied Will.

"Well, that wasn't my first thought, but it's true," answered Connor. "What I was going to say was just that the water was going to be very cold."

"I think I like your one better," Will responded. "Hey!" he shouted again. "If you're there, then tell us what we must do!"

"The one who can control his own environment," said an echo, "can harness the good within."

"Just great," moaned Will. "I hate those cryptic responses. What's that supposed to mean? Harness the good? It doesn't make any sense."

By this time the water had reached their necks and within minutes they would be submerged below the surface.

"I guess we're really bad at this, Will," said Connor as his head disappeared beneath the water.

"Connor, no!" Will shouted as he scrambled to grab his friend, but it was too late as the undercurrent dragged Connor away and he was gone.

Will took a deep breath and sank to the bottom. What little light there was shone down on Connor, showing him lying inert and lifeless upon the tower floor.

"Connor?" Will tried to call out but as he spoke, his lungs began to fill with water.

At first he tried to fight the inevitable but quickly lost hope as he slowly began to lose consciousness. Gracefully he started to sink to the floor but a nagging feeling in the back of his mind forced him briefly to open his eyes. In that split second of survival, he once again heard an echo speaking to him.

"William," it called, "he who can control gravity. Free your mind and the environment will be your saviour."

Will sensed he had nothing else to lose and so closing his eyes once more, he cleared the fear from his mind. As he did so, he sensed a new kind of energy expanding throughout his body. With this renewed life force bubbling through his veins, he reopened his eyes and realised he could breathe in the water. Sensing his own salvation, he shot a glance at his friend and saw Connor was about to pass over into Judgment, not as its saviour but as one about to be adjudicated. Moving as fast as he could through the water, Will was soon by his side and immediately became aware of what he must do. Calmly, he laid both hands upon Connor's chest and with a sense of relief, Will discovered he could emit a warmth of energy into his friend. This burning essence immediately woke Connor and he curiously looked into Will's eyes and waited for the next instruction.

"I'm going to pull us to the top. Just hang on," he told Connor, and although they were both still submerged, the command sounded as clear as though this was a normal conversation.

Connor was in no position to do other than as he was told, and so he waited patiently for Will to grab him and swim them both towards the top of the tower. With the strength of an Orca, Will soared through the water like a fish and soon both he and Connor were resting comfortably on dry land, spewing water from their lungs and replacing it with fresh, clean air.

"What happened?" asked Connor as he tried to process the last few minutes through his mind. "Did I drown?"

"I don't know," replied Will, but as he spoke, he felt a sharp pain shoot up his left forearm. "Aaah," he moaned.

"What is it?" Connor queried. "Are you okay?"

Just as quickly as the pain had started, it stopped and as Will looked down at his arm, he saw an ancient tattoo, reminiscent of Egyptian hieroglyphics.

"Well done, young master," said the robed figure that suddenly appeared before them. "You have pleased the Higher Powers, and they have given sanction to you. The passageway to the Judgment World is yours, and although it did take a little longer than we had hoped you got there in the end."

"Where did you come from? Where is this place? Who are you? Is this the mark?" Will gabbled on in a single breath.

"So many questions," was the reply. "Some I cannot answer, but two I will explain. You now have the mark of passage. You have passed the challenge set before you, and Judgment awaits your visit. You have learned the evolution of your power. In the Judgment World, your soul energy will permit you to harness your environment. It is of great surprise to us, though even more beneficial, that you are able to share your energy with those around you.

"As to my identity! There is nothing more mysterious than I am your guide, an aide to help you through the tests bestowed upon you."

"What did you mean when you said I could share my energy with others?" asked Will.

"You took the oxygen from the water, allowing you to breathe," replied the guide, "but then you granted Lord Connor the same gift. Once your lungs were full, you were then able to focus on this evolution of skill. For that, the Higher Powers have granted you passage into the Judgment World but do not think you have mastered this new art. I must warn you that this is only a small demonstration of your true potential. The rest you will discover on your travels." For a moment he paused and then looked at Connor. "There is still one task that remains, Lord Connor. To face this challenge, we must take the stairs." And with that he started to make his way up a rickety, spiral staircase that twisted and turned its way to the top of the tower.

Connor immediately followed and Will, still relieved that he had fulfilled his part of the task, dawdled behind.

"This way, Lord Connor," said the guide as he pointed to a concealed door at the top of the stairs.

As Will looked up, he noticed that the visibility had suddenly changed and where he could once have seen his hands in front of his face, he was now surrounded by complete darkness.

"Connor?" he called out. "Are you up here?"

With no response, he stumbled forward and felt his way around the stairs. He sensed it part of the mission to accompany his friend, wherever his task took him.

"So I just go through that door?" He eventually heard Connor ask their guide.

There was no response and as Connor turned around, he found he was alone. All he could hear was a shuffling sound as Will slowly made his way up to join him.

"I hate it when he does that," said Will as he looked up.

With no one to ask for advice, Connor turned back towards the door as it slowly began to open. A shiver ran down his spine as he thought over what could possibly face him but in his usual optimistic manner, he consoled himself that they had survived the first ordeal and would succeed again.

Carefully, he stepped through the open door and found himself outside on a square, flat roof. Located on each corner was a pillar rising endlessly above and way out of sight. As he tilted his head back to look up, he could not decide if that was actually sky he could see or an illusion created for the purpose. Was he in fact even standing on the roof of the tower? Cautiously he stepped forward, expecting the unexpected.

"Hey! Wait for me!" shouted Will as he threw himself through the small gap of the door, but no sooner had he stepped out onto the roof than an energy field materialised before him.

This cut the square roof in half, leaving Will on one side with the exit and Connor stuck on the other with the rest of the open roof.

"This can't be good," Connor mumbled to himself as he realised he had now been cut off from his friend.

The task defined for him was obviously something he had to do alone and, if he was not mistaken, one of combat. As Will prodded at the force field, sparks of electricity crackled around the barrier but still it refused to waver. His effort to break through was futile and no matter where he moved around his part of the roof, there was simply no way in to help his friend. All he could do was watch and hope.

Suddenly, without warning, the sky darkened and a torrent of rain began to fall, blurring Connor's vision and making the surface slippery underfoot.

"Will?" Connor shouted above the noise of the rain. "Are you still with me?"

"Nowhere else to be," his friend replied.

"Good," said the Dream Lord. "Then keep your eyes open. I've a feeling two pairs are going to be better than one."

No sooner did he finish speaking than he heard above the seamless rain an intense ripping sound, similar to that he experienced when meeting the Razars for the very first time. As he looked up, he saw the blackened clouds above peel open to expose a portal.

"Oh no," muttered the Dream Lord to himself. "Not again. Will, you're about to get your first glimpse of a Razar."

"Anything I can do?" asked his friend.

"Not from that side of the barrier," Connor replied, "but your vision might help a lot."

Adapting himself to the situation, Connor turned his attention skyward, and as he watched, he saw a single Razar drift slowly down and land with a thud on the roof. The wet surface beneath his feet affected the perfect landing. It slid a little on impact but quickly acclimatised to the weather conditions as it put a hand to the ground to steady itself before standing up to its full height.

"What the . . . ?" mouthed Will quietly.

Having met this adversary once before, Connor was un-moved by the image and instead waited for the first strike. On his last encounter, they had been eager to attack and he had no reason to think this would be any different. With its victim close at hand, the Razar lashed out its tongue but Connor was prepared for the move and sidestepped to avoid the blow. Unfortunately, his concentration on the fight did not take into account the amount of rain that had been falling and he slipped on the watery surface, causing him to slide towards the edge of the building. Luckily, he just managed to steady himself as the rain continued to cascade off the roof. Hauling himself up, Connor turned to face his enemy once again just as the Razar's sharp tongue hit him on the arm. He yelled from the sudden stinging impact as the force of the blow knocked him off balance and over the edge of the roof. Miraculously he did not fall as he felt a couple of invisible steps support his weight.

"Thanks, Will!" he yelled as he rushed forward back onto the roof.

With Connor unable to teleport, Will had doubts of his own dream energy responding and he was relieved to see that his gravity force had actually worked.

The Razar, despite the torrential rain, was not about to let Connor go and thrust another tongue attack at him, this time by gripping his leg and throwing him across the other side of the roof. The rain though acted in Connor's favour as it slowed down his speed and deposited him only metres away from Will, who could only watch helplessly.

"I see what you mean about tough," he said to Connor. "How do you expect to kill it? I mean, the only way I can ever see you matching it is by having the same powers."

"That's it, Will," Connor exclaimed through the energy field. "Thanks."

"What?" asked his friend. "The bit about not being able to match it?"

"Not that part," confirmed Connor but before he had an opportunity to explain, he threw himself to one side to avoid yet another attack.

Quickly he scrambled to his feet and steadied himself. The Razar was about to spit out again when Connor sensed a new type of energy surge through his veins. Moving his head to one side, he flung it forward and as he did so, he opened his mouth. A razor sharp tongue whipped out and cut through the arm of his attacker. Shocked by the instant assault, the creature stood motionless as it moaned in pain.

"That is so cool!" yelled Will in excitement. "How the hell did you do that?"

There was no time for Connor to explain or rest on his laurels as he rushed forward, throwing his entire body into the creature. The impact caused them to lose their balance, slide along the floor and over the edge of the building. Unable to control his own momentum, Connor found himself following the path of his attacker. Without thinking, he spat out his tongue again and wrapped it around one of the pillars as he slid past. It temporarily stopped his fall, leaving him dangling helplessly over the edge. For a moment or two, he hung there before adjusting to his situation, and then slowly, bit by bit, he began to recoil his newfound weapon and at the same time pulled himself to safety. As his fingertips reached the edge of the roof, he carefully clambered over to safety. With his feet firmly on solid ground, he stood up, released his grip from the pillar, and withdrew the tongue. A huge smile filled the expanse of his face, and as it did so, so did the rain-laden clouds disappeared, leaving a sun-kissed rooftop.

"That was so cool," said Will again as Connor walked over to join him. "Guess you've passed the test as well?"

The answer to that was definitely no as the energy field remained fast with Connor trapped on the other side of it.

"Why hasn't it lifted?" asked Connor as an electrical pulse crackled around him when he touched the invisible shield.

"You're asking me?" replied Will, also somewhat puzzled by his friend's imprisonment. Suddenly he saw something.

"What's that?" he asked pointing to an image on the far side of the roof.

Connor turned around and saw a black slime begin to ooze from one of the pillars. As they both stared, it began to form into a shape where two blood red eyes stared back at him.

"Oh, come on!" exclaimed the Dream Lord. "Will gets water, and I get all this. Really? How fair is that?"

Unmoved by Connor's exasperation, the slimy creature threw its arms forward, throwing a mass of gloop in his direction. The substance caught the Dream Lord by the arms and snugly wrapped itself around them, vowing never to let go. The ruler of Sublin yelled as he struggled to get free, but the slime only tightened its grip. Meanwhile from the other side of the roof, the creature slowly moved towards him. Again Will was helpless as he watched in horror. Suddenly Connor cried out, and as he did so, he transformed into a puddle of melted slime.

"Connor?" shouted Will in terror. "What's happening?"

There was no response as the creature stepped into the puddle of what was once Connor and sucked it into his own form.

"Connor?" Will screamed again as he tried to get through the invisible barrier, but the image of his friend was nowhere to be seen, just the effigy of black slime.

Will watched helplessly, praying that Connor had an answer to this attack as the blooded eyes flickered and then an agonising screech emitted from what could only be its mouth. It was in pain, and the longer Will observed, the more confident he was that his friend was somehow attacking the creature from within. Defiantly it stood its ground, writhing and quivering as its outer layers began to peel away with each vibration. Over a matter of minutes, more and more of the slimy skin flew from the body, until the creature could bear it no longer and began jostling and rotating in an effort to stop whatever was attacking it. The efforts however were futile as the sensation it was experiencing became unbearable and it finally stumbled backwards and fell off the roof.

"Connor," moaned Will dropping to the ground, horrified by what he had witnessed.

His friend had gone and he was alone.

For a few moments he remained silent and then got to his feet. Staying on the roof was not going to bring Connor back and throwing one last glance across the arena, he suddenly noticed the remains of some of the slime that had been left behind. For a moment it lingered inert, but then to Will's surprise, it started moving and collecting itself into a puddle. Holding his breath and barely hoping, he continued to watch as the pool of ooze metamorphosed into a bodily shape and turned into the image of his friend. Gradually, bit by bit, the slime melted away and there standing before him was Connor.

"What the . . . ?" was all Will managed to exclaim.

"Well. That was interesting," said Connor as he walked over to his friend. "Can't say I've ever fought an enemy from within before."

Connor looked at Will. Will's mouth dropped open from shock. "What?" asked Connor.

"You really don't know?" queried Will.

"Know what?" was the response.

"That you turned into slime and that thing absorbed you," explained Will.

"Get out of here," joked Connor.

Will shook his head slowly, but before Connor had the opportunity to say anymore, he fell to the ground from a surging, burning pain running through his body. Instinctively he gripped his forearm and as he looked, he saw the hieroglyphics appear. Instantly the energy wall disappeared and Connor and Will heard a voice echo through the air.

"You have done well and understood with open minds the learnings thrown upon you by the Higher Powers."

The pair looked around, and there, standing in front of them once more, was the hooded figure.

"How come you always show up after the danger has passed?" asked Will. "A little help might be useful once in a while."

"What learnings?" asked Connor who had been trying to process the statement.

"Dream Lord Connor," said the man, "you are full of so many surprises. We did not expect you to have such a powerful presence so soon. You are truly unique."

"In what way?" queried Connor again. "I merely did what I had to do in order to survive."

"And that is the most amazing thing," continued the guide. "You have learned to draw in the energy of things around you and use it for your own purposes. It will be a learning process for you but for the time being, once you have made physical contact, you can replicate that force to defeat your enemies. Your soul is truly amazing. Go forth into the Judgment World and take one person by your side."

"How will we know our way?" asked Connor.

"Did I not say I am your guide?" said the figure.

"Then you'll come with us?" queried Will.

"No," replied the being. "I cannot but a guide comes in many guises, and you will find one to take you through the Judgment World. Hurry now. As always, the window of opportunity is very limited." And with that, the hooded man disappeared for the last time.

"Wait!" yelled Connor. "How are we supposed to get back?"

There was no answer, instead they suddenly found the tasks had taken toll upon their bodies and drained their physical energy, so they sat down, closed their eyes, and drifted off to sleep. The first real, restful sleep they had experienced in many years.

5

And So It Begins

"Lord Connor? Master William?" said a voice in the back of their minds.

The Dream Lord slowly opened his eyes and, as he did so, began to focus upon two small figures leaning over them. Lord Thisabow looked concerned and then smiled at Connor's response.

"What happened?" he asked them as he looked over at Will who was also just coming around. "The last thing I remember was being on the roof of the tower and . . ." But before he had finished his sentence, he looked down at his arm and rubbed it.

"Yes, Lord Connor," said Lord Thisabow. "You have both done very well and completed the tasks set before you. You now both bear the mark to allow you passage into the Judgment World."

"Well, it wasn't really a test," said Will as he got to his feet and dusted himself down. "More like a look into the future and seeing the sort of power we'll have in the Judgment World."

"Speak for yourself," said Connor. "You didn't have to fight a Razar or the Black Slime,"

"That's true," admitted Will, "which only proves my point."

"Which is?" asked Connor.

"Why couldn't the Higher Powers just tell us our strengths, rather than putting us through the big show?" Will grinned.

"Because," interrupted Connor who understood the reasoning of the Higher Powers, "the experience was to prove to ourselves our true potential."

Will thought for a moment and then nodded his agreement. He was once told of an old Wake World adage. It went "seeing was believing," and now he was a confirmed convert to the appreciation of his own powers.

"Lord Thisabow?" asked Connor. "The hooded man we met in the tower mentioned to us the privilege we had earned of taking a guide, someone who had knowledge of the Judgment World. Do you know of such a person?"

"I do indeed," said the old Hallucium. "There was a time when I would have readily accepted the challenge myself. Our skills of melting into any reality make us your prime candidate. However, as much as I would hate to admit it, I am much too old these days for such excitement and would only slow you down."

He then turned towards Vanisheo and proudly laid his hand upon his son's shoulder and smiled with the pride of any father.

"I would entrust such an important mission to only one person and that is my eldest son, Vanisheo," said Lord Thisabow. "His loyalty to you, Master William, is unfounded and in these dangerous times, he has agreed to take on a new role and guide you through the Judgment World. When he was a child, he spent many hours playing hide and seek through the pathways of reality, including the Judgment World. Since Volnar took control its contours have undoubtedly changed, and it has been many years since my son's last visit, however, I am certain he will be a great asset to you."

"My dear Lord Thisabow," said Connor kindly, "we are indebted to you for your generosity. Vanisheo is a good son and you must be proud of him."

Lord Thisabow did not respond for fear of showing emotion but looked fondly at his son instead.

"I will not let you down, Father," replied Vanisheo before turning to Connor and Will. "It is an honour to be chosen as your guide, my lords and I will pledge my allegiance until the end if need be. First, with your permission though, I must go home and say my goodbyes."

"You need no sanction from us," replied Connor. "It's we who are honoured to have you by our side. Say your goodbyes and take as much time as you need. We've business of our own to attend to anyway. During our tasks of understanding we were also told we could take a companion each, the names of which were decided before we left, so now it's time to go and collect them. There is, however, one more favour I ask of you, Lord Thisabow," added Connor.

"Ask away, my lord," replied the Hallucium.

"Whilst Jasmine and Kustos leave this world, they have asked Lady Eva and Lord Frederick to keep safe the Waterfall Kingdom," Connor paused for a moment as if to ask an impossible question. "Can you please watch over them and keep them safe? At least as best you can."

"I feel my task is the easiest of all." Lord Thisabow smiled. "Take heart that I will play my part." And with that, he and Vanisheo melted back into the forest.

A lingering voice floated from the direction they had taken.

"I shall meet you both at the great tree at nightfall," it said before drifting off into the wind.

Connor and Will looked at each other and smiled.

"Are you ready?" asked Connor.

"As ready as I'll ever be," confirmed his friend.

"In that case," Connor said with a grin, "I think it's time to take another trip."

Taking Will's arm, he closed his eyes and in a second, they were both within hearing range of Lady Eva and her daughter. For a moment, they stood quietly, hidden from view. The conversation between mother and daughter appeared to be one that should not be overheard and so they discreetly kept their distance. Only Connor could hear each syllable spoken.

"So your mind is made up then?" He heard Lady Eva ask. "There is nothing I can say to make you change it?"

"I am afraid not, Mother," replied Jasmine. "I go where Kustos goes, and Connor needs him right now."

"And you, dearest Jasmine," said her mother sadly, "does he need you as well?"

Jasmine blushed slightly at her mother's insinuation but continued with her reasoning behind the decision anyway. Connor also felt a sense of embarrassment as he realised how much he relished Jasmine's company.

"It is not like the Great War," she told her mother. "Connor and Will were new to our world, and their powers unproven. Now they are great warriors and can protect themselves; besides, I will not be alone. Kustos will be by my side and he has sworn to keep me from danger. Do not fear for me, Mother. This battle must be finished once and for all and I believe in my heart that we are the chosen ones who can do it."

Lady Eva looked intently into her daughter's face and smiled. She recognised the look of determination and realised nothing she could say would ever make Jasmine change her mind.

"In that case," she said warmly as they turned and stared up at the two suns burning majestically in the bright, blue skies, "you have my blessing, but it will not stop me worrying about you all."

"Nor would I want it any other way." Jasmine smiled as she learned over and kissed her mother gently on the forehead. "I too will worry about you and Father while we are gone. You are not as young as you used to be and looking after the Waterfall Kingdom can be a very taxing task."

"I am sure your father and I will manage," laughed her mother.

Just then Lord Frederick and Kustos appeared. They had been attempting to fish in the river while discussing the state of Sublin.

"Is the food ready yet?" they asked.

"Not unless you caught something," laughed Jasmine as she jumped up from her seat to greet her husband.

"How was the fishing, my dear? Did you catch anything worth eating?" Lady Eva asked Lord Frederick.

"Fishing was very profitable my lady," replied Kustos as he dropped a bag full of fish before her.

"So when do we eat?" asked a voice from behind them.

The four of them turned around and smiled as they saw both Connor and Will walking towards them.

"My my, Lord Connor, Master Will," exclaimed Lord Frederick. "Look at you two, all grown up. Sublin must be agreeing with you."

"As with you, my lord," replied Connor, "I'm pleased to see you both looking younger than ever."

"Such flattery will get you everywhere," laughed Lady Eva as she walked over to Connor and hugged him. "I am sorry that fate has called upon you again so soon," she added.

"Don't be, my lady," replied Connor. "As pointed out by my good friend over here," he said, waving a hand in Will's direction, "it goes with the territory. As Dream Lord of Sublin, it's my duty to protect. My only regret though is that I must borrow both your daughter and Kustos to complete the task."

"We know you would not ask unless it was absolutely necessary," interrupted Lord Frederick, "and believe me, we have tried to talk them out of it, but, like you, they understand the meaning of loyalty and responsibility. If only Eva and I were younger—"

"If you were younger, my lord," replied Connor, "your destiny would still be the same. We are relying on your skills to keep order in Sublin and the Waterfall Kingdom in our absence. A task as difficult as the one we are about to face."

"Thank you for your confidence in an old man." Lord Frederick smiled.

"No, thank you, my lord," said the Dream Lord. "Knowing that you're here to protect Sublin has made my choice easier. Deep in my heart I've always feared that trapping Volnar between worlds would not be the end of his villainy. I have now been proven right but with help from the Higher Powers and my friends, I know we'll end this once and for all."

"Do not be so hard on yourself, my lord," said Lord Frederick as he and his wife sat down. "This could not have been foreseen. Many have been punished by enslavement between worlds and lived their entire existence behind the invisible bars. Volnar is the only one I have ever known to escape and just because it has never happened in the past, does not mean it was a bad plan. All that can be done is to rectify the problem. Which I have every faith will happen one way or the other. Come," he ordered, "sit and eat. Fighting on a full stomach is the only way to go into battle. Panlash . . . set two more places for lunch."

Panlash, standing discreetly some distance away, quickly rushed forward and laid another two places on the old wooden table before standing back and waiting for further orders. Jasmine took her place next to her father, and as Connor walked past her to sit with Kustos, she grabbed his arm.

"What happened?" she asked as she noticed the tattoo.

"That's our ticket into the Judgment World," interrupted Will, "bestowed upon us by the Higher Powers."

"Is this true?" Jasmine asked Connor.

Connor nodded and then went on to explain, "It was a necessity to prove to them that we're able to survive in the Judgment

World and when they were satisfied with our efforts, they marked us with their key of acknowledgment."

"Looks painful if you ask me," said Kustos, who despite his knowledge of the world was unfamiliar with the art of skin painting and tattooing.

"Trust me, Kustos," replied Will as he recalled the moment it was etched into his skin, "you have no idea."

"So now you have the key?" said Jasmine. "What is the plan?"

"I'm glad you asked that question." Connor smiled as he noticed the sun's rays catch the golden streaks in her hair and emit a halo around her head, like an angel. "At nightfall," he continued, "we're to return to Oakhanagan. There we'll meet our guide."

"And who might that be on such a dangerous mission?" asked Lord Frederick.

"Prince Vanisheo," replied Connor proudly.

"I cannot say that in all my years I have heard of this person," replied the Lord of Mallusion.

"Oh, he isn't a person," interrupted Will. "He's the prince of the Halluciums."

"A Hallucium as your guide?" reiterated Lady Eva in disbelief. "Many people of this world pass on to their next journey without ever seeing a Hallucium, let alone spending time with one. Such an honour has been bestowed upon you all. The Higher Powers must have great faith in your abilities."

"I wouldn't go so far as saying great abilities," answered Will. "I just think the four of us are probably their last best hope."

"I think I like Lady Eva's version better, Will," laughed Connor, "but either way, we've a battle before us that's not reared its head in this world for many years. One I know we mustn't fail and with you, Kustos, Jasmine, and our allies on the other side, I sense it'll provide many perils, where all our skills will be required. Vanisheo has the most important task—to ensure we all return home."

"That's a bit deep for you isn't it?" Will asked Connor. "Sounds like a king going into battle."

"Sorry," apologised Connor. "I didn't mean it to be my last speech. I just wanted you all to know how much I appreciate the sacrifice you're making, that's all."

"Lord Connor," Kustos grinned, "do you not know us well enough by now? Have we not fought shoulder to shoulder against the most impossible odds?"

Connor nodded as he recalled the battle on the plains of the Great Waterfall Kingdom. In those days his knowledge of his skills was limited and his arm-to-arm combat no more than that of a novice. Kustos had patiently spurred him on.

"Then why doubt," Kustos continued, "that we would not readily take up our arms to protect those that pass from this world to the next?"

"Oh, I didn't have any reservations," replied Connor. "I just wanted you all to know how grateful I am that you're still prepared to risk it all for our darkest mission yet."

"But is that not part of the challenge?" asked Jasmine. "To ensure what others see as a mindless mission is merely another hurdle to overcome?"

"Forgive my daughter," interrupted Lady Eva. "Her imagination always saw two sides of an option but enough of death and doom. There will be plenty of time to reflect over that. Let us enjoy the food that has been laid before us and have a normal, pleasant afternoon of company and conversations."

"Well said, my dear," smiled Lord Frederick.

"I agree," said Kustos as he looked lovingly at his wife. "Today must be a good day. Spent with friends and loved ones to create memories that can be etched in our minds until the passing of time."

The meal was amazing, an infusion of dishes that could be named as a favorite for every person sitting around the table. From then on, the relaxed feeling of the afternoon continued with storytelling and laughter and even a few snippets of information that Connor and Will divulged about the Untouched Forest. It could not have been a more magical time for the six friends. Only when the long shadows began to etch their way across the table did their reality return.

"I suppose it is time for your assignment," said Lord Frederick sadly as he looked across at his daughter, happily snuggled under Kustos' arm. "This day has been a day of wonderful memories. One I will cherish until the end of my time. My only wish is that we can repeat these moments on your return."

Connor got up from his chair without a word and walked over to Lord Frederick. He took his hand and kissed the royal ring before moving over to Lady Eva. Casting ceremony aside, he gave her a huge hug.

"Look after our world," he told her.

"I promise we will take good care of Sublin in your absence," she confirmed. "You just take good care of my daughter and son-in-law?"

"You can rely on me," replied Connor as he grabbed Will's arm and dragged him a little way off.

"I think they need some family time," he told his friend quietly.

Will agreed and as they walked away, he heard the quiet tones of Lord Frederick speaking with Kustos.

"Take good care of my daughter, Kustos," he almost pleaded. "She is the illumination of this kingdom. Do not permit it to be extinguished?"

"My lord, Lady Eva," replied Kustos, "I will protect her with my life. Without my dearest Jasmine, the light in my heart would also go out." And out of normal custom for him, without warning he hugged them both as though they were his own parents.

Lady Eva blushed at his open affection and watched him walk away to join Connor and Will, leaving Jasmine to say her final farewells alone.

"You don't have to prove yourself, my child," said Lady Eva with tears in her eyes. "This is not your fight. Please, will you not consider staying here with us?"

My dear mother," began Jasmine, "and you, Father," she quickly added, "You have always taught me to follow my heart, even if it takes you down many dangerous pathways. I have to do this. Kustos is my husband and I cannot be parted from him ever. Besides, this will be my final test before I allow myself to settle down and make you grandparents. I cannot do that if my husband does not return. You know our powers will be much stronger in the Judgment World and your thoughts will always be there to guide me."

"It is true, my child," said her father as he hugged her tightly. "Our powers do increase outside of Sublin and up until recently, I could contact my father, who was a Judgment Oracle. If he has not moved on, seek him out and show him your lineage. I know he will help you."

"Jasmine, my dear," called Kustos gently, "it is time for us to leave."

Jasmine turned to her parents. Tears filled her large brown eyes.

"It will not be that long," she told them as she hugged them for one last time.

Then without a second glance, she ran off to join Kustos.

"She will come back, my dear," smiled Lord Frederick as he grabbed his wife's hand in an effort to quell her fears. "If my father received my last message, he will be there to meet them when they arrive."

In silence the royal couple watched as suddenly the small group disappeared before their eyes.

6

Into the Unknown

"You're getting really good at that," said Kustos as they dematerialised in front of Oakhanogan.

"Thanks," replied Connor. "It's always nice for a bit of flattery."

"What's happened here?" gasped Will as he stared at the old tree lord.

The others were immediately drawn to the vision and instead of Oakhanogan's friendly eyes peering out with parental care, an exposed opening, running at a forty-five-degree angle and two metres up from the base of the trunk, was visible. Cautiously they looked inside and saw, off in the distance, a tiny light.

"Quickly, Lord Connor, Master William," came a voice from within, "we do not have much time to make the transition."

"Who said that?" Kustos asked as he looked around.

"Vanisheo!" declared Jasmine. "It was Vanisheo."

Connor looked at Jasmine quizzically. Never before had she mentioned any knowledge of the prince of Hallucium.

"Jasmine, sweet Jasmine," cooed Vanisheo as he appeared, "so many years have passed since our last meeting. I am only sorry our union had to be on this occasion."

"Me too," smiled Jasmine, "but even so, it is so good to see you again."

Vanisheo quickly turned his attention to the others.

"Come, come," he urged them. "We do not have much time to catch up. We must hurry." And he quickly disappeared through the tree trunk.

Connor obeyed immediately and began to squeeze in behind the Hallucium through the slender opening.

"How do you know Vanisheo?" asked Kustos as they followed the Dream Lord and his friend.

"Many years ago," replied Jasmine, "when I was just a girl, I found him wandering through our forests. He had got lost whilst playing hide and seek with his friends. I helped him find his way home but he made me promise not to tell, for fear of the Hallucium reputation. I have never told a soul of our meeting. Not even my parents."

"I told you Kustos, women are a mystery," said Connor over his shoulder . "You think you know everything about them and then they surprise you."

"If that is the worst of your secrets, my dear," Kustos answered, "then I am a very lucky man."

Jasmine was about to reply when suddenly the entrance expanded into a room.

"Here we are," announced Vanisheo. "This room leads to the portal of the Judgment World."

"Are we still in Sublin?" asked Will as they looked around.

The walls were smooth and white and only a single flame was visible, emitting a dull, gentle, glow, barely illuminating the room.

"Yes . . . and no," replied the Hallucium. "This is the twilight of our worlds. We are neither in Sublin nor the Judgment World. Up ahead is the main entrance to the portal, but we must be quick. It will not wait for dawdlers." And he rushed forward as he melted from view.

"Where did he go?" asked Kustos.

"He does that a lot," Connor assured him. "He has the ability to melt in and out of realities, but have no doubt, he's never very far away."

"I can hardly see a thing," said Jasmine as she screwed up her eyes in an effort to focus. "The light is so dim."

"Hang on," said Will, "I think I can do something about that."

Focussing on the flame, he concentrated hard, and as they watched, bit by bit, it began to burn a little brighter. Satisfied with his efforts, he swung his arms in front of him like a magician, and every wooden torch in the room burst into flames. It was only then could they see the magnitude of the twilight room. At the far end in front of them ran a swirling staircase, ending its majestic path with two, large, solid doors. Etched upon each portal were some unusual markings and an indent the size of a forearm. Protecting the stairway at intervals were four stone statues. Each stood about eight feet tall and was armed with either an axe or a Thor-like hammer. Their frame was that of a Herculean god, but each head bore the resemblance of a different beast.

"Well, they look friendly," surmised Will sarcastically as he carefully weighed up the muscular frames.

"Up there." Connor pointed, looking at the doors. "Look. Some of those symbols are similar to the markings on our arms and if my hunch is correct, by matching them up, we'll open the doors."

"I can make out some of the other symbols as well but not enough to read," replied Jasmine as she peered at the hieroglyphics.

"Then perhaps we should take a closer look?" suggested Kustos as he moved forward.

"It is alright. I am sure I have almost deciphered it," said Jasmine and then shouted with some urgency. "Wait, Kustos!" she yelled. "Do not move!" But her warning came too late as his foot touched the first step.

Like an electrical charge had surged through his body, he was thrown backwards and landed softly into Connor and Will. The three of them then lost their balance and ended up in a heap on the floor. Embarrassed by the collision, they quickly struggled to their feet just as they heard a graunching sound, like stone grating upon stone.

"I have a very bad feeling about this," said Will as he looked up.

"The writings warn that we must ask permission to walk the stairs," Jasmine told them.

"And you decide to tell us now?" replied Will.

"I am sorry, Master William, my ancient hiero is not as good as it should be," apologised Jasmine.

"Don't blame yourself," said Connor as he pulled Kustos to his feet. "It's no one's fault. What we have to do now though is work out a plan to get past the guardians."

As he spoke, the four statues slowly formed a line and step by step made their way towards Connor and his friends.

"This is not good," moaned Kustos as he pushed Jasmine behind him to protect her.

"Yes . . . and no," replied Connor, who by his comment obviously had a plan. "Look at it this way," he continued, "one-to-one odds are better than we've ever faced before."

"How do we stop them? They're made of stone," asked Will.

"Yes . . . and stone breaks, doesn't it?" Connor grinned. "Spread out. Take one each and see how you get on. If you need help, just yell."

Connor took the lead and shouted at one of the guards to gain his attention.

"Hey you!" he challenged. "C'mon on over here!"

The statue immediately changed direction and raised his axe in preparation of a fight. Connor slowly backed away whilst the others coerced their own stone guardian. Once he was fully satisfied the odds were even, he extended his own Cinxi swords and parried them in front of him. Still the statue continued to step forward until Connor was backed up against the wall.

"Jasmine?" he called. "Can you mind alter?"

"I am sorry, Connor," she apologised from the other side of the room. "I cannot penetrate the stone to see if they in fact have a mind to change."

"Oh well," said Connor as he resigned himself to physical combat.

Just in time, he noticed the swinging stone axe come gliding towards him and deftly he sidestepped the weapon as he raised his swords to clash with the granite exterior. They clanged and sparked as the blades slipped effortlessly off the hardened surface.

"Hey you!" shouted Jasmine as she threw a small rock at the guardian to distract it.

The abuse had little effect, and as she watched in horror, she saw the stone warrior swing his axe towards Connor.

"Connor!" she warned frantically. "Look out!" But the caution came too late and with full impact the solid axe hit Connor on the side of his face.

A split second too late Connor saw the weapon looming before him, and he braced himself for the impact. The blow glanced off his skin, and without a word, the statue turned away and moved towards Jasmine. She was already trying to dodge a hammer attack from her own adversary and panicked when she saw another approaching her.

Connor could not believe his luck, nor understood why the impact from the weapon had not caused him bodily harm but as he looked down at his hands and feet, all his questions were answered. He had taken on the consistency of his foe, just as he done during his test for the Higher Powers.

In fear for his life, Jasmine took a moment to check on Connor and was amazed to see his latest form.

"How did you do that?" she asked as she suddenly realised she had acquired a second guard.

"Do what?" he replied as he swiftly made his way to her side.

"You turned yourself to stone," she told him.

"Didn't I tell you about my new skills?" he grinned as he grabbed her hand and dragged her away from the two guards who were slowly moving towards them.

Kustos had also realised that the one–to-one tactic was not working, and he quickly attempted to manoeuvre his way to Will's side.

"Perhaps fighting together would be—" He was about to finish his sentence when he felt a presence behind him.

"Kustos, look out!" shouted Will.

Kustos glanced briefly around and could feel the movement of air as the swinging axe got closer.

"Just keep running forward," instructed the Dream Warrior. "I'll do the rest."

From past experiences, Kustos had learned not to question Will's demands. As he continued to move forward, he saw Will throw his hands out and move them upwards, creating a stairway of gravity. The Realm Lord kept running and as he did so found himself elevated into the air by the invisible steps. On reaching the top, Kustos took a leap of faith and found a gravity bubble waiting to collect him and return him safely to ground.

Whilst Kustos was attempting to outrun the stone statue, Will used his other hand to bombard it with his own gravity projectiles, forcing it to momentarily lose balance and fall back.

"Thank you, Master Will," gasped Kustos. "You have saved my life once again."

"Think nothing of it," replied Will, still finding the adoration of his skills somewhat embarrassing. "Your time will come to re-pay the debt; I've no doubts about that."

"I fear we are outnumbered in this fight," admitted Kustos.

"No," answered Will, "we just need a different strategy, that's all."

Meanwhile on the other side of the room, Jasmine and Connor were encountering the same difficulties. Although the statues were slow in movement, their massive size made them awkward to outrun or fight. Until a new plan could be put together, their only option was simply to stay alive.

"Jasmine, get behind me!" ordered Connor as an axe swung dangerously close to their heads.

She did as she was instructed but placed her hands on his shoulders so she could just peer over to one side to see what was happening. Again the axe cut through the air, missing them by inches.

"When I say duck . . . just duck," he told her.

She was about to acknowledge his command when he yelled, 'DUCK!' They both threw themselves to the ground. As they did so, the axe swung above them. The stone guardian threw so much effort into the attack that, because the blow did not hit a target, it swung uncontrollably around, hitting a second guard across the neck. Immediately there was a crashing sound as stone met stone, before the head of the guardian split from its stony body and shattered on the floor. Pleased with their achievement, Connor turned his attention to the second soldier.

"Well, that's one down," he told Jasmine.

"I am not sure. Look!" she replied as she pointed to the headless body still swinging his hammer aimlessly around.

"Oh, no!" moaned Connor, not noticing the other statue slowly working his way behind them. "Give us a break? Will, Kustos, how are you getting on?"

"Not a lot better," Will confirmed. "All I can do is knock them off balance but they keep getting back up." And he turned to

Kustos for his opinion of the situation but as he looked, he noticed an odd glow around Kustos' body. "Are you okay?" he asked him.

"I feel very strange, Master Will," he replied. "I can feel my dream energy bubbling within me, yet I am not consciously trying to conjure it up. I remember you saying our power was useless."

"Well, not useless," Will confirmed, "just different. How does it feel?"

"It feels amazing," he confirmed.

"That's great," oozed Will. "It appears you're calling upon your soul energy. Embrace it, use it, and sort these stony warriors out."

Kustos searched his mind for a way to tap into his power and then sensed the advice that Will had given him was the truth. It was now up to him to use that control and get them through their first ordeal.

"I have a plan," announced Kustos confidently. "Lord Connor, take care of my beloved Jasmine. We will be there to help you soon."

"Well hurry," urged Connor. "It is getting increasingly difficult to dodge these guys."

Kustos had already recognised the urgency, and soon the four of them were back-to-back in the centre of the room, surrounded by the guardians.

"I hope your plan's a good one?" said Connor as he ducked away from a swinging axe.

"Trust me, my lord," he answered, "it is. Now all of you get to the ground."

Without a second thought or doubt, Will, Connor and Jasmine dropped to the floor, leaving Kustos the only person standing. En-circling him was an aura of mysterious blue electricity, flashing and cracking against the ceiling as it waited for his command. Very slowly, Kustos took in a deep breath.

"Kustos?" said Jasmine softly.

He looked down at her and smiled, and in that split second, she knew that everything was going to be alright. Slowly he moved his arms out sideways, his palms away from his body. When fully satisfied with the position, he swung his arms until his hands finally met. The impact of the joining caused a powerful clapping sound as a sonic field spread rapidly away from his body like a ripple on a pond. A massive vibration of sound followed. Connor, with his acute hearing, heard it long before the others and covered his ears in an effort to defer the pain. A few seconds later, Will and Jasmine did the same. As the sonic pulsation hit the guards, they began to quiver and then, without warning, exploded, shattering into thousands of tiny pieces. Aware of what was about to come, Connor quickly threw an energy shield around them just in time to watch the remnants of stone crash against the invisible barrier. As the last piece of rock slipped to the floor, he dropped the shield, and Kustos held out his hand to assist Jasmine to her feet.

"Wow! Kustos!" exclaimed Will as he got to his feet. "That was awesome, man."

"It's some feeling, isn't it?" said Connor as he looked around at the devastation.

"It scared me at first," admitted Kustos, "all that power. Yet I felt invincible and now a little tired. Is that normal?"

"I think so," Connor told him. "When Will and I completed our tasks in the tower, we both fell asleep. Unfortunately though we don't have that luxury, so if you think you can manage, we must continue the journey."

"I will not hold you up," declared the king as he brushed the dust from his tunic.

"Nor did I ever doubt it." Connor smiled. "You've got to wonder though," he added as he started to walk up the stairway, "if you can create this type of devastation, I just can't wait to see what power Jasmine can conjure up."

Jasmine was not listening. She had already taken Kustos' hand and was brushing some dust from his hair.

"I am proud of you." She smiled lovingly.

"I am only glad I had the strength," he told her as she led him up the stairs.

"Hey! Guys?" said Will, who was idly kicking the rubble around. "Wait for me?"

At the top of the staircase, the four of them stood before the doors and studied the hieroglyphics.

"Does it say anything?" Connor asked Jasmine.

"I'm sorry no," she replied shaking her head. "The only sentence I can read was that of the guardians. The rest of the symbols seem to mean nothing."

"Well, not exactly nothing, Jasmine," interrupted Will. "They're replicas of those on our arms."

"And that dear friend," announced Connor, "is probably what it says—place here. All we have to do is put our arms on the indents and with any luck, wait for the doors to open."

"I hope you're right," replied his friend. "After the count of three then. One . . . two . . . three."

As Will finished counting, both he and Connor leaned forward and placed their arm into the notch in the door. At first nothing happened and just as they were about to remove them, pain shot through their arms.

"Oh, my God!" Connor shouted, followed by his friends agonising screams of, "Let go!"

"You must not remove them," ordered Kustos.

"That's easy for you to say," replied Will. "It feels as though my arm's being cut off."

"You must have faith, Master Will," encouraged Kustos. "After all, did you not tell me once there is no gain without pain?"

Will was about to answer when Jasmine interrupted with screams of delight.

"It's working, it's working," she advised them all. "Please hold on Lord Connor, Master Will."

Connor too had felt the slow movement of the door and although he had first thought it was wishful thinking on his part, the sudden confirmation from Jasmine told him it was not his imagination. Gradually, bit by bit, the doors opened and as they did so, they released the painful grip upon Will's and Connor's arms. The sudden movement forced them to lose balance, and both dropped to one knee as they quickly rubbed the life back into their limbs.

"Well, that wasn't pleasant," admitted Will as he stood up.

"Did you expect it to be easy?" Connor grinned.

There was no response as the four of them stared into darkness.

"This must be the point of no return," Connor told them. "If any of you have doubts about continuing the journey, please tell me now."

"We have no doubts." Jasmine smiled as she held Kustos' hand.

"Nor me, old friend," replied Will.

"In that case," added Connor, "I think it's time to go."

In unison, the four looked around and briefly perused the devastated room behind them, then, as if fully satisfied with the recent events, turned to each other and smiled. Without a word, they stepped into the darkness.

7

One Step Beyond

"I wish there was better light," said Kustos, enshrouded by the blackness of an unlit room.

The comfort of the cold feel of metal beneath his fingers was the only consolation he could take from walking into the unknown. Even the faintest hint of light, emitted from a small crack in the ground, did not raise his hopes as the Realm Lord quickly assessed that they faced yet another door.

"It is a door," he added as he turned the handle, "and surprise of all surprises, this time it is open. Perhaps our luck is changing?"

Cautiously he gripped the handled and pushed. Without any obstruction, it opened and a flash of illumination erupted from within the room.

"What is this place?" asked Jasmine as she followed Kustos in.

"Looks like a woodcutter's cabin to me," said Will as he looked around, and sure enough, it did resemble the fairy tale image of the woodcutter's cottage.

The cabin was devoid of any furniture, but a warming light came from a fireplace burning happily in the grate. There were no windows. Instead, three doors decorated three of the walls—one directly ahead of them, one to the left of them, and the other to their right.

"Master Will, Lord Connor," came a voice in the air, "I am glad you managed to find your way past the warriors."

"Vanisheo!" exclaimed Will, relieved to see a friendly face. "You know that phasing in and out of reality thing you do could be a useful asset to us here?"

"I am sorry, Master William," apologised Vanisheo. "It is not my place to interfere. I am merely your guide."

"Yea. Not if we really need you though, surely?" exclaimed Will.

Before the Hallucium had a chance to answer, a robed figured materialised before them.

"It is time," it told them.

"You!" exclaimed Connor. "I didn't expect to see you again."

"Nor I," the figure confirmed, "but here I am anyway and so are you, and I also see you have brought some assistance. Let us hope they will serve you well in the Judgment World."

"You know this being?" asked Kustos as he tried to gain a definitive vision of the figure.

"Yes," replied Will. "Sort of. He was our very vague guide in the tower."

Oblivious of Will's scathing statement, the illusive figure continued to speak.

"I will take Lord Connor," he suggested, "and Vanisheo can escort Master Will."

"Wait," ordered Connor. "Take us where?"

"Your rooms await you," advised the robed being. "Now please, Lord Connor, we do not have much time. Who will be your aide in the Judgment World?"

"Hang on," Will interrupted. "You mean we can't all go together?"

For the first time since their meeting, the robed figure showed some sign of emotion and apologised for the next part of their journey.

"I am sorry," he explained, "but the rooms are only set for two, the one who bears the symbol of the traveller and his companion. I know this is not an easy choice but please decide with haste. Time is running out."

"Yea, yea, it always is," said Connor as he looked at Kustos and Jasmine.

The decision was a hard one to make. Both were his friends, who without a second thought he would lay down his life for as they had done in the past for him, and to separate them in what could be their final days was more than he wanted to do. After a short time of deliberation, he spoke.

"If I must choose," he said, "I'll take Kustos. I fear I'll be faced with the most danger, and I wouldn't want to force dear Jasmine to face such a foe."

"No wait, Lord Connor," interrupted Kustos. "I understand your reasons to protect my wife, but I trust her life with you. In the past we have fought together side by side. If you are my friend, please grant me this favour."

Connor was finding the situation most uncomfortable. Both Jasmine and Kustos had valuable powers, but he feared more for her life than her husband's.

"Do you want to come with me, Jasmine?" Connor asked her.

She nodded and replied, "If it pleases my lord, I would prefer your company. Please do not be offended, Master William, but I am far more familiar with the ways of the Dream Lord."

"Hey!" replied Will. "No worries on my part. Besides we're bound to meet up on the other side, so I doubt it'll be for very long."

Jasmine threw her arms around Kustos and whispered in his ear. He smiled and kissed her and then wiped the tears that were forming in her eyes.

"We will be together soon," he promised her.

Connor and Jasmine wasted no time and immediately walked over to the robed guide who was still patiently waiting. They permitted him to lead them to the door on the left. Jasmine turned for one last time and mouthed, "I love you" to Kustos. Connor also turned back and smiled at Will.

"See you on the other side," he told him. "Try to keep alive on your own."

Will was about to reply but it was too late. They had entered the room, and the door closed quickly behind them.

"Come, Master Will, Lord Kustos," said Vanisheo. "We must take the right door. Have faith in your beliefs, and everything will work out for the better."

Bemused by the decisions they had been forced to make, they followed without a word, and, like their friends, they disappeared behind the door.

Jasmine was gripping Connor's hand so tightly he felt his fingers begin to cramp up.

"It's okay, Jasmine," he told her gently. "There's no danger here. Isn't that so, old man?" he queried from the robed figured but received no reply. "So where are you taking us anyway?" Connor added . . . but still nothing.

Instead the figure merely quickened his pace, so Connor and Jasmine had to hurry to keep up with him. As they wandered through the well-lit corridor, they could see rows and rows of doors. All were similar, but none were signed.

"I wonder where these doors lead to?" queried Jasmine who had now lost her sense of fear and had permitted her curiosity to take over.

"Behind each door is as many races as there are realities," came the reply. "Just like Connor and Will, they have all earned their right into the Judgment World and back again. These doorways are their links to their next path."

"But why would you want to voluntarily go into Judgment?" asked Jasmine.

"Many have their reasons for wanting early access," confirmed their guide, "but you are different, Lord Connor. For the first time in my known history, someone has craved access that was not in their best interest. For this alone, I believe you will succeed."

Connor felt flattered by the statement and took some comfort in the words. If nothing else, at least someone had faith in their suicidal mission.

"Ahh . . . here we are!" the being suddenly announced. "A very nice room, this one."

He reached into his robe and retrieved a large key. Carefully he placed it into the lock and turned. Slowly, the door opened, and as it did so, the key evaporated from view.

"Please, Lord Connor, Lady Jasmine, enter," he urged them.

Together they peered into the open doorway and looked inside. It was a bedroom. A four-poster bed stood majestically in the centre of the room, and a blazing fire burned in a large stone grate. Soothing warmth and comfort from the yellowy flame bathed the room, and both Jasmine and Connor felt drawn to it.

"Umm . . . what are we supposed to do in here?" asked Connor somewhat confused and embarrassed by the connotations.

"This bed is of the finest craftsmanship and dressed with the purest of silk. It is designed for perfect comfort," replied the guide. "Its purpose is the transition from this world to the next. You and Jasmine must lie side by side and close your eyes. Only then will your dream energy be absorbed by the fire, forcing your soul energy to replace it. At that moment, the fire will once again absorb the energy, leaving your bodies as lifeless shells. Then and only then will you be pulled through into the Judgment World. It is not a pleasant experience, nor would I have you believe so, but then it is but a small price to pay for such an important assignment. Be safe, my lord, my lady. There is much counting on your success. More than you can ever imagine."

His voice slowly softened as the door closed behind them, and he disappeared.

"I don't like this," announced Connor, "not the whole lying on the bed next to you thing but—"

He did not finish the sentence as Jasmine put a single finger over his mouth.

"Ssh!" she assured him. "It will be fine. We have each other and therefore are not alone. Besides, do you not think Will and Kustos must follow the same procedure and will undoubted be waiting for us? They would not think twice about the request."

"I guess so," Connor admitted, "but I want it noted for the re-cord that I lay down next to you in the interest of this mission."

"Your reasons are duly noted, Lord Connor." She smiled as she climbed upon the bed and lay down on the soft furnishings.

"Are you coming?" she asked as she patted the mattress next to her.

Connor stared at her. She looked so determined as she rested and yet was still perfectly groomed, despite their latest ordeal. Her long blond hair spread out across the pillow and over her shoul-ders, resting lightly against the fresh white linen blouse that was loosely fitted over a tighter-fitting tube top. This was designed to absorb the heat in winter and keep cool in the summer. Even her white linen trousers over white shorts appeared unwrinkled by wear and the lightweight shoes, capable of any surface but still flexible for speed, remained unscathed from any previous battles.

"Sure! Why not." He smiled as he climbed next to her.

She reached out and took his hand.

"Ready?" she said.

"As I'll ever be," he replied.

Together they closed their eyes and almost immediately began to feel their dream energy drain from their bodies. The room lit up as their power unified as one and was absorbed into the flame, only to be replaced by the force from their soul. Jasmine began to moan as this energy was also dragged from her. Pain shot through their frames as it battled to remain encapsulated within the warmth of their bodies. Agony became their strength as it began to get the better of them, and with one last thrash of power, their life force was extricated from each body and absorbed again within the flame. Now all that remained were two lifeless corpses lying side by side.

�֍ ✤ ✤

"Master Will, Master Will, Wake up!" said Kustos as he shook Will by the shoulders.

Slowly Will opened his eyes and stared up.

"You gave me quite a scare," continued Kustos. "I thought I had lost you."

"It takes more than that to get rid of me, I can assure you," replied Will as he sat up, "although I have to admit, that really hurt."

Will looked around and sighed.

"Oh man," he said. "Have we actually gone anywhere?"

In front of him was a long empty wall finishing someway off in the distance with a single door decorated with some unrecognisable writing. Above them red and orange skies of twilight shone down upon them, whilst behind them the darkness of night was waiting to drag them back into oblivion.

"I guess the only way is through that door then?" he said to Kustos who was looking around for some sign of his beloved Jasmine.

"Where is Lord Connor and my dearest Jasmine, Will?" he asked. "Where is Vanisheo?"

Will had been so preoccupied, it had not occurred to him they were alone, and just as he was about to answer, a familiar voice drifted from behind them.

"Lord Connor and Lady Jasmine will take a separate path," it said.

"You!" challenged Will as the robed figured appeared. "What have you done with them?"

"It is alright, Master Will," interrupted Vanisheo quickly as he appeared behind Kustos, "they are safe."

"What in the name of Sublin is going on, Vanisheo?" demanded Will. "Why's this guy following us?"

Vanisheo did not speak but instead the robed figure took a step forward to face both men.

"Allow me to finally introduce myself," he said. "My name is Joshua." And with that, he removed the hood from his head to expose his true features.

Surprisingly enough he had a human face, short brown hair, and dark eyes. By the look of his skin, he was probably in his late thirties to early forties, although age in any of the worlds was not always a reflection of looks.

"I was once an Oracle of the Judgment World," he continued, "performing tasks in the Judgment Halls."

"Forgive me for interrupting," said Will, "but with such a reverent job role, what possessed you to give it up?"

"The choice, I fear, was not mine," said Joshua as though he had not heard Will's question. "One day, I heard a whisper in the air, trying to communicate with me, asking for assistance to walk the path of redemption. The request appeared honest enough, but my senses warned me that the essence was an evil soul, and so I took it upon myself to notify the other Oracles. Unfortunately, I was too late. One of my brethren had weakened under false promises and allowed the being through. Many of us disagreed with such a decision, and so a rift amongst the Oracle was caused. Some of them joined this evil monster. Volnar was his name. Others, like myself, had heard his reputation and fled in fear of our own safety. Those more naïve amongst us stayed to face their final Judgment."

"So how did you get here?" Kustos asked.

"With help, I managed to escape. It was by sheer luck that I met the one who pulled Volnar through into the Judgment World. He had knowledge of the passage into Sublin and showed me the way. There I stayed hidden until you and Connor came to change this course of evil."

"Who was this person who freed you?" asked Will.

"His name was Armon, a victim in the history of time and a pawn for Volnar. Every time the Evil Lord had need of something, Armon was always at hand, but that I also cannot get into right now. All you must know is that Armon is in hiding, and, this William is where your journey lies."

"Me? Why me?" asked Will.

"Through that door," pointed Joshua, "is the path of redemption, the one chance where those of sinful history can redeem themselves before the Oracle and find a heavenly pathway. The route is not an easy one, and many dangers can prevail, but Armon took that chance to hide until you came for him, Master William."

"Again, I have to ask . . . why me?" reiterated Will.

Joshua did not answer the question, instead merely pointed again at the closed door.

"This is where you must go," he ordered. "Only you can help Armon regain everything he has lost."

"But what about Connor and Jasmine?" queried Will, still unconvinced that his destiny lay elsewhere.

"It is not their destiny but yours. It is my responsibility to show you how to contact Armon," Joshua told him. "As consolation of your separation, your thoughts can reach your friends, and I will teach you. Please, let us join hands, so I can relay the assignments."

Vanisheo stood back while Kustos and Will took Joshua's hands.

"Vanisheo," ordered the Oracle, "you must join us as well. Your destiny also lies within these paths."

Vanisheo did as he was instructed and grabbed Will's hand one side and Joshua's on the other, completing the circle.

"Now focus your mind's energy," Joshua instructed. "Picture a room where we all can meet. Connor, Connor?" he called.

⚜ ⚜ ⚜

Connor opened his eyes and quickly focussed on Jasmine's peaceful face.

"Jasmine," he called softly as he carefully touched her shoulder, "we've made it through. Please wake up?"

Jasmine opened her eyes and smiled briefly and then sadness filled her face.

"What's the matter?" asked Connor.

"I see we have reached our pathway," she said, "but I do not see Kustos or the others. We are lost."

"Lost is a meaning for not knowing where you are," Connor told her. "We at least must assume we've reached our destination."

As Connor looked around, he saw the endless, blank wall with a door some way off in the distant. The sky above them held a twilight hue and behind them was the darkness.

"We have to go towards the light, dear Jasmine," he said as he helped her to her feet.

Together without a word, they walked towards the door. Writing was sprawled untidily across it as if written in a hurry.

"Can you read it?" Connor asked her.

"Sort of," she replied. "It says something about 'to walk the path to Judgment you must first show bravery.'"

"Well, that doesn't sound—" Connor did not have a chance to finish his sentence as Jasmine grabbed his shoulders and smiled.

Together in their minds they heard familiar voices.

"Connor . . . Jasmine? Can you hear us?" they heard as a vision appeared of a room.

Standing together in a circle were Kustos, Will, Vanisheo, and Joshua.

"You?" replied Connor directing his accusation at Joshua. "What's going on and why aren't we together?"

"Chill out, old man," joked Will. "This is Joshua, an Oracle of Judgment. That was until Volnar turned up. Then he came back to Sublin to wait for us."

"Too many eyes, too many ears, my lord," explained Joshua.

"Jasmine, are you alright?" asked Kustos with concern.

"I am fine, my love," she replied. "Connor has been nothing but a gentleman."

"So, what happens now, Joshua?" asked Connor cutting to the chase. "What plans are laid out for us?"

"My lord," he replied with respect of the Dream Lord's title. "Master William and Lord Kustos must come with me. Their journey must take a different path from yours, if we are to have any chance of being victorious."

"What references can you provide that encourages us to trust you?" asked Connor. "How do we know this isn't a trap and that you're not also working for Volnar?"

"There is nothing I can do to prove my trust, my lord," replied Joshua, "but you are a man of great judgment. You must have faith that I am here to help. It is imperative that we find Armon in the

Judgment World. His only real crime is being of weak mind. A slave to Volnar's bidding but yet a potent being, if the curse can be lifted. Master William has the power to release Armon from the Dark Lord's clenches and use his strength to bring him down."

"What do think, Will?" Connor asked his friend. "Can we trust him?"

"I can't say for sure," Will answered, "but what I do know is that we don't have a plan now we're here, and Joshua does. If there's a slim chance that Armon can help us, then we have to take it. I mean, let's face it, Volnar was difficult to contain in Sublin. I really hate to think what he's capable of in the Judgment World."

"Okay," replied Connor, "if you're sure that's what you have to do, then go with Joshua, but if you're off chasing down Armon, what pathway lies out there for Jasmine and me?"

"I honestly have no knowledge of what trail you have been sent on," admitted Joshua. "My instructions came from the Higher Power. What I can tell you, though, is that you must find the one they call Hunter. He was awaiting final sentence in the Judgment Hall that day Volnar stormed the halls. In all the confusion, he managed to escape, the only person still alive to have performed such a feat in the history of Judgment. It is imperative that you find him, as we need his knowledge to lead us back into the Halls."

"But did you not say you were an Oracle?" asked Jasmine. "Would you not know the way back?"

"Unfortunately not," replied Joshua. "The Hall of Judgment is the single most important place this side of existence. This alone means it must remain hidden. As soon as any Oracle leaves, its location is immediately wiped from their minds. As its true function in the Passover of the mind is a one-way gate, it must always remain safe at all cost. Once you sit before the Oracle in the Judgment Halls, your future is determined, and you pass on, never to return. The whole idea of an escape from the halls is unheard of, however, and if luck is on our side, Hunter would still have retained the memories of its location."

"You mean you do not actually know for sure that Hunter can help?" asked Kustos, finally breaking the silence.

"Sometimes," said Joshua with a smile, "you must take that leap of faith, as I'm sure Lord Connor and Master William would agree. A slim chance is better than nothing. I do understand how it looks from your point of view. This is not ideal, but what did you expect? There was only ever going to be a fool's hope in this mission. Looking over your history, I have seen what faith has done for you in the past and for this reason alone, I believe it will work. I would not be here if I thought it was futile."

"Okay," replied Connor reluctantly, "Jasmine and I will search for Hunter although the chances of him being on this path are very small."

"I think," Joshua pointed out, "you will find you first clue close by, hiding in the shadows. I am sorry, I wish I could do more, but I have used what little influence I had left to lead you to where you are now."

Connor hardly felt surprised that Joshua had arranged their passage in the direction of Hunter, and for the first time since reawakening in the room, he felt a certain peace, an understanding that he was on course to his own path of destiny.

"We must be off," Joshua suddenly announced. "Time is not on our side. We will contact you once we have news of Armon. In the meantime, you and Jasmine must swiftly move on. Remember to avoid discovery by Volnar as best you can. There is a war going on in the Judgment World but at all cost, try not to get involved. Your destiny is far more important. We must all reach the Judgment Halls and face Volnar once more. Be safe, Lord Connor, Lady Jasmine." And as his words lingered in the air, he lifted his hood over his head and walked out of the room.

"I don't like this plan very much, Will," admitted Connor, "but it looks as though we've little choice. Look out for each other and keep your heads down."

"You know me," Will said with a grin, "I'm the Dream Warrior with the best teacher ever by my side. It's you and Jasmine that must be careful."

"We will, Master Will," interrupted Jasmine. "Just look after my dear Kustos."

"Come on, Jasmine," said Connor. "We'd better try and find Hunter although I've no idea where to start."

"Wait, Connor," ordered Will. "Vanisheo," he said turning to his friend, "can you guide Connor and Jasmine through their task?"

"Of course I can, Master Will," answered the Hallucium.

"Then please, my friend, show them the way?" asked Will.

"Lord Connor, Lady Jasmine," Vanisheo said as he looked sadly at Will.

He was reluctant to leave his friend but understood the importance of the request

"Please wait for me," he told Connor. "I will join you shortly." And turning to Will, he hugged his leg tightly. "Take care, Master William," he said as he released him. "I do not want this to be the last time we meet."

"Nor I," Will smiled. "Now go." And with that Vanisheo disappeared from his side, and in his mind's eye, within seconds, Will saw him reappear beside Connor.

"Thank you, Vanisheo," said Connor as the Hallucium materialised beside him. "Your presence is gratefully appreciated. Be safe, Will, Kustos, and contact us at the slightest sign of trouble."

Connor turned to open the door, and as he did so Jasmine took one last longing look at her husband.

"I love you, Kustos," she said. "Please do not do anything that will get you killed."

"Those days have gone, my love," replied Kustos. "We will be together soon enough. Just find Hunter, and we will seek out Armon. Then we can be together once more."

Jasmine smiled at Kustos' response and turned to joined Connor.

"Come on, Master Will," urged Kustos as he watched Jasmine leave. "I just want this over."

"Me too," replied Will. "Oh and, Kustos?"

"Master Will?" he answered.

"Just call me Will," said the Dream Warrior.

"As you wish, Will." Kustos smiled as they left the room.

8

The Road to Darkness

"So I guess we need to walk through the door in order to reach the Judgment World," suggested Connor. "I've no idea what to expect. Are you ready, Jasmine?"

"I am," she said as she tried to turn the handle. "Huh? It's locked," she added.

"So even the first step of the journey is causing a problem," concluded Connor as he looked above them, "and I don't rate our chances in trying to scale the walls either. This isn't a very good start to a mission now is it?"

"Lord Connor, Lady Jasmine? Are you there?" said a faint voice from the other side of the door.

"Is that you, Vanisheo?" asked Jasmine. "Can you see why the door will not open?"

"I can, my lady," replied the Hallucium. "I do not understand why, but a metal bar has been placed to prevent entry."

"I guess someone knew we were coming," interrupted Connor. "Are you able to lift it, Vanisheo?"

"I am sorry, my lord," apologised the reality spirit, "it is too heavy for me on my own."

"Then let me try something," suggested Jasmine as an idea came to mind, and she concentrated on her soul energy as a way of assisting.

To her surprise and relief, it began to swirl around her body, and then suddenly she turned into a blue, transparent, ghost-like figure.

"Wow! That's spooky," joked Connor. "What are you doing?"

"I feel my psychic energy growing stronger," she told him and without further explanation walked cleanly through the door to other side.

"Jasmine, Jasmine!" Connor called frantically.

He feared he had lost her before their mission had even started, but his reaction was unfounded as the door suddenly flew open, and there standing before him was both Vanisheo and Jasmine.

"Come on, Connor," she reprimanded, "we do not have all day." And she grabbed him by the arm and dragged him through the door.

"Well, you look as though you're back to normal," replied Connor as he looked at her smiling face.

The blue aura had now disappeared and her solid form was once more ready to take on the next challenge.

"Thanks for helping us find Hunter, Vanisheo," he added as he noticed the Hallucium standing by her side.

"I would help you, my lord, with my very last breath," he replied.

"I know you would." The Dream Lord smiled kindly. "But let's hope it doesn't come to that and, . . . Vanisheo?"

"Yes, my lord," replied the spirit.

"Just . . . call me Connor," added the Dream Lord. "My title is not important, even less so here."

"Connor?" interrupted Jasmine. "We are losing the light of day. Look?" And she pointed to the lowering light as it began to disappear behind a small clump of trees. "We must find shelter and plan."

"I think I recognise this place," mused Vanisheo as he looked around. "If my memory serves me well, there should be a village not far from here, in that direction." And he pointed over to the left.

Relying on the Hallucium's intuitive powers, they hurried off in the direction he had shown. Darkness was almost upon them and the unknown of this new world began to unsettle Jasmine and Connor. Even when they approached the village, their mood did not improve. It was obvious by the deathly quiet that it was deserted and had been for many years. Tumble-like weed blew across the dusty road, and shutters to the old, wild west-type homesteads, rattled on their hinges as they flapped uncontrollably in the wind. In the middle of the main street was a stone well. Its bucket dangled helplessly within the structure, swinging silently backwards and forward, only occasionally scraping the stony sides.

Cautiously, they walked through the buildings and as they looked, they saw in the distance another wall blocking the pathway. This time though with no visible sign of exit.

"Hello," shouted Connor as his voice echoed around the empty town. "Is there anybody here?"

"What happened?" asked Jasmine as she continued to look around.

"I do not know," answered Vanisheo sadly. "This place was once a vibrant town. Full of life and friendly faces. It always used to throw the best parties in the dry months, better than any other in this area, but now it looks as though no one has lived here for years."

"How long ago were you here?" enquired Jasmine. "Because the natural order of progression could be the reason for this desolation."

"No, my lady," replied Vanisheo, "this is not a usual evolution, as not so many cycles of this planet ago was its heart still beating."

"We'd better keep moving," suggested Connor un-nerved by the sensation of fear that was beginning to crawl up his spine. "The sky is turning and soon it'll be completely dark."

No sooner had he spoken than the last glimmer of light disappeared from the sky, and the shadows of darkness began to creep their way down the deserted, dusty road. Out of the quiet, a cry was heard from one of the buildings.

"Quick! Over here!" shouted the stranger. "You must stay in the light. It is your only protection."

Slowly the shadows sneaked through the village, and growls and cries of an evil presence resounded eerily throughout the hollow shacks. Jasmine, Connor, and Vanisheo looked at each briefly then started running towards the nearest building. Snapping jaws of shadows behind them broke the now still air, but they dared not stop to look. The darkness was only inches from them, and once consumed, they sensed the mission would be over.

With one last final effort, Connor grabbed Jasmine and Vanisheo by the arms and thrust them through an open door, following close behind. Less than seconds later, it was slammed shut as the malevolent entities crashed into the wooden barrier, depriving them of their latest victims.

Connor caught his breath and looked up. There before him stood a man.

"Thank you," Connor said as he stood up and laid a hand upon his shoulder in an act of friendship. "That was close."

As he looked around the room, he noticed many lanterns illuminating every corner. Shedding light and barring the darken shadows. A huddle of adults and children sat comfortably in the centre, eating and chatting quietly, oblivious of the evil waiting outside.

"Who are you?" asked Connor.

"We could ask that of you?" was the reply.

"Well, we are no mystery," admitted Jasmine, and then she caught the warning in Connor's eye. "We are travellers trying to outrun the war," she lied.

"Well, we are Wake Worlders," said the man, a little more relaxed now that the introductions were over. "It was our choice not to take the path of Judgment and so we made a home for ourselves here."

"What was that outside?" asked Jasmine, as she dusted herself off and joined Connor.

"None of us know who they really are," was the answer. "For no one has ever seen their true form and lived to tell the tale. All that is known of the evil is that they live in the darkness, hiding amongst the shadows, just waiting to pounce. Wherever night time shadows form, so does the malevolence lurk."

"They are sinful souls that have no world," explained Vanisheo as he suddenly understood what they were facing. "They use the darkness to travel around. I did not realise they still existed. On my last visit here, the Oracles were working on banishing them. I can see now that did not happen."

"You know this world, my friend?" asked the stranger. "Then you must also be aware that they have increased in numbers. The new Judgment Oracle no longer has an interest in this troubled place, to rid it of such evil. It relishes in the darkness taking over Judgment."

"I cannot believe it has changed so much," muttered the Hallucium as he reached out and grabbed Jasmine's hand for comfort. "It is far worse than Father ever imagined."

"Then you are familiar with this current plight?" the trio was asked.

"Familiar of another time," replied Vanisheo, "when the Judgment World was controlled and it was safe to roam whatever path had been laid out for you. It breaks my heart to see how much it has changed."

"And ours also," replied the man, "but changed it has, and we must make the best of it. Our reason for this existence was an easy one but what brings you three to this world? You do not look as though you are trying to avoid the path of Judgment."

"Looks can be deceiving." Connor smiled, not wanting to give too much away to perfect strangers. "But where are our manners? I must apologise. My name is Connor, and these are my travelling companions, Jasmine and Vanisheo. We've come to this world to find the one called Hunter."

"Hunter?" echoed the man. "Why no one can find Hunter, unless Hunter wants to be found."

"We *MUST* find him," implored Jasmine. "We dare not fail."

"Such bold words from one so pretty," replied the man.

"And what is that supposed to mean?" asked Jasmine as she rested her hand strategically on her hip to express her disapproval.

A couple of the men stood up, brandishing their swords, and Jasmine quickly moved behind Connor.

"Hey, hey, hey," said the Dream Lord as he raised his hands in submission. "We mean you no harm, and if you can't help us, then please, just lend us a lantern or two, so we may continue our journey past the next wall."

"You must forgive my son," said a voice from the corner of the room. "His manners wane when the shadows creep across our homes."

Connor looked around the room and could just make out the image of an old man in a corner as he scrambled to his feet and moved further into the light.

"My name is Goldsmith," he explained. "We are the only survivors of this town, destroyed by the armies of Volnar as they cleansed the world of any remaining goodness. We fought to retain our freedom but paid an expensive price. So many lives were lost and with it the hope of ever rebuilding the happiness we once had."

Connor thought for a moment and then decided a little bit of hope might encourage the survivors to help them.

9

Time for a Plan

"I'm Connor of Sublin," he told them, "and this is Lady Jasmine of the Waterfall Kingdom. Vanisheo here," he said as he pointed to the Hallucium, "is the prince of Hallucium. We've come to the Judgment World to try and rid you of this evil."

"I know your name," said the old man. "Your reputation precedes you. Stories of your victories have travelled throughout this world."

"But how?" asked Connor, amazed that anyone would have heard of him.

"Up until a day or two ago a man had been waiting for you here," came the reply. "He kept telling us you would come, and that it was his destiny to join you and rid Judgment of the Oracle known as Volnar."

"Who was this man, and where is he now?" asked Connor.

"He would not tell us his name," answered Goldsmith, "as he said it would be safer for us not to know."

"So where is he now?" interrupted Vanisheo.

"He has been taken by the darkness," replied the old man, "but we think he might still be alive as sometimes in the still of the night we hear his screams."

"Where do they come from? Do you know where he is being held?" asked Jasmine.

"We know," was the answer, "but it is of little use to you. He was taken to the bottom of the well, a perfect strategic hold. That is where the darkness tortures him as part of their own entertainment, but whether his wails of pain are merely images of the past, trapped within the gloom, we cannot say for sure."

"Then I'll have to go and find out," said Connor. "Please, let us have one of your lanterns, and then we shall leave you in peace. For your kindness and help, I will promise one thing . . . we will end this destruction in your lives."

"That is suicide," exclaimed the first man. "Father, we cannot let them go down there alone."

"That is true, my son," replied Goldsmith, "but it is not their choice to force any of you to take up arms and face these deadly creatures once more. Only you can make that decision."

"Then I will go with them and help," interrupted another, "and any man that wishes to join me will have my admiration as a true warrior."

"I can't ask you to risk your lives on such a foolhardy mission," said Connor, "but let it be known that those that wish to rid the Judgment World of Volnar will have the appreciation of not only the whole of Sublin but of the other two worlds within the system as well."

"This is not just your battle, Lord Connor," replied the volunteer. "It is our lives too and an opportunity to fight back and take what is rightfully ours. Any man who wants to join me, say aye,"

A few men in the group responded and clambered to their feet to join the instigator of the assignment.

"It seems a decision has been made then, Lord Connor," said Goldsmith. "This is Bow," he said as he pointed to the first volunteer. "He is a good man and will lead you down the well and through the tunnels."

"I am Fazer," said another as he stepped forward.

"And my name is Duke," announced the third.

"Thank you, my friends." Connor smiled. "Your bravery is much appreciated. I only hope I've not given you false hope?"

"We know the risks, my lord," said Fazer. "I would rather die trying to defeat the darkness than hide like a fox from the hounds."

"In that case," answered Connor, wanting to hold on to their enthusiasm while he could, "let's go. We can't waste a moment longer. Jasmine, Vanisheo, don't stray? Stay close to my side." And he handed them each a lantern.

"I do not think there will be any chance of that," announced Jasmine as she grabbed Vanisheo's hand. "I have no intention of letting you out of arms reach. I know you have offered some insane plans in the past, Connor, but this one, so far, tops the list."

"We will be fine, Jasmine," smiled Vanisheo nervously. "Vanisheo will protect you, and if all goes horribly wrong, I can always melt us out of existence to some place else. If the stress does not get to me that is."

"You can do that?" she asked, now feeling a little more comforted by an escape plan.

Vanisheo said nothing more but winked at her and smiled again.

"Come? We must go," instructed Bow as he picked up a lantern and headed for the door.

"Good luck," said Goldsmith to his son. "You are going to need it."

During their discussions and volunteering, Connor noticed how quiet it had become outside, and rather than take comfort from the lack of noise, he sensed they should move on as soon as possible.

"It seems a little too quiet out there," he acknowledged. "I doubt we could be this lucky that the darkness has moved on."

"You are right, my lord," replied Duke. "They think they can draw us out if we believe they have left. We fell for that just once and lost several of our family. Never again will we underestimate their devious minds."

"Keep your lanterns over head," ordered Bow, "and stay in the light, however dim it may appear to be. This will be our only defence. At the bottom of the well is a small tunnel. This is where the darkness likes to settle and wait. If we can create sufficient light, we should be able to force them out. It is dangerous but what suicide mission is not?"

"So far I like your plan, Bow," said Connor, "but how do we get to the bottom of the well?"

"That is where I come in," interrupted Fazer as he threw a huge rope ladder over his shoulder.

"If I didn't know better," added Connor, "I would get the impression you were prepared for this event."

"In a way, yes," replied Bow. "The stranger waiting for you had unbreakable faith in your ability, and once he was taken, we thought you might want to rescue him. All we had to do was watch and wait for you to arrive."

"Again, I can only thank you for your perception," answered Connor, "and hope we're not a disappointment to the image that has been portrayed."

"Never, my lord," interrupted Goldsmith. "Your bravery spans farther than you could ever imagine, and if you fail to overthrow the Dark Lord, we know it will not be through lack of courage."

Bow realised this was his cue to get the mission started, and putting his hand on the door handle, he issued his orders.

"We will go out first, my lord, and set up the ladder," he told them. "When you hear us call, run like the wind towards the well. The light will probably be sufficient to keep the darkness at bay, but it will not deter them from trying to entice you into their world. Fazer, Duke, are you ready?"

"I have been ready since I was born," replied Fazer bravely.

"Then let it begin," answered Bow. "Everyone here get to the back of the room and burn those lanterns brightly. We do not want a straying entity to find its way in."

The small crowd of people did as they were instructed and huddled tightly together with their backs against the wall. When Bow was satisfied with their safety, he opened the door and the three men ran out. Growls and screams could be heard as the darkness snapped within inches of their ankles, but the golden rays emitted by the lanterns discouraged it from getting any closer. As the men strode forward, a cold fearful sweat started to run down their faces. Images of evil drifted across their path and then quickly dissipated in the glow of their lights. One slip was all it would take to drag the human forms into their world of obscurity.

Bow was the first to reach the well, and he called out to Fazer, "Give me the ladder, Fazer!"

Fazer removed the makeshift ladder and threw it to Bow. As he did so, his lantern dropped from his other hand. His protection had been removed and the darkness instantly swooped, engulfing the figure into a pit of desolation, slicing and cutting across his flesh. Duke was only a step behind, and in a single movement, he grabbed Fazer by his collar and dragged him towards the well. What light the single lantern threw was just enough to pull Fazer back from the depths of the dark.

Bow in the meantime had focussed his mind on the task bestowed upon him, and although the darkness nipped and pecked at his half-shadowed figure, it did not sway his determination.

Instead it made him work that much quicker, and soon the ladder was attached to the well and hanging limply inside. As soon as Duke and Fazer reached him, he threw his lantern into the well to illuminate the depths below. The three men huddled together under the one remaining lantern, praying the glow of the flames would be enough to keep them safe.

"Lord Connor! Now!" shouted Bow above the eerie cries.

Connor opened the door and was just about to leave when a voice from the shadows offered another form of defence.

"Take this, my lord," it said, as a bottle rolled along the floor and landed at his feet. "It is my own concoction of oils, an explosion that will scare even the biggest monster."

"Thank you," replied Connor as he picked it up. "Now, Jasmine, Vanisheo, keep those lanterns burning and stay close."

With that, he grabbed Jasmine's wrist and dragged her into the night. Blocking out the danger and focussing on her task, she held the lantern high above her head so shards of light fell over her and Connor. Vanisheo gripped the bottom of her blouse as he struggled with his own oversized lamp.

The malevolent darkness, sensing the importance of the trio, dared to test the rays of light by slicing and cutting across their path in an effort to draw them into the night. Connor was undeterred by their attack as he concentrated on his mission of all of them reaching the well.

"Good to see you," exclaimed Bow. "Now you have done the easy part, how about the next stage of the journey?"

"Bring it on, my friend, bring it on," said Connor.

"I have created a light down in the well, but the ladder is hidden by shadow. This will be where the darkness will aim to strike," Bow advised them.

"I have an idea, Connor," interrupted Vanisheo. "I am small enough to ride your back. Let me hold the lantern as you climb down the ladder. Once at the bottom you can shelter in the rays. I do not need a light to phase through reality and can reappear back here to cover Jasmine and the others as they join you."

"You can do that, little pixie?" asked Bow.

"I am no pixie," replied Vanisheo defiantly, "and yes, my skills are such that any place within the universe can be my home."

"Apologies, young friend," said Bow. "I have not seen or heard of such a being."

"I am not young by your standards," continued the Hallucium trying not to take offence again, "but apology accepted. We are a secret people, and you had no reason to know of our existence."

"Where do we go when we reach the bottom?" asked Connor.

"I will lead," offered Bow.

"I can't ask that of you. Bow, nor Duke and Fazer alike," replied Connor. "You must protect your own people. Your bravery will act as an incentive to their survival."

"But we can help." interrupted Duke. "We can guard you for as long as you require."

"I know you can, Bow," smiled Connor as he rested his hand upon Bow's arm. "Your bravery is not questioned here but this is not the pathway written for you. Your destiny has chosen a different route."

Bow thought for a moment over the words and understood what Connor implied.

"In that case, my lord," he said, "let me at least paint a picture of your route? The well will be devoid of water. Only during the rainy season will its levels rise, so once you have reached the bottom you must take the tunnel to the storage room. Pass this room and continue to the other side of the wall, into the river. There you should find your friend."

"Connor," whispered Jasmine as she listened to Bow's plan of action, "do not make me climb the ladder alone? Let me join you and Vanisheo?"

Connor was about to protest over the safety issue of climbing down together but could sense the nervousness in her voice.

"Vanisheo will climb your back, Jasmine," he told her, "and I will carry his lantern."

"Thank you," she replied with relief.

Connor climbed over the side of the well and gripped onto the rope ladder with one hand. He then held out the other to take Vanisheo's lantern. He found some loose rope by the ladder and attached one end to the handle, so the lantern hung down his back and onto his belt. When all was in place, the Hallucium quickly climbed up on Jasmine's shoulders.

"Am I too heavy for you?" he asked her.

"Of course not," she lied, knowing that this was their only way of survival.

If the truth was known, Jasmine did find the burden of the Hallucium weighing down upon her shoulders, but fear of climbing without Connor forced her to remain quiet. Once Connor was out of view, Duke assisted Jasmine over the side and handed her the lantern.

"Be careful, my lady," he told her.

Calmly Jasmine slowly began to lower herself down. Every so often she felt a nip at her feet, and she shrieked as the shadows snapped at her.

"Do hurry, Connor," she urged as the light from his lantern cast shadows upon the wall. "This is getting extremely irritating."

Connor looked up to quell her fears, and as he did so, he heard an urgent shout from above as a body dropped past him and hit the ground below. Jasmine, taken by surprise, slipped and lost her footing, forcing her to tumble downwards. Reacting without thinking, Connor put out his hand and casually grabbed her arm, then mustering up his strength, he swung her back towards the ladder, where she managed to get a hold.

"What was that?" Connor shouted up.

"It was Duke," cried Bow. "The shadows pushed him over the edge. Can you see him? Is he alive?"

"I have a few bruises," came a voice from the depths of the well, "but otherwise I appear alright."

"Stay in the light, Duke," ordered Connor. "We'll soon be there."

With that, both he and Jasmine quickened their pace. Each step took them closer to the bottom but at the same time gave the impression their destination was no closer. Unrelenting nips and bites slowed their pace and each rung of the ladder became harder to take. After many minutes of timeless travel, Connor could just decipher the outline of Duke's physique.

"We're almost there, Jasmine," he told her. "Don't look down."

Not taking his own advice, he took another quick glance at the silhouette as it balanced precariously in the light of the lantern. Fully satisfied that Duke was safe for the time being, Connor continued to climb until a piercing scream echoed around the stone walls, and the blood in his veins froze. The cry was one of pain and fear and forcing himself to look down once more, Connor was just in time to see Duke dragged from the light as it went quiet. Moments later a severed arm hit him on the side of the face, and he knew then that there was no hope of a rescue. Duke had gone and by now his lifeless form was probably a feast for the hungry souls. Connor's only wish was that the brave human would not suffer.

"I am sorry, Bow," said Connor sadly. "Duke is gone. There was nothing I could do."

"No! This cannot be true," cried Bow. "He was standing in the light. How could the darkness cross the line?"

"I can't answer that," replied Connor. "You know these creatures better than I."

"You must put an end to this, my lord," said Bow angrily. "Do not let any more helpless souls suffer by the hand of such evil. Please end the torment?"

"Go, Bow, "Connor ordered firmly. "Take Fazer and go back to your people and keep safe."

Bow was about to object but saw the injured body of his friend hanging limply over the well wall next to him. Picking up Fazer and throwing him over his shoulder, he looked down at the well for the last time.

"Be safe, Lord Connor," he said as he leaned over and then was gone, removing the last remnants of light above Connor's head.

10

Finding a Friend

Completely alone, they continued to descend the ladder and before he knew it Connor felt the solid ground beneath his feet. Howls and cries of pain growled from within the darkness, and whispers rested lightly through the stale air.

"No . . . one . . . is . . . coming. Tell . . . us . . . why . . . you . . . are . . . here?"

"Do not let the words taunt you," warned Jasmine as she joined Connor.

Taking her advice, Connor took the lead once more.

"This way," he ordered as he picked up the lantern and shone it before him.

There, as Bow had described, was a tunnel, dark, dank, and small, just large enough for one person at a time to squeeze through.

"Stay close to me, Jasmine," he added, "and keep those lanterns burning."

Although initially the thought of the well had frightened Jasmine, as time went on she no longer feared it. All was beyond their control. This was what they had been destined for and already the path of failure or success had been written, so there was little left to worry about.

Thankfully, slowly but uneventfully they squeezed through the stony passageway until they finally reached a doorway at the end.

"This must be the room that Bow told us about," Connor whispered for fear of waking their enemy.

"The door is locked," said Jasmine as she turned the handle.

"Then can you not use your physic power?" asked Vanisheo who suddenly appeared beside them.

"I do not think that would be very helpful," replied Jasmine. "The door has no lock and must be sealed by some sort of magic."

Connor leaned forward and peered through a crack in the wall. Through his limited vision, he could just make out another pathway leading towards a dim light. There, sitting before it, marring some of its glow, was a figure; its identity hidden by the dead man's shroud that covered his head. From time to time the light fluctuated in the breeze, and screams of agony sang upon the air.

"Well, this is definitely our room," announced Connor quietly, "and past it must be the way out."

"But how do we get in?" asked Jasmine.

"I have the method," replied Connor softly, "and a plan, but everything will happen fast. Just follow my lead and don't stop for anything."

Jasmine hated Connor's on the fly plans but knew there was no other way, so taking a step back, she allowed him to work as she watched with interest. Reaching into his pocket, he retrieved the small bottle of oils and emptied part of its contents into a small gap in the stonework. Then, ripping a small piece of linen from the bottom of Jasmine's blouse, he lit it from the glow of his lantern. Small flames quickly licked around his fingers as the fabric blackened from the heat. At this point, he waved it over the oils and stepped back.

"Turn away," he ordered.

Quickly Jasmine and Vanisheo averted their eyes and as they did so, a loud boom echoed behind them.

"Wow! That hurt," said Connor rubbing his ears. "Good hearing does have its disadvantages sometimes."

As they turned back to face the door, it still stood its ground, but a small crevice had appeared in the wall beside it, just large enough for them to squeeze through. Carefully Connor threaded the lantern onto the other side of the wall then pulled himself in. Jasmine followed suit. Vanisheo took a more traditional route and disappeared, only to reappear beside the Dream Lord. With the two lanterns boosting their vision, the trio swiftly made their way towards the seated figure.

"Where do we go from here?" asked Jasmine as she noticed a large number of wooden crates blocked the only other exit.

"Umm. That's a point. I hadn't actually thought that far ahead," admitted Connor.

At the sound of his voice, the figure stirred.

"What trickery is this?" he asked. "Have you not tortured me enough?"

"This is no trick," replied Jasmine softly. "We have come to rescue you."

"Be still, my friend," said Connor, "while I untie you." And with that Connor leaned over and removed one of his knives from his boot and slit the restraining ropes.

"Lord Connor? Is that you?" asked the man.

With the lantern held above his head, Connor removed the cloth bag from the stranger's head.

"Durban!" he echoed in disbelief. "It's good to see you again and alive. Can you walk? We must leave."

Durban eagerly went to stand, but his legs gave way. Taking some of his weight, Connor helped him to his feet.

"I am glad our efforts were not in vain." said the old soldier weakly. "We found out you were coming, and I was entrusted to help you track down Hunter. I came from the other side of the river, but in my carelessness, the darkness lured me into the shadows and kept me here as bait. At first I thought they would consume me, but when they did not, I feared they also knew of your plans and intended to use me. I was distraught with myself, and vowed I would not let them take you because of my inadequacies, and so I held on to warn you."

"You did well, old friend." Connor smiled. "You've yet again protected us, so we were able to enter this world unseen. Unfortunately, only four of us could cross the path into Judgment, so our tactics must be as underhanded as our enemy. Vanisheo here simply appeared of his own volition." And he pointed to the Hallucium who was hovering near them. "I'm aware that our numbers are too few to make a difference at the moment, but that will change. Kustos and Will are on the far side of the world looking for Armon, while Jasmine and I are tasked to find Hunter."

"I know, my lord," replied Durban. "Lord Fortis has planned to meet them there."

"Fortis?" exclaimed Jasmine as loud as she dared. "You mean Kustos will be reunited with his brother, as he was before he became a Dream Stealer?"

"Yes, my lady," said Durban as he tried to smile.

The bruising on his face, caused by the torturous darkened entity, was painful and reminded him of the endless hours he had spent at their mercy.

"Time for reminiscing must be saved for later," interrupted Connor. "We've been lucky so far, but we dare not rest upon such laurels. Stand back and hold the lanterns."

Jasmine and Durban took a step back and gripped the lanterns as though their life depended upon it. Removing the bottle from his pocket once more, Connor shook it to establish the contents. Half of the liquid still remained, so taking careful aim at the blocked doorway, he threw the bottle. A clink of broken glass echoed in the silent room as the liquid slowly oozed out onto the wooden crates. Taking one of the lanterns, he then threw it in the same direction.

"Wait, Lord Connor!" yelled Durban when he realised Connor's plan. "That is not a good idea."

His warning though came too late as a huge explosion forced its way out through the stone. Stale air sucked through the new opening was quickly followed by a gush of fast moving water.

"So now you tell me? Grab the lanterns!" shouted Connor as the waters began to swirl around their feet. "We mustn't lose the light."

"All is lost but one," Vanisheo advised him as he clambered up on Jasmine's head and held the lamp above his own.

Noticing Durban's excitable splash, Connor realised he could not swim and quickly grabbed him by the scruff of his neck in order to keep his head above the ever rising water.

"Relax," he told Durban, "I'll keep you a float." But as he spoke, he felt the nips and pinches to his legs from their adversaries beneath the water.

"Keep moving, Jasmine," Connor told her. "You must keep safe."

Tiny slash marks appeared across his face as the safety of the lantern drifted further away. They were almost at the mercy of the darkness.

"My lady," whispered Vanisheo, "we must go back. Connor and Durban are almost consumed by the shadows. They will not stand a chance and neither will this mission."

Jasmine immediately turned around and began kicking against the current. Vanisheo wobbled with each thrust but soon anticipated the movement as they swam closer. Within seconds, the brilliant rays illuminated the space before them, and as they touched the blackened shadows, the darkness recoiled in pain.

"Jasmine . . . no!" ordered Connor. "You must escape. The future of the Judgment World is in your hands."

"No it is not," she retorted angrily. "I am not the Dream Lord. It was not me that earned the trust of the Higher Powers. I am disappointed in you, Connor. I did not think you would give up so easily."

"You infuriating woman," moaned Connor. "How does Kustos put up with you?"

"He does not question my decisions," she replied calmly. "Now both of you, grab hold of me."

Durban reached out and managed to put an arm around her waist. Connor with his spare hand touched her shoulder and looked into her face. A serene smile covered it and knowing her friends were now by her side, she opened her mouth and screamed. A blue light immediately appeared and quickly surrounded the four friends.

As Connor watched with interest, it increased in brightness. So much so that he was forced to close his eyes. Now trusting totally in Jasmine's power, Connor felt himself being pulled forward against the flow of water and daring to look, he saw them float through the damaged doorway. What he also saw was Jasmine standing several metres in front of him beckoning them on. Confused by her vision and the direction he thought they were taking, he glanced behind, and there within arm's reach was Jasmine swimming effortlessly through the water with Vaniseho perched precariously on her head.

"What in the name of Sublin is happening?" he asked her.

"My soul energy," she told him. "I find it is getting stronger the longer I am in this place."

"I felt that part of me must leave my host," said the image standing before him, "and then I found myself in two."

"We must keep going," Jasmine answered from behind. "I can see a light ahead, and our faithful lantern will soon burn out."

The alternate Jasmine ahead of them continued to pull them forward, and finally they reached the end of the tunnel. With one last push from the swirling waters, they fell over the side and down a watery-type slide, landing in the river below. It was peaceful and calm, and apart from their ungainly entrance and the splashing of water running from the tunnel, hardly a ripple touched the surface. One by one they swam to the riverbank, with Connor still dragging Durban along. Upon reaching the sides, they pulled themselves ashore. Connor made a note to himself that on his return to Sublin, everyone would learn to swim, just in case of times such as this.

Jasmine got to her feet and smiled at her twin.

"Thank you," she told herself.

"No, thank you," was the courteous response as the doppelganger took a step closer and began to merge back into the original figure.

When fully absorbed, Jasmine fell to the ground exhausted. Connor pulled himself up on one elbow and leaned over to her.

"Are you alright?" he asked.

"A little tired," she admitted, "but otherwise I am fine."

"In that case," replied the Dream Lord, "we'll rest for a while. You must tell us, Jasmine, when you are ready to travel."

"A moment or two," she answered, "and I will be as good as new."

"I am indebted to you, Lord Connor and Lady Jasmine," interrupted Durban as he wrung the water from his sleeve. "You have risked yourselves to save my life."

"And me!" interrupted Vanisheo. "I held the lantern. Without the lantern you would have been taken."

"How true, Vanisheo." Connor smiled. "Without your courage, we would have all been lost."

Vanisheo puffed out his chest with pride and smiled. His bravery had finally been rewarded.

"We need to figure out what we need to do next," stated Connor. "Now we've rescued Durban, how do we find Hunter?"

"My willingness to help, Lord Connor," began Durban, "was my knowledge of this world, but where the Hunter can be found is as much a mystery to me as you. I am sorry if this disappoints you."

"It doesn't disillusion me." Connor grinned. "You've already given up your chance of Judgment to be here now. How can that be a failure of character?"

"But I thought . . . ," began Durban.

"You thought wrong, my friend," said Connor. "I'd no illusion that this path would be simple. A victory has been accomplished today by bringing you to safety. The rest will follow, planned by the hand of fate."

"Thank you, Lord Connor," echoed Durban.

"There's no need for thanks," he answered, "but there is one command I wish of you."

"My lord, anything," replied the old warrior.

"Please call me Connor," was the response.

11

The Other Side
of the World

"Look at that," said Will as he peered precariously over the cliff. "Is there an easy way down?"

"I am afraid not, Will," replied Joshua, "nor is it very inviting, once you reach the plains."

As Will, Kustos and Joshua looked out they saw the battle-fields below, dotted with masses of beings the size of ants.

"What's going on?" asked Will as he continued to watch.

"There is no control now in the world and any major strength will force its power upon the weak," replied Joshua. "Only those wise enough to stay hidden will survive."

Out on the fields far below them, the Razars were taking on the humans. These, like the small group Connor had recently encountered, had once decided to forgo their own Judgment and live in the outer realms forever. This though was not the outer realms and the ruthless dominions of evil were destroying the illusions of peace wherever it passed. The humans from the Wake World were greatly outnumbered and even more under armed. The Razars not only had their lethal tongues but were also calling upon their soul energy and creating ice and heat blasts. The humans with their meagre swords had little defence. It was not a fair fight and the sounds of death lingered on the blood-stained air as it wafted up the cliff face.

"We must do something," said Kustos as he automatically readied his Cinxi swords.

"As hard as it might seem, my lord," replied Joshua, "we cannot interfere. It is imperative that your presence in this world remain a secret for as long as possible."

It was not the answer Kustos wished to hear but the only one he knew to expect.

"What happens to the dead?" asked Will. "I mean, we're already in the Judgment World and you said they refused the chance of judgment the first time, so where do they go when they die? Do they get a second chance?"

"Their choices are the same," Joshua advised them, "if they have shown enough of their true souls. They still have the option to go to the Judgment Halls and be given their final judgment, though I doubt if that would be my choice. At least not since Volnar has taken control."

"And the other option?" asked Will.

"Well, the alternative is non negotiable," answered Joshua. "You are sent directly to a hell dimension without room for an appeal. Judgment is instant based on your past history."

"There does appear to be another choice," Kustos replied as he pointed down to the battlefield. "Look."

There emerging from the shadows, were the Soul Crunchers, grabbing the essence of any victim within their path. Razar and human alike suffered under their power.

"Do you recognise any of them?" asked Kustos. "Did you not say they were once like you?"

"I take offence, Lord Kustos, that you would liken me to one so dark," replied Joshua.

"I apologise, Joshua," answered Kustos quickly for fear of upsetting their guide. "I did not mean to identify you with such evil. I merely suggested your knowledge of the person."

"I was quick to judge," apologised Joshua, "and now understand your words. Please accept my own regret?"

"Forget it, guys," interrupted Will as he tried to break the uncomfortable conversation. "But as a matter of interest, do you recognise any of their faces, Joshua?"

"Their features are unknown to me," admitted Joshua as he looked, "but that is not to say we were not once friends. The souls of their enemies have aged them and drowned their contours into that of an ancient man. What I do not understand is why they risk their indiscriminate lives to raid this world. This battle should be of no interest to them."

"But isn't that what Volnar wants?" asked Will. "Causing endless fighting between remaining races can only strengthen his armies."

"I suppose it does," mused their guide as he looked on. "I suppose it does."

Together for a moment they continued to watch the mindless deaths. Their eyes struggled to keep up with the eternal mounds of mixed fighters. The only consolation they could take from such atrocities was that they were well out of reach.

Slowly Will perused the desolate panoramic view until he noticed a small stone building on the edge of the battlefield. Chained inside was some form of being.

"Look." He pointed as he screwed his eyes up to focus. "Who or what is that?"

Kustos and Joshua quickly moved along the cliff until they could just make out the features of the captive.

"A Butterhawk!" mumbled Joshua. "What is it doing here?"

"Whatever the reason is negligible," interrupted Will. "It looks as though the battle is moving towards it. We must do something."

"Do what?" queried Joshua. "Carry out some amazing rescue attempt and get caught up in the melee?"

"I guess there's one thing you don't know about Kustos and I," replied Will in his determined manner. "We don't leave people behind."

"But they are not people," reiterated Joshua. "They are Butterhawks."

"And they are?" interrupted Kustos impatiently.

"They are . . ."

Joshua began to explain and then carefully thought of his answer. With the Butterhawks on their side, it might make their journey that much easier.

"They are a race of beings that live in the skies," he began. "Before Volnar took control of this world it was their duty to watch over the realms from above. They would observe until they saw someone or something get out of control, then using the powers given to them by the Oracles, they would glide down and nominate them for Judgment.

"I thought you told us no one outside of the Halls knew where Judgment was?" said Kustos. "So how could they send them there?"

"It is like being arrested in any world. The order is issued and the enforcers come and take you away," answered Joshua. "Only here, instead of the enforcers collecting you, Judgment itself would appear and suck you into the Halls."

"What happens if the Butterhawks get it wrong?" asked Kustos.

"Wrong?" queried Joshua. "Oh, they never get it wrong," he confirmed adamantly.

"So their presence on the ground would not be a welcome one then?" said Will.

"Most definitely not," emphasised Joshua. "There would be no mercy if they fell into the wrong hands."

"And by the wrong hands . . . you mean those guys?" asked Will.

"Well, yes, my lord," answered the guide.

"Then I suggest we go and save the Butterhawk," recommended Will as he watched the fighting move slowly closer towards where it had been tethered, "especially as it doesn't appear to be in the position to save itself. Why doesn't it just fly away?"

"You cannot see it from here, Will," Joshua told him, "but they do not have a full expanse of wings. They are known as Butterhawks because their wings are similar to that of a butterfly seen in the Wake World. From an on looker's point of view, they have no wings but merely a tattoo etched across their shoulders and down their back. The colours are most vibrant and striking, and every single design is different. When the time comes to move away, the tattoos open out into a set of small wings made of thin, chitonous membrane that picks up the air currents and glides gracefully upon the thermals of the skies. For this though, they need a lifting spot and there are only six hot spots throughout the kingdom that can create sufficient turbulence to soar them into the skies. The nearest one from here is the fire valleys of the Volcanoes, a good few leagues away."

"Then we must help the Butterhawk get back to the valley?" said Will.

"This is not our fight," replied Joshua. "We must not get involved but take advantage of the situation and use it as a distraction."

"I disagree with that completely," replied Will angrily. "If the Butterhawk isn't supposed to be here and you said yourself this battle shouldn't really be happening, then it suggests there's more to this than meets the eye. We have to rescue the Butterhawk. I feel it's important. Don't ask me how, I just do. You agree with me, right, Kustos?" he added as he turned to his friend for support.

"Joshua is right, Will," answered Kustos sadly. "This is not our fight."

"Did that stop Connor and me when we helped Sublin?" asked Will.

"No, Will, it did not," replied Kustos, and he looked from Joshua to Will, then to Joshua again. "Will is right also, Joshua. This might not be our fight, but we cannot stand by and let the Soul Crunchers deliver the Butterhawk to hell when it cannot protect itself."

"And how will you get down there then?" asked Joshua.

"I can do that," volunteered Will. "No problem."

"And even if you successfully reach the plain, the building is still probably a mile away. Do you expect to run through the battle-strewn fields without getting stopped?" replied Joshua unhappily as he contemplated the even more suicidal suggestion than their mission.

"We have to try, Joshua," Will told him. "I'm a Dream Warrior, and it's my duty to protect. I won't walk away from this."

Joshua was about to protest again when Will suddenly grabbed both his and Kustos' wrist and leapt off the side of the cliff. As he did so, his gravity force created a slide leading down to the valley. The three of them skimmed effortless down, ending with a gentle jump to the ground. For the moment their presence was undetected, and they cautiously began to edge their way around the battlefield.

"This is going to take forever," exclaimed Kustos. "Take care as you move through the fighting."

"Where are you going?" asked Will.

"I will meet you there," explained Kustos. "I can get there far quicker than you."

"But how?" asked Joshua.

The Realm Lord did not wait to enlighten them of his plan. Instead he turned and began to run straight across the battlefield. Within several steps, Will and Joshua heard an almighty bang as Kustos broke the speed of sound and his image was now a mere flash in the distance. Only the display of flaying bodies thrust aside as he sliced through them was an indication of the pathway he took.

"That is so cool," oozed Will as he ran through the trail of dust Kustos had left in his wake. "Come on, Joshua, before they realise what's happened."

Kustos quickly reached the stone building only seconds later and carefully came to a stop on the far side of the construction to listen what was going on inside. The elevated anguished echo of war screams above the battle cries filled his ears, but still he heard the words from someone in the building.

The prisoner was undoubtedly a woman but regardless of the torture she had endured so far, apparently she was still refusing to talk.

"Tell us where he is," snarled one of the Soul Crunchers.

"I do not know who you are talking about," replied the Butterhawk. "My task is to deliver Judgment, not spy upon the living."

To get a better assessment of the situation, Kustos carefully looked along the wall and managed to find a small crack, just large enough to peer inside. From this slender vision, he could just make out the silhouette of four figures, presumably all Soul Crunchers. For a moment one was barring his view of the Butterhawk, but then he moved out of the way, and for the first time, Kustos caught a glimpse of the strange, new race.

The prisoner was beautiful. Long, black, shiny hair hung over her well-tanned shoulders. Huge dark eyes peered out of the slender face, invisibly etched with lines of fear. There was little doubt she had been scared by her encounter with her captors. Her clothing was not unlike that of a normal Wake World teenager parading along Waikiki Beach but to Kustos it seemed strange and somewhat revealing for her gender. The dirty white bikini top and shorts were complimented by a thick, well-shaped belt supporting two empty knife harnesses on either side of her waist. The weapons lay innocently on an upturned box in the far corner of the room that was acting as a seat. From the back of her shoulders, he could just make out the small subtle wings that Joshua had told them about. They were an infusion of blue and lilac hues swirled in circular patterns across the membranes that were slightly irregular in shape, to accommodate her clothing. It was hard to believe that despite their delicate facade they were still capable of keeping her in the air.

With his first impression of the Butterhawk, he knew their decision was right and that at all costs, she had to be rescued. The task could be simple with the right type of plan to outsmart the malicious Soul Crunchers. To clear his mind from the vision and in order for the ideas to appear, he stepped back slightly from the building. To his delight, he noticed on either side a decrepit stone stairway leading to the roof of the construction. Opportunity had been kind to him and shown a means of attack. Unaware of the time available for the plan and not daring to wait for reinforcements from Will and Joshua, he quietly climbed the old ladder. Step by step he effortlessly scaled the structure, ensuring that he kept his body low and out of view, especially once he reached the top. Once there, he could just make out the images of his friends as they weaved through the battlefield. Help was at hand but still, in his mind, some way off to be of much use.

Cautiously, he crawled across the wooden roof and peered through the ill-fitting struts. This location gave Kustos a better view of the Soul Crunchers, and the images of their eyeless faces brought back unpleasant memories of his first encounter in Sublin.

"This woman is not going to talk," said one of the captors. "Let me take her soul. You have already had a fill from the battle outside."

"Silence!" ordered another. "Leave us now! Wait outside until told otherwise. You can feed on anything that passes."

The fact the other Soul Crunchers took notice of the order told Kustos that he was their superior, and he watched as the remaining three moaned amongst themselves before walking out of the building and slamming the door in protest behind them. Once alone, the Soul Cruncher turned on the Butterhawk.

"This is your last chance, Butterhawk," he sneered. "Tell me what I need to know, or you will suffer the same fate as your friends. Trust me, their souls tasted pure and sweet and blended well within us. Were you so foolish to think you could hide amongst this battle? Did you not realise that once we had tasted Butterhawk soul it created a connection with your race? You cannot hide from us now. So tell me—where is he?"

The woman, drained by her experience, lifted her head slowly.

"Just because your horde of evil-smelling drones managed to catch me off guard does not mean my race is weak. Even if I knew the information that you wanted, I would rather die than give it up." And she spat into the Soul Cruncher's face indignantly.

Slowly he wiped the spittle away with the back of his hand and sneered at her, and then thrusting his arms forward on either side of her body, he leaned over and opened his mouth. The dislocation of the jaw enabled him to completely consume her head without hesitation. Slowly he began to suck the soul from its shell.

The sudden attack took her unawares and she screamed as the pain of her life force being dragged from her body stimulated every cell of her being. Kustos knew from previous experiences that there was no time to wait, and throwing himself through the roof, he landed on the unsuspecting Soul Cruncher, pulling him to the ground in the fall. The Butterhawk's senses told her this was a rescue attempt and she continued to scream in an effort to drown out the noise of the fight. Fortunately, it worked. With her cries and the sound of battle carnage outside, the remaining Soul Crunchers were unaware of the melee within the building.

Quickly Kustos scrambled to his feet, grabbed the prostrate Soul Cruncher and threw him against the wall. He hit it with a solid thud and slid slowly to the floor.

"Hurry," ordered the Butterhawk. "The key is over there on the floor."

Recovering the key as instructed, Kustos had to pass the inert Cruncher and he gave the body another kick just to be sure it was no longer a threat.

"Please hurry," urged the woman again as Kustos began to unlock the chains. "The others could come in at any minute."

"Are you alright?" asked the Waterfall Lord as he reached out to unlock her wrists.

"I will be, thank you," she replied as she eyed her rescuer up and down. "You cannot be part of this world?" she added.

"What makes you say that?" asked Kustos.

"Chivalry is unheard of here," she answered. "Anyone in Judgment has only one agenda . . . themselves."

Suddenly the Realm Lord heard a sound behind him, and as he turned around, he saw the Soul Cruncher looming over them both. The Soul Cruncher was still nursing the pain in his head caused by Kustos throwing him across the room and his disgruntled mood had urged him to attempt the theft of two souls instead of just the one.

There was no time to react, and Kustos and the Butterhawk found themselves clamped in a vicelike grip, as the essence of their life was dragged involuntarily from their bodies. Darkness began to blacken their vision and Kustos was convinced all was lost, until suddenly, without warning, their energy began to return. Their attacker emitted an agonising scream, and as they watched, he melted into a pile of ash upon the floor.

12

What a Surprise?

"You really ought to pay more attention, little brother," said a voice from within the room. "When you think an enemy is down, do not trust your instinct. It might not mean he is ACTUALLY DEAD. Not in this place anyway."

"Fortis!" cried Kustos as he ran across the room and threw both arms around his brother.

"I am sorry I took so long," apologised Fortis. "I got a little caught up with things." And he pried himself out of the hug to look at his younger brother.

"Err, excuse me," interrupted a gentle voice. "Could one of you fine warriors free my other wrist?"

"My apologies," replied Kustos as he went back to the Butterhawk.

"Thank you," she said, as he put an arm around her shoulder.

Her wings instinctively folded back and Kustos felt the strange sensation of the membrane on his hand as he helped to steady her.

"My name is Camella," she added.

"Come we must go," urged Fortis, but as he spoke the door flew open, and the remaining three Soul Crunchers burst in.

Slowly they edged their way forward towards the Butterhawk and her new friends, preparing themselves to feast upon their souls but as they stepped closer, the wall behind them blew outwards and a strong gust of wind, apparently responsible for the damage, died down. When the dust had settled, Kustos could see the images of Will and Joshua standing in readiness.

"What did we miss?" asked Will as Joshua bent over to catch his breath.

"Not too much yet," replied Kustos as he and Camella backed away towards them. "I think the worst is about to start. Your timing could not be better."

One of the Soul Crunchers became impatient and seeing Fortis standing alone made a run for him. The prince, however, was already prepared for such an attack. He charged up his power, causing flames to emit from his body, which subsequently transformed him into a human torch. The Soul Cruncher, naïve to such a weapon, was undeterred by the metamorphosis and foolishly continued to advance. Through the lashing flames, Fortis smiled and reached out to touch his enemy. An agonising scream reverberated around the room as the heat transferred throughout the Soul Cruncher, causing him to crumple and immediately turn to ash. At the demise of the creature, the stolen souls within his frame exploded out into freedom, crying and screaming as the disorientated essences searched for their hosts. When none were found, the disillusioned souls resigned themselves to their fate and evaporated into the atmosphere.

The remaining Soul Crunchers, having watched the fate of their brother, approached Fortis with far more caution as the fire around him died down. Despite their limited brain capacity, they had seen enough to know that only by working together were they likely to steal the fire man's soul and so, drawing upon their own inner power, they began to suck in unison towards Fortis. With

Camella drained by her own experience and Fortis slowly giving in to the supremacy of the Soul Crunchers, Will and Joshua were left to take control.

To everyone's surprise it was Joshua who appeared to understand the situation and, warning Fortis to drop to the ground, he began his own retaliation. Standing calmly before the enemy, he placed his hand upon his chest and scrunched it into a fist. After several seconds, he removed it, and as he did so, a mist of energy materialised. Moulding it carefully into a ball of light, Joshua held it gently in his hands before throwing it in the direction of the Soul Crunchers. As it travelled through the air, it began to expand large enough to engulf the assailants and trap them within its force. There was no escape, and all the Soul Crunchers could do was stand and accept their fate. The essence of Joshua squeezed and crushed until their lives and souls had been wrenched from their solid frames, causing them to implode, leaving no trace of their existence.

"What did you just do?" asked Will as he helped Fortis to his feet.

"It is not magic, Lord Will," replied Joshua. "Remember, I am still an Oracle of this world and can pass judgment on whoever walks its earth. I simply turned their own skills upon them and cancelled out their entire subsistence. With such little time to spare, my only regret was that I could not save the souls they had devoured."

"Remind me never to get on your wrong side," joked Fortis as he dusted himself down.

"So you are one of Kustos' brothers?" asked Will.

"That's me," smiled Fortis. "Guilty by all accounts."

"Your reputation of bravery was well recorded," continued the Dream Warrior, "and for that you are held in high regard. It was understood that your dark path of the Dream Stealer was not of your doing and should not be a reason for your punishment. You've already helped Connor and for that I'll always call you my friend." And he held out his hand to seal the friendship.

"Thank you, Lord William," answered Fortis as he took the hand and shook it profusely. "That means a lot to me."

"Well, now the admiration society has met," interrupted Kustos, who had been sitting with Camella all of this time. "I think Camella might need some help."

The three of them then turned and walked over to where Kustos had rested the limp form of the Butterhawk. She looked pale and dark shadows had appeared under the eyes of the unblemished face.

"She doesn't look good," Will stated, "but what can we do? Isn't this where a woman's touch would solve the problem?"

"I only know of basic wound repairs," said Kustos. "Not something like this."

"Stand back and give her room," ordered Joshua as he made his way forward.

Gently he placed his hand upon her forehead and closed his eyes. Camella instantly opened hers and screamed.

"Let it out, my dear," said the Oracle. "Let the pain leave your body."

The Butterhawk screamed once more before going quiet and a minute or two passed before she slowly opened her eyes again.

"Thank you, kind Oracle," she said sweetly to Joshua. "You have rid me of my torment. I am indebted to you and to your friends for such a foolhardy rescue."

"You know?" grinned Will. "You're one handy person to have around." And he placed a hand upon the shoulder of the Oracle to show his gratitude.

Joshua turned to Will and smiled.

"That is the first time I have ever seen you smile, Joshua," said Kustos. "Is gratitude a funny cliché to you?"

"No, no, my lords," replied Joshua. "The joke is all on me. For the first time, I see what has happened here. You are truly amazing, Lord Will," he smiled again. "Even in dark times you find something good to appreciate. I can see now why you are the key to ending all of this."

Camella focussed on her rescuers from Kustos to Fortis and then Will. Her mouth dropped as she stared at the strong image of the Dream Warrior.

"Hello! I'm Will," he told her as he tried to overcome the embarrassing moment, but she said nothing and continued to stare. "Are you okay?" he continued, now even more concerned by such dedicated attention.

The others looked from Camella to Will and then back to the Butterhawk again.

"Yes, yes," she hastily replied. "I am sorry. It is just that you look . . ."

"Look like what?" queried Will. "Do I have dirt on my face?" And he wiped his hand across his forehead.

"No, no," replied the Butterhawk as she struggled to her feet, "it is not important."

Her leather boots had loosened in the earlier scramble, and she tightened the straps below her knee before straightening up. She wobbled and Kustos grabbed her arm to steady her.

"We must move now, Lord Will," ordered Joshua. "Your detour is over and we must find Armon."

At the mention of Armon's name, Camella backed away from the group.

"You know of Armon?" she asked.

"We do but why should that be such a surprise?" interrogated Joshua.

Camella did not reply. Instead she turned to run away.

"Wait," ordered Will calmly. "I'm Will, Dream Warrior of Sublin. I've earned my passage to this world with my friend Connor, the Dream Lord. We've left our home where many years ago we won a war against Volnar the Shadow Lord. Connor banished him to between worlds by using the Tukurak knife. We thought then that would be the end of him but have since been informed that isn't the case. Connor and I have come to finish the path that fate had started for us. It was Joshua here that told us of Armon's involvement. We don't wish to harm him, but it's written in his destiny. He's one more task to complete. My quest is to find Armon and bring him to Connor, whose path has taken him down a different track. He must find Hunter, who's rumoured to know the route back into the Judgment Halls."

"It seems a lot is weighing on your shoulders, Will," replied Camella as she stopped and looked at him. "We cannot talk here. Ears may be listening."

"How about the other side of that wall?" suggested Kustos as he pointed to the fifteen-foot stone barrier some way off in the distance.

"To go over it is not a good plan," Camella informed them. "Many battles are taking place along the turrets. It would be too dangerous to get involved. Besides it is far too high to scale."

"For you guys maybe." Will smiled. "But for me . . . a piece of cake."

"This is no place for magic tricks," the Butterhawk scolded. "Draw attention to yourself and every race will want to end your life without a second thought."

"Then what do you suggest?" asked Fortis.

"We use the tunnel," recommended Joshua.

"Yes. The tunnel," reiterated Camella. "It is our only chance."

"Wait, wait." interrupted Fortis, in complete disbelief of the suggestion. "The Tunnel of Absolution? Are you crazy?"

"Only when on a suicide mission," replied Joshua dryly.

"So what's so scary about the Tunnel of Absolution?" asked Will.

"It is a passage that leads through to the fire paths, those which we are seeking, but it does not come without a price," Fortis answered. "It is a means of access designed to confuse you and play on your fears and insecurities. It will test the most hardened of souls for proof of strength to overcome temptation."

"Yes, that is true," agreed Joshua, "but if you clear your mind and have no fear, your passage will be a safe route."

"Well, I do not like it," said Fortis.

"Like it or not, dear brother," said Kustos as he slapped Fortis on the shoulder. "Our choices are very limited and time is not on our side."

"Put like that," interrupted Will, "I see there's only one answer. We have to use the tunnel. Now . . . where is it?"

"Its entrance is over there, through the battlefield behind this building," explained Camella. "Just to one side, about two-thirds through, is a ditch. This is the entrance but take heed, one foot inside and there is no turning back."

"We will need to split up," suggested Joshua, "just in case some of us do not make it through the field. It will soon be dark and during this time, the battles here will draw out the more unsavoury characters."

"Well, I can run," stated Kustos.

"And so can I," confirmed Fortis.

"In that case," replied Joshua, "I will follow best I can. What path will you take, Will?"

"I'll go with Camella," he answered. "If you think you can carry me, I'm almost certain I can get you into the air. I've the power of wind, which should create enough turbulence for you to glide."

"I am a lot stronger than I look." Camella smiled. "And it will be good to take to the air again. I hate walking."

"So we shall meet on the other side," said Kustos as he placed an outstretched hand before him.

Fortis and Joshua followed suit and then Will and Camella completed the circle.

"Be safe, my friends," said Will, "and watch your backs."

With that Kustos broke away and started to run. Just like his previous effort, a loud bang echoed in the skies as he picked up speed but fortunately the unexplained noise did not deter the fighting and no one bothered to stop to investigate.

"Wait for me, little brother!" shouted Fortis as he ran after Kustos through the flaying bodies his brother had left behind.

His speed was fast but not on the same scale as Kustos and he ducked and dodged the occasional sword as it swiped the air at anything that moved.

"Good luck to us all," said Joshua as he followed them.

His speed was easily inferior but the dust cloud that the two brothers created with their swift movement was sufficient shelter for Joshua to pass through without challenge. Left alone, Will turned to Camella.

"Are you ready?" he asked her.

She nodded and he awkwardly placed his arms around her waist. Closing his eyes, he concentrated and as he did so, a wind around their feet began to stir. Camella raised her wings from her shoulders and as the breeze increased and caught the delicate membranes, it lifted them from the ground. Within seconds they had picked up speed and soon were gliding gracefully through the air.

"We will be there soon, Will," she assured him. "Just hold on."

Effortlessly they soared above the battlefield. Below, Will could see Joshua weaving his way through the fighting, still unharmed. Kustos and Fortis were nowhere to be seen. The only conclusion was that they had reached their destination.

Without a word they continued to fly and only the thoughts of their next encounter were uppermost in Will's mind. One of them at least had to make it through the tunnel. Failure was not an option.

13

Hidden in a Grain of Sand

"We've been walking through this desert for hours," complained Connor as they trudged through the bleak environment. "Are you certain there's a city here, Vanisheo?"

"I am," confirmed the Hallucium, "although I have not been here for many years, and over time the landscape has taken on many changes."

"It is true, Connor," agreed Durban. "The city is almost deserted now. Only the most stubborn of settlers have refused to leave. It is my hope that someone will have some knowledge of Hunter."

"I hope you're right," replied Connor, "otherwise we may have wasted valuable time. Jasmine?" he asked her, changing the subject, "have you managed to contact the others yet?"

"I am afraid not," she replied sadly, "although I do know they are still alive. I can feel their presence. I suspect my powers are more controlled than theirs and should they be distracted in some way, they would not be able to pick up on my thoughts. I will try again later."

"So we just keep walking then?" Connor moaned again.

"And walking," reiterated Durban as he smiled at the Dream Lord.

Jasmine suddenly stopped and then stepped forward slowly.

"Is everything alright?" Vanisheo asked her.

"I do not think so," she whispered as she shook her head. "I cannot shake this feeling off—that we are being followed."

As she spoke, the wind suddenly picked up and tiny sand granules began to whip around them, swirling into the air and joining the rest of the sandstorm that was now beginning to erupt.

"What's that?" Connor asked as he grabbed for Jasmine's arm to try and lead her to safety.

"We must keep moving!" shouted Durban above the noise as he pushed off to take the lead.

No sooner had he made the suggestion than the sand before him took the formation of a large human hand and punched him in the chest. The impact took Durban by surprise, and he lost his footing and stumbled. Without thinking, Connor quickly reached out and somehow managed to break his fall, but at the expense of his own safety as he found himself suffering an attack from behind, forcing him to trip into Jasmine.

Not restricting itself to the warriors, the sand formation grew up in front of the princess but before it had a chance to strike, she changed into her ghost-like form, grabbed the shape and threw it to the ground. For a moment it took a solid form and briefly showed the profile of a body, before collapsing into a pile of sand. Fearing Jasmine was too powerful, the sand being again tried to attack Connor but the result of the fight was the same. Since touching Jasmine, Connor could now mimic her skills and seeing the success of her spectre image, he followed her example.

"What's going on?" he shouted above the noise of the howling wind.

"I do not know," replied Durban as another blow sent him tumbling towards Connor.

"I cannot see what it is!" yelled Vanisheo, who up until this point had managed to avoid any conflict.

Durban staggered to his feet and felt another sharp blow across his face, forcing him to lose balance yet again and fall to the ground. Amongst the sandy mayhem, he touched his face and felt the blood drip between his fingers. Even more aware now of the urgency of their fight, he moved to get up but stopped as he heard the sound of something coming towards him. In fear of moving the wrong way, he remained static and as he waited, a whooshing of steel flashed past his ear and buried its tip into the sand beside him. Quickly Durban sat up and was just in time to see a figure dressed in the robes of a ninja standing before him. At first he thought this was their attacker but as the silhouette began to punch and kick into mid air, he knew the adversary was still at hand. Like a practise session in the gym, the lithe being parried and thrust against an invisible foe and then, just when Durban thought the effort was futile, a single blow lashed out at chest height. The impact caused the sand to flatten out and slide along the ground until it stopped at Durban's side. As it came to a halt, an image suddenly appeared. Like the figure helping in their fight, it was a Ninja but dressed in a sandy, yellow uniform to enable him to blend into the desert environment. Briefly, he stared maliciously at Durban. Dark, ruthless eyes glared out of the desert disguise, wishing death upon anyone who dared gaze upon him. The warrior, so preoccupied by Durban's façade, did not notice the other ninja silently run to the captain's side. It gathered a sword from the ground as he moved and without hesitation or remorse, thrust it into the sandy, coated body. The sand man writhed in pain as the blade penetrated and then, without warning, he suddenly disappeared.

"Thank you," Durban said as he got to his feet.

The ninja said nothing but handed him the sword as the granulated sand erupted once more, spewing several sand ninjas into their path.

"Make your stand, old man," the ninja told him, as the warrior hurried over to Connor and Jasmine.

In their own desperate way they were trying their best to combat the invisible attacker and having briefly seen the demise of the sand ninja, knew now exactly what was expected of them. Like street mimes pretending to fight, they continually missed their mark and only when the black ninja joined forces did the blows begin to find an impact point.

"What are you doing here?" the ninja asked Connor as a defending kick met with thin air.

"I could say the same of you," said the Dream Lord.

"It is not me they are trying to kill," replied the ninja. "So if you want my help, you will answer my questions."

"But how do I know I can trust you?" Connor queried.

"And how do you know you cannot?" came the answer.

"Okay, fair enough," said the Dream Lord. "I guess I can go with a little bit of faith here. We're trying to find someone," he added as he dodged a blast of sand, "and we believe he might be here."

"No one has come through here for many months," responded his new ally. "Not since Volnar caused so much pain and suffering."

"Who are we fighting?" asked Jasmine as she stumbled from a shove in the back.

"These are the Sand Ninjas," came the reply. "They hide in the desert and live any way they can. Anyone passing through these lands will be attacked without mercy. To them you are just another meal."

"You mean they will eat us?" asked Jasmine, barely believing what she had just been told.

"Meat is a short commodity around here," said the Ninja. "To them you are the succulent steak they have not tasted in years."

"Well, that is just nasty," moaned the princess as she floundered with another blow.

Vanisheo rushed over to help Durban, who despite the fact he had a weapon, was still finding it difficult to actually hit a mark. Determined to be of help, the Hallucium picked up sand and began throwing it around, hoping he might catch someone in the eye, but instead it merely became lost upon the swirling winds, which only added to its strength.

"How do you see them?" asked Connor as he stumbled again.

"You must slow down your mind," the Ninja told him. "Concentrate on the now and they will become visible."

Jasmine immediately obeyed and with little effort immediately saw the sand people around her.

"I see them," she said. "Dare I say . . . a lot of them."

At first Connor did not find it so easy but feeding on Jasmine's energy, he soon discovered their enemy. To fight such acrobats would take more skill than Connor possessed and so borrowing a little force from the ninja, as he now found he no longer needed contact to feel the connection but merely needed to absorb when in close proximity, he started to lash out like a black belt. He made sure he did not take too much energy from the ninja and, because of that, felt confident they could take on the enemy.

"I see them as well," he admitted. "Let's not waste any time here."

Jasmine looked at Connor and the Ninja and then turned her attention to Durban and Vanisheo. They were easily outnumbered and despite their valiant efforts were fighting a losing battle.

"I think we should even the odds," she announced. "Are you with me, Connor?"

Connor immediately knew her plan and as he watched, she split herself into two. She nodded at Connor and held out her arm for him to touch.

"Don't worry about it." He smiled. "I don't need that anymore—just don't drift too far away." And with the renewed skill, he focused hard and split apart.

The ninja looked in disbelief.

"Clever stuff, do you not agree?" Durban shouted to the ninja.

There was no response but merely a studied looked at the two Connors.

"My friend," said one of them to their ally, "please protect the others over there. Jasmine and I can finish off here."

The ninja, still bemused by the strength of the soul energy, nodded and quickly joined Durban and Vanisheo.

"Jasmine, my dear," said a Connor, "shall we finish this?"

"Yes, please," echoed the two princesses in unison. "I am tired of all this and besides the sand is getting everywhere."

Now fully aware of the sand ninjas, Connor and Jasmine felt confident that they were evenly matched but the more fighters they managed to take down, the more that replaced them from the sands below. During the fight, one of the Connors glanced over at Durban and Vanisheo to check on their progress. The outlook was not good as the old captain had been caught off guard while one of the sand ninjas slowly sneaked up from behind. On approaching his prey, the warrior flicked his arms and two sharp knives appeared from the wrists. Connor could do one of two things. React or warn his friend of the imminent danger. He took the first option and decided to protect Durban.

Without a second thought, he started to run and as he did so, jumped into the air. By using the shoulders of the sand ninjas, he stepped from one to another like stepping-stones across a stream until he finally reached the last one. Then he sprung himself off with all the strength he could muster and stuck his foot forward. At the same time, he warned Durban to raise his shield. Instantly the liquid metal protection engulfed them, leaving Connor outside to fend for himself. Thuds and pummelling bounced back off the shelter as sand projectiles hit the surface and fell harmlessly to the ground.

Connor's landing was just as he had hoped for as he struck a sand ninja in the chest and forced him to the ground, burying them both in the sand. The Dream Lord choked and coughed as the tiny granules filtrated into his lungs and with little chance of finding the enemy on home territory, he forced himself to the surface.

"Durban!" he shouted as he tried to focus. "I can't see. Drop your shield."

The old captain immediately obeyed and as the liquid protection fell away, Connor retrieved two knives from the sand.

"All of you drop . . . now!" ordered the Dream Lord.

Again there was no hesitation as Durban, Vanisheo and the ninja flung themselves to the ground. In the split second it took for them to fall from Connor's view, he had thrown his weapons forward, killing two sand people who were waiting to pounce.

"Did we get them?" asked Durban.

"See for yourself, my friend," smiled Connor as the inert bodies materialised before them.

In the other part of the battle, the two Jasmines and the other Connor were fighting bravely but their split energy was quickly tiring from the exertion.

"Connor!" yelled Jasmine. "Your other you and I could use some help," she added.

"Go!" said the ninja softly. "We can manage from here on."

"Thanks," replied Connor as he got to his feet and dusted himself off.

Hurriedly he made his way towards his counterpart but was stopped by a couple of sand ninjas emerging through the swirling sands. Despite his endless parrying and defensive moves, even he could see he was no match for the multiplying numbers, and as he looked across at Jasmine and himself, saw they would soon be surrounded. Behind him, Durban and Vanisheo were also in a similar situation. If they were to escape the attack, he would have to think fast.

With his mind more determined on preservation for than desperation, an idea came to him and he called to his split personality.

"Connor?" he ordered. "Over here?"

The counterpart was about to object, but then he sensed the plan mulling through the other's mind and turned to Jasmine and smiled at her wryly.

"Give me a minute," he told her. "Then I'll return your skill."

"If you are sure?" she replied trustingly. "But please be quick. I do not know how long we can contain them alone."

Satisfied that Jasmine could cope, he turned to join himself and jumping from shoulder to shoulder of the unsuspecting sand ninjas, he soon found himself within arm's reach of his counterpart. Taking a final leap, he reabsorbed himself back into Connor, providing a single entity to stand his ground.

"Take your power, Jasmine, now!" he yelled above the melee.

In the distance Connor noticed her nod, and with full potential surging through her veins, she turned to fight the group around her. However, even with her strengthened power, she was still no match for their adversaries.

The Dream Lord was quick to notice the plan had failed and ordered her to stall for as long as she could, so he could provide her with support. In the meantime, he tried to force his way back but the path was blocked by a small faction of ninjas all prodding and slashing at his form.

Jasmine glanced across at Connor and then her other self. She knew she was in trouble and, like Connor, would have to find another way to destroy her enemies. Without fear or any indication of a resolution to her predicament, she merged back into herself and briefly watched the battle going on around her. Tranquillity ran through her mind and then pumped into her veins, embodying her with an air of serenity. She then knew instantly what had to be done and as she continued to stand her ground, the sand people around her stopped what they had been doing. Thinking she was easy prey, they began to encircle her.

In complete control of the situation, she took a deep breath, composed her karma and started to focus on the task mulling around in her head. Slowly she closed her palms and ripped them backwards to her chest. The motion caused a reaction as the sand ninjas before her collapsed to the ground. Blood began to seep from one of the bodies, staining the golden sands beneath with the dark, red colour of death. The other warriors turned and stared whilst a single ninja dared lean down and pull the body aside. There, lying on the ground, encrusted with the grains of sand, was a heart, still pumping its final beats of life. A large cavity was exposed within the torso of the body where it had once been housed. The assassins looked at one another in amazement and noticed Jasmine move her hands again. In defiance, they stupidly took another step forward closer to her, hoping this would cause a distraction whilst some of their brothers dared an attack from behind. Jasmine, however, had already sensed the danger and pushed her right hand forward and upwards. As she did so, the faction behind were raised from the ground and thrown over her head into their comrades standing before her. Her focus of survival was now dedicated towards all of the ninjas, and as she turned and casually walked towards Connor, bodies were cast aside to make a pathway.

Finally the strenuous ordeal was over and as she reached the Dream Lord, she sensed the energy drain from her body and her legs go weak. Connor knew the signs all too well and took a step forward just in time to catch her before she hit the ground. Scooping her up in his arms, he ran back towards Durban, Vanisheo and the black ninja.

"You were amazing, Jasmine," Connor told her as he helped her back onto her feet. "Kustos would have been proud of you."

"I hope so, Connor," she whispered weakly. "It did not feel right to kill those men but our mission here is far more important than a single life. Oh, how I hate war," she added.

Considering the fact his race were passive beings, Vanisheo had worked out a way to sense the sand ninjas and was easily holding his own.

"There are too many of them, Connor," he said as the Dream Lord approached him. "We cannot win this fight."

"We must," replied Connor. "We can't let Volnar stop us at the first hurdle. There must be a way."

No sooner had he uttered these words than the Sand people stopped in their tracks, listened for moment and then turned and ran away, leaving the five standing alone. With the exodus of their assailants, the sandstorm subsided and Durban could just make out in the distance a dust ball rapidly approaching.

"Razars!" he shouted.

"Can it get any worse?" asked Vanisheo.

"We have to go . . . NOW!" Connor told them as he carefully rested Jasmine on the ground.

Gently he laid his hand upon her forehead and closed his eyes. As he focussed on rejuvenating her energy, a blue light emitted around her body and flashed in ebbs and flows as Connor's strength passed through her. Suddenly she opened her eyes and smiled.

"That is enough, Connor," she whispered softly. "I will be fine now."

Carefully he helped Jasmine to her feet and took a few breaths to renew his own energy, then looked off into the distance.

"We must find that abandoned city and take shelter," he told the others. "The sand ninjas will not be able to hold off the Razars forever."

"I know the way," the ninja advised. "Followed me." And without waiting for a response, ran off in the opposite direction from the battle behind them.

Durban and the others were unsure but Connor was convinced the ninja was a messenger of good.

"Our new ally hasn't let us down yet," he told his friends "so we must trust our own instincts on this right now."

Accepting Connor's faith in the stranger, they picked up pace and ran off after the ninja. With the sandstorm no longer present, the burning rays of the sun beat down upon their heads and with each step slowly drained any enthusiasm or energy they might have had.

"I need to rest," gasped Vanisheo sometime later as he stopped and sat down. "My legs are not as long as yours."

"Why have you stopped?" asked the ninja. "We must reach the city before we are caught."

"We need just a moment, please," pleaded Connor as he joined Vanisheo. "We've been travelling for many hours and our energy levels are failing."

The ninja did not approve of delay but seeing Jasmine and Durban stop as well, realised that further reprimand would be futile and giving in to their weaknesses, took a moment to rest.

"Vanisheo!" asked Durban. "What do you make of this city we are trying to find? Is it safe?"

"It was once a beautiful place," Vanisheo mused as he recalled the whitewashed buildings, glistening in the sun. "I cannot believe all has changed."

"It did not happen overnight," interrupted the ninja, "but over a period of years. Many fled to save their lives, whilst others refused to be bullied. I will not permit the evil of Volnar to force me from my home." And with that, the ninja began to unravel the head protection.

Everyone stared in dismay when the long, black, tresses of a young, beautiful Asian woman fell over her shoulders.

"Is there a problem?" she asked impatiently.

Everyone in unison shook their heads politely and then thanked her for coming to their aid. They hoped the change of subject would avoid any questions over their surprise at discovering her to be a woman.

"My name is Nuwa Lin," she told them.

"It was you I sensed following us through the desert?" exclaimed Jasmine.

"I am afraid it was," she replied, "but I had to be sure."

"Sure of what?" asked Connor.

"A few months ago," continued the ninja, "I heard a whisper. It was about a small group of people that would be travelling this way. The reason for their visit was not known, only that their presence here would end the misery of this world. I had to be certain you were the ones that rumours had spoken of."

"And what was your intention once you discovered who we were?" asked Durban, somewhat defensive on behalf of his friends.

"I merely wanted to help," confessed the ninja. "I know this desert and it is not a safe place, but for a non-worlder, it is even more perilous."

"For your consideration we thank you," interrupted Jasmine. "We would not be here now but for you."

"I would not say that was strictly true," replied the woman. "From what I saw of your skills, your powers are far superior to many of Judgment."

"So what's your story?" asked Connor. "Are there others like you? Didn't you want to take the Judgment path and therefore decided to set up life outside?"

"Not exactly," Nuwa Lin replied sadly, as she drew a circle in the sand with her foot, an action to avoid eye contact. "I . . . sort of, well, used to work for the Oracles of Judgment. It was my task to watch those that wandered the path searching for one last chance of a happy ending. If I saw anything I thought was untrue, I would report to the Oracles. Many lives were in my hands, even my own and those of my people." And whilst reminiscing over her fate, a large tear rolled down her cheek.

"What happened?" asked Vanisheo. "Are we going to meet more of your kind?"

"Most of my people have been slaughtered at the hand of Volnar," she told them. "I fled into hiding when the armies marched through. There was nothing I could do at that time. Now I only go back to the city when there is a need. I cannot tell you how many of my people are left but I am certain some managed to escape."

"I am so sorry," apologised Vanisheo sadly, as though the demise of her race was his fault and he shuffled over to her and hugged her leg.

"What of the Sand Ninjas?" asked Durban as he looked briefly behind to see if he could catch a glimpse of the Razars.

Fortunately, the only view he caught was a dazzling horizon as the sun continued to burn down upon the sands.

"Many years ago," began Nuwa Lin, "when I existed in the Wake World, I lived in a small village in the China mountains. It was a peaceful place, cut off from manic civilisation, a happy, timeless existence. As time went by, several other villages grew up around us and, in time, asked if we wanted to join them and expand into a city. After much discussion amongst our elders, it was decided that we did not want the change and so my father, the head elder of our village, declined their offer. Many of our own people were not happy with this decision and it split us into two. Those that disagreed with the verdict left to join other villages, whilst those of us that stayed behind struggled to survive. Naively, we thought we would be left alone but one night we were attacked, and many of us were slaughtered in our sleep. A statement of power had been declared and very little resistance was offered from us and other villages that tried to help. The mountains of China ran with blood in those days.

"When I awoke, I found myself before the head of the Oracle of Judgment, along with others from my village. We were given a choice, to pass in peace to our chosen path or stay behind and help the Oracle ordain judgment on the sort of people that had taken our lives. Once more this split our people. I continued to work for the Oracle as did my father and the rest of my family, but others refused to work with him, as they held him responsible for their deaths. Instead, they fled into the desert to build a city—the hub of progress they never managed to create in the Wake World. For their own protection they lived beneath the sands and over time metamorphosed into what you fought today."

The story was almost unbelievable but the serious tone in which it was delivered confirmed its truth. No one spoke. There was really nothing to say. All it proved was everyone in their lives at some point suffered pain and when their time to pass over arrived, their judgment would truly reflect the life they had led.

Nuwa Lin looked up at the sky and noticed several white, fluffy clouds forming on the horizon.

"Come," she said, "we must keep moving. It looks like rain and rain in a desert can be a very dangerous place."

"Really!" asked Connor. "Rain . . . in a desert?"

"Do not sound so surprised, Connor." The ninja smiled. "After all you have seen, you dare question nature?" And with that she turned in readiness to move on.

"Wait!" he ordered. "How do you know who I am?"

"This is not the time, nor place," said Nuwa Lin as she ran off, leaving her voice to fade upon the wind. "We must get to Hunter," she added.

"And how do you know we're looking for Hunter? I didn't give you his name," he added but the ninja was either too far ahead to hear him or refused to acknowledge his question.

The four friends looked at one another and then at the fading dust trail in the distance as Nuwa Lin headed towards the city.

"I guess we'd better follow," Connor told them as he helped Jasmine to her feet.

"After all, she is our only lead to Hunter," Jasmine reminded him.

14

A Test of Faith

Camella swooped down elegantly and gently touched the ground with her feet. Feeling the lack of motion, Will opened his eyes.

"Are we there yet?" he asked as he steadied himself.

"Yes," she answered and pointed to an area to the left of them, "over there is the entrance." As she finished talking, something caught her eyes, so she knelt to the ground and ran her hands over two faint imprints on the grass. "It looks as though Kustos and Fortis have already passed this way. Look!" she said, showing Will two sets of footprints.

"So one down and two to go," said Will with a smile.

Camella cocked her head to one side as she tried to understand the phrase then accepted it as something quite unimportant. Instead, she looked Will up and down, again taking a mental picture of his image.

Will could sense her curiosity and waited for some type of question but nothing was asked and rather than stand in uncomfortable silence, he felt impelled to say something.

"Guess it's us next then," he told her.

She looked at him again and smiled. Not an emotion of happiness but one that attempted to apologise for the dangers they were about to endeavour.

"I know that splitting up is not the ideal solution," she said, "but trust me, it is probably for the best. This way, any fear and anger is divided and because of that, we might make it through. Come on!" And without waiting for Will to move, she walked off.

Quickly he hurried to join her as they passed a number of bodies strewn along their route, an aftermath of the ongoing battle. Aware of their lack of weapons, Will scoured the blood-stained grasses and noticed a flickering of light reflecting from the setting sun.

"Look over there, Camella," he suggested as he pointed to the evidence of dazzling colours. "What are those?"

Casually she walked over to the inviting light and picked it up.

"Hmm!" she mused to herself but just loud enough for Will to hear the dulcet tone. "ice blades! Now these will come in very handy." She smiled at him as she placed them carefully in the empty knife holders resting lightly on either hip. "We must not waste time," she added as she rejoined Will and before he had a chance to speak, she began climbing down into a large hole metres from where they were standing.

It was well hidden and could easily be mistaken for a large rabbit hole. That was if rabbits actually existed in Judgment.

"This is where we must enter the tunnel and make our way to the fire lands. Are you ready?" she asked him.

"As ready as I'll ever be," he replied.

In that case," Camella warned, "clear you mind and think of nothing."

Will did as he was instructed and peered into the darkness.

⚘ ⚘ ⚘

The cave was damp and ill lit and a stale, rancid smell lay heavily in the still air. Black water trickled slowly down the rugged rock walls, and from time to time, Lingel beetles rushed across the wet floor. Kustos had been in some pretty unsavoury places in his time but recalling them did not improve his journey or his mood. For hours, or that was how it felt, he trudged along the only pathway shown to him until finally, with great relief, he reached the end. There in front of him was a room supporting six doors in a semicircle around the walls. Kustos scratched his head as if to determine which door he should choose but no immediate answer came to him. Instead, a gust of wind blew around the room and scattered a shadow of darkness, blocking out what little light there was. His visibility was reduced to nothing, and in the obscurity, he could hear the cries of desolation.

"Choose a door and suffer your fate," it told him over and over again, chanting incessantly, nagging away at any decision he was going to make.

Remembering Camella's warnings, he tried to clear his mind and let his instincts make the final choice. Blinded by the darkness, he carefully walked towards his left and turned the handle of the first door he came across. Effortlessly it opened and he walked through. There was now no turning back, especially when the door slammed behind him, locking him away from any possible retreat.

For the time being, the shadows in the Room of Doors sensed its first task was complete and slowly filtered back from whence it came. It knew it had to prepare, for others would be coming, treading the same path and making the same mistakes.

With the barrier of darkness now removed, Kustos walked forward. Dazzling rays of light enticed him on and as his eyes adjusted to his new surroundings, he realised he was back in Sublin, outside the Great Walls of his own kingdom. He told himself this could not be true but as he looked, he could just make out some

figures in the distance. The suns of Sublin were in full glory, illuminating every blade of grass and stone with their brilliance, even
dazzling Kustos' vision and marring the features of the people
before him, yet he sensed a familiarity of their presence. One he
could not explain but one he sensed must be treated with caution.
As each step brought him closer, he saw three teenagers. Two were
boys and the other a beautiful young girl. They were teaching each
other how fight with Cinxi swords.

"Hello," said Kustos in a friendly tone as he approached.

He was hoping that his presence had not scared them but he
need not have worried as the youths were undeterred. Instead the
three of them immediately stopped what they were doing and
stared at Kustos. Their smiles of contentment fell from their faces
and an evil stare of hatred clouded their eyes.

"Father!" they said in unison.

"Father?" echoed Kustos in confusion.

⚙ ⚙ ⚙

Fortis was the next to enter the Room of Doors and ignoring
the incessant mantra, spent little time thinking about his options,
He merely reached out and chose the first door on his right. He
thought the elected access was of his own doing but the darkness
knew exactly which way he must turn and guided him on to his
own personal pathway. Without hesitation, he walked through and
once inside, heard the door slam behind him. There was no way
back . . . only forward.

For a moment he waited for the light to settle and as his eyes
became accustomed to his surroundings, he realised he was on the
Island of Kusp standing before the Dream Portal. With curiosity,
he walked towards it. He knew not why, it just seemed the obvious
option. With every step he noticed the unkempt pathway and over-
grown, luscious flora. Silence deafened his ears as not a single

bird warbled its songs of joy or contented bees buzzed. There was no doubt in his mind that no man had passed this way for a very long time.

"What has happened here," he thought to himself, but before he could find the answer, he felt a blow from behind knocking him to the ground.

Quickly Fortis turned around and was just in time to avoid another attack. Reacting on the presumption of another blow, he scrambled backwards and got to his feet. His attacker took a step forward and smiled.

"Hello, Fortis," he said.

Fortis stared in disbelief. The image before him was familiar and yet he could not recognise the figure.

"Who are you?" demanded Fortis.

"Why," replied the man, "has your easy life made you so blind? Do you not recognise the soul? You are me, or should I say . . . I am you."

⚜ ⚜ ⚜

Kustos stood before the three teenagers and studied their faces. They had called him father and yet he knew this could not be true.

"Father?" he asked them. "How is this possible?"

"It is what it is, Father," one of the boys told him.

"Why have you come back?" asked the girl. "You were never there for us before. You ran away because you were scared. So why now have you come back?"

"What is your name?" Kustos asked the young girl.

"Has it been that long you do not remember?" was the response.

"Jasmine and I had always said that should we be blessed with a girl, we would call her Ophellia," mumbled Kustos, more to himself than the teenagers.

"So you do remember," snapped Ophellia angrily as she raised her Cinxi swords in a threatening manner. "You left us. Why? Were we not the dew upon your grass? You told our mother that Grandpa and Grandma were not dead and that you could bring them back to us. For you it was better to chase their ghosts than live your life and love your family. You failed us and Mother. It was us that had to listen to her crying herself to sleep, night after night. How could you be so selfish, Father? We hate you for what you did. You never loved us or Mother, so while you have the chance, we suggest you leave. Stay and we will kill you where you stand."

Kustos' children took their stance, and one by one, they raised their swords.

"This is impossible," Kustos told them. "I love your mother more than life itself and I would be the proudest father in Sublin if you were the fruits of our love. I would never leave any of you to fend for yourselves."

As Kustos proclaimed his own defence before his children, it suddenly occurred to him Camella's warning.

"My fears," he said aloud to the sky, "you are playing on my fears. Is that the best you have?"

Despite his challenge to the Tunnel of Absolution, the two boys parried their swords high and charged them with blue energy before rushing towards their father. As they reached within feet of an attack, the energy died.

"It is lucky for me they are still young," Kustos thought to himself. "They have not yet harnessed their full potential." And picking up a loose rock on the ground, he threw it at the children and knocked the training swords away, snapping the thinner metal in half.

⚜ ⚜ ⚜

"Fortis, poor Fortis," said the image of his imagination, meta-morphosed in the guise of a Dream Stealer. "You were left in Judgment, when you could have been so much more in Sublin. What a waste of our talent."

"I never wanted to steal that energy," he shouted at himself. "My will was not my own and I was weak. It was only my dear brother that released me from my torment . . . but I am stronger now. I will not be coerced back into darkness."

"Do not pretend that you have forgotten how the power feels," sneered the Dream Stealer. "All those lost dreams . . . the en-ergy . . . the power. Remember how it gave you an unbelievable sense of complete euphoria as it ran through your veins."

"I will not be that creature again," Fortis told the stealer.

"You cannot hide your feelings from me," laughed his alter ego. "I am you. I know you fight the cravings of power every sin-gle day but here it is no longer necessary. Quench your thirst, stay and feed once more." And with that, the Dream Stealer pointed to the Dream Realm entrance. "Just take that step, Fortis."

Fortis tried to fight against the uncontrollable urges, but he still found himself pulled towards the entranceway. The fire in his soul began to burn once more and the cravings of the stolen en-ergy burned his eyes, as smoke smouldered from their sockets. He could not deny the feeling was exhilarating and step by step he moved towards the other image. For others it looked as though Fortis was still in the room, but to the prince, it was the Dream Portal entrance enticing him in. Leading him into the fate of a bot-tomless pit shrouded in darkness.

"Yes! Yes!" encouraged the Fortis Dream Stealer. "Closer you must go."

"Why did you come back, Father?" asked Ophellia as she attacked him. "This is not your life, nor do we want you here. Do you think because your destiny helped to resolve the Great War of Sublin with the Dream Lord, that you would be loved forever? That is not the case. You are not wanted here."

The teenagers, although young, were well schooled in the art of fighting and despite their inexperience, Kustos found it difficult to defend himself. Perhaps the fact they were supposed to be his children played upon his mind but either way, he found himself being pushed back towards the river running around his lands.

"It will never be like this," Kustos tried to tell them. "If you were my children, I would love you forever."

"You say that now," spat Ophellia, "but when the time comes you will leave. You always leave."

"No! No! I will not," Kustos assured them as he took another step back, each time moving closer to the hunter's trap, bedecked with upward spikes, waiting to claim its next victim.

Kustos had to be calm. He knew that this was playing on his own insecurities and to survive, he had to overcome them.

⚜ ⚜ ⚜

"Come on, Fortis," urged the Dream Stealer. "Just a few more steps."

Fortis saw the entranceway and stopped. This was not the man he had become.

"I will never go back to the Dream Portal," he told the Dream Stealer as he turned and looked at him. "I will never be you. I have no problem with addiction, nor do I crave the power it once gave me. I have a purpose to my life. I will stop the one who forced me down that road." And he grabbed the Dream Stealer by the shoulders and started to shake him.

For a moment, their eyes met and Fortis briefly saw the emptiness within the shell before it turned to ash, blowing in the wind. Immediately the island vanished, and all that remained was the darkened pit, waiting for him to enter. Quickly he took a few steps back and as he did so, a disturbing laugh echoed around him. Taunting him and challenging his strength.

At the far end of the room, a door flew open, filtering light into the shadows. With barely a moment to lose, he ran to it and without hesitation walked through. Instantly it slammed behind him.

❖ ❖ ❖

Kustos had bruises and cuts all over his hands and arms, caused by defending himself against the children. He knew he was far more skilled than they in the art of fighting but he dared not lay a blow upon their form, for fear of injuring them and so he did the next best thing until he had a plan and tried to avoid every one of their blows.

"We will kill you. Father, without remorse," they echoed as they forced him back towards the pit of stakes. "How could leave your own children?"

"Enough!" shouted Kustos suddenly, and to his surprise, the children stopped. "I know what you are doing," he continued as he looked up at the sky.

Ophellia followed his glance to see who he was challenging but saw no one.

"I am not chasing my mother's or father's ghosts," he said angrily. "They are gone and I would never leave my family on such a foolish whim. I will be the best father I can. I will teach my children, discipline them and love them. I am no longer scared to take on that commitment. I can see these children need guidance and I will lead them by the brightest light. Do you hear me?" he added.

Silence filled the air and the teenagers stared at Kustos in dismay.

"I will be your father," the Realm Lord told them, "and your friend. I will be there always until the sands of time invite me to join your grandparents."

His children looked at one another and then back at Kustos. Ophellia began to cry, the wails of a broken heart, craving for attention. Kustos smiled at them lovingly as one by one they faded into oblivion. Sublin also vanished and he found himself once more in a room. The hunter's pit was still behind him, waiting for him to fall, and just like his brother before him, he moved away. A menacing laugh lurked in the shadows as a door before him opened. With nowhere else to go, Kustos walked on as a hand reached through the open door, grabbed him by the wrist and pulled him through.

"You took your time, little brother," laughed Fortis as the door closed behind them.

"Fortis!" Kustos smiled with relief. "Am I glad to see you. Have the others made it through yet?"

"I'm afraid not," Fortis told him. "We are the first but at least it gives us more time to rest. I am certain this is where we all shall meet up as it appears to be the main route into Infernato."

As Kustos looked ahead, he felt the uninviting warmth of fire. Its craggy rocks soared high into the orange sky, never showing where the rock formation ended and the skyline began. Lava slowly oozed from every crevice of the inhospitable lands, forming a river of spitting fire and treacherous pools. It reminded Kustos of the Island of Kusp where Fortis met his demise.

"I too dislike this place, brother," Fortis told him as he watched Kustos survey all before him. "It reminds me of memories I wish to forget."

❧❧❧

"Look ahead," Will told Camella. "A door's opened. I guess that means we have to walk through."

"Wait!" replied the Butterhawk nervously. "It could be a trap."

"And it could also be our passageway through the tunnel," Will told her. "Either way, we don't have a choice." And he grabbed Camella by the hand and dragged her through.

"Remember!" she shouted as persistent chanting swirled through the darkness. "Clear your mind. Do not give it any memories to prey upon."

❧❧❧

The door closed behind him and as it did so, Joshua strutted into the room. The darkness screamed out at him in fear.

"Why are you here? Why are you here?" it echoed before evaporating into the shadows.

Joshua was far more relaxed than the others and casually wandered towards one of the doors. Once his choice was made, he opened it and walked through.

"Okay!" he challenged. "Give me all you have got."

Reluctantly the door closed behind him.

15

Whose Fault Is That?

Will and Camella found themselves in yet another room, and as the door shut behind them, it began to vibrate. An ambient voice bounced backwards and forwards off the walls, warning them that the worst was yet to come. The quaking of the floor began to increase; they struggled to retain their footing and as they looked, to their dismay, the ground around them dropped away, leaving them trapped on a small circle of stone beneath their feet.

"What the . . . ?" Will began to ask but before he could finish the sentence, their circular respite began to escalate toward the ceiling, throwing them both to the ground as it soared upwards.

As they lay upon their backs like helpless turtles, Will noticed the spikes protruding from above.

"That can't be good," he told Camella, above the grinding sound of stone upon stone, "but don't worry, I've a plan." And he harnessed what air he could within the room and directed it up to the ceiling.

The impact forced it to rip apart as they escaped out into the atmosphere above until, finally, their stony escalator stopped as it reached the upper level. Will scrambled to his feet and took Camella's hand as he helped her up.

"Where are we?" he asked her.

"I do not know," Camella told him. "This is not Infernato or the Tunnels of Absolution. I do not recognise any of this."

Again, they looked around and saw nothing but Orange skies and fluffy summer clouds.

Joshua walked through the room and as he did so, noticed the two pits on either side of his walkway. One was a dark, bottomless hollow, the other a hunter's trap with wooden stakes decorating the ground. Both were similar to those in Fortis and Kustos' tests. A door at the end of the room beaconed to him, and rather over-confidently, Joshua walked on. Just as he was about to enter the next room, he heard footsteps behind him. He turned around and found himself face to face with a soul cruncher.

"What on earth!" he exclaimed as he stared at the image.

The figure reflected back was an illustration of himself.

"So, what do we do now?" asked Will, devoid for the time being of any plan of action.

"I do not know," replied Camella. "Are you certain your mind was clear?"

"I think so," he replied, trying to remember what he was thinking about as they entered the room.

He was convinced his memories were nothing like this.

"I'm sure this wasn't me. What about you?" he asked her.

"My mind was very clear, I promise," she told him. "I would not dream of putting you in this environment."

"Well, one of us managed to conjure this up," he answered.

As he spoke, dark clouds began to form in the sky and thunder echoed around them; a sudden familiarity popped into Will's mind.

"I've a horrible feeling about this," he whispered in Camella's ear. "This I think I do remember."

The Butterhawk said nothing but looked at him. Fear reflected back from her eyes. Will obviously knew of this scenario and by his tone, it was not a pleasant one. As they continued to stare at the evolving storm, lightening crackled around them, missing their tiny platform by inches. Camella jumped and squirmed as the electricity sent static through her wings, causing an uncomfortable sensation over the membranes.

"I do not like this," she told Will. "When will it stop?"

"Your guess is as good as mine," he assured her.

Just then a lightning bolt pushed through a cloud, heading towards Camella.

"Look out!" Will shouted, and as he did so, he flung his arms towards the Butterhawk and controlled the wind around her, lifting her away from the platform. With her quick reflexes, she extended her small wings to steady herself. Only seconds later, the lightning crackled and spluttered in the exact spot she had been standing, leaving a mass of dirt and grit on the ground. Camella, on the other hand, glided on the air as she watched in horror.

"That could have been me?" she exclaimed nervously.

"Would I let anything happen to you?" Will told her. "I'm a Dream Warrior and one of my roles is to protect pretty young women."

Camella blushed at his inference but still enjoyed the intimation.

❖ ❖ ❖

"You should have stayed in the Judgment Halls, my friend," said the Soul Cruncher to Joshua. "You are too fainthearted for the realities of life. Eating souls is far more of a pleasure than judging them and permitting them to live on."

"I could not stay behind," Joshua told the Soul Cruncher. "I am not that weak to shy away from my responsibilities. I left the Judgment Halls to find a way to stop this madness. We have been given a job, defined by the Higher Power. I will not allow you to discredit that."

"Sorry you feel like that," replied the evil twin and with that, he opened his mouth and began to suck the soul energy from the Oracle.

Joshua felt his life force being dragged from his body and called upon his own energies to defend himself. Using his powerful strength, Joshua fought back against the Soul Cruncher. The dark being was not strong enough to battle such a force and quickly relinquished his efforts, exploding into a mass of tiny particles. Even though Joshua had won over his hidden fears, he sensed there was still a danger as the impact of the Soul Cruncher's demise had caused a pressure vacuum in the room, throwing Joshua off his feet and towards the bottomless pit.

In desperation, he made a frantic grab for the sides and in doing so, just managed to grip the edge with a couple of fingers. He was a solid man and the mass of his body outweighed his sense of survival as his fingers began to slip slowly away. There was little left he could do but await his fate until the moment of his demise arrived. Accepting destiny had dealt her final hand, he waited patiently until, out of nowhere, two strong hands grab his arms.

"I've got you," Fortis told Joshua calmly as they swung gently from side to side of the pit.

"But who has you?" asked Joshua as he looked up and saw the prince hanging over the edge of the pit.

"That would be me," struggled a voice way above them.

"Pull us up, Kustos," yelled Fortis. "I am certain we would not like what is below."

Slowly the two comrades began to move upwards towards the opening of the pit and as each finally appeared at the top they saw Kustos, straining with all his strength. Fortis scrambled back on the ground and quickly pulled Joshua to safety.

"Quickly, to the door!" ordered the Realm Lord as he helped his brother to his feet.

Fortis pushed Joshua up and dragged him along.

"Thank you," the Oracle gasped as he ran. "How did you know I was in trouble?"

"Kustos heard the explosion and at the same time a door opened to us," he was told. "We figured it was no coincidence, so we looked inside and saw your hand gripping onto the edge of the pit. Believe me . . . someone wanted us to rescue you."

"What of Will and Camella?" asked Joshua.

"Not yet my friend but I believe we will see them soon." Fortis smiled as they reached the door and threw themselves through, just as it closed behind them.

℥ ℥ ℥

The dust cloud settled and from the air, Camella caught a glimpse of the being who had made such a theatrical entrance. It was Volnar and only then did it occur to Will why their present situation felt like déjà vu. The Shadow Lord's arrival was the same magnificent appearance he had made all those years ago, on that fateful day on the battlefields of the Waterfall Kingdom. He had not changed a bit. Eleven feet tall, his evil, piercing eyes stared out through the feature-less mask that covered his face. Cranial spikes jutted skyward from his hairless head and above the mask that hid his true identity, three red diamonds perched together on his forehead. They glistened in the light's reflection as if a beacon of their importance. These pretty pieces of glass contained the source of his power, his dream energy and rumour had it, only their destruction could possibly bring the end of the Dark Lord's existence. Apart from his gems of power, he was clothed in much the same way as many years before. His upper body was protected by wide, bio-like shoulder pads, terminating in his metal armour. Interlinked, chain mail gloves protected his hands with a final accessory of razor sharp spikes around each wrist. To compliment the smaller weapons, he finalised his ensemble with a blade protruding from each boot.

"I think we could be in trouble here," Will told Camella.

"You know this creature?" she asked.

"This . . . is Volnar, the guy we're all trying to stop overrunning Judgment," he advised the Butterhawk.

She gasped in disbelief. She had heard of his name and the evil he had caused to the Judgment World but she never expected to meet him face to face.

Volnar quickly recognised the Dream Warrior and raised his arms in preparation of an attack as he moved towards Will. Will in turn immediately called upon his elemental powers and pushed his hands forward to create a mini hurricane around the Shadow Night Lord. His efforts were not as effective as he had hoped and, apart from slowing the enemy down, caused little injury.

"Damn. It's not working," cursed Will to himself as he dropped his hands.

The conjured wind immediately stopped.

Volnar said nothing, no goading or verbal abuse. Instead, he continued to walk slowly towards Will. Aware of the imminent fight, the Dream Warrior took a step backwards and balanced precariously on the edge of the platform.

"Will! Look out!" yelled Camella as she changed direction to swoop closer to Volnar.

Without thought of her own safety, she reached down to her knife harness and retrieved one of the ice blades, then held it out in front of her as a protective move. Out of the corner of his eye, Volnar noticed the minor irritation and threw an energy bolt in her direction. It hit her squarely in the chest and caused her to lose momentum as she spun backwards before falling towards the ground.

"Camella!" shouted Will as he jumped off the platform and into the air.

With perfect timing, he caught her by the waist as she fell and using the wind as a cushion, he manoeuvred them back to the platform.

"Are you okay?" he asked her as they stood down.

"I think so," she replied. "Just a little shaken."

Will smiled at her with relief as she posed him a question.

"How are we ever going to destroy him?" she asked.

"Don't worry," Will assured her. "I know the what, not yet the how. Do you see the three red diamonds on his forehead?" he added.

Camella nodded her acknowledgement of the glittering decoration.

"That's the secret of his power," Will told her. "They act as a blockage to his energy. All we have to do is destroy them."

"And that is all?" she asked and then thought for a moment. and smiled. "I think I have a plan. I can sense where the air currents flow around this area, so if you can get me up into the sky, I can distract him. That might give you an opportunity to go for the diamonds."

Will was not keen on using Camella as a decoy. After all, he knew what Volnar could do and feared for her life.

"It is our only choice," she told him.

Reluctantly he agreed. Calling upon his power of gravity, he summoned it from within and circulated it around the Butterhawk.

Once more she soared up into the sky and recognising a nearby air current, glided upon the breeze. Like a bird she swooped around the sky, encroaching closer and closer on Volnar. The enchanting human butterfly caught his attention and delighted at a little sport, he threw an energy bolt at her. Deftly, she turned on her side as the energy beam whizzed close by, singeing her hair as it passed. Again, she turned her body once more and swooped down towards the Dark Lord's angry stare.

With Volnar's attention now diverted, Will conjured up his gravity power once more to quietly raise some loose rocks from the ground and throw them towards the distracted Volnar. Controlling their speed was an easy trick as they moved slowly and effortlessly through the air. As they reached closer to their target, Will shouted across, "Hey Volnar! Want another piece of me? The Dream Lord isn't here to save me this time."

Volnar turned to face his abuser and as he did so, Will instructed the rocks to accelerate. Due to their size, most of the impact had little effect. Only the largest of the rocks caused any damage as it struck one of the red diamonds. A cracking sound echoed around the still air as the jewel fell from its setting in pieces. Volnar stepped back as a surging pain raced through his body. Still stunned by the innocuous attack, he had little time to compose himself as another projectile damaged a second stone. This time the injury had more of an effect as the Dark Lord collapsed to the floor in his weakened state. Enraged by such an attack, he forced himself to his feet and ran towards Will, charging up his body as he moved with his damaging lightning bolts.

"Camella!" shouted Will. "Your blade!"

It was then she understood the final part of the plan as she withdrew another ice blade from her harness and dived towards Volnar. Blinded by anger, he did not notice the Butterhawk as she swooped towards him with her hand outstretched. Through the lightening shield she went until she reached the Dark Lord. Then, as the opportunity presented itself, she struck the last and final diamond on his head. Almost immediately, as the weapon touched the energy stone, Volnar melted into the darkness.

Surprised by such a quick reaction, Camella hit the ground, rolled lightly over before stopping and clambered to her feet.

"Sorry," she apologised as she looked at Will. "Not my normal style of landing."

"I figured that," he smiled but as he spoke, their platform began to drop.

Picking up speed, Will dropped to the ground and crawled over to Camella, who by this time had lost her balance and was sitting on the floor. Protectively, the Dream Warrior put his arms around her tiny frame but as the platform got nearer to the room, it began to slow down, until finally it came to a standstill. They looked at each other and laughed.

"Clear our minds, aye!" said Will.

"I think we did pretty well together," exclaimed Camella as he helped her to her feet.

For a moment they stood in silence as they heard the malevolent sound of laughter emitting from the dark corners and then, without warning, an open door appeared at the far end of the room.

"Do you think you can jump from the platform to the floor?" asked Will.

"I can now," replied Camella over the sinister hilarity.

They held hands and together jumped, landing on the other side of the doorway.

"Finally," said Kustos as he patted Will on the back. "What took you so long?"

"Volnar, that's all," Will told them.

"Volnar?" echoed Fortis, as he remembered his slavery under the Dark Lord's rule.

"Not the real one," confirmed Will quickly. "I wish it was. Then this whole nightmare would be over."

"Did you think it would be that easy?" asked Fortis.

"Don't be ridiculous," replied Will. "It's never THAT easy."

"So where do we go from here?" interrupted Kustos. "We've passed the test, so what is expected of us now?"

"I think now," interrupted Joshua, "is the time Camella tells us what she knows about Armon."

"I will, without hesitation," Camella replied, "but may we rest first down by the heated springs? I am not used to such adventure."

"I think we could all do with a little time to prepare," Will said with a smile. "I know I do."

"Very well," said Joshua begrudgingly.

Time he knew was not on their side but if Will had just faced the wrath of Volnar then perhaps he had earned himself a respite.

"Thank you," replied Camella as she led the way.

16

Solarium and Frezicus

"That is where we need to go." Nuwa Lin pointed as the others finally caught up to her.

From the top of the sand dune, they could just make out in the distance the outer walls of Solarium. A once vibrant city now deserted with only the bravest of inhabitants daring to take shelter within its boundaries.

"Look!" said Durban as he pointed skyward.

Dark, rain-laden clouds were collecting their strength and advancing rapidly towards them.

"It is how I said," explained Nuwa Lin. "Rain clouds over the sandy planes. We have no choice but to keep moving."

"Just two questions before we go," demanded Connor. "How do you know of me and of our mission to find Hunter?"

"There is no sinister reason for my knowledge," Nuwa Lin told him. "I have known of your plans for some time. For many years, we have been waiting for someone to rescue us from this plight and when the whispers on the desert winds sang your name, I knew you were that saviour. Your destiny was to search the pathway to the Judgment Halls, where hope could be restored once again. As for your name, I heard it spoken during the fight, so I am afraid there is little mystery there. You are the Dream Lord and Will is the Dream Warrior. Both of you have faced the wrath of Volnar before and won and now you come to end his rule here in Judgment . . . forever."

"Well, that's the plan," replied Connor. "We vowed to release all from his clutches."

As for Hunter," the ninja continued, "we have met. It was my responsibility to hide him until the time was right to reappear. I found the traveller wandering the open desert. Lost and confused. Fortunately, as luck would have it, an opportunity arose to take Hunter to a safe place before the sand ninjas emerged. It was only then I learned the part this being had to play in the demise of the Dark Lord."

"And that was?" asked Connor.

"Hunter had escaped the Judgment Halls, a miracle that not often happens to anyone, let alone a Wake Worlder," the ninja added.

"So where is Hunter hiding now?" interrupted Jasmine. "We must find him and go back and join our friends."

Nuwa Lin said nothing but looked at Connor and smiled.

"What?" he asked her as he tried to read the look.

"It is nothing," Nuwa Lin replied before turning her attention to rest of the explanation. "The path to Hunter is a long and arduous one. Pass the city of Solarium and into the ice lands of Frezicus. Here, there are two ice mountains. Between them, in its ancient glory, is a single lonely tree. Hidden in its gnarling trunk can be found a secret entrance into the belly of the mountain. That is where Hunter can be found but please heed my warnings. He has not seen a living being for many years, so you must tread carefully when you approach."

Connor wanted to know more but before he could ask, Nuwa Lin urged them to move on.

"We must make haste now," she told him as she watched the menacing clouds rapidly approach.

"It is only a little rain," Durban pointed out, not sure why the ninja was making such an issue.

"A little rain on grasslands can be a refreshing welcome, but in the desert, it can mean death," Nuwa Lin told them dramatically. "Water on these sandy grains will encourage the graves of quicksand to rise. With many years of waiting, they will be only too happy to swallow you whole. We must not drop our pace, as this would only encourage the hunger. Quickly, we must leave." And her voice trailed off in the wind as she ran down the dune, away from the heavily laden clouds, towards the only route into Solarium.

The others remained speechless as Connor bent down towards Vanisheo.

"Come, my little friend," he urged. "Jump up on my shoulders and I'll be your mule."

"My lord," exclaimed Vanisheo, "I cannot take advantage of this opportunity."

"Yes, you can," Jasmine assured him. "If we are all going to make it to Solarium, your little legs will need assistance."

The Hallucium looked down at his childlike limbs then over to the stalwart figure of the Dream Lord.

"I see your point, Connor," he admitted as he lightly climbed the doubled frame and sat astride his shoulders.

Almost immediately, Connor stood up and started to run off after Nuwa Lin. Jasmine and Durban were already ahead of them and as the ninja looked back, she slowed her pace a little for the others to catch up to her.

"Whatever happens," she told them, "we must keep moving."

No sooner had the warning left her lips than the first few drops of rain begin to fall. At first the sprinkle of light drizzle refreshed them from the dusty heat of the desert but as the droplets began to increase in size, they felt like bee stings, slapping against their exposed flesh.

"Keep moving. Do not stop," Nuwa Lin warned them again. "I will look out for Connor and the Hallucium."

With each bead of rain that hit the ground, a sigh of expectation filtered through the air and as their vision blurred because of the intensity of the storm, moving through the sand felt like trudging through a bog. With each footstep, Durban dragged himself along until his footing started to give way. For fear of falling through the ground, he stopped and then decided to take much larger strides in an effort to overcome the danger. Jasmine noticed the difficulties he was experiencing and carefully watched each movement that he made so that she could mimic his pathway. With great determination, they painfully moved forward, forcing themselves through the now driving rain. Intent on her mission of survival, Jasmine did not notice that Durban had come to a sudden stop and she bumped into the stationary frame.

"What is it?" she shouted above the noise.

"Look! There in front of us," Durban pointed.

There before them was a displacement of sand, whisked into a whirlpool as it twisted and coiled the wet, slushy sand into gaping jaws, attempting to entice them in.

"We cannot pass it," Durban told Jasmine, "and it is far too wide to jump."

"I have an idea," she suggested. "Let us take a run up and jump. I can use my energy to throw us forward. It will be more than enough to help us clear the pit."

"I hope you're right, my lady." Durban smiled as he took her hand and carefully led her back a few metres. Briefly, they looked behind towards where Connor, Vanisheo and Nuwa Lin should have been but a curtain of torrential rain blurred their view. "I am sure they will be safe," he told her.

"I am certain too," Jasmine smiled before shouting out the order. "Go!" she screamed above the noise.

Together they began to run towards the pit and just as they reached the edge, they took a huge leap forward. Jasmine threw her arms out and as she did so, lifted herself and Durban high up into the sky. The rain, still beating heavily against their frames, forced Durban back towards the ground just clear of the whirlpool of sand. Jasmine however, was not so lucky, as her lithe figure dropped inches short of the far edge of the hole and quickly began to sink into the sand.

"No!" Durban yelled in disbelief as he watched helplessly.

His frustration though far outweighed Jasmine's composure as she realised the danger she was in and thrust her hands into the sand to try and push her body out. Unfortunately, the action did not work and she found herself swallowed further into the pit. Disappointed by such a response, she let out a cry. Durban thought it was a scream of desperation but as he watched, he saw another image of the princess split from the top of her head. As the second Jasmine floated into the air, she took a leap forward, grabbing Jasmine by her blouse as she went. By reaching safety herself, the spectre Jasmine mustered her last ounce of strength and dragged the princess to the side of the sand pit and safety. Jasmine lay on the ground and caught her breath, while Durban looked in a stunned silence before dragging her to her feet. As soon as it recognised she was safe, the second image rapidly absorbed itself back into the princess.

"Phew!" she smiled. "That was a close one."

"I wish I knew how you did that," Durban said as he held her arm to support her.

"So do I," she replied.

The others—Vanisheo, Connor, and Nuwa Lin—were not too far behind but still struggling against the weather. Only the Hallucium was undisturbed by the downpour as his tiny frame was an asset in the conditions and so he climbed off Connor's shoulders to make his own way towards Jasmine. Lightly he pranced across the sodden sand, barely causing an imprint or disturbance on the ground.

"Thank goodness you are alright," exclaimed Jasmine. "Where are Connor and Nuwa Lin?"

"I can just see them over there," replied Vanisheo as he pointed in the direction he had last seen his friends.

Jasmine peered through the pouring raining and managed to make out two shapes in the gloom. Both were still ploughing side by side through the heavy rain. Connor dropped back a little just as Nuwa Lin reached the pit. Predictably, she took a huge leap, whilst seconds later Connor followed, jumping higher into the air and landing gently on the ninja's back. He rested there momentarily before leaning down and pushing off from her shoulders. As he flipped over her head, he grabbed her by the arms and flicked her past him over the pit. Together they rolled on impact to the land and got to their feet.

Jasmine and Durban watched their acrobatic feat in amazement, but Nuwa Lin was oblivious and reprimanded them for resting.

"We are almost there," she told them. "We cannot stop now but must keep moving."

"Come, Vanisheo," said Durban as he bent down. "It is my turn to give you a lift."

Vanisheo did not argue. The short journey he had taken on his own had tired him out and he was appreciative of the assistance. Quickly he climbed the soldier's shoulders and gripped around his neck. Together the team dodged and swerved the quicksand holes that randomly appeared, until they finally reached the edge of the rain cloud. Here they were all relieved to see the walls of Solarium—an emotion that was soon short-lived, for as they waited, an unexplained rumbling from beneath warned them to remain still. A single step forward would have been their downfall as the noise grew in vibration and the sand before them gave way, revealing a bottomless drop.

"I have this," Jasmine told them all. "Just trust me. Start running, and I will do the rest."

Without a word they did as they were instructed and once they reached the edge of the drop, she threw her arms up into the air and pushed her friends across the ravine. Unselfishly, Jasmine yet again was unable to project herself across and found she was falling into the chasm.

Connor always knew when his friends were in danger and immediately sensed she was in trouble. Turning around, he was just in time to see her disappear into the gaping hole.

"Oh no, you don't," he said to himself as he flung his arms forward.

Like some magician's trick, Jasmine floated back into view as Connor gently placed her on the ground next to him.

"It is lucky for me you can absorb other energies." She smiled as she hugged him. "Thank you."

"I promised to protect you, remember." He smiled too, relieved that his power had worked.

The team watched together as the rain clouds evaporated, and the flaming sun once more decorated the sky. In the blink of an eye, the landscape had returned to the arid desert they had recently become familiar with.

"So how do we get in?" asked Connor, turning his attention to the endless miles of sandstone wall.

The enclosed gates, rusted in place over eons of rainstorms, were immovable, and any hope of scaling them was defused by the razor wire that embellished the top.

"Guess they weren't expecting visitors," he announced as he studied the gates more closely.

"There is a way in," Nuwa Lin assured him as she noticed the disappointed look on his face. "There should be a rope ladder a little way up from the gates."

Conscious of the Razars not too far behind them, they quickly made their way past the gates in search of another entrance. Suddenly screams of panic from within wafted over the city walls.

"I thought this place was supposed to be deserted?" asked Vanisheo as he grabbed Jasmine's hand.

"It was . . . I mean it is," the ninja told them, but as she spoke, a rope ladder dropped before them from the top of the wall.

"Nuwa Lin. Nuwa Lin," whispered a voice from above. "Quickly."

The ninja thought for a moment as she tried to recognise the voice and then grabbed the rope and swiftly ran to the top of the wall.

"Father!" she exclaimed in disbelief. "I thought you were dead?"

"Any explanations can come later, my daughter," he replied. "There is not much time, and we must get you and your friends away from Solarium."

She looked at her father and tears of emotion welled up in her eyes. For many years Nuwa Lin had assumed she was alone, devoid of family and friends, yet in an instant all of that had suddenly changed.

"The Razars are here, my child," her father continued, "along with the Soul Crunchers. Someone must have warned them of your journey. It is Hunter they seek?"

"But how do they know of my involvement with Hunter?" she asked. "Only few are blessed with such knowledge."

"One of them has betrayed your trust, but who can wait for another day," said the old man. "We must get your friends through the city and into the ice lands of Frezicus. It is only a matter of time before the truth is discovered, and when it is . . . there must be some distance between them."

"Connor!" yelled Nuwa Lin from the top of the wall. "We must hurry. My father tells me there is an army here searching for Hunter. It will only be a matter of time before the secret is learned."

Connor sensed the urgency of their situation and quickly climbed the rope ladder. Then leaning over the side, he urged his friends to join him. One by one, they clambered up out of the desert until all were standing on the top of the wall. Silently they jumped into new dangers lurking within the city.

"Lord Connor." The ninja's father bowed. "My daughter and I will lead the way. Many tunnels below the city foundations will be your escape. Follow them to the end and do not turn back. I am certain my daughter will know the way from there."

"I cannot take the path with you, Connor," Nuwa Lin suddenly announced sadly. "But I will give Vanisheo the directions to find Hunter."

"You're not coming with us?" asked the Dream Lord.

"I'm afraid my journey with you all must end here. I need to stay with my father and hold off the enemy for as long as we can. It is imperative you reach Hunter before they do. If legend is true, then only you can decide the fate of this world."

"Your bravery will be rewarded," smiled Connor to the ninja. "Without your help we wouldn't have reached this far. Be careful and be vigilant so that we may meet again."

Nuwa Lin smiled and beckoned Vanisheo to join her, whilst the others moved away to give them privacy. Once alone, she quickly whispered the directions to him. Occasionally he nodded at the recollection of certain milestones.

When fully satisfied that the Hallucium understood where they were to go, she ordered them to follow.

"It is done," she said. "Now follow me?"

With her feet barely touching the ground, Nuwa Lin lightly led the way, carefully stopping and checking every few yards that the route was clear. Off in the distance, the sound of a bloody battle ensued, as the small army of brave Ninjas pitched their wits against the forceful Soul Crunchers and Razars. Screams and yells, mingled with blood curdling cries, echoed eerily around the otherwise silent city. Noiselessly they moved around the empty, tiny streets until they reached a dead end . . . or so it appeared. Without a word, Nuwa Lin's father stepped forward and tapped out a pattern across the brickwork. When fully satisfied with the completion of the ceremony, he moved back. Almost instantly an eruption broke through the silence as a crunching of stone upon stone filled the air. Several minutes it continued until finally a doorway slowly began to reveal itself.

Behind the opening was a small room. It had three walls. On one, coats and rucksacks hung in preparation for a journey. In the floor was a single orifice leading into the depths below.

"These coats may not look the height of fashion," pointed out Nuwa Lin's father, "but will keep you warm in the ice lands. Within the packs is food and water, sufficient to sustain you for many months, but beware, a single mouthful will sustain you for a day. Now take the provisions and go."

"Thank you both," said Connor as he backed into the room. "Especially you, Nuwa Lin. Without your help we wouldn't be here. I wish you well and safe keeping in the battles to come. I hope the paths of Judgment will let us meet in less evil times."

"That is my wish also," said the ninja with a smile, and as she did so, the wall began to solidify, encasing Connor and his friends forever. Just as the last brick was about to be placed, Connor caught a final glimpse of the street and saw a Razar and Soul Cruncher heading towards the unsuspecting ninjas.

"Nuwa Lin!" he shouted urgently, but the wall was complete and his warning unheard.

"I am sure she will be fine," said Durban as he handed Connor a coat and pack. "She is a skilful fighter. I cannot see a Razar getting the better of her."

"I hope you're right, Durban," replied Connor angrily. "HE is going to pay for the deaths he's caused. Come on, let's go." And he put on his coat and climbed down the ladder.

The tunnel below was dimly lit, but there was enough visibility to see the endless corridor stretching before them. The width was no wider than two abreast and the low ceilings enhanced the feeling of enclosure.

"I guess we just have to follow this to the end," Connor surmised as he helped Jasmine from the ladder.

"But how far is that?" she asked as she wriggled next to him.

"I've no idea," was Connor's response as he moved off.

As they walked along in silence, they heard the sounds of fighting in the streets above. Every so often, vibrations of the battle caused grains of earth to slip through fault line cracks in the ceiling as an avalanche of weight bore down upon it.

"I hope the tunnel holds," whispered Durban as the claustrophobic walls began to close in on him.

No sooner had he voiced his wish than Connor quickly stopped.

"Everyone, down to the floor, now!" he yelled.

Durban reacted to the command but Jasmine failed to heed the urgent warning. Instead, she saw a sharp tongue heading towards her. Unfazed by such a spectacle, she metamorphosed into the ghostlike figure and drifted out of harm's way.

"It's a Soul Cruncher and Razar," said Connor to the others under his breath. "Leave this to me." And he stood up and walked towards them. "Hi," he said casually as he approached.

"What are you doing here?" asked the Cruncher.

"Us?" asked Connor. "Umm . . . just in the wrong place at the wrong time, I guess. Found this tunnel and thought we'd pass through. So if you'd be so kind, can you just let us pass?"

"Enough of this nonsense," ordered the Cruncher. "You know where the Hunter can be found, do you not?"

"Who?" queried Connor sarcastically.

"Do not try my patience, boy," demanded the cruncher angrily. "Where is the HUNTER?"

"If I knew, I wouldn't tell you. Not with that attitude. Didn't your mother ever teach you manners?" replied Connor and in response to the Soul Cruncher, he lashed out a Razar-like tongue, striking the enemy in the legs and causing him to topple backwards into the Razar.

Together they fell to the ground as Connor jumped onto the Cruncher and kicked him spitefully in the head, causing him to lose consciousness instantly. With only the Razar to contend with, the Dream Lord flicked out his tongue again and this time struck the creature across the eyes. It howled in pain as it realised the helplessness of his situation.

With the enemy now distracted, Vanisheo, Jasmine and Durban hurried past, leaving Connor to safeguard their route. Once they were out of harm's way, he lashed out again at the Razar, this time hitting him viciously across the throat. Again a scream of anguish emitted from the injured creature as the Dream Lord turned around and quickly followed his friends. His timing was impeccable as the tunnel roof groaned in sympathy of the Razar and collapsed, entombing the injured soldiers of darkness. For-given in thinking they were safe, the Dream Lord glanced back. To his horror, the rest of the tunnel ceiling started to erode and as he continued to watch, he noticed it sweep closer towards them.

"Run!" he shouted when he realised the danger they were in.

In the distance, he could see another ladder leading upwards. Reaching it with little time to spare, he leapt to reach the rungs halfway up the wall and scrambled quickly to the top. Once reach-ing the hatch, he tried to ease it open. Years of time had taken its toll on the fixtures and they stuck fast.

"Durban," he said as he leaned down, "I can't break through. The latch won't budge."

"Move aside," ordered Durban as he squeezed through. "I think I might just have the tool to rectify this problem."

As he reached the ceiling, he flicked his hand upwards towards the hatch. Liquid metal flowed slowly out and turned into a wide, shiny blade. Its cutting edge was lethal as it tore a hole through the hatchway but the latch still remained jammed.

"Hurry, hurry," urged Vanisheo. "Everything is falling down around us."

"We're having a little trouble up here," Connor told him, "but Durban's doing his best."

"Best, best?" questioned the Hallucium frantically. "You are the best, Connor. Have you forgotten your teleporting skills?"

With so many other skills to his armoury, Connor had com-pletely forgotten his most valuable ability, the art of teleportation and within seconds, he was standing the other side of the hatch. Taking the lock in both hands, he pulled with all his remaining strength.

"It's too heavy," he shouted through the hole that Durban had managed to pierce.

Just then Vanisheo appeared beside him and smiled.

"Perhaps another set of hands will help?" he offered. "After three. One . . . two . . . three."

With final countdown completed, together they both pulled upon the hatch, and inch by inch, it began to move.

"Durban," ordered Connor, "push from the other side."

Once more Connor and Vanisheo pulled and Durban pushed with all his might. At last, it gave a reluctant groan and flew open. Without a moment to loose, Durban grabbed Jasmine by her arm and pulled her through just as the tunnel below crumbled into a pile of dust.

"That was way too close for comfort," said Connor as he stood up and dusted himself down, before helping Jasmine to her feet.

With danger temporarily over, they looked around and found themselves in yet another room. This time though there was a window, its view blocked by condensation. Connor rubbed his sleeve against the glass to clear it and looked out. The visibility outside was little better, as driving snow swirled around in the howling winds.

"I take it this is Fresicus," announced Connor as he continued to stare into the whitened landscape and then to his left and right. "This must be a lookout tower," he told the others as he joined them. "Apart from one or two other towers along the walls, the view is not quite how I expected it to be."

"And what did you imagine of an ice land?" asked Vanisheo.

"I don't know," the Dream Lord mused, "perhaps a little less frantic."

"The ice lands are known for their beauty," Durban told him. "I think we have just arrived on a bad day."

"Seems every day's a bad day around here," joked Connor, "and without you guys to make it bearable, I think I'd have gone mad ages ago."

"You know we would not have it any other way," Jasmine told him.

"We will always fight by your side, Connor. It is imperative to restore the balance between good and evil," Durban added. "Come, let us find Hunter and meet up with the others. Then we can put an end to this abomination that Volnar has caused. I sense our friends are still alive and pursuing their path so let us do the same." And he patted Connor on the back like a father would his son.

17

Too Hot to Handle

"I have to say," announced Will as he splashed Camella, "this stream is so relaxing. It's a pity we can't stay here forever."

"The purity of this water is renowned throughout Judgment." Camella told him. "It will revive the most distressed traveller. If you drink it, it makes you feel as though you never require sustenance ever again. Try it?"

"I do not mean to be the one to remind you but there is much work to be done here and we must move forward," interrupted Joshua from the riverbank. "We need to know about Armon. It is important that we find him. Please, Camella, we need any information you have."

"You are right, Joshua," she replied as she splashed Will one last time. "We must move on."

Slowly she swam towards the riverbank, and as she stepped out of the water, her clothing and delicate wings, which looked like nothing more than a pretty tattoo on her back, instantly dried.

"I will explain all I know as we continue," she added as she wandered off towards an arched doorway they had not noticed before. "This will take us to the ash fields," she told them. "The journey from then on is a treacherous one. So be vigilant. Once we reach the other side of the fields, we must use the stone walkway. Either side of this is the flowing lavas of the inner world, bubbling and spitting as it tries to entice unsuspecting travellers into the jaws of death."

"Well, that's a bit dramatic, isn't it?" said Will as he stepped out of the water.

"Perhaps so," admitted Camella, "but I just did not want you to see the journey without its dangers. A footstep wrong could be your downfall."

"I get it," said Will. "We have to be careful. So once we've passed the stone walk of death, where do we go from there?"

"Once on the other side," she continued, "there is an entrance-way into the fire mountain. We must take the path that leads to the top. From there we shall go back to my homeland, the Kalus Kingdom." For a moment, she paused.

"Is that where Armon is hiding?" asked Kustos.

"Armon," she said, oblivious to the question, "now he is another story. How he got to the fire mountain, no one could ever discover, but one day, whilst taking in the views, my friends and I found him wandering around, confused and lost. He was very weak and kept mumbling something about the wrong doings he had committed. His heart bore so much pain of regret that the devastation of his actions was killing him. I can only assume the reason he had not passed on through Judgment was that his evil deeds were so dastardly and his punishment retribution to roam forever, so he could lament his lifetime in Sublin. It was Armon who told me of Volnar and how the Dark Lord played with his mind and altered his realities of life, causing him to become a puppet. I cannot say more on this matter, for that is not my place but what I can tell you is that we took pity on him and flew him back to the sky kingdom. He has been hiding there ever since."

"And you never doubted his story?" asked Fortis.

"No," replied Camella. "You would have to see the agonising torture he was going through to understand our reasoning. We are a people of great belief in faith and thought his arrival was not by accident and that one day he would have a part to play in some higher event. Up until recently, we did not know what it was. Only when Volnar appeared in Judgment and started to wreak havoc did the light begin to shine. Full acceptance that Armon was a pawn in future events was enhanced by a rumour of some visitors from Sublin, who had earned the right of the higher powers."

"Okay," said Will. "So I get the mystery behind Armon but was it by accident we found you?"

"Again no." The Butterhawk smiled. "As stories of your journey reached our kingdom, I took a few men to search the lands, in hopes that you might hold the key to Armon's redemption. In my naivety, I did not realise how far this knowledge had travelled and we found ourselves being hunted by Razars and Soul Crunchers. At first I thought they were looking for you but one by one, as my men were murdered, it occurred to me that they knew we held the key to Armon's whereabouts and that Volnar would go to the ends of this world to get him back.

"Eventually, I was the last one left. I clung onto the thought that if I could find you, I might stand a chance of survival but the evils of Volnar's forces had spread and I found myself trapped. When Kustos turned up and rescued me, I knew then that fate had played her hand and was trying to give us an advantage. Now that I have you here with me, it is imperative we get back to my home. Armon is waiting and I know he is eager to help."

"See, Joshua," Will said with a grin, "aren't you pleased we rescued her now?"

"I have to admit that I was wrong but caution is not a punishment," replied their guide. "My focus was on the retrieval of

Armon and returning to the Judgment Halls. It clouded my assessment of the situation."

"Hey!" interrupted Kustos, in a very Connor-like manner, as he rested his hand on Joshua's shoulder. "We take it that is you apologising then?" he said. "Right or wrong, it does not matter; the outcome is, we have Camella, and we now have the knowledge of where Armon is hiding. Things are definitely looking up for us. As soon as we get to Armon, we can contact Connor and the others and see how they are progressing in finding Hunter. I know in my heart they are still alive and still following their path. It will not be long before we are together again."

Camella stopped before entering the doorway.

"I have not been here for a while," she told them. "So I do not know what the ash fields have in store for us."

"Whatever is there," said Fortis, "is of little consequence. We must get to Armon at all cost."

"If you are certain then?" she asked them again.

No one replied, so she gave the order to move on. "Alright then. Let us go."

As they walked through the archway, another door pushed its way up from the ground and sealed itself against the stonework, blocking the path behind them. Any thoughts of turning back were no longer a viable option and so they turned their attention to the way forward into the ash fields.

Over time Will had seen many strange sights but this one simply took his breath away.

"What happened here?" he asked Camella as he surveyed the view.

Stretched for as far as the eye could see across the ash fields were thousands of statues. Some were human and others were races that none of them recognised. As he studied them more carefully, Will was horrified to discover they were once alive but now appeared preserved in ash, still bearing the look of terror upon their faces.

"These are the many that have chosen this path and failed the tests it has cast upon them." Camella told them. "Their punishment of failure is as you see—frozen in time by the ashes of Infernato and destined to accept a punishment of endless desperation to their lives. They are the lost causes that have no place for final Judgment, either in a hell dimension or one of heavenly bliss."

"I remember a lava-encrusted nation of people back in the Wake World," said Will as he carefully poked one of the figures.

"So you understand the punishment then?" asked Camella.

"No, no, this was no punishment." Will assured her. "If it was, then it was one of nature. An entire city was covered by lava and ash when a nearby volcano erupted. It was in a place called Pompeii, in Italy, I think."

"But they survived?" Camella queried.

"No, they all died," Will told her.

"Not these," answered the Butterhawk. "Touch them and see."

Will pulled on one of the fingers of a nearby statue and the arm came away in his hands, permitting an essence of energy to escape. Instantly the human effigy crumbled into a pile of ash on the floor.

"They were covered alive as their punishment," Camella explained, "but over time, their outer shells have died, leaving their souls trapped within this ashen covering."

"What is that?" asked Fortis, as he pointed to the summit of a huge mountain rising majestically into the sky.

A small image of life was making some kind of gesture toward the heavens.

"If I am not mistaken," interrupted Joshua, "I would say it is a Soul Cruncher but what he is trying to do, I cannot explain."

As they watched with curiosity, a flash of light, injected from the sky, filled the entire field and when the dazzling rays had melted into the day of light, the figure was gone.

"Well, that was strange? What did he do?" asked Will.

"I have no idea," replied Joshua, "but whatever happened, I feel it cannot be good. We must hurry and reach the mountain entrance." And he quickened his pace under his own instruction.

The others followed as they picked their way through the museum of statues. Only their footsteps were heard as they lightly walked upon the ashen ground. Suddenly Kustos heard a noise.

"What was that?" he asked the others. "Did you hear something?"

On finishing his sentence, he spun around as he felt something touch his shoulder.

"I think I know what the Cruncher has done," he announced with panic in his voice. "Everyone, get together, now!" he shouted.

As they turned to face Kustos, they noticed the figures begin to shift. Inch by inch, they moved their encrusted frames towards the group, as an eerie mumble sang upon the gentle winds.

Kustos was the first to react, and he punched one in the head. Instantly it shattered, spewing ash upon the ground and its soul into the air.

"Keep hitting them," Kustos ordered the others. "They simply fall apart."

Will lashed out at the approaching army but was soon surrounded. In an effort to escape, he tripped and lost his footing, forcing him to ground. Almost in an instant, the figurines were bending over him, attempting to pour ash into his face, blocking his nose and mouth. Camella quickly realised the danger and turned her attentions to come to his assistance as she kicked them one by one to dust.

"Do not let them bring you down," she warned Will as she pulled him to his feet. "They try to suffocate their victims into submission."

"And now you decide to tell me?" he replied.

"I cannot see the walkway to the other side!" shouted Fortis above the noise of smashing chlorastrolite. "There are too many of them."

The only sure thing they knew was they had not reached the edge of the field and as they fought their way forward, they discovered they were somewhat off course. Instead of a stone walkway spreading before them, they were faced with the bubbling, spitting lava, swirling around on the underflow currents. Joshua surveyed the landscape and was relieved to see their escape was not actually that far away from them.

"Over there," he said as he pointed. "About half a mile away, I would estimate."

The others glanced quickly across and then began fighting their way towards the walkway. Will, in his eagerness, stepped too close to the lava flow and a couple of tiny stones tumbled into the river as he moved away from the edge. No sooner had the last pebble been consumed by the greenstone than a regurgitating growl echoed around them.

"That cannot be good," said Kustos as he looked across the river of fire.

To his dismay and heart-stopping horror, a large wave erupted from the bed of lava and spewed out a creature of amoebic dimensions upon the ground. At first, it took no form but then it collected its lava and took shape. As the fiery exterior melted away, a gigantic creature rose to its full height and stared directly at Will.

Out of its flat, featureless face peered two charcoal black eyes, surveying the opposition as they stood in disbelief. Its lizard-like body supported two pointed ears on its head and a spike protruding from its forehead. A long, scaly tail swished impatiently from side to side as smoke emitted from its heated body.

"It's a Fire Hog!" shouted Camella as they continued to fend off the ash people. "You must have woken him up, Will, when you teetered on the lava edge."

"So it's my fault then, is it?" he shouted back. "But he must be half a mile away, how could he have heard me?"

"They are light sleepers and the smallest disturbance can wake them," Camella told him, "and believe me, they do not like to be woken suddenly. It puts them in a really bad mood."

Before Will could ask any further questions, another huge wave exploded from the river and a second Fire Hog appeared and stared directly at the Dream Warrior.

"I think they like you," Fortis said laughingly.

"Well, I wish they didn't," replied Will. "Does anyone have a plan, especially as it looks as if they seem to be blocking our only route out of here?"

"Do you not think they already know that?" Camella replied. "That is why they are not coming to us. They know if we want to leave, we will have to meet them face to face."

Fortis grinned to himself as he disposed of a nearby figure and then spoke, "I have a plan. Camella, Will, and Joshua, work your way towards the walkway as best as you can but do not let those ash things get you." Camella nodded her agreement and smiled.

In a strange way, she sensed what Fortis had in mind.

"Come on, little brother," Fortis said to Kustos. "You and I are going to deal with these Fire Hogs. Come with me?"

Kustos nodded as both took off in a sonic run and with the speed they were moving, they dashed through the ash figures, melting their shells into piles as they passed by.

"You know, Fortis," said Kustos as he ran alongside his brother, "for just once, I would like to get somewhere without facing danger."

"Aah, little brother, said Fortis with a smile, "you have a lot to learn about Judgment. This is the roughest path you will ever experience. Never expect it to be a relaxing walk in the countryside."

Within less than a minute, they had reached the stone walkway and briefly looked back. They could see Camella and the others still fighting their way towards them, clearing a pathway through the punished souls. Confident that their friends were safe, they turned their attention forward and saw the two creatures standing their ground across the stone pathway. Together they stamped their feet impatiently as they waited for the two princes to approach.

"So what is this plan of yours?" Kustos asked.

"Well, we leave the others and take the two hogs on alone," replied Fortis.

"And that is your great plan?" his brother exclaimed. "Any other details I should know about?"

"Not really," he said as he turned to pulverise another statue. "Don't these things ever give up?"

"They are the least of our worries," interrupted Kustos. "You have told the others we would deal with the Fire Hogs, so we had better think of a way to get rid of them and fast."

"Hmm," mused Fortis and then smiled. "I think I have got it."

"Well, are you going to share?" asked Kustos impatiently.

"That lava river," pointed out Fortis. "The current is running extremely slow. Now if we could find a way to speed it up and then somehow wrestle the lava beasts back into the current, it could carry them away. Then we can all make a run to the entrance."

"There's a lot of ifs and coulds in that plan," answered Kustos and then yelled a warning, "Look out!" as he shoved Fortis to the ground.

A large newly created rock landed inches from his body

"Are you alright?" asked the Realm Lord as he pulled his brother to his feet. "It looks as if those creatures can suck rock formations out of the lava with their tails and catapult them at us. That is not very friendly."

"No indeed," said Fortis, "but they cannot do that if we run right at them. Come on."

Without thinking, Fortis made a charge forward, and Kustos, not wanting to be left behind, swiftly followed. As they approached the creatures, a barrage of rocks were launched in their direction and it took all their skill to jump and roll from left to right in an effort to avoid any impact. Fortis was the first to reach their target and leapt at one of the creatures, landing unceremoniously on its head. Steam was seething from it and despite Fortis' resistance to heat, it burned through the soles of his boots.

Kustos was about to follow in his brother's footsteps but Fortis shouted a warning.

"No, Kustos!" he ordered. "They are too hot for you to handle. Even I am struggling."

Taking heed of the warning and trying to avoid a collision with the second Fire Hog, Kustos quickly change direction and slipped to the side of the creature. A large tail came crashing towards him, and he just managed to roll out of the way to safety before the attack began again.

Fortis could see his brother was in danger and still holding on to his Fire Hog's ear, he managed to throw a couple of fireballs at the second lava monster. They successfully made the optimum effect, as it stopped its attack on Kustos and slowly made its way over towards its partner, growling and grumbling as it moved. With tiny arms, it pushed and shoved towards Fortis and at one time managed to lay a blow upon him. Smoke emitted from the prince's arm and he cried out as the burning pain surged through his flesh.

"I have had enough of this," moaned Kustos as he got to his feet.

Conscious of what little time they had, he raised his arms out sideways and then thrust them forward suddenly, in a clapping motion. Immediately a blue, sonic energy field emitted. It was so intense that when it reached the Lava creatures, it threw them backwards, forcing them to end up in a heap on the ground. Fortis' grip was unhinged and he was thrown through the air, only to land heavily not far from his brother. Painfully he scrambled to his feet and limped over to join Kustos.

"That is it," exclaimed Fortis. "Can you direct your sonic clap towards the lava flow? If you can speed it up, we can then force them back into the river."

Kustos did as his brother instructed and focussing hard, took aim in the direction of the lava flow but as the sonic force reached the substance, it simply absorbed any real strength it held, increasing the current to a slightly quicker flow.

"I do not think that is going to work," Kustos announced.

"Have faith," Fortis told him. "Try again but this time three or four claps at a time."

"If you think it will help," said Kustos, "but I feel my power ebbing away, so let me see what I can do while I still have the strength."

"No pressure, little brother," Fortis warned him, "but you might want to hurry. I think they have got a second wind."

As Kustos and Fortis watched, the Fire Hogs got to their feet and began cautiously moving towards them. They had been hurt once and wanted to make certain it did not happen again. Sensing that the brothers were weakened by their attack, one of the creatures took control and quickened its pace.

"Hurry, Kustos," urged Fortis, in a clearly panicked tone.

Kustos took a deep breath and clapped his hands in a rhythm of four. When the last pulse hit the lava, the shock wave was sufficient to change the speed and ripples of swirling liquid, creating waves upon the surface. Concerned this would not last for any length of time, Kustos and Fortis quickly turned their attentions to the creatures. One had already used its initiative and taking advantage of Kustos' focus elsewhere, it silently approached. Fortis saw him just in time and dived to the left. Kustos, on the other hand, was a little slower to respond and the hog's tail caught him as he tried to slide out of the way. Instead of jumping to safety, Kustos found him himself falling over the edge of the walkway. In the nick of time, he managed to grab the side as his body dangled dangerously close to the lava river below.

Fortis saw their adversaries direct their attention towards Kustos but he was too far away to be of any help.

"I thought you were going to handle this?" said Camella as she and Will pulled Kustos to his feet.

"We are." Kustos grinned as he gave the Butterhawk a quick pat on the shoulder before running back to help Fortis.

"I think they'll be okay," announced Will to Camella as he turned back to face the ash people.

"Well, I hope they will finish it soon," replied Joshua. "These statues just keep coming."

Leaving his friends to hold off the ash people, Kustos joined his brother.

"Roll away from the beast!" he shouted at Fortis.

Fortis was relieved to see his brother safe and noticing him preparing to create another sonic clap, rolled behind his brother as protection. In the meantime, Kustos raised his arms and clapped his hands together as hard as he could. The impact was devastating as the resonance echoed violently around. Camella fortunately saw Kustos out of the corner of her eye just as he was about to perform the act and instinctively reached out and grabbed Joshua and Will and dragged them to the ground.

The discharge of power undulated through the air like the ripples upon a still pool. Missing the prostrate bodies of Camella and her friends, it hit every standing object and shattered the remaining ash people into piles of dust. In the other direction, the sonic wave smashed into one of the Fire Hogs, throwing it over the side of the walkway and into the lava river below. The rapid current was now far too strong for the beast to fight, and it growled and protested vehemently, as it was swept away. The second creature was far luckier as the blast merely knocked it from its feet to land unceremoniously on its tail.

The efforts of the final attack had drained Kustos of his strength and he fell to his knees from exhaustion, right into the path of the now infuriated creature. It had scrambled back onto his feet and was thumping his way angrily towards the Realm Lord. Camella sensed something was wrong and quickly stood up. As she turned around, she saw the danger Kustos was in.

"Fortis!" she yelled. "Catch."

She retrieved an ice blade from her belt and threw it toward Fortis. Catching it in one hand, he made a run towards the approaching hog and, once within a few feet of the monster, jumped into the air. As before, he landed on its head and held on tightly to his ears. In frustration with the uninvited guest, the creature gyrated and shook in an effort to throw him clear but Fortis held on for all he was worth as he attempted to steady himself, in order to make some sort of attack. For what felt like hours, the prince struggled with the beast until an opportune moment presented itself. Pulling the ice blade from his mouth, he thrust it into the creature's head and quickly jumped away. As he landed safely on the ground, he turned around to check on the devastation he had caused. The blade had already begun to react and the creature gyrated in agony as the freezing powers of the blade began to work. Slowly, inch by inch as Fortis watched, the beast began to change from a dirty brown flesh into an ice blue statue, until it was completely frozen. With the Fire Hog now immobilised, Fortis took a run and jumped, landing on its chest. The creature lost its balance and toppled, shattering on the ground in pieces. Fortis got to his feet and casually kicked away one or two of the ice shapes as he looked to retrieve the ice blade but within seconds, the shapes had turned into water, then steam, before evaporating into the air.

Camella broke his concentration as she called to him from the edge of the walkway.

"Fortis!" she yelled. "A little help over here, please?"

Piles of demolished ash still lay on the ground but an influx of mindless ash people still continued to advance.

Fortis picked up the ice blade and jogged over to Kustos.

"How are you doing, little brother?" he asked as Kustos sat on the ground.

"I am getting there, brother," he said. "That effort took more out of me than I thought, but I should be alright in a while."

"We cannot wait that long, I am afraid," said Fortis. "Joshua? Can you give Kustos an energy boost?"

"I will see what I can do," replied their friend.

"Alright, Kustos," suggested Fortis, "once Joshua has worked his magic, you will need to clap your hands once more and separate the walkway. We need to be on one side of it and those ash people the other. Joshua," he added running over to the guide, "let me take your place here so you can help Kustos."

Joshua obeyed the instruction and hurried over to where the Realm Lord was sitting.

"There are too many of them," Camella complained as she struggled to contain the numbers. "We can never beat all of them."

"We will not have to," Fortis assured her. "Once Joshua has injected some energy into Kustos, we will fall back and join them. If my plan works, they will not be able to follow us."

Joshua by this time had laid his hands upon Kustos' shoulders and was passing his power into his body. The lord was quick to recover and scrambled to his feet.

"How are we doing, Joshua?" shouted Fortis.

"We are almost done," the Oracle advised him.

"Fortis!" yelled Kustos. "Get the others over here?"

Fortis did as he was instructed and, in turn, helped the others to run away. With his friends now safe, Kustos put out his arms with his palms facing downwards. For a moment he held the position and charged the sonic blast, then waited. When fully satisfied he was ready to act, he took one last look at the approaching ash people and let out a cry before slapping his hands towards the ground. The shock wave tore through the stone like a thin sheet of paper and as they all watched, the path before them began to crumble away.

Kustos was the closest and as the walkway disappeared into the lava river, he found himself losing balance. Two pairs of hands quickly reached out and pulled him to safety.

"Thank you," said Kustos as he looked from Fortis to Will.

"Let's hope we don't have to come back this way," stated Will, as Fortis and Kustos looked at him and smiled.

For a moment they all relaxed, thinking that danger had passed but as Joshua reached out to infuse Kustos once more, a fire rock came hurtling towards them.

"Look out!" yelled Will, as he threw a couple of gravity bubbles at the rock and forced it off course.

"Now what?" moaned Joshua.

"It looks as though someone isn't happy," replied Will as he pointed to the other side of the lava bed where a fire hog was jumping up and down in agitation.

"How did he . . .?" Kustos was about to ask as another rock came flying their way.

Again, Will simply deflected it away.

"We have to reach over there," announced Camella as she pointed to a distant entranceway.

Joshua pushed Will out of the way and took his place supporting Kustos. With Fortis on the Realm Lord's other side, the two began to run, half dragging Kustos along.

"Go now!" ordered Will as the barrage of rocks became more frequent. "I'll cover you."

The five of them struggled along the uneven path, dodging and sidestepping the ammunition of stones. Will was using his skill as he held a level of gravity above his friend's heads. Eventually they reached a safe distance away and stopped to catch their breath as they watched the Fire Hog steam in frustration.

"Well, that is that then," smiled Fortis.

"Not quite, I fear," announced Camella as she studied the entrance.

Will wandered over to join her and noticed a slight dilemma in their latest situation.

"It is blocked, Will," she told him. "This has been done deliberately."

"Of course it was!" replied Will calmly. "So what have we got? On first impression, it doesn't look good but there must be a way. We haven't come this far simply to turn back, which I might add, is now totally impossible anyway."

Camella said nothing, for fear of showing her own disappointment. Instead, she walked over to the boulder and inserted another ice blade into a crevice. As she waited, nothing happened.

"The boulder is too large," she sighed.

"What about using the other one as well?" suggested Will. "Would that work?"

"It might," she agreed hopefully. "Fortis? Do you still have the blade?"

"Of course, my lady," he replied as he joined them.

Kustos and Joshua also followed just in case there was something they could do to help.

"It is good to see you up and about, Kustos." She smiled. "Your skills were greatly appreciated. Will, take the ice blade from Fortis, and when I tell you, force it into the large crevice at the back."

Will did as instructed. He took the weapon from Fortis and stood beside the boulder, waiting patiently for the next command. When Camella had positioned herself the other side of the boulder, she smiled at the Dream Warrior.

"Now, Will, now!" she ordered.

Simultaneously they jammed their blades into the rock and stood back. At first, nothing happened but then they heard the faintest sound of cracking ice. Within seconds, the stone had been changed into an ice ball. For a moment it stood in white-blue glory, before shattering into pieces and evaporating against the warm lands.

"Well done, Will," the Butterhawk praised as she walked over to him and picked up the other ice blade.

Without thinking, she replaced it in her harness.

"We must move on," she urged the others. "We need to get to the top of the mountain while there is still sufficient heat to get us home."

Without another word, the others looked at one another and walked into the dark entrance of the fire mountain.

18

Hunter

"I can't see anything through this blizzard!" shouted Connor above the noise of the snowstorm.

"I am so cold," moaned Jasmine as the bitter winds whipped through her coat.

Connor and Durban quickly made their way either side of the princess and tried to protect her from the arctic weather.

"Vanisheo?" shouted Durban. "Are you certain you know where you are going?"

The Hallucium's small footprints barely left an imprint in the frozen snow and were quickly covered by the blizzard. Suddenly Durban stopped as he bumped into a tiny figure before him.

"Not this way," Vanisheo suddenly told them.

As the three of them tried to focus through the white sheet of driving snow, they managed to see a huge drop several feet before them.

"How do you not feel the cold?" asked Durban as they waited for their next instructions. "You don't even have a coat."

"We have but a small presence in this existence," replied Vanisheo, "so the basic things of hot and cold we do not feel. Now back in Sublin is a different matter altogether." And he started walking again.

This time he changed direction, but even so, the blizzard winds still blew violently in their faces, swirling all around them.

"Well, I wish we could do the same," announced Durban as they followed him once more.

For what appeared like hours, they battled with the gruelling elements, draining them of every ounce of energy they possessed and freezing their skin to their bones. When they thought things would never get any better, the snowstorm suddenly stopped as if someone had flicked a switch and there before them, displayed in blazing sunshine that dusted the fallen snow with warmth, were the two ice mountains. Even more encouraging, just as Nuwa Lin had described, was the lonely tree standing between them.

"You did it, my friend." Connor laughed in delight as he picked Vanisheo up and hugged him. "Well done."

The Hallucium smiled as Connor returned him to the ground and felt an inner satisfaction that, despite his own doubts, he had actually managed to follow Nuwa Lin's instructions and bring them safely to the mountains.

"How could anything survive out here?" asked Jasmine as she shivered again. "This land is so cold."

"That is why it is the perfect place to hide a wanted being," suggested Vanisheo.

"So what do we do now?" asked Connor. "Where's the entrance?"

"We must get to the tree as quickly as we can," Vanisheo told them. "We have been blessed with good visibility, so let us take advantage of that."

The others did not argue with the Hallucium. The atmosphere was cold and walking through the deep snow was difficult; however, their vision was good and no longer did the frozen wind hit them in the face. Still though, it took almost another hour of silence before their destination looked within arm's reach. Only then did Vanisheo speak again.

"Come," he encouraged them, "we are almost there. We must quicken our pace, for I fear another blizzard will soon be upon us."

The others looked to the mountaintops, and there, peering over their summits, were the early signs of grey clouds, brimming with snow, excitedly waiting to fall. The recent memories of their last encounter were enough to urge them forward and before long they reached the foot of the tree. Drained by their exertion, they sat down and Connor opened his rucksack and took out the prepared food. He took a bite and, after chewing it a little and swallowing it, found his hunger had been fully satisfied.

"This is good," he told Jasmine and Durban. "You should try some."

Realising how hungry they both were, Jasmine and Durban took out their own food and bit into it. After a single mouthful, they also both felt full.

"So, do you really think this Hunter guy will be able to show us the way into the Judgment Halls?" asked Connor.

"I do not know for sure," replied Durban. "I certainly hope so, especially as we have come all this way."

"Connor!" exclaimed Vanisheo.

He had been standing a little way off and beckoned to the Dream Lord.

"I am sorry to disturb you," he apologised, "but I need your help to draw some markings on the ground."

"Looks like I have some work to do," Connor told the others as he got to his feet. "Take advantage of the rest. I'm sure we'll soon be moving on."

He placed his hand gently on Jasmine's shoulder and she smiled back at him.

"Without her," Connor thought to himself, *"I wouldn't have the confidence to be who I am today. I'm truly blessed to have her as my friend."*

Quickly turning away, in case his thoughts betrayed him, Connor walked off to join Vanisheo.

"So what are we drawing then?" he asked the Hallucium.

"Nothing," said Vanisheo quietly. "I just wanted to talk to you alone."

"Don't ruin my good mood," Connor joked and then saw the look on his friend's face. "Just tell me, what's bothering you?"

"I think we may have been followed," Vanisheo told him softly, for fear of being heard. "I have been seeing shapes behind us for many hours. I thought we might have lost them through the blizzard but it was not to be. Hours later, I sensed them again. I did not want to say anything before as the others look so tired, and the hope of finding Hunter and joining the others were uppermost in their minds but now I know there is no choice."

"Okay!" said Connor slowly, as his mind began to race, searching for a plan. "We always knew this wasn't going to be easy. There's no reason to think we'll not find Hunter but you're right about the others being tired and in no shape to fight. How long do you think it will take to open the entrance?"

"I have but one symbol to write in the snow," Vanisheo told him, "and then the entrance should show itself."

"Okay," Connor echoed again. "Now we have a plan. You get started on the symbol and I'll collect the other two." And with that, he casually wandered off towards Durban and Jasmine.

"Come on, you guys," he said as he helped Jasmine to her feet. "Rest time over. Vanisheo is almost done, so it's time to move on."

No sooner had Connor finished his words than all of them felt a vibration beneath their feet, followed by a huge grinding of stone echoing around the valley. As it stopped, they noticed lowering into the depths in front of Vanisheo were two staircases, one leading to each mountain. Quickly they rushed forward and as they reached the Hallucium, another rumbling filled the air. The creation of the stairways and the separation of the ground had caused an avalanche from each summit, and the heavy snows from above were relinquishing their hold.

"What mountain is he hiding in?" asked Connor urgently.

"I do not know," replied Durban. "Pick one. We have a fifty-fifty chance of getting it right."

"Okay," shouted Connor above the noise, "the right staircase . . . no, the left, definitely the left."

Happy with his decision, Connor grabbled Vanisheo and Jasmine by their wrists and dragged them down the left stairway. Durban followed quickly behind. When they reached the bottom, they found a metal door blocked their path. As expected from their previous experiences, it was locked. Connor looked up, saw the fast approaching snows and tried to focus on a new plan.

"Now what?" he asked his friends.

Nobody spoke. Instead, Jasmine removed her heavy coat and turned into her ghost façade. With ease she walked through the barrier and a few seconds later, there was the sound of chinking metal as bolts were sliding through their fittings. Seconds later the door flew open.

With no time to waste, Durban and Vanisheo hurried through the open door, while Connor retrieved Jasmine's coat and followed, closing the door behind him. Quickly they secured the bolts and stood back just as the full strength of the avalanche hit the stairs and tumbled towards the door. A final thud and vibration advised them that their exit was now probably concealed by tons of snow and ice.

"You're certainly a handy woman to have around," said Connor as Jasmine returned to her normal self.

She bowed her head in acknowledgment of his compliment and took her coat from him, then gracefully slipped it on and did up the buttons.

"I guess we have to go this way," announced Durban as they all looked at the long, winding tunnel before them.

"I hope my choice was right," stated Connor.

The others looked at him and he shrugged his shoulders.

"Just kidding." He laughed. "Of course it was. What was I thinking?"

Considering Connor's speed of choice, Durban, at the time, was not so certain of the decision but said nothing. Instead, he led the way slowly along the tunnel. Their vision was quite limited, as the only light they seemed to have shone down through tiny crevices in the ceiling. Connor thought it might have been light from the upper world but considering the weather above he could not be sure. They had not been walking for long when another door blocked their way and to their surprise this time, it was unlocked. Durban pushed it opened.

"Wow!" exclaimed Connor as they walked through. "This is amazing."

Inside was a room without a cciling exposing the elements through the mountain summit. The sun shone down upon the irregular walls of ice, splintering it into a myriad of light, casting rainbow colours that bounced across the crystallised stone.

"This is beautiful," Jasmine mused as she looked around. "It reminds me of home and our beautiful waterfalls."

"I have to admit," agreed Connor, "it is pretty spectacular."

"Strange we are so exposed," declared the princess, "and yet it does not feel cold. If I had to hide from the world, then I think this would be the place. It seems so peaceful here. The only thing missing is life but I suppose it is far too cold for anything like that."

"Hello!" shouted Durban as he walked around. "Is there anyone here?"

There was no reply, instead his voice echoed around the colourful walls and faded into the distance.

"This is not it," Vanisheo told them. "Look! There is a path that leads a little higher up the cavern."

"I see it," replied Jasmine, "and look." She pointed to one side of the room where a small house was resting precariously on a ledge halfway up the chamber.

Carefully they took the trail and followed its route around twists and turns, until they reached a resting ledge. Here they looked out across the cavern and noticed on the other side a lake, the brightest blue anyone had ever seen before.

"How beautiful," exclaimed Jasmine as she watched the cascading waterfall oozing from the mountaintop and gracefully dropping into the waters below.

"This must be the wrong place," announced Durban as he looked around. "It is far too quiet. Whoever once lived here must have moved on."

"Come on," commanded Connor, "let's check out the house. There might be some clues to its inhabitant and their whereabouts."

Turning their back on the view, they trudged up the rest of the pathway until they reached the house, and wiping the frost from the window, they peered in.

"I don't know," mused Connor as he looked at the furniture and belongings inside. "It seems VERY lived in to me."

Just then they heard a sound and instantly spun around to see a figure before them.

"It's okay," said Connor as he raised his hands in submission. "We won't hurt you."

It was difficult to define the being, as it wore a huge oversized coat from head to toe with a hood pulled over its face. What little part of the face had been exposed to the elements was protected by dark glasses. In its hand was a blade but the stance it took was more of fear than attack. Durban took offence at the posture and preparing himself for any eventuality, turned his liquid metal into spikes around his body. Vanisheo and Jasmine took a step back.

"Wait! Wait!" ordered Connor. "Just be cool. Now everyone relax. We're not here to hurt you; we simply want to talk."

Durban stood down, and his barrage of spikes disappeared.

"My name is Connor," said the Dream Lord as he moved slowly forward. "We're not here to hurt anyone."

The figure said nothing but edged back, still swinging the blade in front of it as Connor tried to approach.

"Be careful, Connor," Durban warned him. "That is a fire blade. You can touch it but never let it pierce you skin, or you will turn to ash."

"Thanks, Durban," replied Connor. "Great information but not helping."

"Just thought you should know, that is all," moaned Durban to himself.

"We're looking for someone," Connor continued as he took another step forward. "His name is Hunter. Do you know where we can find him? We've come to try and stop the chaos caused by the one they call Volnar. We need to get into the Judgment Halls and Hunter is the only one that can lead us there."

The figure said nothing but lowered the fire blade.

"Please can you help us?" implored Jasmine. "We do not have much time."

"It's okay, really it is," said Connor as he walked still closer.

"I am Hunter," said the figure as it lowered its hood and undid the coat. "You should not have come here. I can help no one."

"But you're a . . . a," Connor stuttered.

"A woman, yes I know," replied Hunter. "It is far easier to hide when the evil that hunts you is looking for the wrong person."

Hunter had brown hair and looked as though she was in her forties. She was about five feet tall and slim in build and her blue eyes and perfect complexion gave softness to her face.

"My name's Connor," he announced again, "and this is Jasmine, Durban, and Vanisheo."

"What a strange little creature," said Hunter as she stared at Vanisheo, "although everything in this reality appears to be odd."

"I am a Hallucium," said Vanisheo firmly, somewhat upset by being called strange.

"I did not mean to be unkind," apologised Hunter. "It has been so long without visitors my manners are a little rusty. My name is Ashley Hunter but I'm afraid, I am not the one you seek. I cannot help you." And she walked to the door of her house and unlocked it.

"Joshua told us that you knew the way to the Judgment Halls," said Jasmine as she peered through the door.

"Please come in," invited the woman. "Would you like some boiled water? It's fresh. I have just been over to the lake and made it with my fire blade."

The four of them walked in and found somewhere to sit, as Ashley took her blade and stabbed the wood to make it burn. Instantly it caught alight, and soon a cosy fire was burning in the grate. She then poured out some water and placed the cups down by each of them.

"I mean . . . it's not that I don't want to help," she said sipping her drink, "it's just that I can't. It's that simple."

"I'm not sure that I follow you," said Connor. "We were told you'd be our guide."

"Then you were misled," Ashley replied. "I do not remember how I got away or where the Judgment Halls are located."

Connor was taken aback and disappointed by the response and felt in that split second that their time had been wasted. Even so, deep down, he was certain they would not have been sent on this mission if it were a meaningless cause.

"Jasmine," he said breaking the silence, "see if you can contact Kustos and let him know that we have found Hunter. Explain to him what you've heard here today."

Jasmine smiled at him, put down her drink and excused herself as she made her way outside.

"She might need help," said Durban as he followed her through the door.

"I will also join them," said Vanisheo sensing that Connor needed to be alone with Ashley. "Those kids could get into all sorts of trouble without me." He laughed as he closed the door behind him.

"I sense your disappointment, Connor," said Ashley when they were alone. "I am so sorry."

"That isn't it? Is it?" asked Connor.

"I do feel as though I have wasted your time," she told him, "but you are right, there is something else. I feel we have a connection. I can sense your energy. Have we ever met before?"

"Not to my knowledge," Connor answered, "but I know what you mean. I also sense something familiar about you. Unfortunately, it won't bring us any closer to the Judgment Halls, so if you'll excuse my questioning, perhaps we can glean at least some information that might be useful. Can you tell me what you last remember about the day you escaped?"

"Hmm," she mused as she lay back in her chair and closed her eyes. "So long ago and memories fade, but I will do my best."

For several minutes there was silence as she clawed through the memories in her mind, then, without warning, she opened her eyes and smiled.

"I do remember some things," she told Connor. "I remember lying in this really decadent room on the most comfortable bed I have ever tried. The door was locked and yet it didn't bother me because I felt no compulsion to leave. I was safe and at peace with myself. Food was served by men in robes and when I asked them where I was, they smiled and told me not to fear the great Oracle of Judgment and that I would soon be judged. He would send me to a place that represented my inner self. Their response appeared so genuine that not once did I question it.

"Then, one night, while I was resting, lost in my own thoughts, I was disturbed by screams of sheer panic, followed by a thunderbolt. The door to my room flew open and exposed the hallway outside. For days I had not wished to leave that room but curiosity got the better of me and urged me to take a look, so I got off the bed and peered out. To my horror, I saw bodies strewn everywhere and as I stepped into the corridor, I realised that my room was one of many thousands. I can remember looking up and around and seeing endless levels of rooms connected by walkways, stretching as far as the eye could see.

"Suddenly, panic took over as I heard footsteps running from behind. I turned around to see who was there, and they started chanting, 'Judge her as evil, judge her as evil.' They were not the friendly robed men I had met before and I hoped this was just a nightmare but the stench of such creatures that filled my nostrils was enough to warn me of danger. I ran, not knowing where I was going but determined enough to evade the chants of 'Judge her as evil in the name of Volnar.' It felt like hours that I was running and each time I dared a glance behind, my pursuers were still on my scent.

"After that it all seemed a blur. I cannot say exactly what happened but the next thing I remember was falling and then waking up in a strange town. From there it all gets really hazy. A young girl found me. Her name was Nuwa Lin. She helped me and finally hid me here with her fire blade. She warned me that a great evil wanted me dead and it was my purpose in life to stay here and be safe. One day someone who needed my help would come.

That someone, Connor," she said as she smiled, "is you. I do not remember anything more but I do believe that I am meant to stay with you and help. I have been alone many years and whilst waiting for good or evil, I have trained myself the best way I knew how. I have to admit, I am relieved you were the first to find me."

"You mean you've been here on your own for all that time?" asked Connor. "I'm not sure I could handle that."

"It was a case of having to I'm afraid," replied Ashley.

Just then Jasmine reentered the room with a look of relief upon her face.

"Kustos and the others are fine," she smiled. "They are currently entering a mountain, in the fire lands of Infernato. They saved a woman called Camella and as luck would have it, that proved to be a very good move. Oh and Kustos says Will is quite smitten by her. She knows where to find Armon and is leading them to him and to add to it all, Fortis has joined them. This has made Kustos very happy."

"Well, that sounds like good news to me," answered Connor. "What did Joshua say?"

"He said that we still need Ashley, even though she could not remember the path. That, he said, would return in time," Jasmine continued, "and I also got the impression he was not as surprised as the rest of us when I mentioned Hunter was a woman."

"It seems then," smiled Ashley, "that not everyone was fooled by my façade."

Suddenly a piecing scream echoed around the mountain.

"What was that?" asked Hunter. "Who followed you?"

Durban burst through the door. "It is Razars and a Soul Cruncher, but how is that possible?" he asked.

"I don't know," replied Connor. "Nor do I intend to hang around and find out. You must come with us, Ashley. We'll protect you."

"It appears my choices are limited," she replied. "Lead the way."

Vanisheo peered out of the door to check on their safety and was shocked by how quickly the creatures had found the path.

"I think there might be a problem with our plan," said Vanisheo. "We are trapped. They are almost upon us."

Connor took a quick look and saw a small army of Razars charging towards the door.

"They look different from the others we have seen," Jasmine pointed out as she sneaked a glance through the window.

"I have seen these creatures before," Ashley explained. "A few years ago, I was out in the mountains when I was set upon by creatures such as these. They wrapped their tongues around my legs, which quickly went numb. When I looked down, I saw they were beginning to freeze. If it wasn't for the fire blade, I would have been frozen to death. I hate to say this but two of them were bad enough, a whole army will overwhelm us."

"Is there another way out of the house?" Connor asked. "It must have been built with a secret escape route, especially with the danger you were in."

"How did you know?" replied Ashley. "There is another way out of here. If you put out the fire and lift the stone slab beneath the grate, you will find a small escape tunnel down to the river on the other side of the cavern."

Durban wasted no time in pulling a blanket off the bed and smothered the fire. Then with Vanisheo's help, they dragged the embers out of the grate as Jasmine felt around the edge of the stone floor beneath.

"I have found the seal," she announced to the others. "Durban, help me lift it out?"

Durban did as he was instructed and taking most of the weight, dragged the square stone out of the fireplace.

Just as Ashley had said, there was the escape tunnel.

"There is not enough time, Connor," explained Vanisheo as he peered out the window. "They will soon be upon us and surely follow our path."

"But I've a plan." grinned the Dream Lord. "How long will it take you to melt the others out of existence and back to Will?"

"It will take a little time to find Will, but it can be done and in all honesty, out of existence would be safer than here right now," Vanisheo replied.

"Then do it," Connor ordered him. "Durban, you take Jasmine, Ashley and Vanisheo down to the river."

"But what about you?" asked Durban.

"I'll give you the time you need," answered Connor.

"I am not leaving you," replied Jasmine.

"You must," he urged her. "You must meet with the others and help with the mission. Kustos will be waiting. Now get out of here and take Ashley with you. I'll follow as soon as I can."

Jasmine hurried over to Connor and hugged him. As she did so, she left an imprint in his mind where Will could be found, should he survive long enough to teleport away.

"You must go," he ordered her gently as he pried her away and wiped the tears from her eyes.

"Go, Jasmine," Durban instructed. "I will stay with Connor. You must get Ashley and Vanisheo to safety."

"Before I leave," said Ashley as she stepped into the hatchway. "Please take this." And she threw him the fire blade. "I think it might be of more use to you right now."

Connor reached out his hand and plucked the blade from the air then carefully slipped it through his belt. As he and Durban watched, the three of them, one by one, disappeared from view. Only Vanisheo stopped briefly and looked back.

"I will look after them," he promised as he closed the hatch behind him.

"I trust you have a plan?" Durban asked Connor once they were alone.

"Well, to survive would be a good start," he answered.

"Do you even know how to control your teleporting in this world?" said Durban.

"Not really," Connor confessed. "I've had a lot of trouble in that department and it drains my energy far worse than at home. I was sort of hoping that if we gave the others some time and then managed to get out of here ourselves, I could focus on the teleporting when things were less frantic."

"Then that sounds like a plan to me," said Durban as he patted Connor on the shoulder. "Let us show them what we can do." And with that, he called upon his metal energy and created a number of blades protecting his body.

Connor moved to the door and kicked it opened. As he did so, Durban threw his metal blades at the oncoming army of twelve. The armoury took them by surprise and as each projectile reached its mark, the Razars dove out of the way to avoid injury. Quickly, the old soldier recalled his fluid weapon in preparation of the next assault, whilst several of the Razars scrambled on the ground.

"Well done," encouraged Connor, just as Durban created a metal shield around them.

A Razar tongue viciously attacked, and as the weapon hit their shelter, it quickly began to freeze over.

"Drop it!" yell Connor as he made a break towards the army.

The fire blade now rested comfortably in his hand and as he dodged the oncoming tongues, he sliced proficiently through them, cutting the enemy as he moved. The injured Razars dropped to their knees as they writhed in pain, giving Durban an opportunity to follow safely behind. Both warriors were now exposed to the remaining army as Connor attempted to slice their tongues with his fire blade and Durban raising his liquid shield to take the impact of the attack.

Slowly they forced their way through the remaining few and soon found themselves on the lower levels near the entrance to the cavern. Together they looked to one side of the entrance and noticed a small hole dug to the measurements of a man.

"I assume that's our way out then," said Connor as he pointed to the discovery.

"There are too many of them to fight," replied Durban. "We need to put some space between them and us, so you can get your head together to use your teleporting skills."

No sooner had Durban finished his sentence than he begin to experience some numbness in his foot and ankle and as he looked down, he saw a serrated tongue wrapped tightly around his boot. Connor was also experiencing the same sensation but he instinctively sliced through the appendage with the fire blade, just as the Razar made a jump towards him. Unconsciously, Connor raised the weapon and stabbed the creature in its hand. Almost instantly, it turned to ash and scattered across the white, cold ice.

"I think we could be in little trouble, here," Connor told Durban as they were quickly surrounded.

A Soul Cruncher stepped forward and stood menacingly before the Dream Lord.

"Where is Hunter?" it demanded to know.

"Hunter?" queried Connor. "Who's that?"

"It does not matter if you do not speak," warned the Cruncher. "I can devour your soul and find my own answers."

Connor and Durban were forced to kneel and both closed their eyes in preparation of their imminent demise but instead, a horrific scream resounded around the cavern. Connor looked up just in time to see a stream of souls released from the skull of the Soul Cruncher as it fell to the ground. It was dead.

Taking advantage of the reprieve, Connor elbowed Durban in the ribs.

"Come on," he said urgently. "We need to go."

"Go? Go where?" asked Durban as he noticed the confused and panicked state of the Razars.

"Away from here," answered a familiar voice as two arms helped Connor to his feet.

"Nuwa Lin," he said with a smile, "your timing is impeccable."

"My father said you would be in need of help," she replied. "So here I am."

"And we are very glad to see you," replied Durban as he flung his arms around her and gave her a hug.

"We must go . . . now," Nuwa Lin instructed. "The Razar will soon discover the ruse quickly enough and even we will not be able to out fight them then."

I agree," replied Connor. "We must meet with the others and this time I hope you'll join us?"

Even in the brief moments that had passed, the Razars took control once more and saw the three standing before them. Nuwa Lin was well prepared and with the speed of light, she ran towards them, dodging the lethal weapons and confusing the attacker.

"I will join you, Connor," she shouted over her shoulder, "but first we must get out of here."

Again they were outnumbered as the three began to fight their way through. Their only hope of survival now was to gain some time for Connor to teleport them away.

19

The Magnum Rescue

"Jasmine will join us soon," Kustos told Camella with some relief in his voice, "but we must get to the top of the mountain and wait for them before we can go on any further."

Camella said nothing concerning Jasmine and the others but merely kept to the plan in her mind. If Kustos was convinced they would soon be able to join them, then it was up to her to see they made it to the mountaintop in safety.

"We must keep walking," she told them. "We will soon be in the centre of the mountain where many pathways lead to the top. We must move with caution as danger can lurk in any guise."

Vigilantly the five of them walked through the entrance into a nearby darkened tunnel. The only light was an orange glow some distance away. Kustos suspected the lava flowing through the soul of the mountain might cause it. Eventually, with careful footing, they reached the base. It was as stunning as the ice-cold cavern that Connor had encountered but instead of freezing icicles reflecting a multicoloured light, it bounced off the pockets of lava churning slowly through the ancient stone, creating a yellow and orange hue. It offered a warm and calming effect, potentially giving a false air of safety. As Camella had told them, many pathways led from the centre to other caves and walkways. The complex of tunnels was almost the size of a city on its own.

"Psst, Camella," said a whisper from one of the caves.

The Butterhawk turned around and immediately burst into a huge smile as she went running off.

"Ruthus!" she screamed with delight as she threw her arms around the figure. "You are alive."

"You ever doubted otherwise," replied the Butterhawk as he pried himself away from her.

"Not for one second," lied Camella as she dragged Ruthus back to her friends. "These are my friends," she added.

Ruthus had ill-kept blond hair and a golden tan but despite his unruly looks, from a woman's point of view, he was extremely handsome. He was not too tall but his body was well toned and strong, and he wore a dirty white vest that allowed his extensive wings to expand when required. Their patterns, unlike the soft tones of Camella's, were vibrantly red with the silhouette of a black opened-mouth jaguar exposing its sabre-like teeth. The images would project a fearsome, angry warrior to any assailant.

"I thought you were dead," admitted Camella. "When the Soul Crunchers took us by surprise, I thought they killed you."

"You think something like that could take me down?" he asked Camella boastfully. "I escaped with a few bruises but otherwise I am fine. It was you I feared for the most. I wanted to come after you but was forced to hide out here." It was only then that Ruthus noticed the others quietly eyeing him up and down.

"Where are my manners," giggled Camella as she realised the awkwardness of the situation. "Ruthus, these are my friends, Joshua, Fortis, Kustos and Will. They are the ones rumoured to have come from Sublin. It was Kustos who saved my life. They are looking for Armon."

Ruthus eyed them up and down as they each introduced them-selves but it was not until Will presented himself that he stopped and carefully studied the image before him.

"Hi, I'm Will," he announced casually.

Still Ruthus said nothing but continued to stare at the Dream Warrior.

"I've been getting that a lot lately," Will added. "Camella looked at me in exactly the same way when we first met."

"I am sorry, Will," apologised Ruthus. "It was rude of me to stare. I have been here for what seems like an age and all I want to do is get home."

"Ruthus is my brother," Camella interjected as she tried to break the uncomfortable silence.

"I gotta say," said Will, "you have a pair of cool wings there, Ruthus."

"Thank you, Will," replied Camella's brother, embarrassed by his own reaction at the introduction of Camella's friends.

"Please, Ruthus," urged another voice, "we must get out of the open."

As they all looked suddenly around, they noticed several small faces appear in the lava river and then one by one, a number of creatures emerged out onto the path. As they did so, the lava ran off them like water, collecting in a puddle around their feet.

There were five small beings and on first glance could be eas-ily mistaken as children. Their skin was a burned, brown colour with smoke continually smouldering from their hair; their clothes were made from hardened, molten rock.

"Who are they?" Kustos asked Ruthus.

"They are the Magnum," he replied. "They live under the lava river, so we are told. We believe an entire city beneath the flow ex-ists, but we are unable to visit the place to verify this. From time to time, they like to walk upon the surface, and it is here we have made friends with them. They provide us with the extra warm currents we sometimes need to help us back to our kingdom."

"You must get out of sight," they echoed in unison. "Please. Let us lead you into safety, so we can work out a way of getting you back home. Now that help has arrived perhaps we have a chance of saving the Elders."

"Elders?" asked Camella. "What has happened to them?"

"They are prisoners of the Soul Cruncher," the Magnum replied. "He found a way to force our mother and father to the surface, where they were taken to the top of the mountain. It appears the Soul Cruncher up there has stolen just enough of their soul energy to keep them under control, and you know what that means?"

"No!" replied Will and his friends together.

"That means the Soul Cruncher also has control of the lands," answered the Magnum.

"In what way?" asked Will innocently.

"In every way," they replied. "Our Elders control all creatures and elements within this land, so now the air currents and lava flows belong to the Crunchers."

"Why have they chosen now to kidnap the Elders?" asked Camella.

"Because of you," replied a Magnum as he cried a few tears of lava, "they caught and tortured one of us and now know that you have knowledge of Armon. Realising that these lands were the closest to your home world and your only route through, it would be easiest to catch you here. It is our entire fault the Elders are their prisoners."

"Oh no!" cried Camella. "What have I done? I have brought this downfall onto the entire fire lands."

"We do not blame you and your people, Camella," said another of the Magnum. "We do not know why Armon is so important to Volnar but he obviously is. For this reason alone, it must mean there is hope in destroying the evil one. All we ask of you and your friends is that you help us rescue our Elders. Then we can try to repair the damage to our world."

"Of course we will help," replied Will as he stepped forward to show himself. "Do you know where they're being held and how many guards there are?"

"We sent one of our best spies to the surface," announced another Magnum.

Heatron stepped forward and bowed his head in acknowledgment of Will then proceeded to explain his findings.

"The news is not good I am afraid," Heatron told them. "All our major routes are guarded by a new breed of Razar. They do not have a razor tongue but spit out lava balls and their skin is hot to the touch. To us this is not a problem but you, my friends, would find the experience most unpleasant. On my travels I have found only one route free of eyes but it comes with many dangers. It is behind us across the lava river and through a tiny crevice in the mountain. The route leads around the outside and up a very difficult path. Not impossible you understand but full of dangers such as faltering paths, high winds and avalanches.

"Around the summit is a small number of Razars, perhaps four or five at the most. This is where the Elders are kept in a cage, suspended over the centre of the mountain, a perfect viewpoint to see the entire lands. There you will find the main Soul Cruncher. Oh and I nearly forgot, there are also four Fire Hawks encircling the skies."

"Fire Hawks?" asked Will. "What are they?"

"In normal circumstances," continued Heatron, "these birds are usually friendly but if the Elders are not controlling them, it means the Soul Cruncher is using them for their own purposes. The Fire Hawks are exactly as they sound, a bird of burning flames, leaving a trail of fire across the midnight skies, a most glorious sight for anyone to see."

"I can see a problem immediately," said Kustos. "You said that our best route was on the other side of the river but how are we going to cross it?"

"We had already thought of that. If you look over to other side, you see there is a huge, ancient pillar. We thought, with help, we could knock it down across the lava flow," said one of the Magnum. "We think it should be tall enough to span the two banks. Our only problem is we would need at least one of you to help."

"Fortis," asked Joshua, "do you think you could withstand such heat to get across?"

"I think the lava will penetrate even my toughened skin," replied Fortis, "but I do not see we have an option. I will help you," he told the Magnum.

Cautiously he studied the river and assessed the distance between the two banks. It was too far for him to jump and far too wide to swim, so he decided to combine the two.

"Alright!" he exclaimed as he looked at the others. "Wish me luck."

The Magnum had already returned into the lava and was bobbing swiftly across to the other side of the bank. Fortis took a deep breath and then ran. Using his accelerated speed, he sprinted towards the edge and then jumped. With the extra height the technique had given him, he turned his body into a dive and disappeared into the lava halfway across the river.

"Do you see him?" asked Kustos as he peered intently into the lava.

"I am afraid I do not," replied Ruthus.

"Come on, Fortis," urged Kustos, worried for his brother's safety. "Stop playing around and show yourself."

For a moment no one spoke and only the sound of popping and glupping lava filled the cavern. Kustos continued to stare into the red heat, concern playing on his mind with each second that passed. Suddenly, they heard a huge gasp for air as Fortis pulled himself out of the lava and fell onto the bank. His arms and body were smoking profusely and he was taking in huge gulps of air, but otherwise he appeared unscathed. Within seconds, the smoke had cleared and Fortis got to his feet.

"Are you alright?" Kustos yelled across the river.

Fortis stuck his arms up into the air and smiled.

"You are crazy!" Kustos shouted back. "You had me worried."

Having regained his strength from the test, Fortis walked over to the pillar. In its day, it was probably erected in order to support an important building but now, as years had passed, it stood silently waiting to be of use once more. The Magnum was already in position at the front of the pillar, leaving just enough space for Fortis to squeeze in.

"Are you all ready?" he asked.

His small team of workers nodded in unison, so Fortis gave the order.

"Alright, NOW!" he demanded.

At first, despite their efforts, nothing happened, but as the momentum of their endeavour continued, dust and aggregate began to crumble from the foot of the pillar and it slowly gave way from its footings. Eventually gravity took over, and the pillar collapsed into the bubbling river, causing the workforce to fall to the ground. The column splashed as it was absorbed into the lava and for a few seconds, it vanished from sight before floating up to the surface again. It was not quite long enough to reach the other bank but rested precariously upon the top of the lava flow, held in place by a small amount of the original daub footings.

"We must weigh this end down," Fortis told the Magnum, "so the others can walk it."

The Magnum understood the command and settled themselves comfortably at the base of the pillar to keep it in place.

One by one, the others carefully jumped onto the column and precariously scaled across to the other side. Once or twice the structure slipped as a violent surge of lava rushed through the river but fortunately no one lost their footing and without further hitches they all arrived safely on the bank.

"Good job, brother," said Kustos as he pulled Fortis to his feet. "You gave me quite a scare for a moment."

"I am pleased for your concern, Kustos," Fortis smiled. "It is good to have someone to care for your welfare."

"I am sorry to interrupt," apologised Heatron, "but the gap to the outside world is over there. Behind those rocks is hidden the exit," he said, pointing to a pile of rocks strewn randomly in their path.

"Are you not coming with us?" asked Will.

"We are not fighters, Will," Heatron replied. "And as much as we would like to help, we fear we would only be in the way. We will stay here and see if we can distract the Razars within the mountain. Once you reach the top, you must kill the Soul Cruncher. With him dead, you simply need to cut the Elders loose and let them drop. They will land within the Lava River and regain their energy and control. I am sorry there is not more we can do."

"You have done enough," confirmed Will. "We'll rescue your Elders and try at least to bring some sanity back to your lands."

"Thank you, Will," replied Heatron as he held out his hand in appreciation. "Good Luck." Then, turning his back on them, he lowered himself slowly into the lava to join his friends.

"I doubt if this is going to be easy," said Will, whilst Kustos began to remove the rocks and expose the opening.

"Is anything ever easy with you or Connor around?" smiled the Realm Lord.

When the opening was finally uncovered, both Kustos and Will looked in.

"Wow!" echoed Will. "Heatron wasn't kidding when he said the crevice was small."

From what could be seen, the entranceway no bigger than the width of a teenager and at the end, some distance away, was a faint glimmer of light.

"I guess the sooner we get this done, the sooner we can go to Camella's kingdom," announced Will as he squeezed his body into the tiny opening and slowly crawled along.

One by one they struggled through the narrow tunnel until they all eventually reached the outside of the mountain. The walkway, if that is what it could be described as, was barely a person wide and wound around to the summit like a helter-skelter. An unpleasant hot wind hit their faces as it picked up momentum around the pyramid shape of the mountain and lashed against their bodies in an effort to cause them to fall. Slowly, they began to edge their way up and as they looked towards the top, they saw a ring of fire encircling the outline.

"They must be the Fire Hawks," assumed Will, but no one answered.

Everyone else was far too preoccupied with clinging to the crumbling path.

In silence they continued to follow the pathway up, until it suddenly disappeared. They stopped and stared at the sheer drop before them.

"It looks as though they found the pathway after all," said Kustos as he looked around for another route up but there was nothing in visible view. "So now what?" he asked.

Will also checked out the situation and then shook his head in agreement.

"I've no idea at this point," he admitted. "For me, I don't think it is a problem, but for you guys . . . well, that could be another story."

"So how do you think you can get up there then?" asked Fortis, more out of curiosity than anything else.

"Well, I don't have a problem, or at least I don't think I do," replied Will. "Many years ago, I dreamed I could walk up the shear side of a building at a ninety-degree angle. I'm almost certain I can make it happen again. I'm also confident that I could take Camella and Ruthus with me. They can act as the distraction while I try and kill the Soul Cruncher."

"Are you crazy?" exclaimed Kustos. "Don't answer that. How do you expect to get past the Razars and kill the Soul Cruncher on your own? You need us."

"I know it won't be easy," admitted Will, "and believe me, I'd rather we were all there together to take this on, but that isn't going to happen. If we're ever going to reach the Kalus Kingdom, we have to work with what we have."

"Well, personally," interjected Joshua, "I do not like it but cannot see what other options we have."

"Thank you, Joshua," applauded Will. "A man with some vision. Camella! Ruthus! Will you help me?"

"Of course we will," replied Camella. "You did not need to ask." She smiled.

"Once we have rescued the Elders," said Will, "I will be more focussed on helping Camella and Ruthus to come down and collect you."

Kustos was not happy but knew it was of little consequence to complain. The plan was the best they had, and he had to believe that Will could pull it off.

"Good Luck!" he said sadly as he turned away.

Fortis touched his brother's arm in reassurance then looked at Will.

"Do not do anything more stupid than normal," he warned him. "If it gets too dangerous, run away and come back to us. We will look for another method of attack."

"Be careful, Will," Joshua said softly.

20

A Great Escape

Taking one last look at the mountain summit, Will then turned his attention on Ruthus and Camella. He flung his arms outwards and upwards towards the sky and, as he did so, took command of the elements around him. The Butterhawks instantly took flight as they felt the air below them fill their wings. It was good to feel the breeze caress them once more as they rose up into the skies.

"I will send you higher when I reach closer to the top," Will told them. "In the meantime, stay out of view."

Will jumped up and grabbed a rock above his head, then waited. Within seconds his gravity energy began to surge throughout his veins to his fingertips. His hands felt as though they were glued to the granite stone as he scrambled to find a footing. The instant he took a foothold, his confidence rose, and he knew that the experience of his wall walking had returned. Comfortable with the angle, he put one foot before the other and quite soon he was jogging up the side of the mountain, whilst Camella and Ruthus hovered by his side. The others looked on in amazement.

In less than no time, they had reached the top and stopped a few metres from the summit.

"I will help you go higher," Will told Camella and Ruthus, "so you must distract the Razars but watch out for the Fire Hawks. Do you still have the ice blades, Camella?" he asked her.

She nodded and removed two from her pouch before handing one over to Ruthus.

"Be careful, brother," she told him.

Ruthus took the blade from her and studied it.

"A rare specimen," he replied. "I dare not ask how they came into your possession."

"Nor should you," she scolded playfully.

Will clambered over the final stages to assess his position and could just make out the mountain summit with a huge central opening. There, suspended above it, was a cage containing the four elders. From what he could see, the Elders were similar to the Magnum he had met earlier. The only thing that differentiated them from the others was their dark red eyes and the wrinkles of flesh that had spanned the eons of time.

Over in the far corner the Soul Cruncher was standing, his back facing Will as he surveyed the fire lands stretching out before him. In a one-to-one fight, his positioning would permit the element of surprise, but this was no easy battle as four Razars paced up and down around the centre opening of the mountain, prepared to repel any attack. Slowly Will pulled himself onto the mountaintop and scrambled across the ground on his stomach until he was safely hidden behind some rocks. The plan now was clear. He would work his way over to the Soul Cruncher and hope he could take him by surprise.

"Are you ready?" he whispered to the Butterhawks.

"We are ready," replied Camella softly.

As quietly as he could, Will threw his hands forward and, utilising the heat around him, created a warm current of air. Camella was the first to sense it and drifted high above the mountaintop, exposing herself to the Razars. Ruthus followed swiftly behind.

They caused the desired distraction as the Razars quickly spotted them and yelled and roared at the Butterhawks swooping above them. The disturbance alerted the Soul Cruncher and he turned and glared at the Elders. Manipulated by his control, they called upon the Fire Hawks and urged them to attack. A squawk of acknowledgment was all that was heard as they dived towards the two Butterhawks.

With all eyes now on them, Will stood up and made a run towards the Soul Cruncher. Unfortunately, the creature noticed his movement and turned around undeterred to face the enemy. Will grabbed a couple of rocks as he moved and threw them towards the Cruncher's eyes. It was only then that he remembered the creature was devoid of vision, so instead of blinding him, it merely pinpointed his own location, as the long arms swung in the area of his footsteps. The Dream Warrior was almost within arm's reach of the Soul Cruncher when he felt a surge of extreme heat rush pass him. He quickly stopped and turned around and saw a Razar coming towards him, spitting lava balls as he moved. Looking around, Will saw the perfect cover and threw himself to one side, to hide behind a large outcrop.

"Come on, boy," encouraged the Soul Cruncher as he tried to home in on Will's heavy breathing. "Let's you and me have a little chat."

Meanwhile, up in the skies, Camella and Ruthus had their own problems to face. Not only were they trying to dodge the heat of the Fire Hawks but also the lava balls emitted by the Razars.

Since being rescued by Kustos, the once battle-shy Camella had now become acclimatised to war, and unperturbed by their predicament, she used her ice blade as a bat and swiped at the lava balls as they whizzed towards them. One by one as her efforts improved, the fiery weapon evaporated and turned into steam on impact.

"I really do not think this is a plan," Ruthus told her as he dodged another projectile.

"Stop grumbling," Camella reprimanded. "At least we have a fighting chance."

Will, in the meantime, was not progressing very far at all. As he crouched behind a rock, attempting to stay out of sight of the Soul Cruncher and any of the other Razars who might decide to join in the fight, he knew his chances were getting slimmer by the minute.

"Come on, boy," the Soul Cruncher coaxed, "if you tell me what the Butterhawks know, I promise you will have a painless death."

Will did not respond but instead peered cautiously around the safety of his rock and caught sight of the Razars congregating together. Their plan, he figured, was to try and bring Camella and Ruthus down. Without thought for his own safety, he looked skywards and watched Camella gliding across the currents as she dodged the Fire Hawks and evaporated the barrage of lava balls. Things were not looking good.

"Camella!" he suddenly shouted urgently as he noticed a Fire Hawk flying extremely close to her in an attempt to singe her delicate wings. "Look out."

She had no time to react but Will did. He thrust his hands forward and raised them towards the skies. In the split second it had taken to perform the motion, a strong gust of wind lifted Camella higher into the air, whilst the Fire Hawk struggled to combat it and lost control. Panicked by the lack of momentum, it fluttered frantically in the air but the wind was too powerful to manage and it found itself falling towards the ground. A streak of burning fire lit up the sky as the bird descended, extinguished only by the heavy thud of its body as it hit the solid mountainside.

"So there you are, boy!" acknowledged the Soul Cruncher as his keen hearing picked up on the rescue Will had made.

Without thinking, Will ran towards him, picking up speed as he moved. Their bodies collided with a loud thud and he grappled with the enemy, using all the force he could muster, throwing the Soul Cruncher and himself over the central opening of the mountain towards the lava river below.

Camella watched in horror as she saw the Dream Warrior tumbling to an imminent death, and without a thought for her own safety, she swooped down after him. Out of the corner of his eye, Ruthus noticed the dramatic dive and cursed under his breath as he dodged an assault from another Fire Hawk. He could not help his sister in her death-defying attempt.

The Soul Cruncher, smug from his own satisfaction at capturing Will, attempted to save himself and instinctively let go of his prey but the action came too late as he dropped too close to the river for any real salvation. Still oblivious of the danger he was in, the Cruncher screamed in agony as a burning sensation crept up his legs. Briefly he looked down and saw his wrinkled flesh melting into liquid and merging with the molten lava not far below. Any efforts he made of stopping his fall were futile as the increasing heat began to liquefy the rest of his flesh from his bones. Will stared in disbelief and realised his own imminent death as he tried to raise a gravity pod to soften his fall . . . but nothing happened. His only conclusion in that short time was that the heat must have had an effect on his skills. All that was left was to except his fate. Looking again at the lava below, he noticed the features of several Magnum as they waved their arms frantically. To him, it appeared a final farewell gesture and just as he had made peace with himself, two hands grabbed him by the shoulders and tried to whisk him away.

"Got you," said Camella as she struggled to straighten up from the dive but the angle was too acute and the air currents too weak to lift them from danger.

Aware of their peril, Will held out his arms and hoped he could produce a cushion of heat to slow their pace. It worked and once their drop was reduced to a slow float, he conjured up more heat to create a current of air and lift them once more up into the sky.

The Magnum below cheered with relief.

"Phew! That was close," announced Will. "Thanks."

"That was stupid," Camella told him angrily. "I could . . . I mean we could have lost you."

"I'm sorry," apologised the Dream Warrior. "I didn't think."

"Then please do so next time," she pleaded.

Within seconds, they reached the summit of the mountain and Camella called out to her brother to cut down the Elder's cage but he was far too busy eluding the Fire Hawks from the skies and the Razars from the ground. He dare not take the risk.

"Give me your blade," Will ordered Camella. "Drop me to the ground, and I'll cut them free."

"My pouch," she told him. "Take it from the pouch on my belt."

Skilfully she swooped lower to the ground whilst Will carefully removed the weapon from her belt. When in position, she released her grip and he rolled in a controlled manner across the ground before coming to a halt. Slowly and surely he steadied himself as he got to his feet and waved to Camella. Convinced of his safety, she glided off towards Ruthus to see if she could assist him. The Razars, mesmerised by her movement, watched her rejoin her brother. Then, as if they had received an instruction to act, they began once more to spit their lava balls at them.

Obsessed with the Butterhawks above them, the Razars lost the focus they had on the Elders as Will moved stealthily towards the cage. Quietly he rested the ice blade upon the holding rope and watched as it turned into frozen twine. Then he took the blade once more and sliced through the weakened cord. Detached by its holding, the cage immediately fell towards the lava river below, and as Will leaned over the side to watch, he saw it crash into the liquid and sink to the depths of the riverbed. For a moment, he thought he saw Heatron waving his thanks but in a split second the object had disappeared beneath the surface and was gone.

All that was left to the plan now was for Will to destroy the Razars. He sized up the situation, looking up into the skies and noticed the remaining Fire Hawks still attacking the Butterhawks. He was disappointed. He had hoped that the rescued Elders would be able to resume control and call the off the birds.

"I thought they'd stop now the Elders are safe," Will called up to Camella.

"I do not think it is their fault," she told him. "I think the poor creatures are so confused they will attack anything."

The Razars preoccupation with the Butterhawks was soon altered as they noticed Will conversing with them. An opportunity, in their minds, had now arisen for them to destroy the Dream Warrior.

"You and your brother go back to the others," Will ordered. "Wait for my signal, and I'll bring you back up here."

"That is suicidal!" she yelled at him. "You cannot take them on alone."

"Just GO!" Will commanded.

Unhappy by the order, Camella and Ruthus reluctantly vanished behind the mountaintop, with the Fire Hawks in hot pursuit. Their only chance now of losing the birds was to draw them back to the others and get Fortis to take them down.

"Okay," said Will to himself when he was fully satisfied he was alone, "I have to stay alive long enough to take the Razars out. A little crazy perhaps, but what plan isn't?"

Any fear he might have felt was now gone. He knew what had to be done and despite the fact the four Razars were approaching him, he still had every faith in his ability to prevail, even more so when he saw the comical way one of his enemy spun around whilst still spitting its lava balls in every direction. Will ducked quickly behind a rock to protect himself as the bombardment of lava bounced off the mountain. Every so often, he cautiously peered out from his hiding place to see what was going on and soon noticed that three of the Razars had fallen behind. As he continued to make his assessment of their plan of action, a flash of light ripped across the sky, momentarily blinding Will and the Razars. The Dream Warrior blinked profusely to clear his vision, and as he focussed, he saw Jasmine standing to his right. On his left were Vanisheo and another, unknown to him. His own assumption was it had to be Hunter.

"Jasmine . . . look out!" Will cried as he noticed the lava balls winging their way towards her.

She turned her head to see the danger and saw the projectiles making their way towards her. Unfazed by such an attack, she turned herself into a ghost, permitting the lava to simply travel through her body. Will was speechless as he watched her raise her hand and pick the Razar up from the ground, then when she was satisfied with the hold, she threw him through the air and over the mountainside. The effort she had to use to attempt such a feat was excessive and as the Razar fell to his death, she stumbled weakly towards Will as her energy drained away.

"Quickly," urged the Dream Warrior as he caught her and staggered back behind the rock. "Being out in the open is not a wise move, but believe me, I'm really glad to see you here." He smiled.

"This is Ashley Hunter," Jasmine told him as she introduced the stranger.

Will said nothing as he peered around the rock.

The Razars had also taken cover and were bobbing up from time to time, spitting lava balls in their direction in the mere hope of hitting someone.

"Well, that should keep them busy for a while," explained Will. "Forgive my manners. It's a pleasure to meet you, Ashley." And he held out his hand. "If you're here," he added, "where's Connor and Durban?"

"They had to stay behind to give us a chance to escape," interrupted Vanisheo.

Will hugged his friend tightly with relief for his safety.

"The Razars attacked us at Ashley's home and they were unable to follow us. Connor promised to be here, so do not worry, Will," Vanisheo added.

"I don't have any doubts on that score." Will grinned as he noticed Jasmine's strength return. "In the meantime, Vanisheo, I want you to take Ashley and Jasmine back down the mountain to Kustos. Melt yourself back to them and wait for my signal. I need to clear the way for Camella and Ruthus to take us to the Kalus Kingdom. Armon is waiting there."

"I will not leave," replied Jasmine emphatically. "You cannot fight these creatures alone. I will help you."

"Do not try to disagree with her, Will," warned Vanisheo. "She always gets her own way in the end." And with that, he grabbed Ashley's hand and was gone.

"So I guess we're on our own then," remarked Will as he turned to Jasmine. "Could you use your telekinetic power to force the rest of the Razars over the edge, like the last one?"

"I am afraid not," she replied. "It takes too much of my energy."

"Hmmm . . . then hold this," he said handing her the ice blade. "I'll try and manipulate their lava and fire it back at them, but to be honest, I'm finding it quite difficult to harness my energy in this world."

"What is this for?" replied Jasmine as she took the blade. "What am I supposed to do with it?"

"It's an ice blade," answered Will. "If you stab a Razar with it, it'll freeze them from the inside out, and in this heat, they'll evaporate into nothing but a puddle on the floor." And with that, he stood up and started to dodge the erratic lava balls. "Oh and another thing," he shouted back, "don't let them touch you, or they'll burn the skin from your bones."

"That is not very friendly," replied Jasmine as she also stood up to face the enemy.

A Razar had already seen her move and was making his way very slowly towards her but undeterred by the opposition, Jasmine picked up some rocks and walked towards him, randomly throwing them to try and delay an attack. The Razar's thoughts were focussed on one thing. She would make a fine prize, even if it meant taking the brunt of the rocks as they hit their skin and smouldered before falling to the ground, one way of retaliation without harming her. She was outnumbered and firing lava balls directly in her path would also slow her down and more than likely eventually overcome her.

Jasmine however was not so easily swayed and reacting to the assault, she raised the ice blade before her and stopped the weapons in mid flight. As they hit the knife, they sizzled on impact and immediately evaporated into steam.

"Hmm, that is interesting," she mused to herself as she watched a Razar draw closer.

With each step that he made, he swung a hammer-type weapon around his head, dangerously near her body. Without a thought she changed into a ghost and the confusion it caused enabled her to dodge the deadly blows. Unfortunately, the Razar did catch her off guard and she lost concentration and returned to her normal state, where she tripped and fell. From the corner of his eye, Will saw her fall and tried to reach her but his own attacker was also swinging a weapon that made it increasingly difficult to escape.

With Jasmine on the ground, the Razar moved in to apply the final blow but she managed to miss the attack by rolling from side to side as the weapon hit the ground. With luck still on her side, she tried to roll away but she hit a rock blocking her path. This provided sufficient time for the hammer to find its mark. As it slammed down onto her delicate frame, she split into two as each Jasmine rolled to safety.

Will and the Razar stopped in amazement as they watched her get to her feet. Both Jasmines were identically stunning, each holding an ice blade. Suddenly jolting back to the reality of the situation, the Razar took a swing at one of the Jasmines but as he did so, the other ran around behind him and stabbed the ice blade into the top of his neck. The creature screamed in agony as the freezing element within the blade began to seep through its veins and solidified it into a frozen statue. It took only moments before melting in the heated atmosphere.

Will was relieved and impressed by her battle abilities but was having problems of his own in containing one of the other Razars. He dodged from side to side to avoid the hammer but there was little room for movement and each attack took the Razar closer to him. It was Jasmine's turn to see the danger Will was in, so she collected her other self and tried to manoeuvre to a tactical advantage. The third Razar however, had been watching the fight and was now spitting a barrage of lava balls in an attempt to stop her progress.

Will by this time was backed into a corner with the Razar directly in front of him and the edge of the mountainside beneath his feet. There was little left to do but close his eyes and accept his fate. Blood pounded in his ears as he heard the hammer swishing and the sound of lava balls as they flew through the air towards him. It would soon be over, or so he thought but as each second passed, he felt no pain. He opened his eyes slowly and saw the shiny surface of a liquid metal shield protecting him and holding fast as the lava balls hit and fell to the ground. Without thinking, Will began to feel his energy boil and suddenly, without warning, he burst into flames, like a human touch.

"Ready, Will?" said Durban. "Let me know when I need to drop the shield."

Will looked around and there beside him was Connor and Durban.

"It's good to see you, my friend." Connor smiled. "Now show us what you can do."

Will nodded to Durban as the shield fell away and he threw his hands forward. Fire emitted like a bullet from a gun as it hit the Razar and knocked him down. Taking full advantage of the fallen enemy, Will continued to walk towards it, pummelling continuously as he approached.

"Connor!" screamed Jasmine as she struggled against the Razar. "Help me!"

Connor moved to assist her but Nuwa Lin raised her arm across his chest.

"I have this one, Connor," she told him as she ran towards the creature.

Her movement was so fast she was almost invisible to the eye.

"Duck, Jasmine!" shouted a voice from out of nowhere.

Jasmine quickly slowed her mind and saw that Nuwa Lin was there, so obeying the instruction, she threw herself to the ground and covered her eyes. The ninja continued to run and jumped over the prostrate figure and into the Razar. Taken unawares by the fast, invisible attacker, the creature was helpless as Nuwa Lin punched and kicked. Her moves were so fast into the creature's body that the heat it emitted had no time to take affect against her skin. Flailing arms and confusion was all the Razar could offer as he was forced back towards the edge of the mountain.

"Nuwa Lin!" Jasmine shouted, as she raised her head to watch. "Catch!" And she threw her the ice blade.

The ninja jumped and spun around as she caught the blade in her hand, then using all the force she could muster, she stabbed it into the Razar's head as she landed softly on the ground. As instant as the last ice blade when it hit the target, it froze the liquid in the creature's veins before turning its flesh to ice. The frozen statue stood before her as she raised her leg and kicked it hard into the chest. The impact of her blow was sufficient to break it in two and before the top half of the body touched the ground, it had melted and evaporated away. Nuwa Lin bent down and picked up the ice blade.

"I like this," she said with a smile as she walked over to Jasmine and helped her to her feet.

"It is so good to see you again." Jasmine smiled at the ninja. "And you as well," she added as she joined Connor and Durban.

Instinctively she hugged Connor and kissed him on the cheek before hugging him again. She also smiled and mouthed the words thank you to Durban.

Whilst all the greetings were taking place, it occurred to Nuwa Lin that Will was still fighting the last Razar and his energy of fire was beginning to fade. Although little effort was required to finish the creature off, Will had found himself in a similar situation as earlier, struggling to keep his balance on the edge of the mountain.

"Will!" she shouted she started to run again. "Drop down . . . now."

On demand, he dropped his guard and fell to the ground, just as the ninja ran quickly past and leapt into the Razar. Already precariously placed, it lost its balance and fell unceremoniously over the mountainside leaving Nuwa Lin to skilfully adjust her balance and land safely on the ground.

Durban ran to Will and grabbed him just in time to prevent him from slipping over the edge.

"It's good to see you, Will," said Connor as he helped Durban and his friend to their feet.

"Durban," Will said, "am I glad to see you. Perfect timing as always."

"I also find it good to see you again, Will." Durban grinned.

"And who's the new warrior?" Will asked Connor as he noticed the lithe figure of the ninja standing with Jasmine.

"This is Nuwa Lin," announced Connor. "Without her help we wouldn't have completed part of the mission. She showed us where to find Ashley and came to our rescue back in the ice mountain."

"It's good to meet such an accomplished fighter," said Will as he held his hand out to her.

She took it lightly and shook it.

"Anyone that can watch Connor's back is always a friend of mine. I have heard many stories about you, Will," she replied. "And the honour of meeting a Dream Warrior is all mine."

Embarrassed by such an acclamation, he turned his attentions to the matter at hand and walked over to the edge of the mountain.

"We have to get the others up here," he told them. "I'm certain Kustos would like to know that his wife is safe."

And he looked at Jasmine and smiled.

"I am sure he would." Jasmine grinned as she hugged him.

As she released him, he leaned over the side and called out, "Is everybody all right down there?"

A faint response drifted towards him.

"We're fine," they replied.

"I'll raise the currents for Camella and Ruthus. Vanisheo, can you bring the others to me?" Will asked.

"Yes, I can," answered a voice from behind and he turned around to see Fortis, Kustos, Joshua, and Vanisheo all standing beside him.

Jasmine rushed to greet her husband, her arms outstretched, longing to feel his protective arms around her once more.

"Fortis!" Durban grinned as he punched his shoulder. "It is good to see you again. Allow me to introduce Nuwa Lin."

The ninja bowed her head in reverence of the prince and then noticed Joshua, standing beside Will. Immediately she dropped to one knee. Her action confused the others and they stopped what they were doing to wait to see what was about to unfold.

"My lord!" she said softly. "The Great Oracle of Judgment, we all thought that Volnar had killed you."

"Great Oracle!" Will and Fortis echoed together but Joshua ignored them and continued to focus on the ninja.

"My child, please rise?" Joshua replied kindly. "Your valour has already proven you need not bow to me."

Nuwa Lin stood up and accepted the praise, then smiled. The Oracle was safe and it looked as though the mission was going to plan. What else could there be that could trouble them? From far below drifted a faint voice on the wind.

"What's going on up there?" asked Camella.

"Oh good grief," exclaimed Will. "In all the excitement, I'd forgotten about the Butterhawks. Forgive me, my friends." And with that he raised his arms.

A warm current circulated around the Butterhawks and their wings, unfolded from their backs, began to quiver as the urge to take flight took over. Within a minute both Camella and Ruthus had landed either side of Will.

"So what did we miss?" Camella asked as she sensed a great revelation had been announced.

"Joshua's the Great Oracle of Judgment," Will told her. "Well, according to Nuwa Lin, that is."

"And who is she?" queried the Butterhawk as she eyed the ninja up and down.

"Just a friend that Connor picked up along the way," confirmed the Dream Warrior. "Apparently she saved their lives and helped them find Ashley Hunter."

"So part of the adventure has been fulfilled?" smiled Camella.

"Yep," agreed Will, "we're halfway there."

"So you are the high and powerful Judgment Oracle?" said Connor. "Why the façade?"

"I will explain everything," Joshua told him, "but not in this place."

"Joshua is right," interrupted Camella. "It will not be long before other Razars will track us here. We must leave the mountain."

"And any suggestions how?" asked Connor. "It looks as though only two of you can fly, and you can't carry us all."

Camella ran over to the centre of the mountain and peered down. Quietly at first but then building in momentum, she started to hum until a beautiful tune resounded around the silence. Her hypnotic voice was gentle and fresh and rested calmly on their ears. As the song came to an end, Camella saw the Magnum Elders rise above the river below. They waved at her and she waved back before stepping away from the edge. With an understanding of what was required, the Elders joined hands and within seconds had conjured up the spirits of the river. A gigantic rumble rocked the mountain. This was followed by an intense rush of heated air, spewing from above the heads of the Elders into the sky and through the fluffy white clouds. Ruthus looked up and began to hum a different tune that penetrated the nimbus and faded upon the winds. Moments later, several Butterhawks descended from the skies towards them.

"Camella, Ruthus," said one of their kinsmen, "we are so glad to see you have outwitted our enemy."

"You should have more faith in us." Camilla smiled. "And the friends we have managed to collect along the way."

"Enough admiration," reprimanded Ruthus. "We must all return to Kalus . . . now. The survival of this world depends upon it."

"I will take Will," volunteered Camella as she stood protectively by his side. "Ruthus, you can take Joshua. My friends," she added to the rest of the Butterhawks, "choose one of the others to transport home."

In turn, each Butterhawk introduced themselves to Kustos and the rest of the team and advised them of the procedure required to take to the air.

"You must hold onto me, Will, the best way you can," Camella told him as she unfolded her wings once more and without a second thought, he gently took hold of her hand. "When I say run," she continued, "we must run towards the centre of the mountain and then jump up into the hot air. Whatever happens, do not let go."

"You can bet on that one," Will said as they ran forwards.

When they reached the edge of the mountain cavity, Camella let out a shriek of delight as she stretched her wings out as wide as they would go and they swooped up into the clouds and out of sight. Taking his cue from his sister, Ruthus instructed Joshua of the technique and quickly took to the air, following Camella into the atmosphere.

"Come, my fellow Butterhawks," he shouted as they soared upon the currents, "pick up our friends and follow us to Kalus."

Up into the skies the flock of Butterhawks flew, carrying with them their precious cargo. Those without a rider simply followed behind, protecting the group from any further attack.

21

A Memory of Time

"Our kingdom is just beyond those gates," announced Camella as they approached the city boundary. "We must not delay but get to safety quickly. We may have been followed."

"Well, I'm not going to Kalus until Joshua tells me exactly what's going on," said Connor emphatically. "We've all risked our lives on his instructions and now, for once, I want the truth."

The other Butterhawks hovered together in silence, holding their passengers and waiting in expectation of a reaction. All of them were keen to know the answer.

"So you're the Great Oracle of Judgment?" continued Connor. "What does that mean and why is Ashley so important? No offence meant, Ashley," he apologised.

"None taken, Connor," she replied.

"You are right, Connor. I cannot expect you all to risk your lives on faith alone. There was always going to be a time for explanations," replied Joshua. "As you have quantified, I am the Oracle of Judgment—not just an Oracle but THE Oracle, the highest of them all. In the only hope of saving Judgment, I have left my people behind. For this, believe me, I am not proud but it was the only way I could see any chance of a future for any one of the three worlds."

"So why didn't you tell us from the start?" asked Will. "We still would've helped you."

"I know that now," replied the Oracle, "but I was fearful of betrayal. There were too many eyes and ears watching my every move. The day Volnar attacked was an unforgettable one. I had been warned by my friends in the Judgment Halls but arrogance clouded my mind. I was the Great Oracle and the most powerful being in Judgment, or so I thought. My only adversary was Volnar, and he was trapped between worlds. Even if he did manage to break free, I felt he was no match for me . . . but I was wrong. He had a following in every world and all it took was the weakened mind of an age old friend to bring him back."

"Armon," echoed Camella in disbelief. "When I found him, he was the picture of a broken man, unable to barely stand alone. How could such a being bring about the downfall of the Judgment World?"

"I know your thoughts, Camella," said Joshua, "but Armon was merely his puppet. It was Volnar pulling the strings. He sent Armon to me, pleading for help. Telling me he felt an energy pulling him in two. I know now but all too late, it was Volnar draining him.

The day *HE* stormed the Halls, assisted by his army of Razars, I became aware that my power alone could not contain this enemy. His strength and allies were more than a match for me, so in complete helplessness, I watched as he slaughtered any Oracle that stood against him. Even my own family and friends were either destroyed or converted, and I did nothing to help. I was one against an entire army and thought only of my own safety; I fled and hid, until such time as I thought I could make a difference.

As I was leaving the Judgment Halls, I saw a door open and Ashley wandering the hallways. The look upon her face expressed it all. Bewilderment confused her sense of survival. I heard the Soul Crunchers behind us threatening to kill her, though I did not understand why. For some reason, she was important to Volnar and if nothing else, I felt I had to protect her from him. I knew the corridors of Judgment like my home and using that, we managed to escape the Halls. Once outside in the open, I used every last ounce of my energy to split us apart. It forced her to reappear somewhere else in the world, somewhere that I had no knowledge of. If she was that important to Volnar, I had to be certain I could not betray her whereabouts if ever captured. I knew her memory of the Judgment Halls would be erased. It was the fate of anyone who managed to leave but I felt, with no logical reason, that she was an integral part of the battle ahead.

Rumours of her escape seeped from Judgment and in the best interest of our world I spread the word that Hunter was a man. I only hoped it would keep Ashley safe until I could figure out my next move. To my relief, I learned of the actions of Fortis and Durban and how they managed to speak with you Connor and I prayed this meant there was still some hope left in this world for its redemption. I risked a meeting with the Higher Powers and presented my case. In their wisdom, they granted me access to Sublin. There I was given the opportunity to test you and Will on your skills and decide whether or not you could help. Your performances were better than I hoped for. It gave me a glimmer of optimism that the Judgment World could be saved."

"So if you knew Ashley wouldn't remember the way back to the Judgment Halls, why did you send us to find her?" asked Connor. "I mean, if she's that important to Volnar, wouldn't it make more sense to keep her hidden?"

"It is her destiny to join us," replied the Oracle. "I do not know what part she has to play but I know that it is vital to our success. If I had told you the truth, would you have spent so much energy in finding her?"

"But why me?" asked Ashley. "I'm just an ordinary person. Why would Volnar want me?"

"That I cannot answer, Ashley," replied Joshua. "I am working on instinct. Volnar wanted you dead at any cost and in my experience of him, he never gives an order unless it fits into his plan."

"Regardless of the explanation," interrupted Will, "aren't you forgetting something? None of us know where the Halls of Judgment are."

Joshua grinned for the first time since relaying his story.

"I am the Higher Oracle," he said with a smile. "This is my world. My memory of many lifetimes cannot be erased. I will take you there when the time is right."

"Are you satisfied now?" Camella asked Connor nervously.

Her senses were tingling, and she feared for their safety, still exposed and visible.

"You know, Joshua," said Kustos, "I may not like the fact you kept this from us but I do understand why you did it. Sometimes we are forced to make impossible decisions in a moment. I know it could not have been easy for you but you did the right thing escaping. Your friends and family in the Halls would have understood that."

"Thank you," replied Joshua. "Perhaps one day I will forgive myself but not until this is over. Now please, Camella, Ruthus, take us to your kingdom."

Camella did not wait for Connor to approve but swooped lower as she led the way towards Kalus.

"Yes, my lord," she whispered as she flew.

For several minutes they travelled on, until they finally reached the city gates. Two Butterhawks guarded the entrance and huge smiles spread across their faces when they recognised Camella and Ruthus.

"It is good to see you again," shouted up one of the guards. "We had all but given up hope for you both."

"It is good to be home." Camella smiled as she reached the gate. "We have brought some guests to our city; please let us in."

The two guards did not waste a moment and began to manually turn the huge wheel holding the gates in place. Very, very slowly they began to move, and an inch of light escaped the kingdom. As the opening widened, blazing beams lit up the skies, dazzling the waiting visitors.

"Please follow me," instructed Camella as she gently landed on the ground and walked forward.

One by one, Connor and his friends began to adjust to the iridescent light and within seconds caught their first glimpse of the Kalus Kingdom. Directly in front of them stood a small village that had been built around a large well. Butterhawk children were playing and laughing in total innocence of the havoc outside and in their excitement, every so often, flittered a few feet from the ground. A warm, vigorous breeze continually whipped around the stone-built houses, trying to loosen the securely fasten roof tiles and windows creaked as they flapped open and close.

Off in the distance, high above, was a colossal white cloud resting peacefully in the bright blue sky, protecting a temple-like structure towering up into the atmosphere.

"That is the home of our rulers," pointed Camella excitedly as she grabbed Will's hand and dragged him towards the village. "They can oversee the whole kingdom from up there. Ruthus and I live with them."

"Will they mind us just dropping in then?" asked Connor.

"They have been away for many years," replied Ruthus.

"Then how do they know what's going on?" asked Will.

"Oh, they keep in touch." Camella smiled. "Come on. The best way to see our kingdom is in the air," she added with pride, "Besides, the Temple of Clouds will be your resting place for the time being. We will provide you with food and comfort before meeting with Armon."

"Then take me up." Will grinned as he tightened his grip around Camella's hand in preparation of flight.

Comforted by his closeness, she once more headed towards the currents and quickly rose from the ground. As they glided through the air, Will could see how beautiful and peaceful Kalus was and understood why Camella and Ruthus had risked their lives to find them. Volnar would undoubtedly destroy this paradise and leave it as a ruin just like so many other cities he had laid waste to in the past. As they silently flew over the rest of the kingdom, he noticed the smaller hamlets throughout the large expanse. A glistening river flowed gently below them. Will was about to ask where its source was when he noticed a large grey rain cloud, permanently situated at the far end of the kingdom. Cascading like a waterfall in the sky, water fell endlessly, replenishing the river.

"Amazing, huh?" Camella asked Will with pride.

"I'd say," agreed Will.

"The cloud draws its water from a huge ocean below then feeds our river that eventually flows back into the sea at the far side of the kingdom. Our people call it the Waterfall in the Sky."

While Will continued to take in the sights, it crossed his mind what a contrast there was between Kalus and the devastation and horror the land-based kingdoms were experiencing. It must have taken a real miracle to protect such a way of life.

"We are here," announced Camella finally as she lowered them both to the ground so they were standing on the steps of the temple.

Will looked around and saw his friends not far behind.

"Come on," she ordered him gently as she walked off.

Like a puppy following its master, he ran to catch up with her just as she reached the entrance.

"Camella!" exclaimed a guard. "Thank judgment you are safe. I see you have brought—" And the guard stopped as he stared at Will.

"I get that a lot around here," said Will as he stepped forward. "I'm Will." And he held out his hand in friendship.

Before the guard had an opportunity to speak, Connor and the others had joined them and the guard's attention was diverted to greeting the additional visitors.

"Please," Camella implored the guards, "my friends and I are tired and hungry. Arrange for the guest rooms to be readied and a banquet laid out in the dining hall."

"Camella?" asked Joshua. "Where is Armon? I need to speak with him."

"He is in the courtyard, my lordship," said one of the guards as he bowed. "It has taken us months to convince him to sit and relax by the fountain. Come, I shall take you to him."

"Thank you," replied Joshua as he turned to Will. "Will, I need you to escort me. I think it is important that you meet with him."

Connor stepped forward and put his arm across his friend's chest as if to advise him otherwise.

"It's okay, Connor." Will grinned. "I'll join you all shortly. Don't eat all the food before I get back?"

Connor sensed that Will was in control and smiled.

"Be safe, my friend," he told him as he lowered his arm.

"Come," invited Camella, "let us eat and exchange the adventures we have experienced." And she walked off to the top of the stairs.

Slowly she turned back and looked at Will, then smiled

"See you soon," she mouthed silently.

"Come, Connor," said Ruthus as he patted him on the back. "Will and Joshua will be fine. You are all safe here."

Reluctantly Connor took the stairs and followed the others into the temple.

"Why is it so important for me to meet Armon?" Will asked Joshua once they were alone.

Joshua said nothing but followed the guard through another set of double doors. As they walked along, they were greeted by two enormous statues. The images were of two Butterhawks, one male, one female and Will assumed they were the lord and lady of the realm. Casually they wandered up another set of marble stairs where he could just make out the images of his friends as they disappeared from view.

"Please, my lords," implored the guard, "this way please, through this door." And he led them through a doorway at the back of the enclosure.

"I will explain everything," Joshua told Will as they wandered along the corridor, "just as soon as you have met Armon."

Idly Will gazed out of the windows as they strolled along and saw clear blue sky and fluffy white clouds below them.

"I think you must be wondering how we have managed to escape the horrors?" questioned the guard.

"Well, it did cross my mind," replied Will.

"We are protected by the cloud," came the response. "Many have tried to find the pathway of Kalus and even more have failed. The cumuls is our guardian and hides us from the other realms, whilst still enabling us to keep abreast of what is going on." For a moment there was an awkward silence, and then the guard spoke again.

"Aah, here we are," he said. "Just go through the door and into the courtyard. Armon will be waiting. If you would excuse me, I must check on your friends. I will collect you when it is time." And with that, he hurried off back down the corridor.

Cautiously Will opened the door and breathed in deeply. An aroma of sweet smelling fragrances tantalised his nostrils, as did the visuals of the various different flowers. Slowly they walked along the path leading to the centre of the courtyard and a sense of calm drifted over them as though the stupor of the amazing flora had melted every bad feeling and memory from their minds.

Finally, they reached their destination and there before them was a huge fountain engulfing a stature of a young Butterhawk. His arms were outstretched and fresh glittering water ran down the wings and back into the fountain. Around the statue was a circle of seats. One was taken. A man was seated with his back to them and without a word Joshua and Will approached him and sat down.

The visage of the man was pathetic as he waited in silence. His medium-length brown hair was brushed forward in a side part, exposing even more of his pale face, which was drained of any real life or emotion. He was dressed in a brown, long-sleeved tunic with loose-fitting trousers and open-toe sandals. His eyes were firmly shut and by the nasal sounds, he was asleep.

"Armon?" said Joshua as he shook him gently.

The man slowly opened his eyes and took a quick glimpse at Will before turning to Joshua.

"I know your face," said Armon as he studied the image of Joshua. "My memory is patchy in places but you I have met before."

"Yes, you have, Armon," confirmed the Oracle. "We met a long, long time ago. My name is Joshua."

"Yes, yes, Joshua," replied Armon excitedly at suddenly remembering something from his past. "You are a Judgment Oracle. We worked together." His eyes suddenly widened as he recalled the moment and then quickly apologised. "Oh, my lord, forgive me," he begged "you are the Elder Oracle."

"I was once, my friend," replied Joshua, "but none of that matters now. I need your help to stop Volnar."

"Volnar!" Armon shuddered, at the mention of the Dark Lord's name. "I cannot help. He has a hold over me. He is always in my head."

"You just need strength, Armon," Joshua told him. "William, your son, will be that force."

"What?" said Will as he heard his name mentioned.

The old man turned and studied Will's face before shedding a tear.

"My son?" he echoed.

"That's impossible," interrupted Will as he jumped up from his seat.

The memory of his father brought only shame and he did not want to be reminded of it.

"My father was a drunk. He killed a family with his car by running a red light and was then found dead in his prison cell."

"That is the story you were led to believe," Joshua told him quietly, "did it not occur to you why the Butterhawks stared at you so. Why can you not see how much alike you are?"

"You're my father but—" Will blurted out.

So many different emotions were racing through his mind and he found it difficult to keep control.

"Please sit down, Will," said Joshua softly. "I know this is hard for you to accept right now, but all will become clear."

Without argument, Will did as he was instructed and sat down next to Armon.

"Who are you?" Will asked Armon.

"I am your father," he replied.

"But why are you here?" asked the Dream Warrior. "Why haven't you been judged for your crimes?"

"Volnar and I were childhood friends," Armon began to explain, oblivious of the accusations. "As children and youths, we were inseparable but as Volnar grew older, he constantly moaned that his father favoured Valiant over him. The more time that passed, the more his bitter jealousy began to eat away at his heart until he could not mention Valiant's name without hatred in his voice. Despite his efforts to win his father's affection, Volnar was still not offered the title of Dream Lord and on the day Valiant took the position, Volnar swore to reap revenge and show Sublin he was the born leader.

We had been friends for many years, and I thought if I could stay by his side, I would be able to persuade him to see reason and prevent the war he was planning. I was wrong . . . very wrong. His power was strong and as the years went by, he got into my head and I felt weakened by the influence of his hatred for all that was good. I knew it was wrong, but I was completely under his control and lived only to serve.

After the loss of Valiant, Volnar became more powerful and started to execute his plan for total domination. Only when he heard that Valiant had escaped into the Wake World did his confidence waiver a little but even then he had a plan and sent me after the Dream Lord to bring him home.

Eventually I managed to break into the Wake World, through a woman's dream. Her name was Lily and night after night, I would enter her rested thoughts and connect with her soul. She was a sweet and kind person and I felt closer to her than anyone before. The goodness in her was strong and after each visit, I felt the urge to break away from the invisible bonds of my master. One night, Lily somehow managed to drag me via her dreams into the Wake World and when she woke up, I was free. Free from the constant voices in my head telling me what I should do. Away from the prying eyes of my master, I began to live and quite soon, Lily became pregnant. We were both overjoyed and longed for the day when we could hold you in our arms.

Unfortunately though, my happiness was short lived as Volnar sent his Dream Stealers to find me. I could not risk his wrath upon my family and so I left Lily in an attempt to keep her safe. It broke my heart to walk away from her and our unborn child but I dared not risk her being found. I knew my master of old and he would hurt anyone to force me to do his bidding.

To numb the pain of leaving my beloved Lily, I went to the near-est bar but the more I drank, the more I started to remember. All I wanted was to be left in peace, so Volnar and I could go our separate ways. I knew I was too drunk to drive, so when I left the bar, I hailed a taxi. The driver could not speak very good English, so I sat in the front next to him, with the idea of directing him through the town. As we got to the traffic lights, they were red, so I screamed at him to stop. He didn't and instead smashed into an oncoming car. When I came to, I was in the driver's seat, alone in the cab.

Naturally I could not prove a thing. Besides, who would take the word of a drunk? Instead, I was sentenced to prison where the inmates spat upon me for my crime. One night, Volnar came to me in a dream and his power over me returned. He forced me to dream that I would hang myself and when the guards came to my cell the following morning I was found dead, suspended from the ceiling by my belt.

When I finally awoke, I found myself in a Judgment room, waiting to receive sentence. For the best part of my life, it had been a wretched one and I remember thinking that my final des-tination would be a hell dimension but to my surprise, the Oracle had different plans. One night, Joshua came to my room. He told me that I had not killed that family but a Dream Stealer, under the instruction of Volnar, broke through into the Wake World and stole the identity of the taxi driver. It was him that hit the other ve-hicle and framed me for the crime. Joshua offered me retribution to clear my name. All I had to do was work within the Judgment Halls, carrying out any task asked of me.

My sullen heart was lifted when I heard that Volnar had been defeated by the Dream Lord and trapped between the worlds. I felt I was finally free but this was short lived, as one day Volnar ap-peared once more in my head, forcing me to drag him into Judg-ment. I tried to tell Joshua of his plans but he said it was impos-sible and that my mind was playing tricks upon me.

One night, I was walking through the Judgment cells, when I sensed a strong soul energy from the other side of the wall. I do not know who had been waiting but somehow Volnar used this as his opportunity to break a hole into Judgment, a portal just large enough to haul himself through. He drained so much of my energy that when I awoke, death surrounded me everywhere. Panicking that I would be blamed, I ran and by good fortune found a way to escape. The rest I cannot recall with clarity but I do remember wandering on the top of the fire-mountain and dearest Camella finding me. She has hidden me here ever since."

With the story of his life now exposed, like a floodgate of truth gushing through the valley, tears of regret began rolling down Armon's face.

"This wasn't your fault," said Will kindly. "You've been a pawn in the Dark Lord's chess game. No matter what you did to change, he would always have found you. For that I'm so sorry but it was always going to happen. It was your destiny."

"Sorry, Will?" asked Armon. "Why should you be sorry? My regret is twofold. One, I am a weakened mind unable to protect myself against the darkest evils, and two, I did not get the opportunity to see you grow. I should have found a way to be with you and Lily."

"It would not have worked," Joshua told him. "There was no world that could have hidden you. Sooner or later you would have been found. You made the right choice, although I know it was the hardest thing for you to do."

Will fumbled around his neck and retrieved the locket that Vanisheo had given him all those years ago. He opened it and showed Armon the picture of his mother inside.

"My dearest Lily," Armon said as he looked upon her smiling face.

"It is time, Armon," interrupted Joshua. "You and your son must join your energies and confront Volnar. The power you hold will be your strength in your darkest hours. Your familiarity with the Dark Lord is the only chance we have."

Armon was still staring at the photo of his wife and so Joshua decided it was time to leave father and son alone.

"While you try and entertain Will for a few minutes Armon, the rest of us will engage upon a plan of attack," added the Oracle.

"I cannot do it, Joshua," Armon confessed. "I do not have the will power."

"Look!" interrupted Will. "The Dream Lord and I have risked our lives to put an end to this and we need all the help we can get. You're my father and to be honest, I don't know how I'm supposed to feel about that but we need you. If you can help us destroy Volnar for good, then that'll leave us time to get to know each other, to find that bond and rebuild the family we're supposed to be. I'm certainly willing to give it a go . . . how about you?"

"You are right," said Armon as his face began to light up with the sense of life bubbling through his veins. "I would dearly love to get to know you Will and if that means facing my demons, then so be it."

"So you are agreed?" asked Joshua.

Will and Armon looked at one another and smiled. An identical grin spanned across their faces.

"We are agreed," they said together.

"Good, good," continued Joshua. "Then it is settled but first, let us join the others. Your father can meet his allies and understand the strengths we have for reaching the final hour. All we need now is the guard to take us back."

As if by magic, a figure suddenly appeared from the shadows.

"Err hmm," said a voice, "I am here, my lords. I have been here for a while but did not wish to disturb you."

"Good, good," replied Joshua, "then lead on."

"Yes, lead on," echoed Armon as he swung his arms around Joshua and Will. "This is one meal I think I can enjoy."

22

A Surprise from the Skies

"What's taking them so long?" Connor asked Jasmine as his concern for his friend began to grow.

"Give them time." Jasmine smiled. "I am certain Will is safe. Joshua must have needed him for a good reason. We must trust him. He has already proven worthy of our loyalty."

"Besides," Kustos said, laughing as he perused the spread before them, "look at this food. It will give us an opportunity to have a head start on him."

Connor smiled weakly at Kustos' efforts to lighten the mood but still could not help but worry about his best friend. Something had happened, perhaps not physically but he sensed an emotional drain, one similar to his own experiences.

The dining room, compared to other grand kingdoms he had eaten in, was quite small and the long wooden table just managed to fit within the confines of the four walls. At either end of the room were two lit fires, providing the air with pleasant warmth. Two majestic paintings decorated each wall.

"So the lord and lady of your kingdom have two sons then?" Fortis asked Camella as he surveyed the family portraits.

"They did . . . once," replied the Butterhawk. "They were killed during training."

"That must have hit them hard?" interrupted Connor.

"Most training camps come with little danger," answered Camella, "but this was something that could not have been foreseen. Their test was to watch a particular man from the Wake World. His name was Primus. He was a serial killer in his own time and was given a life sentence of imprisonment. One day, whilst in confinement, there was a riot and during the lock down, two guards were inadvertently captured. Primus took it upon himself to protect them until they could be rescued. When normality resumed in the prison, Primus lost his life. He was stabbed one night, by one of the inmates.

Due to a final act of bravery protecting the guards, Primus was offered one last chance of redemption by taking the path of fire. What no one realised at the time, though, was that the man who had killed him was also walking the path at the same time and with him was a group of associates.

When Primus recognised his killer, a fight broke out, blocking the way for others. The two princes, Julian and Cameron, not thinking of their own safety, tried to intervene and were killed in the frenzy.

Ruthus and I were patrolling at the time and managed to track the two down and pass sentence, sending them to the Hall of Judgment, where they were adjudicated and sent to some evil dimension, a place of continual fighting."

"So that is why you and Ruthus live here?" asked Durban.

"Our parents were also killed whilst on duty and the lady and lord took pity upon us and offered their home. They needed an heir to carry on and saw Ruthus and myself as the perfect fit. They have been like parents to us and there is nothing we would not do for them."

Just then the door opened and Joshua, followed by Armon and Will, walked in. Without a word, Joshua sat down, leaving Will and his father to face the group.

"Err, hmm," Will uttered as he cleared his throat. "Armon, this is everybody."

Everyone stood up in turn and introduced him or herself, then, when all was quiet, Will continued.

"Guys," he said cautiously, "this is my father."

Silence immediately fell upon the room as they stared at Will and then at Armon. The similarity was obvious. Standing before them was father and son.

"Well, that's a bit of a bombshell," said Connor as he stood up and walked over to them. "Why don't you sit down and tell us all about it?"

"Connor!" echoed Armon as he tried to recall each name. "You are Will's friend, his brother and his family. I am glad he had someone in his life to stand by him."

"Connor is the Dream Lord," Will told his father.

"The son of Valient?" echoed Armon in disbelief. "No wonder things are the way they are. You and Connor are the good of life, whereas Volnar and I the opposite. Thank you, my lord, for protecting my son."

"You make it sound like a chore." Connor grinned. "Though sometimes perhaps it is." And he winked at his friend. "Our lives were intertwined at birth and over time we've saved each other many times. Please, come and sit down. I want to hear all about you. The only information we have on you is—" Connor looked over at Will who was profusely gesticulating a kill-the-sentence sign and so he immediately stopped. "Umm, please come and eat," he said, changing the subject as he politely showed Armon to his seat across from where he and Will were sitting.

Armon sat down next to Vanisheo who wiggled in his chair.

"Please tell us," demanded Vanisheo, "how did you kill that family and end up in prison?"

An awkward silence echoed around the room and then Joshua began to explain what really happened that night.

For hours they talked and shared adventures of survival and victories and for the first time in a very long time, Armon felt as though he belonged. Ashley also enjoyed the company and with each hour that passed, she sensed a bond between her and Connor. When asked about her experiences in the Wake World, she explained that a barrier had formed around that part of her memory and no matter how hard she tried, she could not break through.

With such relaxed company, the devastation covering the rest of Judgment was almost forgotten until, from out of nowhere, a blast violently shook the room. The group instinctively reached for plates and glasses to prevent them smashing to the floor.

"Camella, Ruthus," shouted a guard as he rushed into the room, "you have been followed. We are under attack."

"Followed? How? That is impossible," exclaimed Ruthus.

"That is irrelevant now," announced Camella as she jumped to her feet. "We must protect Armon and Ashley at all costs."

Reacting to her instructions, they all scrambled to the hallway, just as another explosion hit the temple, shaking it once more to its very foundation.

"What are they using?" asked Kustos as he helped his wife to her feet.

"It must be exploding arrows, my lord," said the guard who had been leading the way.

"But with so much power, where can we possibly hide?" asked Jasmine.

"We'll find a way," Connor assured her. "We haven't come this far to fail now."

For several minutes, they battled to reach the open courtyards; once out of the building and down the stairs, they took a moment to look behind. Billowing up into the sky, some distance away, were clouds of smoke. Camella and Ruthus looked as horror filled their faces.

"Flying Razars," gulped Camella. "I have not come across them before."

"Don't worry," Will told her, "a Razar is a Razar whatever its skill. We'll find a way to kill them."

Suddenly they heard a buzzing noise behind and, as they turned around, were faced with two more of the new species. The hyper action of their bug-like wings had given them away but even so, the group were unsure how they were supposed to fight them. Not waiting for an introduction, the Razars opened their mouths and spat out their tongues, catching Armon and Ashley around their waists. Fully satisfied that their victims were secure, they took flight and whisked them off into the sky.

"Camella," ordered Connor, "take Will and get Armon back. Ruthus, you're with me. We must rescue Ashley."

"But what about us?" asked Jasmine. "Let us help."

"You have to go with the guards and help wherever you can," he told her. "It's our fault that the city has been breached, and we must try and make amends."

Jasmine nodded her agreement, and as she did so, Ruthus starting running alongside Connor in preparation of taking him into the skies. To the Butterhawk's surprise, just as he was about to grab him, Connor's shirt tore at the top of his shoulders, and a pair of Butterhawk wings appeared, supporting the hues of various deep purples. The Dream Lord cried out as his energy took over and then jumped into sky. Like a native Butterhawk, he glided and swooped along the currents. Ruthus stopped and stared in disbelief.

"Stay with me, Ruthus," Connor ordered. "I need your soul energy to keep me in the air.

Camella and Will were already in hot pursuit, and using the currents to their advantage had almost caught up to the Razars. They could see Armon hanging precariously from the creature's tongue just below its body. Unable to break free, he struggled and wiggled in an attempt to slow the creature down, and to a certain extent, it was working. Sensing that a Butterhawk was close, the Razar turned onto its back and pulled out a bow and some fire-bomb arrows. Then, when fully satisfied the range was correct, he started to bombard them with his weapons. Camella skilfully dodged the arrows as they exploded on either side of her.

"I've an idea," Will called up to her as he hung from her grasp. "Can you get us a little closer?"

Thinking for a moment, she looked down and nodded, then found a current that projected them quickly towards the Razar. Anticipating a new attack, it pulled out another fire bomb and aimed it straight at Will.

"Don't dodge this one," the Dream Warrior shouted, just as the arrow appeared on track to hit him. "Let me go," he suddenly ordered, "and be prepared to catch us."

Camella was horrified by his suggestion but had learned to trust his judgment, so she released her grip. As Will fell, he used the air currents around him to slow his fall and drifted gracefully in the air. With time in his favour, he called upon his own gravity to slow the arrow down, and now, with little speed to its impact, he grabbed it and threw it back in the direction of the Razar. Within inches of its body, the projectile exploded, damaging the creature's wings and forcing it to drop its prey as it lost balance and spiralled earthwards. It missed the Sky Temple several feet below and continued falling even further until it hit the ground, creating a dust ball around the impacted area.

With the enemy out of the way, Will fell towards his father and somehow managed to grab him. Camella, who had been watching with interest from above, recognised her cue and swooped in for the rescue. With ease, she grabbed Will under the arms as he gripped tightly onto his father. For a Butterhawk, a single being was an easy courier, but with the weight of two men, Camella found herself rapidly losing height and tumbling towards the ground. Without panic, she quickly racked her brains for a solution, and as the meandering river below came into view, she summoned up what little strength she had left and released her package. It barely gave her sufficient time to find a current and glide herself, in an uncontrolled manner, to the ground. Her own descent was not as she would have wanted, as she landed with force and rolled over on impact. Will and Armon also made an unceremonious landing as they dropped into the river, disrupting the wildlife from its peaceful day.

"Is everyone alright?" asked the Butterhawk as she ran to the riverside. "I am so sorry. I could not take the weight."

Will and Armon swam to the edge and pulled their drenched bodies onto the bank.

"Wow! What a rush," said Armon as he rung the water from his sleeve. "Son, I can see your days are never dull."

Will looked at his father and smiled.

Despite the fact that they had made it this far, they were still in danger of being attacked again, and when Camella looked up to the skies and saw a few of her fellow Butterhawks flying past, she called out for assistance. Her lyrical voice rested upon the winds and reached the ears of a flyer. He immediately recognised the dulcet tones and looked down. Seeing Camella and her friends below, he circled around to approach.

"My lady," he told her as he landed by her side and bowed, "they are attacking one of our biggest cities."

"Are my friends still there?" Will asked, nervously.

"I believe so, my lord," replied the guard.

"We must go back, Camella," Will told her. "They'll need our help. As always they'll be heavily outnumbered."

"Do not fret so, Will." Camella smiled. "We will go back." And she then turned her attention back to the guard. "Take Armon for me," she instructed him. "I will take Will. We must get to the city and help."

"But I cannot soar the currents from here, my lady," he told her as he sniffed the air to try and locate the nearest path.

"That will be taken care of," Camella assured him as she looked at Will. "Just take hold of Armon."

The guard did as he was told and waited. For a second or two nothing happened but then he felt the rustle of a faint breeze as it ruffled his wings. A current had appeared out of nowhere, lifting him and Armon, up into the sky.

"Are you okay?" Will asked Camella as they stood alone.

"I am fine," she assured him "A little shaken from my graceless landing but otherwise in good health. I am more concerned for the dangers prowling the Sky Temple and Kalus."

"I know," replied Will with apprehension, "but at this moment in time, I'm more worried about you."

"I am honoured you take time over my welfare," she said as she blushed, "but we must go and help the others."

"I know—," he agreed, and before he had a chance to finish his sentence, he found himself taking to the air on the gravity disturbance he had created himself.

✤ ✤ ✤

"There they are Ruthus, just ahead," Connor shouted to the Butterhawk as he watched the Razar casually swinging Ashley from side to side.

"Fly higher, Connor," Ruthus advised him. "The currents are faster above us. We might be able to gain on the creature."

Connor did as he was instructed and pushed himself upwards. Immediately, he picked up speed and soon was swooping and soaring like a seasoned Butterhawk. With air on their side and no additional weight, both Connor and Ruthus soon caught up their enemy but the silent attack, which both had hoped for, was short lived. The creature had sensed their approach and had turned on his back to prepare to attack. Taking aim, the Razar released a barrage of fire headed arrows that whistled through the air like a bug bomb. In an effort to avoid the weapons, Ruthus and Connor split up, as the projectiles whizzed past their ears.

"We cannot get close enough to take him," Ruthus shouted above the explosions.

"I've an idea." Connor suddenly grinned. "Create a diversion but don't stray too far away from me. I won't be able to sustain this form without your power."

"You do not make it easy, do you, Connor?" replied the Butterhawk.

"Life would be so boring if I did," answered the Dream Lord.

For a few seconds, Ruthus pondered on his plan of action. The simplest of ideas came to him as he started to wave his arms to attract the Razars attention.

"Hey, over here?" he shouted at the top of his voice. "Do you think you can catch me?"

The Razar, easily goaded by the Butterhawk, turned his attentions on Ruthus and started to shower him with a concentration of arrows. All too quickly, the creature forgot the Dream Lord as Connor silently approached from above. When he was within what he considered a sensible range, he shouted down to the Razar.

"Up here, lizard," he yelled. "Forgotten about me?"

Ruthus quickly backed away as he watched the Razar turn his attention on Connor, bombarding him with what seemed like an endless supply of arrow bombs. Connor was relieved to see he had read the Razar correctly and as a couple of the weapons approached him, he grabbed one in each hand. Avoiding the other projectiles, he then began to fly directly towards his adversary. Panic set in as the creature suddenly realised he was in danger and in an effort to escape, he loosened his hold on Ashley and dropped her.

Ruthus was quick to react to the situation and dived down in an attempt to catch her before she hit the ground. The reputation of his skills had foundation as he caught her several feet from the earth and landed them both in an almost controlled manner. Together they rolled across the grass and stood up. As they looked up, they could still see Connor heading directly toward the Razar. With Ruthus out of proximity, the Dream Lord had lost his wings and was falling uncontrollably towards the ground. Without fear or thought of his own safety, he somehow managed to move within inches of the Razar and force the two weapons into its skull. For a brief moment Connor had the opportunity to steal its image and a pair of wings sprouted from his back once more. This plan, however, had a short shelf life as within seconds of his attack on the Razar he heard the arrow bomb explode, killing the creature and also his means of a safe landing. Instead, he now found himself falling helplessly towards the ground.

Death was never something he had feared and accepting that his time was up, Connor closed his eyes and waited for the impact. To his surprise and relief, it did not come as he felt himself gently rise into the air. He looked up and there was Ruthus smiling down at him.

"That was close. Thanks, Ruthus." He grinned.

"That was by far the craziest plan I have known anyone to come up with." The Butterhawk smiled in adoration.

"I did actually plan that in my head to go a lot smoother," Connor told him as they landed next to Ashley.

"Are you okay, Ashley?" Connor asked her as she hugged him from relief for their safety.

"I think so," she replied.

"I know you probably do not want to fly again, Ashley," said Ruthus, "but we must get back to the others."

She nodded her agreement and as she turned to Connor, she noticed the small butterfly wings protruding from his back once more. Accepting Connor's strange powers for what they were, she smiled.

"Then it looks as though we are ready," she said.

Gently Ruthus held onto Ashley and together they soared up into the sky. Connor quickly followed. For several minutes they flew towards the Sky City, and once within range, they could see a heavy battle taking place around the city walls.

Jasmine had split herself in two as she fought alongside Kustos and Fortis. Vanisheo was wielding his sword with Will and Camella by his side. Even Joshua, Armon and Durban were holding their own against the flying Razars. Although the enemy outnumbered them, every so often, Connor caught sight of a Razar or Soul Cruncher fall to the ground but he was unable to see their attacker. Reminded of a previous battle, he slowed his mind and soon saw the images of a darkened, lithe figure. Her fighting moves were that of a beautiful dancer as she controlled the gravity around her, enabling her to punch, kick and block. Although Nuwa Lin was surrounded by multiple Razars, not once did she appear threatened by any of their moves. Connor smiled to himself at seeing her again, as he and Ruthus landed with Ashley.

By this time the rest of their group had noticed the approach and had managed to manoeuvre themselves together, awaiting further instructions.

"We must get to the edge of the kingdom where the river flows out to the sea," Joshua told them as they all continued to fight. "That is one of the entry points into the Kingdom of Aquamarine."

"And what's there?" asked Will as he parried another blow from a Razar.

"They are the guardians of the passage into the Judgment Halls," Joshua advised them.

"But will they let us in?" asked Connor.

"Without a doubt, I assure you," the Oracle told him. "They are extremely good friends of mine."

"I will find some of our guards to fly you there," Camella shouted above the din of the battle, and she quickly disappeared into the thick of the fighting.

Will was annoyed at her recklessness but was relieved when he saw her returning only minutes later with a small army of men.

Each Butterhawk picked up a non-flyer and took to the skies. Connor was the last to leave the ground and as he looked behind him, he saw a Soul Cruncher about to mount a flying Razar.

"Over there!" the Cruncher ordered. "Follow them!"

Connor knew they were in trouble. If one Soul Cruncher had taken to the skies, others would follow.

"We've got company, Camella," he warned her as he leapt into the air and soared up into the sky.

She looked back and saw a small squadron of flying Razars, each supporting the haggard frame of a Soul Cruncher.

"We are so close to the edge of the kingdom, we must keep going," Camella shouted to all her men. "Do not stop for anyone or anything."

Hanging just beneath Camella, Will managed to glance behind and saw the Soul Crunchers and Razars rapidly approaching. He knew he was the only one who could slow them down, and thrusting his hands forwards, he caused a swirling, howling storm. The uncontrollable winds did as Will had hoped and tussled the enemy around erratically, slowing down their pursuit. With their pathway temporarily cleared, the group of Butterhawks continued to glide until they finally reached their destination.

"We are here," Camella cried a few minutes later.

Familiar with their own boundaries, one by one the Butter-hawks landed until everyone was safely on firm ground. Only then did they all look at each other to see who would instruct them further. Joshua stepped forward. At the edge of Kalus, he cautiously peered over and saw the white cotton wool clouds enveloped by a halo of water spray. A sound of crashing water as it battered against the rocks below deafened any other noise.

"Here they come," Fortis yelled as he saw the Soul Crunchers and Razars appear once more behind them.

"We have to go now," ordered Will as he grabbed Camella's hand.

"I cannot follow you, Will," Camella told him sadly with tears in her eyes. "My wings become weak in the water and if submerged for any length of time, they would shred and evaporate into their surroundings. As much as I do not want to leave you, you must do this without me."

"Then I'll stay," he told her, "and help you fight the Razars."

"That is not possible, Will," interrupted Joshua. "You are the only one who can harness the water and allow us all to breathe. Remember the training I put you through?"

Will looked at Joshua and back to Camella. He knew he was the only one who could take them through the water and even though he did not like the idea of leaving Camella behind, there was little choice.

"Fine," he moaned begrudgingly then added, "When we all hit the water, assuming the fall alone doesn't kill us, don't fight it but let it fill your lungs. It'll be an uncomfortable sensation, and your natural reaction will be to panic but try and relax and just let it happen. Once this is done, I can harness the oxygen from the water and envelop you all in your own invisible air bubble. You must remember though that at this time, I'm vulnerable. My entire concentration will be keeping us alive, so if we're attacked, it's up to you guys to defend us."

"Go, Will," Camella urged him as she kissed his cheek. "Ruthus and my army will hold the Razars off for as long as we can."

"Well . . . don't do anything heroic," he ordered her. "I want you safe. I'm coming back for you so make sure you're here, waiting for me."

"But how will you know where 'here' is?" she asked him.

"Just trust me . . . I'll find you wherever you are."

She smiled briefly before turning away for fear of showing her own emotion. The last thing Will would want was to see some distraught female, proclaiming undying love.

Joshua was the first to step to the edge and look down.

"This is what they call a leap of faith, I suppose," he told the others. "Trust that the water below will cushion your fall. Once in the sea, follow me and stay as close as you can." And with that, he jumped forward and was gone.

The others peered over the side and saw nothing apart from the fluffy white clouds hovering just below them. Kustos took Jasmine's hand and together they jumped, followed shortly behind by Durban and Fortis. Ashley and Nuwa Lin thought nothing of taking the leap forward, leaving just Connor, Will, Armon and Vanisheo.

"Come on, Will," urged his friend, "we have to go."

Will said nothing. Instead, Vanisheo tapped Connor's leg. The Dream Lord looked down as the Hallucium spoke.

"Leave this to me, Connor," he told the Dream Lord. "I will make sure he makes the jump. Please go and wait for us."

Connor knew that his own tactless approach would probably not improve the encouragement and so he took once last glance at Vanisheo, then Will and urged Armon to jump. Together the two of them disappeared from view.

"You must go, Will," Camella urged him. "Judgment's fate is in your hand."

"But what of your fate?" he asked her.

"Trust me, Will," interrupted Vanisheo. "Camella will be waiting for your return."

"Are you sure about that?" he queried.

"As sure as any man," replied the Hallucium emphatically.

If the truth be known, Vanisheo no more knew whether or not Camella would survive the fight against the Soul Crunchers than the next person but as he was not human, he felt his final words were not exactly a lie. Will's mission was not an easy one and at the end of the day, it might be that he was the one who did not return and then any false promises made would hurt no one.

"I'll be coming back for you, Camella." Will told her. "So make sure you're here to meet me." With that, he kissed her passionately on the lips.

An electrical charge buzzed excitedly from one to another, creating an amazing warmth through their bodies. It was a sign that despite the low possibilities of finding someone within the three worlds who was your perfect match somehow the Butterhawk and the Dream Warrior had managed it.

Camella blushed at such a demonstration of affection and smiled as she watched Will grab Vanisheo's hand and jump over the edge.

Her feminine thoughts of love and romance however, were soon short lived as Ruthus interrupted her daydream.

"Here they come, dear sister. I hope you are ready," he said.

"As ready as I will ever be," she replied.

23

Into the Depths of Aquamarine

As Will and Vanisheo landed in the water, they experienced an unexpected sensation. Instead of hitting a solid wall, they felt as though a cushion of air had reached out and gently drawn them into the river. Immediately on impact, they kicked their feet and, as they did so, found themselves gracefully heading towards the others.

The clarity of the water was incredible as they saw their friends paddling their arms to keep them underwater. Bubbles were systematically escaping from their mouths as they struggled to hold their breath.

"Let the water into your lungs," Will burbled to them the best he could, as water sloshed around in his mouth and down his windpipe.

Panic raced through their minds but they obeyed his instructions and once the water began to drain into their lungs, they ceased fighting and allowed the sensation of their waning life seep away.

Jasmine struggled as she tried to gain control and then stopped. All of a sudden, she discovered she could breathe and what fear she had was replaced by the confidence of survival. Having already experienced the sensation before, Connor allowed himself to be taken by the water and calmly swam over to join his friend.

"Camella will be fine," he assured him. "The quicker we get this done, the sooner you can get back to her and tell her about your latest adventures."

Will smiled as he understood the words and then looked around to check that the others were safe. They were fine. Jasmine's hair flowed elegantly around her as she flapped her hands to retain her position. She looked like the most stunning of sirens preying on the lives of men. Joshua was a more comical image as his dark robes wrapped around his hidden body, showing the contours of his well-fed stomach but still providing an air of mystery as his hood continually flopped across his face. Ashley calmly waved her arms up and down to keep her in place, whilst Vanisheo was the strangest of them all. His lightweight body barely displaced the water and his movements were no different from the way he moved on land. The warriors—Kustos, Fortis, Durban, and Armon—were obviously out of place as they flayed and kicked to retain some air of normality but they lacked the finesse that Jasmine was portraying. Connor and Will smiled to each other over the images before them and then beckoned to Joshua.

"Follow me," Connor mouthed as he pushed his way down into the depths below.

Tiny fish dodged around the group as they swam and nipped at their clothing to see what strangers had arrived in their territory. Sea plants swayed majestically backwards and forwards with the current, waving at the newcomers as they passed. Jasmine was mesmerised by such life and colour and was surprised to see how vibrant the seas became, even as the sunlight faded from above.

Endlessly they continued down until finally Joshua pointed to a small gap, barely large enough for them to squeeze through. Connor studied the entrance then, forcing his frame through the diminutive opening, he disappeared from sight. The others wasted no time at all following suit and quite soon only Will and Vanisheo were left behind.

"Are you prepared, Will?" asked Vanisheo as he pushed past.

"Prepared for what?" he queried.

"You will see," the Hallucium grinned.

Once they had all managed to wriggle through the tiny portal, they pushed themselves forward. The tunnel was tight with little room to turn around and so the only way to go was straight on. For some time they slowly progressed through the water-filled passageway, then, without warning, they found themselves heading upwards. Unexpectedly Will's head broke the surface, and he looked around in disbelief.

"Come," said Joshua as he offered Will his hand to assist him out of the water, "Aquamarine is not far now."

Will was speechless as he looked around at the glistening cave, shards of multicoloured lights reflecting against the black, smooth stone. Somewhere above them, the rays of Judgment had filtered their way through, illuminating the cavern like a diamond's prism.

"Pretty impressive," said Will as he joined his friends. "Now where did you say the entrance to Aquamarine was?"

"Why," replied Joshua, "just over here." And he walked off towards the side of the cave then stopped. "Oh no!" he moaned with a trace of uncomfortable surprise. "I cannot believe we are too late."

"What do you mean . . . too late?" asked Fortis. "Where is it?"

Joshua pointed to a large patch of ice frozen into a perfect circle.

"It is down there," he replied sadly.

Connor peered at the patch of ice and then jumped on it to ascertain the density but even his weight did not crack an inch of the surface.

"Looks pretty thick to me," declared Durban as he peered through the ice. "I am not sure how we are going to tackle this one."

"You have no chance of breaking through," said a voice from behind them.

Together, they all spun around and saw an old man sitting upon a flat rock. He was extremely old and his perfect grey hair was cut with immaculate care. Only his faded clothes gave any indication that he had been sitting around for some time.

"I've been here for months and still have not managed to find a solution," he said.

Jasmine started in disbelief as she studied the face in the colourful light, then when she was positive of her assumptions, she smiled and rushed forward to hug him.

"Gramps," she exclaimed between cuddles, "I never thought I would see you again."

"Oh, my dearest Jasmine," he smiled as he pried her away from him. "How beautiful you have become. I have been waiting for your arrival but did not understand the time it would take you."

"So how long have you been here?" asked Connor.

"Time in such a place is hard to define," replied the old man, "but for many months I have waited."

"And how did you know we would be coming here?" asked Kustos.

"I have been in contact with my son for many years," answered Gramps. "Frederick advised me of your journey and with much research from stories I had heard, I deduced that eventually you would arrive at Aquamarine. There have been rumours for many years that the Judgment Halls are located in this area, so it seemed the most logical place to wait. When I finally managed to get myself here and believe me that was a feat in itself, I found the entrance frozen."

"So why didn't you return to the surface?" asked Connor.

"Look at me," replied the old man. "I have seen far too many moons. My lungs could only just get me down here. There was no way I could make a return journey."

"There is no way you could have held your breath for that distance either," interrupted Kustos. "How did you really get here?"

"Good gracious!" exclaimed Gramps as he stared at the Lord of the Waterfall Kingdom. "You have grown into quite a man. No wonder my granddaughter loves you so."

"Do not change the subject." Kustos laughed. "Just tell us how you got here."

"You are right," sighed Jasmine's grandfather. "I did have some help. A friend of mine found some explosive weed. A rare commodity I can tell you. Once eaten, it expands the lungs, enabling you to fill your lungs to the capacity of a couple of hours. The trouble was," added Gramps as he scratched his head, "I only had enough weed for a one-way trip. I suppose I did not really think about the return journey."

"It was amazing you got this far," exclaimed Jasmine as she hugged her grandfather again. "Everyone," she added as she turned to her friends, "this is my grandfather."

"Please to meet you, sir," replied Connor as he held out his hand.

"You must be Connor," said the old man. "You look just like your father at that age. My name is Harry." And he took Connor's hand and shook it profusely.

A couple more introductions were made until Harry came face to face with Armon.

"What is he doing here?" snarled Harry angrily.

"Do not be afraid, old man," interrupted Joshua, quickly trying to diffuse the tension, "Armon is here at our invitation. With the help of his son, Will, they are destined to defend us against the reign of Volnar."

"He has a son?" asked Harry and then recalled the conversations he had over the years with Frederick. "Ahh yes, Will. My memory is not as it once was. I do remember now my son telling me of Will. I believe it was once thought he was the Dream Lord. The bond between Connor and Will is strong, a brother's love that has protected them through good and evil. It is an honour to meet you, Will." And he held out his hand to greet the Dream warrior who had been waiting next in line.

"It is pleasure to meet you, sir," replied Will politely. "It's true that Connor is my family and always will be but now I've found a father I never knew I had and he too has taken a place in my life."

"Can we get over the niceties and find a way of saving Aquamarine?" interrupted Fortis, impatient over the endless introductions.

"Ahh, yes, Fortis," said Harry. "A man after my own heart. Never wants to hang around but always eager to get the job done."

"There is nothing wrong with that," replied Fortis as he tried to defend his impatience.

"Nor did I say there was, young prince," smiled the old man.

"The way I see it," interrupted Durban who had been peering through the solid ice, "it must be between fifty and one hundred metres thick. There is no way we are going to be able to bore through that."

"Out of the way," ordered Fortis as he stepped upon the ice. "I think this is up to me." And with that, he called on his energy and burst into flames.

For several minutes, the fire lashed around his form but even with the amount of heat he was creating, barely a drop of water appeared on the surface.

"It's useless," he finally gasped as his strength faded. "At this rate we could be here for months."

"Perhaps not," said Ashley as she rummaged under her coat. "I think I might have an idea. I managed to recover this." And she produced a fire blade.

"I do not think the blade will penetrate such thickness," replied Joshua.

"Maybe not on its own," interrupted Connor as he turned to Will, "but with Will's help, it might. Do you remember on the fire mountain when you harnessed the fire and heat? Do you think you can do it again?"

"I'm certain I could," the Dream Warrior confirmed, "but even I don't have the power to travel through one hundred metres of solid ice."

"But what would happen if once you have heated the surface, I used my sonic clap?" queried Kustos. "Would that do it?"

"I think that might just work," replied Durban.

"I think you are forgetting something," said Fortis. "Once you execute the plan, you will fry everyone below the ice. The heat will be so extreme, it will cook anything in its path."

"But not if Will uses this directly afterwards," interrupted Nuwa Lin as she retrieved another blade from her boot.

"An ice blade?" asked Will. "But how?"

"Camella handed it to me just before we jumped," the ninja told him. "She said that ice under water might come in handy. Could you not harness the cold after the melt to bring the temperature down?"

"I think this crazy idea might just work." Will grinned.

"Well, it's the only plan we have," said Connor as he winked at Ashley for her contribution. "So we'd better get started. Will," he added, "take the fire blade first and as soon as you feel the ice crack, let me know. I can then pass you the weapon. Stand back everyone, it looks as though we are going to get wet again."

"Kustos, are you coming?" he asked as he and Will walked out to the centre of the ice.

"I would not miss this for the world." Their friend grinned as he joined them.

With the three of them centred upon the ice, Connor handed Will the fire blade and then stepped back a little to give him room to manoeuvre. Closing his eyes and concentrating, Will raised the blade above his head. The invisible energy of his thoughts glowed, as his power entered the weapon. When he was fully satisfied of its strength, he let out a loud cry and slammed down into the ice beneath his feet. At the moment of impact, the blade pierced a few inches into the solid portal and quivered as it stuck fast.

Apart from the initial cry emitting from Will's mouth, silence echoed painfully around the cavern. It was Connor who first picked up the noise, as a gentle crack, barely audible, emanated from beneath their feet.

"It's working," he exclaimed with delight as his feet sunk into a foot of water and steam began to sizzle around them. "Now, Kustos, now!" he yelled as he sloshed his way over to Will to exchange the blades.

Kustos leaned over so he could see Aquamarine many metres below, then he raised his arms out and slapped them together as hard as he could. The sonic impact ripped through the remaining ice, as Connor, Will and Kustos disappeared and in their place a geyser of steam and boiling water spewed up into the air. The others held their breath in fear, waiting for the re-emergence of the trio but no one appeared. Minute after minute went by until they had all but given up. Only when the heat had settled did a ripple of water become visible on the surface of the once frozen portal, and suddenly three heads appeared.

"Well . . . are you coming or not?" asked Will.

A sigh of relief echoed around, as one by one they jumped into the water. When all of them were in, Will once more harnessed his energy and provided them with the ability to breathe. Like fish just returned to home, they excitedly swam towards the bottom, where a small cave awaited their arrival. As the group approached, it suddenly transformed before their eyes into a cavern of great depth and length, mimicking every colour of the rainbow as it reflected the light penetrating from the upper levels. Each ray of sunshine lit up a tiny mirror and every inch of the underwater city was bathed in light.

"Wow," mouthed Nuwa Lin as best she could, "this is the most amazing thing I have ever seen. Look at the colours . . . and the buildings?"

"And the fish," exclaimed Jasmine excitedly. "I have never seen such brilliance before. They are so beautiful."

"Beautiful yes," agreed Kustos, "but unfortunately that does not apply to them . . . look." And he pointed to line of Aqua soldiers swimming towards them.

From first appearance, they were human-like. Only their webbed feet and the gills on the side of their necks gave away their marine origins. Their clothes were made from fish skin and an electric charge encircled the whole group as a protective shield. In their hands they each held a small dagger, created from the teeth of some oversized fish, undoubtedly sourced from within their waters.

"Halt!" ordered the Aqua guards as they approached the group. "Who are you?"

"We're friends," announced Connor as he slowly approached them.

"Friend or foe, we cannot tell," came the reply.

"We're on your side . . . really we are," confessed Will.

"And whose side would that be?" challenged one of the guards.

"Team Oracle," answered the Dream Lord.

For a moment the amphibians stared at their unwelcomed guests. They were not used to seeing so many land people in one go.

"Time here has very little reference to above," the guard replied, "and for all we know, we could have been frozen down here for many centuries. We do not receive uninvited visitors, so go while you still can."

"Wait! Wait!" ordered Joshua as he swam towards the guards.

"My Lord Joshua," exclaimed one of them as he recognised the hooded figure, "Is that really you or some trick played upon my mind?"

"It is me, Joshua of the Judgment Halls," replied the Oracle. "Now please, lower your weapons and stand down. We have not come here to fight but to ask for your help."

An Aqua guard at the head of the group signalled to his team to lower their weapons and as he did so, another swam to the forefront. Following was a woman.

"My Lord Joshua," he said sadly, "what has happened to our beloved Judgment? The last thing any of us remember was a darkened shadow and then our kingdom was frozen from the outside world. We have failed you, my lord."

"As I have failed all of you," said Joshua in reply, "but all will be returned as it should be. As much as I would love to spend time with you, I cannot stay, although once this is over, I shall return. We must get to the Judgment Halls as quickly as we can. Our destiny is there."

"Uhh . . . hmm, Joshua?" queried Fortis as he swam towards the Aqua people.

"I am sorry," apologised Joshua, "over time I have lost my manners. This is Lord Reiser and Lady Sarcha of Aquamarine. They are the keepers and protectors of the Judgment Halls."

Fortis and the others nodded in acknowledgement of their introduction as the Oracle continued.

"Lord Reiser, Lady Sarcha. These brave souls have given their lives to rid us of the great evil," he said.

"I fear it will be a waste of time," replied Lord Reiser. "This malevolence is far stronger than any of us together can destroy."

"But we must try anyway," interrupted Armon.

"I am afraid it is not your effort that we criticise," replied Lady Sarcha. "Without a way into the Judgment Halls, you cannot begin to stand up to Volnar."

"But I thought this was the way in?" queried Connor.

"It was," answered Lord Reiser, "but the pathway to the Judgment Halls has been blocked. Even before we were sent into an ice age."

"Blocked by what?" asked Nuwa Lin with curiosity.

"By a creature so powerful we dare not send any more of our men to face it. Too many of our warriors have lost their lives. It would be inexcusable to risk anymore," replied Lady Sarcha sadly.

"I am sorry for your loss," interrupted Jasmine, "but we have been sent here to a complete a mission and that is exactly what we will do. Does this creature have a name?"

"No!" answered Lord Reiser. "It has no name but we have called it Shivan."

"Well, that doesn't sound too bad," said Will. "What does this monster look like? Why can't it be defeated?"

"It has a large body mass that produces an electrical charge," said Lady Sarcha. "If it touches you, it will shock your nervous system, so you cannot react."

"Doable," interrupted Will.

"But it also has many tentacles. Mesmerising you into submission, they wrap themselves around you and squeeze your life force from your body. To make it even worse, the Shivan can poison. It has the ability to squirt ink at you and when the black liquid touches your skin, it will paralyse every fibre of your body, making you helpless but still alive. When it is hungry, it will eat and your flesh will be fresh. Just how they like it."

"Wow!" exclaimed Connor. "That's a bit graphic, isn't it?"

"You asked for the description," replied Lady Sarcha, "and I merely obliged."

"And so you did, my lady," said Fortis. "It is just as well for us that we like an unwinnable fight."

Everyone started at Fortis in disbelief and then looked away.

"Oh come on, you guys," pleaded Fortis. "When the odds are against us, that is when we are at our best. Besides, it is not as if we have a choice here."

Again no one spoke until Joshua broke the silence.

"Reiser, my friend," he said, "can you take us to where the creature dwells? If we are to kill it, we must start thinking of a strategy."

"If you are really going to do this," said Lord Reiser, "then I will join you with a few of my best men. The problem is as much ours as yours. If we are to release our kingdom from the evils of the Dark Lord, then we must kill the monster. Besides, it will open the way to the Judgment Halls once again."

"If you are going, my love," interrupted Lady Sarcha, "I am coming as well and this time, I will not take no for an answer."

"She sounds just like you, Jasmine." Vanisheo smiled as he swam off after Joshua.

"I am not like that," she replied.

Connor, Will and Kustos looked at each other and smiled.

"What?" retorted Jasmine as she swam behind with her grandfather. "I am not."

24

Through the Maze

For what felt like hours, they swam through Aquamarine, viewing the business of its people as they attempted to rebuild their lives. For many months the people had been frozen in time and only now could they return to the darkened normality.

Stroke after stroke, the group moved on, until eventually the expanse decreased in size and forced itself into a small, dark passageway. The absence of light only added to their trepidation as the memorable glories of the myriad of colour disappeared, enveloping them in nothing but fear.

Familiar with the territory, Lord Reiser pushed himself to the front and led the way. Not a word was spoken as the group sensed the chill of evil in the water. Even when the passageway opened into another large cavern, their spirits did not rise. Through fear of death, the tiny mirrors used to illuminate the seas lay unattended, and even though a splinter of light had managed to penetrate, an aura of desolation still filled the underwater room.

On the far side of the cavern was the only other way out and the route to the Judgment Halls but this was blocked with heavy boulders strewn randomly across the entrance.

"My lord," whispered one of the Aqua warriors as he pointed to the water, "the creature is over there on the bottom. I believe it is awake."

"Where?" whispered Will. "I don't see it."

"It is there, Will, trust me," replied Lord Reiser. "It can change its body mass at will, to camouflage itself from its enemies. If you focus hard enough, you can just make out its piercing black eyes."

Will concentrated in the direction Lord Reiser was pointing and finally established the image of two beady dark eyes peering up into the cavern.

"So when you attacked this creature before," asked Fortis, "did you injure it anyway?"

"I am afraid not," answered Lord Reiser sadly. "We were unable to get close enough to inflict any wounds."

"So we have nothing to work with then," surmised Fortis as he noticed the disappointment on Lord Reiser's face. "That is a good thing though, my lord," he quickly added. "Whatever plan we put together, the creature will not be expecting it."

"Well, whatever we do, Will must sit this fight out," stated Kustos who was desperately trying to come up with an attack. "He must be close but safe. Without him, none of us can breathe. Ashley, Armon, Joshua, I suggest you stay with Will to protect him."

"I'll be okay on my own," admitted Connor. "As long as I stay close to the Aqua men, I can morph into one of them."

As Connor spoke, one of the guards swam off and a ripple of bubbles floated innocently down to the bottom of the cavern. The minute vibration disturbed the creature's sleep and it emitted a high-pitched scream, resounding against the walls as it fully awoke.

Horror seeped through their veins as they watched the Shiven emerge from the murky seabed. Agile for its size, it moved through the water, its tentacles gracefully dancing as it ascended closer to them. The lack of emotion stared out of its lidless eyes. Several of the Aqua guards panicked as they saw the monster approach and found themselves trapped by the flaying tentacles. Connor watched in macabre amazement as their life force was squeezed from their bodies, whilst others became drunk by the insurgence of toxic ink as it swished around in the water. One by one, the unfortunate guards froze from the paralysing substance seeping through their pores, slowly killing them from its lasting effects. Blood oozed from their eyes, ears and gills, until their existence no longer had the will to support life.

"This is going to be a lot harder than we thought!" Connor shouted to Fortis.

With the first line of attack almost gone, only Lord Resier and Lady Sarcha remained. For Connor's sake, it was imperative that they survive and he was just going to suggest they join Will when the Shivan noticed Jasmine and Nuwa Lin and quickly changed direction to intercept.

The ninja was as graceful in water as she was on the land, swimming with ease to avoid the tentacles. It was Jasmine who was more at risk as she tried to dodge the life-sucking appendages. Only Harry's quick thinking saved her life. He grabbed her legs from below and dragged her to the seabed.

Durban and Fortis tried to attract its attention next by swimming around it, attempting to find a weakened spot. If it had one, it was not readily viewable as the masses of tentacles swayed and flowed in the currents, protecting the main body.

Kustos quickly swam off to find Jasmine. He had seen the attack and wanted to make sure she was safe but as he reached the lower levels, he felt something wrap around his ankle. He knew instinctively what it was. He had been caught by the Shivan. Only seconds later he felt another tentacle wind itself around his body, pulling him towards the creature whilst attempting to squeeze the life force from his frame.

Jasmine looked up and screamed in horror as she saw her beloved Kustos fighting for his life. Alerted by her exclamation and greedy for more, the creature turned his attentions on the princess and Harry as it directed more of its tentacles towards them. The old man frantically waved his arms around to try and elude the appendages but still felt something grab his arm and pull him off in another direction. Panic-stricken, he turned around just in time to see Jasmine following the same pathway. Together they focussed upwards and through the murky waters, they could just make out the forms of Durban and Fortis, pulling them to safety.

Kustos, on the other hand, was not so fortunate. It was time for him to make his peace and accept his fate but as the seconds ticked by, he was certain the grip around his body and ankle was beginning to loosen, and he could breathe once more. His vision cleared just in time to see Connor pull an ice blade from the tentacle and smash it into a mass of splinters, which floated aimlessly in the water. Kustos, still stunned by his experience, began to fall but Connor deftly eased himself through the water and caught him. Then with the skill of an Aquamariner, he glided down to where Joshua was hiding.

"Heal him, Joshua," he ordered. "We need all the hands we can get." And as Connor looked up, he noticed the damaged tentacle had regenerated and a new one stood in its place.

"Oh, come on," he moaned out aloud. "Give us a fighting chance here? Lord Resier?" he added who had been hiding behind their electric shield, "this is useless, we cannot kill that thing."

"So what is the plan now?" asked Fortis as he, Durban, Jasmine and Harry joined them behind the electrical force.

"We think we might have one," said a voice from below.

It was Vanisheo and Nuwa Lin emerging from the depths.

"Nuwa Lin and I were able to swim beneath the beast and noticed a huge gill on its underside," said Vanisheo as they reached the others. "I know we cannot touch the Shivan because its electrical charge will kill us but if we could block it, we could drown it."

"And how do you propose we do that?" asked Lord Reiser, not at all convinced by the new plan.

"We need to create a diversion, so its underbelly is exposed," replied Vanisheo. "Then when Nuwa Lin thinks it is safe, she will swim beneath the creature and jam a boulder into its gill, thus rendering it helpless."

"That is madness," exclaimed Lord Reiser, "but at the same time . . . brilliant."

"Which is why, you, my lord, Lady Sarcha, must join Joshua below," interrupted Connor. "You kingdom needs you."

The royal couple did not object. The plan was a foolhardy venture best left to experts who thought nothing of impossible odds and although Connor and his crew appeared a little insane, the rulers of Aquamarine believed in them. With a smile for good luck, they left the group and eased their way to the bottom, leaving the rest to take on the might of the Shivan.

Connor looked around at the ground and decided on the pairing for the diversions.

"Durban," he said, "you're with me. Fortis, you and Jasmine swim on the other side from us. Vanisheo, Nuwa Lin, we'll try and give you as much time as we can but I've a hunch it won't be long before the creature works out what we're doing."

The six of them looked at each other and nodded. At least now they had a plan. All that was left was to execute it or die.

Connor and Durban started the attack and swam off above the Shivan. Its beady black eyes watched them drift across its path and instantly retaliated by thrusting a tentacle in their direction. Connor somehow managed to avoid the appendage but Durban felt the suckered limb begin to wrap around his leg. Prepared for such an attack, the Dream Lord quickly changed direction. Armed with the ice blade, he thrust it into the tentacle, causing the power of the weapon to discharge its frozen force, enabling Durban to smash himself free. Annoyed by such retribution, the Shivan then decided to attack with full force and all its tentacles began to weave their way through the water towards the fleeing pair.

"Go now!" Jasmine instructed Nuwa Lin and Vanisheo. "Swim with care and keep out of sight if you can. You are our only hope."

"No pressure then," replied Vanisheo as he turned to swim away.

Jasmine and Fortis saw them go, whilst at the same time they kept an eye on the monster below and how quickly it grew weary of its limbs being frozen. Rather than progress with the game any further, the Shivan decided to turn its attention to Vanisheo and Nuwa Lin as they swam to the bottom of the cavern. If the plan were going to work, Fortis would have to attract its attention.

"Hey! Over here!" he shouted as loud as he could.

A different noise did the trick, as the Shivan quickly switched its concentration to Jasmine and Fortis, who were waving profusely at the creature. To the Shivan, this was an easy meal, and slowly it moved its tentacles towards them. Fortis quickly focussed and within seconds, he was glowing like the fading embers of a fire, boiling the water around him. The monster was unaware of such an anomaly and thrust a tentacle towards him. It emitted a screeching call as a sensation of pain ran through the limb. Quickly it retracted the appendage from its prey. At first Jasmine and Fortis thought it was a cry of pain but then suddenly, disturbing the murky waters below, appeared another Shivan, nimbly swimming through the water to assist its mate. At the first assessment, this one was much smaller than the monster they had already encountered and its tentacles were far fewer in number. It also appeared that its only weapon was the electrical charge produced as it swam.

Before Jasmine had a chance to warn Fortis, one of the tentacles grabbed him. He spat out a mouthful of water in pain as the current ran through his body. Fearing a further attack, Jasmine's mind raced for a quick solution, but as she was doing so, a sudden pulse vibrated from the seabed below, forcing its way through the water. It missed her by inches as it ripped through the tentacle attached to Fortis. As the princess peered through the blood-clouded water, she could just make out the image of Kustos as he swam back into hiding. His strength had still not fully returned and to join in the main attack would put the rest of his friends at risk.

Jasmine looked longingly as her beloved husband finally swam out of view.

"I think you need us," said a voice from behind and as she turned around, she noticed Reiser and Sarcha floating before her.

"You cannot touch the tentacles," said Reiser. "We, on the other hand, can. We can match the current of the smaller Shivan and keep it busy. Look! See how the tentacle does not grow back. It must be too young to regenerate."

"I cannot express how relieved I am to see you, my lord," replied Jasmine. "We could do with more help for sure."

Meanwhile, Vanisheo and Nuwa Lin had managed to elude both of the Shivans and were now swimming around the blocked entrance to the Halls of Judgment, trying to find a suitable rock to jam into the gills of the largest creature. After a couple of minutes of perusing their choices, Vanisheo settled on a suitable weapon and with the help of the ninja, they started to swim up towards the underbelly of the Shivan. Despite the dispersal of weight in the water, Vanisheo still found the rock heavy and by accident, he released his grip and it slowly sank to the bottom. Annoyed by his own inadequacies, he swam down to retrieve it and, as he did so, noticed a mass of movement on the seabed. He squinted to get a better look and to his horror, realised the bottom was saturated with a whole school of Shivans.

"Err, Nuwa Lin?" he said as loud as he dared. "I think we have an even bigger problem."

Above them, oblivious of the latest development, Jasmine and Fortis were attempting to reach Connor and Durban but the smaller Shivan had somehow sensed what they were trying to do and kept blocking at every opportunity. Even when Reiser and Sarcha tried to distract it, the creature appeared more interested in the earth walkers than the water dwellers. It was as if it understood the threat Reiser and Sarcha were to it.

"Jasmine, look out!" screamed Lady Sarcha as she watched a tentacle from each Shivan lash towards her.

Thankful for the warning, the princess quickly turned herself into a ghost as the limbs went through her without harm but the smaller Shivan, taking advantage of the space between their enemy and the larger creature, nimbly swam through the gap and rested upon the monster's back. To everyone's horror, it then merged within the features, causing a single entity with permanent electrically charged tentacles.

"So now what?" asked Lady Sarcha as she and her husband joined the group.

Connor was about to answer when he noticed Vanisheo and Nuwa Lin swimming out of the murky waters.

"Have you got the rock?" he shouted.

Vanisheo did not answer but quickened up his stoke as he emerged from the depths. Nuwa Lin was almost on his feet.

"Get back! Get out of here," she screamed as she overtook Vanisheo and grabbed him by the arm in an attempt to pull him along.

Connor quickly read their look of panic, and as he continued to watch, he saw a massive ripple in the water.

"Oh no!" exclaimed Connor as he recognised the shapes.

"It cannot be?" echoed Fortis as the creatures slowly swam towards them.

"We must warn the others below," Connor suddenly announced as the urgency of survival buzzed through his veins. "Quickly . . . all of you."

Even before Connor's order, they started to swim as fast as they could away from the creature but with their untimely movement, they caused an undercurrent that only deterred a swift retreat.

"Wait!" yelled Vanisheo to the others. "I have an idea. Try and stay alive a little while longer. I will be as quick as I can." And with that he disappeared below.

"Survive?" moaned Fortis. "What does he think we are doing?"

As Vanisheo swam towards Joshua, he could hear the screams and warnings above as his friends tried to avoid the deadly clutches of the Shivan. Effortlessly he swam towards where the Oracle was hiding and he breathed a sigh of relief when he recognised the old man.

"Joshua! Joshua!" Vanisheo echoed excitedly. "We are in trouble. I need Kustos. Is he strong enough to help?"

"My strength has returned, old friend," announced Kustos, although from the gaunt look on his face he was not exactly telling the truth. "What is happening above?"

"Are you certain you are ready to fight?" asked Vanisheo.

"I am fine, my friend. Now tell me what has happened," replied Kustos.

"There are hundreds of these creatures. Nuwa Lin and I came across them when we were looking for rocks," Vanisheo told him. "We cannot beat them alone. For this we need your power."

"Then it is yours," answered the Realm Lord. "Just tell me what I must do."

"You must follow me," ordered Vanisheo, "but be warned, do not look."

"If Kustos is going," interrupted Will, "then I'm coming as well. I can't just stay here and do nothing."

"Nothing?" queried Vanisheo. "Is that what you think keeping us alive is? Nothing?"

"No, no, not at all," Will quickly replied, defending his response. "I just think I can do more."

"Dear Will," said the Hallucium, "the role you have is too important for us to take any risks. Use your gift to keep us safe." And with that, Vanisheo turned and swam off.

Kustos was only seconds behind.

Will looked up in disappointment and then felt a hand rest gently on his shoulder.

"The Hallucium is right, Will," said Joshua. "Your time will soon come to make an entrance."

25

And What an Entrance?

Up above the creatures, Connor and the others were desperately struggling to elude the Shivans and with every defeat of an isolated limb, another merely reappeared. It was only when he saw Kustos and Vanisheo swimming below that he realised what the latest plan was. The only problem they had was the mass of Shivans between them.

"Vanisheo," Connor called as a gap momentarily appeared between the bodies, "up here, quickly."

Immediately the pair changed direction and took advantage of the route provided from Connor's viewpoint.

"I know what you intend to do," Connor told them, "and I think it's a great idea but for it to work, you need me. Hold on a minute and I'll be ready"

Vanisheo and Kustos watched as Connor focussed on his latest metamorphosis. It was only seconds before he let out a painful cry, as tentacles began to rip themselves through his back. Each appendage spluttered and sizzled as an electrical charge ran through them. The sensation of the transformation was by far the most energy he had ever absorbed and the uncomfortable feeling that nagged through his body constantly reminded him that the shape was only on loan. Apart from that, it was the perfect way to provide a pathway through the Shivans as Connor surged forward to where Vanisheo and Kustos needed to be.

"Follow me," he ordered as pushed on. "The rest of you stay here and try to defend the best you can. Hopefully this'll soon be over."

"Wait!" said a voice.

They all looked around and there was Will swimming towards them.

"I'm coming with you," he told them.

"It is too dangerous, Will," Vanisheo reprimanded. "We cannot protect you."

"The last time I looked," answered Will, "I didn't need protecting and besides, my skills might be of use."

Connor knew from past experiences that there was little point in arguing with Will and secretly he was pleased his friend was around. They had always faced these dangers together and it felt like a good omen that he was there by his side again.

"Come on then," he said with a grin, "but don't get yourself killed."

Will smiled back at his friend, knowing that he had made the right decision and he quickly fell in behind Kustos and Vanisheo and waited for Connor to call.

"Hurry," urged Connor, as he flayed his tentacles backwards and forwards warding off the Shivans. "The pathway won't be clear for very long."

With Connor forcing his way through, the Shivans backed away and in no time at all, they had reached their destination.

"Okay!" Connor finally announced. "We're here. Now do what you are going to do?"

Vanisheo was about to act upon the plan when Kustos caught a glimpse of a Shivan immediately behind Will.

"Look out, Will," he cried, but the warning was too late as a cloud of poisonous ink drifted towards the Dream Warrior.

Despite the force it projected, it suddenly hit a solid bubble and evaporated back towards its owner. The creature, sensing the danger it was in, panicked and moved aside as the liquid metal filtered back into Durban.

"See, Will," Durban reprimanded, "we all could have died then."

"I'm sorry," apologised the Dream Warrior as Durban joined them. "I just wanted to help."

"And you are. Will," replied Connor. "Now, Kustos? Are you ready?"

Kustos nodded as the blocked entrance came into view. All around them were the masses of Shivans as they tried to encroach upon the group, only to be forced back by Connor's tentacles. Above them were Jasmine and the Aqua sovereigns and even Harry and the others had now also joined them. The largest Shivan had stopped moving and was watching the group above him, waiting for a suitable time to strike. Suddenly the choppy waters subsided and the remaining Shivans stopped moving. The stand-off had begun as the gentle splashing of calm waters was heard calmly bouncing against the cavern walls. Not a word was spoken or an utterance of fear screamed.

Kustos ignored the eerie atmosphere and focussed on the entrance as he breathed in and pulled his arms behind him, then, with all the force the water pressure permitted, he slammed his hands forward and created a single beam of sonic energy, directed solely into the blocked entranceway. With such accuracy the beam dismantled the blockage and the rocks gracefully drifted away without further displacement to the water. Kustos fell to the floor, exhausted by his ordeal and watched with weird interest the reaction of the Shivans.

The instant the entranceway was cleared, a unisoned cry emitted through the water as every Shivan immediately headed towards the opening. They moved at such a rate that Connor's tentacles immediately began to retract and as the last creature disappeared through the exit, he had transformed back to his normal form. With the Shivans gone, the water once more returned to normal, leaving the rest of the group to casually swim down and join Kustos and the others.

"So all they wanted to do was go home," said Lord Reiser. "They were just as much imprisoned as we were."

"How could we have been so blind?" interrupted Lady Sarcha. "Underwater is our life. We should have realised their distress."

"Don't be so hard on yourselves," Connor assured them. "If something big and scary attacks you . . . then, in all probability, it's evil. It was an easy mistake to make. Anyway the important thing is that the problem's been solved and the pathway to the Halls of Judgment has been now been opened to us."

"Reiser, my dear friend," said Joshua as he touched the Aqua lord's arm, "when this is all over, I promise I will return and we can sit and talk about all that has passed this day and many more before it. Now that I know your kingdom is safe, with relief in my heart, I can take these brave new friends of mine back to my home."

"Good luck to you all." Lady Sarcha smiled as Joshua kissed her upon the forehead. "We will count the time until your return."

"I too look forward to the future," replied Joshua as he turned to Kustos. "How do you feel, young man?" he asked.

"My strength has return, Joshua," he replied. "Let us go and finish what we have started."

Connor and the others watched as Lord Reiser and Lady Sarcha swam back the way they had all entered the cavern. The doorway to the sea was finally open to them and with their time of isolation, their food stocks had to be running low. For a brief moment, Lady Sarcha turned and waved and then disappeared down the small underwater tunnel. As the distance between them and Connor increased, so did the Dream Lord feel his gills fade away, leaving him once more under the protection of Will's invisible air bubble.

"You're certain those things have swum away?" asked Will once they had all regrouped. "I don't want to meet them again in a tight cave."

"I am certain of it, Will," Joshua assured him. "Now, no more time wasting. We must be on our way as well."

By the tone in Joshua's voice, the others knew better than to question him and in single file, they followed him through the small entrance and into the cave. What little light there was soon disappeared and they found themselves slowly swimming in darkness. Concentrating on their journey, no one dared speak until they finally reached the other end of the cave. It opened out into the huge underworld of the sea, and brilliant sunshine from the terrain above somehow managed to filter its way down and illuminate the seabed like a dazzling sunrise. The cavern itself was vast, and no matter how hard they tried, they were unable to define its boundaries. A calming sound of water splashed steadily as it flowed throughout the sea. Fish and exotic life forms swam obliviously around, unaware that their world had been infiltrated by strangers. Will felt relaxed and yet saddened at the same time, knowing that his visit was not one of pleasure.

For nearly an hour they continued to swim forward, admiring the sights of the tranquil world. Only when Joshua spoke did they remember the true reason for their presence.

"We are coming to the Path of Confusion," Joshua told them. "It is a series of small caves. Please stay near me and copy my every move. In order to reach the outskirts of the Halls, we must take a specific route."

"Do you even know what to expect on the outskirts?" asked Kustos. "I mean, are we going to leave ourselves vulnerable, or will we have time to find somewhere to regroup if we need to?"

"I cannot answer any of your questions, my friend," replied Joshua. "It has been many moons since I was last here. I was hoping we would have time to plan our next move nearer the time. Now if you are ready?"

They all nodded as the Oracle looked at them and then dove down toward the depths of the seabed. For fear of losing the path, everyone quickly followed then, when they thought there was nowhere else to go, they saw a gigantic rock wall before them. They looked around and then upwards but still could not see the top of the rock face. The only conclusion was that somewhere far above, it soared upwards above the surface.

"We must swim," ordered Joshua.

"But where to?" queried Ashley. "I do not see anything but rock."

"You still do not remember, Ashley?" asked Joshua.

Ashley shook her head in disappointment and silently thanked the stars they were not relying on her to navigate.

"We must swim forward," explained the Oracle. "There is a little gap, hidden by an optical illusion. You will not see it but must trust in your instincts that it is there." And he turned and swam towards the wall.

"Is he crazy?" gasped Durban as he followed. "I do not see anything."

The others felt the same but, rather than add their voice, watched curiously as Joshua got closer to the wall.

"Are you sure about this?" said Will as he watched. "I don't see anything either."

Joshua did not waste his breath in replying but instead continued to swim forward until he suddenly vanished from sight.

Seeing the Oracle evaporate from view, the others followed the exact same route and, as they reached the wall, suddenly found themselves on the other side.

"Well, would you look at that?" said Harry, when he realised that he was safe.

"See," said Joshua as he reappeared again, "you cannot always trust your eyes. Come, we have many tunnels and caves to cover and must ensure we do not get lost."

For what felt like hours they followed Joshua and yet little progress appeared to have been made. Most of the tunnels looked the same and only the order they were taking was their safeguard of ever finding the entrance to the Halls again.

One of the tunnels was really small and very little light illuminated the way. As Ashley aimlessly swam forward, she found herself stuck fast. She panicked briefly for a moment as Will and Connor pushed and pulled to ease her through. Eventually she made it and once free, they looked around for Joshua and the others. They were nowhere to be found.

"Oh, that can't be good," exclaimed Will as he looked from side to side.

❖ ❖ ❖

It was Jasmine who realised that Will was missing as she felt an odd sensation within her lungs. Instinctively she looked around and noticed he had gone. Panicking a little as to how they would survive, she pushed past Kustos and the others until she reached Joshua. Grabbing his robe in an effort to slow him down, she pulled it hard and he turned around.

"We can make it on our own," he assured her. "There is not far to go. Just hold onto your breath and follow me."

Clawing their way through the last couple of tunnels, they all frantically pushed upwards, and then, as they felt their lungs about to burst, a gulp of air breathed life back into them.

"What happened?" asked Harry as he got his breath back and pulled himself out of the pool. "Where are Will and the others?"

"They were right behind us," Nuwa Lin told them. "What could have happened to them?"

"What are we going to do, Joshua?" asked Armon. "We need them."

"Then we shall wait," Joshua told them, "and hope they find their own way through the tunnels."

"But you said yourself that was impossible," stated Kustos.

"Anything is possible," added the Oracle.

⚹ ⚹ ⚹

Realising they were lost, Connor looked around to see if he could sense which way to go. When he felt nothing, he asked the others for their assessment of the situation.

"So what do we do now?" asked Connor. "If we get this wrong, we could be swimming around here forever."

"Then it's up to Ashley to find the way," interrupted Will. "She's been here before, so she must remember."

"I cannot," Ashley implored. "There is a sense of familiarity but I do not know the way."

"Yes, you do," said Connor softly. "I believe that's the reason we had to find you. Now . . . close your eyes and relax. Hidden in the back of your mind is the way to the Halls. All you have to do is find it."

Ashley did as she was instructed and closed her eyes. Then, trying to clear her mind, she searched into the depths of her memories but there was something blocking the way, barring her from the knowledge. She knew it was there but she just could not see it.

"It is no use," she cried with frustration. "I cannot do it."

"Yes, you can," Connor assured her again. "Just close your eyes and relax."

Under direction, Ashley shut her eyes as she felt Connor's hands rest lightly on her forehead. Concentrating himself, he allowed his own energy to flow freely into her. The united force enveloped them both, causing a slight iridescent glow around them.

"Wow!" echoed Will to himself as he backed away.

For several seconds the exchange of energy flowed between Ashley and Connor and then suddenly, quite without warning, they both opened their eyes.

"I know the way," Ashley smiled. "I can see it. Follow me!"

Connor grinned at Will as Ashley swum past them and took the lead.

"So what happened?" Will asked his friend.

"I'm not entirely sure," admitted Connor. "I combined my energy with hers and instantly I sensed I was safe. Then a picture came to me and I was back in the Wake World. It was as though we'd never left. You and I were married and our children were best friends. It seemed to be a life we might have had, if not for Sublin."

"That's really odd," answered Will. "In all our years in Sublin, not once have you reflected on what could have been back home. Who is Ashley and what really is her story?"

"I wish I knew," agreed Connor as they continued a little distance back, just out of her hearing. "I'm certain there's a connection although I can't say for sure. For now though we must keep her close. Whoever she is, Volnar desperately wanted her dead, and we foiled that plan. It might be for our own salvation."

As soon as he had concluded his conversation, Ashley started to swim upwards. Without question, Connor and Will followed.

"Oh my . . . thank goodness," exclaimed Jasmine as she saw the trio emerge. "I am so pleased you are all safe."

Alerted by Jasmine's cries, Joshua suddenly appeared out of nowhere and stared intently at Connor.

"She found her own way here," Connor told him. "I think it's all beginning to come back to her."

"Yeah," confirmed Will. "Ashley was fantastic. She suddenly remembered the way and here we are, not sure where here is though." And he pulled himself out of the water and observed a pair of huge, locked doors before him.

"We are close to the centre of the world," Joshua told them as he helped Ashley from the water. "Many miles stand between us and the top of the ocean. Water is the representation of purity and judgment comes from that untainted place. I also can breathe underwater here and have spent many hours cleansing my energy. Unbeknown to Will, I have been assisting in our travels. Without my help, he would have lost his strength a long time ago. These doors you see now lead to the Halls of Judgment, where Volnar resides."

"In the back of my mind I did wonder how you managed to survive without me." Will smiled. "And the fact that my power remained constant."

Even as he spoke, the others did not really understand the implications.

"So how do we get through them?" asked Harry as he walked forward to inspect the doors.

Without a word, Joshua walked over to Ashley and smiled.

"Ashley," he said kindly, "that necklace you are wearing. May I?"

Carefully Ashley removed the jewellery and handed it to the Oracle. It was a simple beaded braid with a wooden symbol hanging from the centre. By its irregular shape it could have been mistaken for a broken charm.

"Here," she said, "do what you must. I have worn this for as long as I can remember and never understood why. It is not pretty, nor does it hold any great significance to me."

"Not to you maybe," muttered Joshua, "but to the residents of Judgment it is a priceless artefact." And with that he removed a similar object from his own neck.

For a moment he fiddled with the two pieces, and when fully satisfied, he walked towards the wooden doors. Now resting in his hand was the shape of wooden key.

"I split this up," explained the Oracle, "before our paths separated. Just in case we were ever caught and dragged back to this point. Despite all the damage Volnar is causing in Judgment, he is trapped within the Halls and has been searching for a way to break the barrier. I believe, Ashley, you hold all the answers, but how or why, I do not know. I hoped that when the key was separated, it would force you to find your way to me, either by your own free will or as a prisoner."

Very slowly Joshua slotted the key into the carved door and turned it clockwise.

"I do not understand what else I can do," admitted Ashley.

"You will . . . in time," Joshua told her as the door swung open, exposing the Halls before them.

"This is no Hall," said Kustos in wonderment. "This is an entire city."

Quickly Joshua ushered them on and, once inside, closed the door silently behind them, sealing them within the Halls of Judgment. Before them was a mass of houses, crammed tightly side by side, for as far as the eye could see. Running rivers wound idly in and out between the structures. The brilliance of their vision offered only one solution—sunlight but where it was radiating from was unclear. Out in the far distance was a white stone building, very much like the one back in Sublin where Will and Connor had gained their passage to Judgment.

"This was once a thriving city," explained Joshua with sadness in his voice. "Home to all the workers and Oracles of Judgment. Their families would live here, creating an air of tranquil life."

As the others looked around, they could see the city was deserted and an uncomfortable silence sent shivers through their bodies.

"Up there," continued the Oracle as he pointed to the tower, "that is the pathway to the Halls of Judgment."

"I do not like this," interrupted Armon as he strained to hear a single sound. "There does not appear to be anyone here, yet you would have expected it to be guarded by Razars and Soul Crunchers."

"I am inclined to agree with you, Armon," said Durban uneasily.

"There is no need to worry," the Oracle assured them. "We are safe here. No one can get in."

"Accept us, that is," snarled Durban.

"So is there . . . like a back door or some hidden entrance into this place?" asked Will.

"No," interrupted Connor, "the only entrance is the one we've just come through."

Everyone stopped and stared at Connor. He was so emphatic with his knowledge of the Halls that it took them by surprise.

"Before we go any further," he continued, "I need to know you trust me."

"You know we do," confirmed Kustos. "You have never given us any doubt not to follow your word."

"But would that change if you thought my motives had been compromised?" he added.

"That wouldn't happen. Not with you," joked Will. "You know we all believe in you."

"Belief might not be enough," said the Dream Lord. "I need to know you trust me, whatever I decide, even if it appears I could be wrong and leading us into danger. I need for you all to accept I've a game plan."

"We have already said that we trust you," said Jasmine. "Why do you insist on more? Why do you try and scare us?"

"My intentions are good." Connor smiled. "You must understand the dangers we are about to face. This is the last stand. I don't know what's going to happen but we have faced Volnar before and know of his might. We must be alert and aware that our task to rid this world of him might not be as rewarding as last time."

"We would not be here if we did not understand the dangers, Connor," interrupted Durban. "And as before, we stand by your side."

"In that case," said the Dream Lord, "it's time to enter the Halls but we don't scurry through secret passageways. We go through the front door. No more hiding or sneaking. Now it's time to stand face to face against Volnar."

The others did not have the same sense of exhilaration about the plan as Connor did but they had declared their faith in his leadership and therefore agreed to head for the tower and in through the front door.

"I hope you know what you are doing, Connor," Joshua challenged. "Follow me and I will take us to the Halls of Judgment. That is where Volnar will be found." And with that, he turned away from the others and started to walk through the city.

A wry smiled covered his face.

26

The Centre of the World

As they entered the tower, the atmosphere changed again and fear began to creep through their minds. Up until that point they had not seen a living creature but as they entered the tower, they saw a group of Soul Crunchers guarding the central door. This, Joshua told them, would lead to the middle of Judgment.

"What are they doing?" whispered Will to Joshua. "Why haven't they attacked?"

"I cannot say," the Oracle answered.

Taking full advantage of the static Crunchers, Connor and Ashley walked forward and opened the centre door. Instead of attacking the duo, the soldiers cautiously backed away. Joshua took full advantage of the situation and moved to the front to take the lead once more. At first, they travelled down yet another narrow tunnel but eventually it opened out into a vast expanse, almost as large as the city they had just passed through. It was comprised of many levels, each with rows upon rows of doors.

"The resting place before Judgment," Joshua told them. "All these doors lead to many rooms, a comfortable holding area. Time in these rooms stands still, and for some, they could wait for hundreds of years. There will be a lot of work to do, when normality is resumed."

Connor and Will looked up and the thought of five-star accommodations came to mind. Every wall was made from the finest white marble, reflecting light as it hit the gold thread running through it. On every available space were vibrant life-like paintings, depicting the history of almost every race across the three worlds. Their eyes drifted from level to level and their attention was drawn to the far end of the chamber, where two golden doors broke the monotony of the clinical marble.

Joshua marched on and the others followed, finding themselves heading towards the ostentatious doors. As they got closer, they realised they were guarded by the different races of Razars. They were lined up in rows of two with weapons armed, but still they did not retaliate as the group walked past. They merely glared their indignation of such an intrusion.

"I am feeling a little uneasy about this," whispered Nuwa Lin. "Why are they not attacking us?"

"He knows we're here," interrupted Connor, "and wants us for himself."

"I think he has probably known for some time," said Harry. "I did not want to alarm anyone but we have been followed since we left Aquamarine."

As they reached the golden doors, two Soul Crunchers broke rank and opened them.

"Remember what I said," warned Connor under his breath as he walked on through, "just trust me."

Once the group had passed into the next room, the doors slammed shut behind them and as they looked around, they saw they had now entered a room similar to that of a Wake World courtroom. Running down the centre was a walkway. On the other side of the room was a stall. A dark figure sat behind it. On either side of the walkway were dimension holes ripped open by Volnar. Jasmine, Connor and Vanisheo recognised one of them as the eerie cries of pain that came from the Shadow dimension, a dimension they had already had the misfortune of experiencing.

"Don't touch the darkness," warned Connor. "A step in the shadows can be your last."

Many of the other dimensions had little indication of location, only the anguish of the punished inhabitants wafted through the air. Elevated on poles above the portals were a mass of hanging cages, confining as many as seven or eight Oracles within the bars. Some were emancipated and dead, whilst others were merely praying for their time to end.

"My dear friends," said Joshua with pain in his voice, "what has he done to you?"

The fate of his friends had taken the determination out of Joshua's step and Connor, alerted by this sudden weakness, took the lead. After a few moments he stopped.

"Everyone, wait here," he ordered. "Armon, Will, and Ashley, let's approach him alone. After all he's gone through great pains to ensure we're all reunited."

"Be careful, Connor," urged Jasmine as she gripped Kustos' hand.

He stopped for a moment before continuing and smiled at her, one she had learned to trust. Every footstep echoed loudly over the noise of fallen souls as they screamed out their pleas from their hell dimension. Bravely the quartet moved on, avoiding the danger beneath their feet, until they eventually reached the dark, mysterious figure. On their approach, he said nothing, and Connor looked back to his friends and shrugged his shoulders.

"My dear nephew!" it finally said. "What took you so long? And look, you have brought some old faces back with you," he added as he lowered his hood.

A pair of eyes stared back at them and as the flickering light caught his face, the distinctive features of Volnar came into view. Time had not treated him well and many deep-set lines were etched into his skin, showing that age had finally caught up with him. His head was now hairless and two hollow black eyes glared malevolently into their faces.

"Uncle," said Connor as he approached the Dark Lord, "what do you think you're doing?"

"Some people were born to rule," he spat, "but you and your father took that away from me in Sublin. I knew my rights though and did not let that deter me. Whilst trapped in the Twilight, I began to plan my return. As luck would have it for me, I stumbled upon a primitive race called the Razars. They needed a leader and I needed an army, so the combination was just perfect."

"It didn't help your looks though, did it?" interrupted Connor, who was getting bored with the self-inflated speech.

"You cannot criticise on things you have not experienced," reprimanded Volnar. "My time in the twilight was unlike any place I have ever been. Hundreds of years have passed since leaving Sublin, and with that time, I planned the perfect revenge. Who would have thought I could utilise the services of my old, back-stabbing childhood friend, Armon. It was far too simple to get him to bring me into Judgment."

"But you must have known we'd come here to stop you," cried Will. "That we wouldn't let your evil and anger rule this world."

"Ahh!" cooed Volnar. "Young Master Will, son of Armon. How little you understand the mind of a genius. I was counting on you all to try and stop me."

A shiver ran down Will's back and he felt uneasy as he listened to the arrogance of their enemy.

"Counting on it?" asked Joshua from way back with the others.

"So, the Great Oracle himself dares to return," replied the Dark Lord sarcastically. "Did you really think you and Armon escaped the Judgment Halls? I let you go. In the same way, Ashley got her freedom. It was all part of my plan, you see. Letting you believe that you had got away was always a guarantee for you to return, bringing with you my nephew and his friend. By reuniting the families, you have given me exactly what I need. Armon and his son are the key. An individual soul has great potential but join it with another member of the same family and its strength is multiplied infinitely. Imagine the soul energy of the Dream Lord and Dream Warrior mixed with their family and it will become so powerful, it could break the seal that has trapped me within the Judgment Halls. Free me to rule the Judgment World and pass sentence on all souls, punishing the good with the legacy of evil, even create my own realities of immorality." And he emitted an eerie laugh of self-satisfaction.

"That is insane," exclaimed Ashley. "Why would you do that?"

"Easy!" replied Volnar. "Every world and dimension needs good and evil to preserve the balance of life but why? Without one or the other, how would you know the boundaries?"

"That is not your call to make," interrupted Joshua. "You cannot play with our existence like that. It has never been one single entity that decided this fate. It is impossible to keep equilibrium otherwise."

"So, it's Will and Armon who have the power to create this new evil world?" stated Connor.

"Not just Will and Armon," reiterated Joshua as he turned to Ashley. "Ashley? What is the name of your sister?"

Slowly and clearly, she ran off a list of names, presumably her family. Only one name stuck in Connor's mind—Emma.

"What was the name of your mother, Connor?" Joshua asked.

"Emma?" the Dream Lord replied. "But Emma's a common name in the Wake World," he quickly added as he stared at Ashley.

A wry smiled covered the Dark Lord's face as he pushed his hands forward towards Ashley. As he did so, she closed her eyes and instantly the barriers blocking her memory were lifted.

"I remember now," she answered. "I remember it all. I was the youngest of all my sisters and because of the age difference, I felt like I never really fit in with them. As a teenager, I thought the mythical age of sixteen would put everything right and I would be accepted as one of the family. Unfortunately, that was not the case because everyone forgot my birthday and in a fit of anger, I ran away, vowing never to look back. I changed my name, so I could not be found and blocked all memory of my horrid family life.

It took years before I finally forgave them and returned back home to try and rebuild the damage I had left behind. After several months, I eventually tracked down my parents but arriving at their home, I was told by the neighbour that they had both suddenly died under unexplained circumstances. When I asked what she meant, the neighbour described how two piles of ash were found in the house with little clue to the whereabouts of my parents. Unable to find any bodies, the police closed the case as a missing persons.

Devastated at not being able to make amends, I tried to find my two sisters, only to discover that one of them had also disappeared under the same strange circumstances as my parents. Panicked by the fear of losing everyone I had known, I went in search of Emma, who I discovered had recently given birth. Excited to meet with her, I rushed off to the hospital, only to find that she too was gone. With an empty hospital room, I assumed that the child had died also.

I was distraught by the lack of enthusiasm the police had in finding an answer and so one night, I broke into the police station and stole their case files. The next day, as I was driving home, something very strange happened. It was around midday and the sun was high in the sky, but behind me a dark shadow appeared, moving at such a speed that indicated it was trying to catch me up. To my horror, I guessed this was the same ending that had befallen my family. It panicked me, that this would also be my own demise and so I accelerated the car to try and outrun the danger chasing me. My lack of driving experience showed and I lost control of the vehicle, broke through the barriers of a bridge and tumbled into the waters below. As I hit my watery grave, I looked up and saw the shadow back away, leaving me to a different fate. The impact was devastating, and water began to seep in, filling the cabin. I struggled to release the seat belt, but it held fast and the unlocked door refused to give way under the pressure. I knew I was going to die and so I closed my eyes and allowed myself to be taken. Time passed by. I cannot say how long, but when I opened them again, I found I was in a large, restful room. A place I felt I never wanted to leave and for a while, I got my wish. Then one day the door swung open and littering the hallway outside was a mass of dead bodies. I was not sure what I should do. I did not even know if I was dead or alive but since I had the ability to walk, I left. That was when I met Joshua."

"You're my aunt then?" asked Connor, daring to believe he had acquired another new member of his family.

"That's right," confirmed Volnar. "Ashley is the last cog in this puzzle, apart from you and me, that is. Can you imagine how I will feel when I take the soul energy of you all?"

Everyone remained silent as they pondered the implications of Volnar's plan. Even Joshua was lost for words. He had been the Dark Lord's puppet and delivered the final key to complete the destruction of the Judgment World. With the combined strength of Connor, Ashley, Armon and Will, Volnar would be able to break the seal and infiltrate the three worlds.

"Do you think we are just going to roll over and let you absorb us?" asked Armon defiantly.

Volnar waved his hand and almost instantly the door opened, and Razars and Soul Crunchers came flooding in.

"You know what?" said Connor, annoyed that he had just discovered his aunt and was about to lose her again before really getting to know her.

Volnar signalled again and this time his army backed off.

"What, my dear Dream Lord?" asked the Dark Lord.

"I'm tired," replied Connor "tired of chasing you and putting you in your place. I've dragged so many people into this battle, I want to put a stop to it. I refuse to do this anymore."

"What are doing?" whispered Will.

"Remember what I asked of you?" replied the Dream Lord quietly.

Kustos was also confused by Connor's confession and tried to move forward but Jasmine pulled him back.

"We have to trust him, my love." She smiled.

"Tired?" queried Volnar. "You have been in Judgment for months. My spies have been watching you. There has been plenty of time to rest. You have done well in my plan so far and only now do you feel tired, nephew?" And he sat down on an ebony throne and pulled his hood back over his head.

"You win, uncle," confessed Connor. "I don't want another standoff. I thought by meeting you face to face, I could perhaps talk you out of your plan but I see now that was foolish of me. No matter how far we travel and where we try and hide, you'll always be there. There's no disguise from pure evil."

The others all looked at each other. They could not believe what Connor was saying. It was almost as if Volnar had some kind hold over him.

"We have to trust him," Vanisheo told them.

Connor looked at Ashley and then at Will and Armon. Will nodded in agreement. Ashley looked at the floor whilst Armon looked back at the others.

"Alright," they agreed.

It was as if Connor had spoken to them, yet no one heard the words. Only Jasmine understood.

"You want our souls?" Connor demanded. "You really want to crunch us and absorb our energy? Then fine." And with that, he moved a little closer to Volnar and knelt down.

Ashley, Will and Armon followed suit until the four of them were in a line. Their heads dropped in submission.

"I do not know what you are planning," yelled the Dark Lord as he jumped to his feet, "but it will not work." And he thrust his hands above his head, causing his hood to expose the ancient face once more.

A blinding light flashed across the room, seeking out every corner, as shadows screamed out in pain. Jasmine and Joshua shielded their eyes in an attempt to see what was happening but the sound of Volnar screaming was all the graphics they needed. As the light disappeared, Volnar stood in all his glory over the inert bodies of the quartet.

"No!" screamed Jasmine as her cries of distress echo around the walls. "This cannot be. What did you do Connor? Why did you give up?"

"He knew he could not beat me," bragged the Dark Lord. "All you see of the Dream Lord now is the shell of his body. The power of the four, bubbles within me and it feels alive."

Realism suddenly hit Fortis of the danger they were in and he urged the others to try and escape.

"We can do nothing for them now," he told Jasmine. "Our only hope of survival is to run and even that I fear will not be enough."

"Have faith," echoed Joshua as he continued to watch Volnar. "That is what we must do."

"Faith!" exclaimed Harry. "Our main hope of conquering this monster has just rolled over and accepted defeat. What good is faith to us now?"

Before Joshua had an opportunity to explain, their gaze was drawn back towards the Dark Lord.

"What is happening?" asked Nuwa Lin as she watched.

Volnar was still gloating over his victory as he rejoiced in excitement.

"I feel the power," he echoed "A lot of power." And then his voice trembled as he soaked up the energy of the foursome. "No!" he screamed "Too much power, too overwhelming."

As he spoke, a glow of brilliance burst through his ribcage and out into the air.

"What is happening to me?" he shrieked in terror.

"I believe Connor found a way to bring you down, my lord." smiled Joshua as he watched in wonderment. "The Dream Lord learned before coming to Judgment how to face the toughest of adversaries. He knew that on the outside they might well be invincible but on the inside their vulnerability was easier to take on."

"Impossible!" shouted Volnar. "I am invincible."

"Perhaps," mused Joshua as he began to approach the Dark Lord, "but you have just absorbed, how did you put it, the strongest soul energy inside Judgment. I think that was a mistake. Now . . . everyone for your own safety . . . move back," the Oracle warned the others.

Still in a state of shock, Jasmine and her friends obeyed and took a step backwards.

"Get away from me," ordered Volnar to Joshua as he got closer. "I will kill you all. Attack them all," he told the Razars and Crunchers but they ignored his command and also backed away in fear.

The glow emitting from the Dark Lord was increasing and with each second that passed, it pulsated into a brighter and brighter light, until it surrounded the decrepit figure. Pain racked throughout his frame as he sensed the anguish of every being he had ever murdered. The torment and agony were unimaginable. He stared into Joshua's face and tears of remorse and pain escaped from his eyes. In those brief moments, he sensed the torture he had bestowed upon his enemies and the wretchedness of his desperation ruptured his body, further allowing the light energy to break out into the open.

The last words he managed to utter were, "What have they made me do?" As he did so, he split into eight pieces. Using the power of the Oracle, Joshua directed them into the dimension holes, separating them from each other, so they could not be retrieved. As each part was sucked into its new home, it hardened into stone. The representation of Volnar's heart was sealed in a dimension, never to be found again. When the last dimension hole was closed, the Judgment Halls returned to their former glory. The shadows vanished and the brilliant of light returned.

The Razars, although large in number, did not have the intelligence to put up a fight and realising they were beaten, they turned tail and ran for their lives, whilst the Soul Crunchers screamed painfully as they returned to their former images. Only the memories of what they had done reminded them of their part in the event.

Everyone now looked over to Connor and his friends as they began to stir.

The Dream Lord was the first to slowly open his eyes, and as he did so, he asked if they had succeeded.

"Did we win?" he queried as Joshua helped him to his feet.

"You crazy fool," exclaimed Will as he opened his eyes and pinched himself, "how did you know that was gonna work?"

"Let's just say it was one of my better gambles." Connor laughed.

"I am so sorry," apologised Ashley as she hugged her nephew. "I should have come looking for you."

"You didn't know," said Connor, "and with my crazy life, I'd have been impossible to keep track of. All I know now is that I've an aunt that I'm extremely proud of. I'm only sorry it took me so long to find you."

"Is it over?" asked Nuwa Lin who did not quite understand what had just happened, even though she had witnessed the event.

"It is over, my brave ninja," Joshua told her. "Connor tore him apart from the inside. This time there is no way back for him. Each piece of him has been scattered amongst the dimensions and will suffer an eternity of pain. It is the price he must pay for his evil deeds."

"And so must we," exclaimed the converted Soul Crunchers as they bowed before their sovereign. "We ask your forgiveness, my lord, for succumbing to the weakness of servitude. So many souls have suffered by our hand, for which we must pay the price."

"You all have demons of your own to fight," Joshua told them. "Times will not always be easy but all is not lost. With retribution comes respect. It was your will that let you down, not your loyalties to Judgment. We can build on that."

Kustos and Durban helped the captured Oracles out of their cages and sat them carefully down before Joshua.

"You, my friends," said the Oracle with a smile, "must take a holiday."

They looked at one another as if they did not understand . . . then laughed. Joshua was not often known for his generosity and whatever experiences had touched him, had certainly changed his outlook to life.

"So, Joshua," said Fortis as he wrapped an arm around his shoulder "if you think you can take it from here, we will be on our way."

Joshua smiled a rare show of emotion from such a reverent figure then laughed out loud.

"I will miss you all," he said, "but I will never forget. Now you have accomplished your mission, I must reconnect to the Higher Powers and tell them the good news."

27

All Good Things

It took a while for Joshua to regain his connection to the Higher Powers and while he was doing so, the others took the opportunity to have something to eat and discuss their epic adventure. Connor was able to learn all about Ashley, Will continued to build up a relationship with his father and Jasmine and Kustos talked over old times with Fortis and Harry. It was a calming conclusion to such a hectic adventure. For them, in that room, time had stood still, etching new memories into their minds.

Finally, their time to leave arrived as one of the Oracles came and collected them and escorted them back to Joshua, who had retaken his place in the Judgment Halls.

"Come, my friends," he welcomed warmly, "today is the brightest day in Judgment. Not only has the balance of life been resumed but through its journey you have all shown your true souls. Fortis," the Oracle continued.

Fortis stepped forward.

"There are many things in your life that we know you are ashamed of," said Joshua. "When you were younger and involved in the War of Sublin, you followed your brothers blindly, never thinking of the consequences of your life. This led you to a dark and evil place. A force much stronger than your own that enticed you into becoming a Dream Stealer. You were seduced by power and greed, much like the one you served. Only your brother's love saved you from the dimensions of hell but rather than accepting your Judgment here, you chose to stay behind in order to protect the balance of life. With my own eyes I have witnessed the goodness within you, barely thinking of your own preservation but the success of this mission. You have proved yourself to be of pure of heart and for that, you *MUST* be rewarded. As remuneration, I will open a path for you to join the rest of your ancestors who have earned their right in the peace dimension."

"My lord!" gasped Fortis. "I do not know what to say."

"I say," interrupted Kustos. "Well done. You have earned it, my brother. I always knew you were one of the bravest knights of our realm and now I have seen it with my own eyes."

"Kustos, Jasmine." Fortis smiled as he hugged them both. "Thank you for everything you have done. You enabled me to redeem myself. I am so proud of you both. Take care of each other and enjoy a long and happy life. I will wait for you to join me, so we can continue with long tales and laughter."

Tears began to fill Fortis' eyes as he realised this would be the last time he could stand with his brother, but with consolation in his heart, he knew that one day they would meet again. Not wanting to forget his brothers in arms, he walked over to Connor and Will and slapped their shoulder in turn.

"It has been my honour to stand by your side, my friends. I hope we meet again in more favourable circumstances."

"Me too." Connor smiled. "Take care, Fortis, and enjoy the next path of your existence."

"Come, Fortis," interrupted Joshua. "It is time."

Fortis turned and faced the Oracle as he watched the wall behind him began to split into two, providing an opening. A bright light escaped into the room, illuminating everywhere but mainly directed around the form of Kustos' brother.

"Follow the light, my friend," instructed Joshua. "At the end of the Hall, turn left. A door will bar your way but gently place your hand upon the door handle and it will respond to your command. Please enter the room and wait for a moment."

Fortis shaded his eyes as he walked towards the portal. Some of the light illuminated his frame as he walked but a small portion of it remained and hovered comfortingly around Durban.

"Durban," added Joshua, "you have also been rewarded for your unselfish actions. You died unfairly in battle but never complained and then refused to accept Judgment when you realised the dangers of its extinction. Just like Fortis, you have earned the right of passage. Please join him."

Durban was shocked by such an accolade but accepted it with the respect it deserved. Hurriedly, he walked over to Kustos and shook his hand but the Lord of the Realm hugged him fondly.

"Thank you, my friend," said Kustos, "for your help in Sublin and here. We will honour your memory, that I will promise."

"Thank you, my lord," replied Durban as he walked over to Connor and Will. "Goodbye, Connor," added the warrior as he shook his hand. "I am sure we will meet again."

"I've no doubt about that," Connor said laughingly. "Trouble seems to follow me around and I can always use the help."

"Durban?" Joshua reminded him quietly. "You must go."

"Are you ready, Fortis?" asked Durban as he joined the prince.

"I guess so," he replied. "How about you?"

Fortis turned for the last time and looked at Kustos, then looked at Durban and smiled.

"Wait!" ordered Kustos. "Fortis, please tell Mother and Father I will join them one day, where we can be a family once more."

"But—," Will was about to say as Connor touched his arm to stop him.

"He can't know his parents are alive in Sublin, Will. Besides, by now they may well be at peace. We have no way of knowing," whispered Connor. "It was their wish to disappear, remember."

"Until we meet again, brother," Fortis said as he waved his final farewell and walked into the light.

Durban paused briefly at the entrance of the portal and took one last glance at his friends then followed. Slowly the wall began to seal until all remnants of its existence had disappeared. With Fortis and Durban now gone, Joshua then turned to Nuwa Lin.

"I have been in contact with your father," he told her, "and he has requested you return to him and continue your work within Judgment."

"My father!" she echoed with a smile on her face. "He is alive? Of course I will return to him. Thank you, my Lord Oracle."

"It is I that must thank you," said Joshua as he reached out and hugged her. "Your dedication to this mission was more than anyone could ask and yet you thought nothing of your own safety but merely the defeat of the enemy. For that I am truly grateful and hope that we can continue to work together for many years."

"For as long as my services are required, I will be there," she answered.

"Then there is nothing left but for my assistants to return you to the surface," replied the Oracle.

Realising that the battle was now over, Nuwa Lin walked over to Connor and smiled.

"It has been an honour to fight by your side, Connor," she told him, "and I am glad it was my destiny to be your guide in the desert."

"Me too," agreed the Dream Lord as he reached out and gently hugged her.

Absorbing his affection, Nuwa Lin stepped backed and smiled. "I will miss you, my lord," she said.

"I could get used to that," answered Connor.

In turn the others hugged her and watched as she left with two Oracles who had been waiting patiently in silence. As she disappeared from sight, Joshua turned towards Jasmine.

"It is time for Vanisheo to take you and your husband home," he told her.

Jasmine had known this time would come, and she turned to her grandfather with tears in her eyes.

"I wish we had more time," she told him sadly.

"That also would be my wish," replied Grandpa Harry, "but you know it was never to be. I am destined to remain here in Judgment and help the Great Lord Oracle. Once you return, your father will be able to teach you how to harness your energy and a permanent link between us can be established. I will be here whenever you need me." And he hugged her tightly before letting her go. "I am so proud of the woman you have become," he added. "You have outshone my wildest dreams. Your grandmother would have been proud of you. Enjoy your life with Kustos, and when your time comes to pass over, I will be here waiting for you."

Jasmine was unable to speak as the emotion got stuck in her throat. Instead Kustos stepped forward and warmly shook Harry's hand.

"I shall take good care of her," he told him. "With every breath I have, I shall protect her from all harm."

"I know you will Kustos," Harry struggled to say as he held back his own tears. "Your heart is good and strong, and I can take consolation that Jasmine has chosen well."

"It is time," interrupted Vanisheo quietly. "We must go. I have contacted my father, and he is waiting to assist us back to Sublin. Come. Please follow." And the Hallucium walked off towards the entrance of the Great Hall.

Suddenly Jasmine wanted to leave and she turned to Connor and Will.

"Please say your goodbyes," she asked them, "so we can return home."

Connor looked at Jasmine and then Joshua and the Dream Lord and the Great Oracle nodded at each other before turning to Will and smiling. They held a secret between them and Connor was about to expose it.

"My dearest Jasmine and Kustos," he said as walked towards them, "we cannot go back with you."

Vanisheo stopped in his tracks and ran back towards Will.

"What?" exclaimed Jasmine in disbelief. "This cannot be true? Of course you can."

"I'm afraid it is true, Jasmine," interrupted Will as he joined Connor. "When our souls left our bodies in order to destroy Volnar, we forfeited the right to return to Sublin."

"That is madness!" cried Jasmine as tears ran down her face. "Joshua will let you return. It is the least he can do for your part in redeeming Judgment."

"I'm afraid, he can't," replied Connor gently as he reached out for Jasmine and pulled her close. "This is one thing that is beyond his control. It saddens my own heart that we can't return but we understood the sacrifices that had to be made. You, Kustos and Vanisheo are truly important to me, to us and I'll personally miss you with every breath that I take but I've fulfilled my destiny and it's now time to move on. I promise that whatever happens, one day, we'll be together again, but until then, I hand Sublin over to you. Honour Will and me by living a full and happy life and when your time comes to take the path, we'll be waiting."

Tears began to prick the back of Connor's eyes as he realised how painful their parting would be.

"It is not fair," cried Jasmine as she hugged Connor tightly. "Why must I lose the important people in my life?"

"You have not lost us," Connor told her, "nor will you ever. We'll always be here when you need us but you and Kustos have a different destiny to fulfil."

"I meant no disrespect to Kustos," Jasmine quickly explained. "I'll love him even when my heart stops beating but I also need you and Will in my life."

"But we'll be in your life," said Connor as he held her at arm's length and stared into her face. "We'll be watching over you and whenever you need us, we'll be there. Now . . . please, Jasmine," implored Connor, "it's time for you to go home."

Vanisheo recognised the awkward situation and ran over to Connor and hugged him. He was so tiny that his arms could only just wrap around Connor's lower leg and so the Dream Lord bent down and very carefully lifted the Hallucium up.

"Thank you, my friend," Connor said to him as he hugged him like a child. "You've been more help to us than you'll ever know. For that I can't thank you enough. Look after my friends and don't be a stranger."

"How could I trust you two to behave, if I did not pop in from time to time?" replied Vanisheo. "Halluciums do not leave their friends, even when they live in another world or dimension."

"Well, I look forward to your return," answered Connor as he carefully rested the little being on the ground.

As the Hallucium's feet touched the floor, he ran off towards Will and jumped. Will was prepared for the action and caught Vanisheo in midair and hugged him.

"Be good, little friend," he said to Vanisheo, "and don't get into trouble. I'll not be there to help you out."

"Trouble!" laughed the Hallucium. "Was it not I that saved your skin?"

Will laughed as he listened to the language and realised the impression that he and Connor had made on their friends.

"Just be safe," Will finally added as he put Vanisheo down.

With a wry smile of response, Vanisheo grabbed Jasmine's hand and walked her away, leaving Kustos alone.

"My dear friend," said Connor as he briefly hugged Kustos, "Sublin is now yours. I hand it over to you. You've taught me and Will so much that without your faith in us, we wouldn't be here now. You've stood by us without question, even when you knew the odds were stacked against us and not once did you doubt my motives. You're truly a remarkable man, one I know your father is extremely proud of. Enjoy your life with Jasmine. Put the battles of darkness to the back of your mind and only recount them as fairy stories to your children. Be safe my friend."

"Be safe, Connor," replied Kustos as he shook his hand. "It has been my honour to fight by your side. I would have followed you to the end of existence if you had asked."

"I think I almost did," answered the Dream Lord. "Now please go, before I start to get dust in my eyes."

One last time, Connor and Will looked upon the images of their friends before the door to the Great Hall closed behind them.

"It will get better, that pain you feel," said Ashley as she walked over to Connor and comforted him.

"I know." He smiled weakly. "And it's not as if I won't ever see them again."

"Ashley!" interrupted Joshua just as another portal began to open in the wall. "You have been granted access to reunite you with your family. Please step into the Hall of light behind me and turn right at the end. Your family will be waiting. You have earned the right. Enjoy the relationship that was once denied you."

"Who would have thought I fought alongside my aunt." Connor smiled as he hugged her. "I'll catch up with you. Don't wait on my account. I think Joshua and I have unfinished business."

Ashley nodded her confirmation of the instruction and smiled at Armon, Will and Harry as she walked away.

"Goodbye," she said. "Thank you for making this happen for me." And before they had a chance to speak, she disappeared into the light.

Once more the portal closed behind her, leaving Connor, Armon, Will and Harry behind.

"Armon," said Joshua kindly, "I would like you to remain here in Judgment with me. There is a lot to be done to restore the order it once had and your help in this matter will clear your debt."

"Then I am honoured for the opportunity," replied Armon as he bowed his head in respect.

"Will!" the Oracle continued. "I have already made contact with Camella and her brother. I would like you to join your father and the Butterhawks and help to restore Judgment."

Will's face lit up at the mention of Camella's name, and then he tried to contain his excitement.

"I'd love to spend time with my father . . . and Camella," he replied as nonchalantly as he could. "Of course I'll stay."

Connor nudged his friend in boyish jibe.

"Camella, aye," he joked. "So you have a thing for the Butterhawk?"

"And you can talk," retorted Will. "From what I hear, you and Nuwa Lin didn't do so badly either."

"I don't know what you mean," replied Connor. "I'm not very good with relationships." And then he winked.

"Connor," said Joshua as he interrupted the juvenile rapport, "that only leaves your reward."

"Reward!" echoed Connor. "I don't expect a reward. What I did was the expectation of the Dream Lord."

"Maybe so," mused the Oracle, "but your sacrifice was more than any Dream Lord before you. For your part in saving Judgment, I would like to give you a choice. You may pass through the pathways of Judgment and be reunited with your family, or you may stay here and help restore the balance. Once this is completed you may then pass over but, be warned, this could take many years to conclude."

Connor looked behind the Oracle, where the portal had once been and where he knew his parents were waiting. Then he looked at Will and Armon and turned back to Joshua and smiled.

⚜ ⚜ ⚜

Jasmine opened her eyes and sat up. Beside her lay the lifeless body of the Dream Lord. Memories of their last goodbye filled her mind and tears began to roll down her cheeks once more.

"Goodbye, Connor," she whispered as she kissed his forehead. "I will miss you."

Without a glance behind her, she climbed off the bed and opened the door. Without a word, she slipped outside, shutting it silently behind her. A long half-lit corridor greeted her but she was unfazed. She did not understand how but she knew her way back and before long, she was pushing another door open into the entrance room. There waiting patiently was Kustos. Already his arms were outstretched, waiting for her. She immediately saw him and ran towards him.

"I love you, Kustos," she whispered with tears in her eyes.

"I know," he replied, "but I also know how much you cared for Connor. Be comforted in the belief he has found peace and so should we."

"I will, my love." She smiled as she kissed him.

Hand in hand they walked to the end of the room. The double doors previously opened by Connor and Will slowly moved. There before them was the swirling stairway with four colossus statues guarding either side. Without a word they stepped forward just in time to see Vanisheo melt back into the Untouched Forest. The doors behind them sealed themselves once more, exposing the marking of passage. Perhaps another era, another day, someone worthy of such an accolade would use them again.

"Are you ready?" Kustos asked his love.

"I'm ready," she said as she smiled.

Together they took one last look at the door and then turned away. A glimmer of light was calling from the far side of the room, and they knew this was their passage back to Sublin and to the rest of their lives.

The Judgment Map

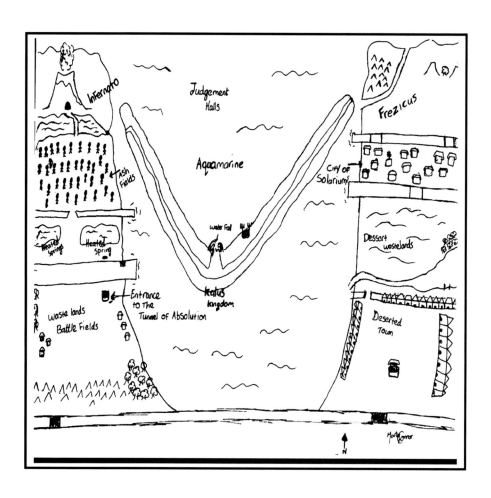

Acknowledgments and Thank Yous

I would like to say a big thank you to King Bad Dog who once again has offered invaluable input to ensure the story line flowed well.

I would like to thank the hard work put in by my publishing team who have spent their time and experience into turning this into a published selling book.

I would like to thank my family and friends whose support has kept me positive even during time when my faith in the story began to waiver. Their encouragement pushed me forward.

Finally but by no means least I would like to thank you for buying and reading our fantasy. My co-writer and I have come a long way since putting together the first two books and as our experience has grown so has our imagination, creating, we hope an escape route for all that read them.

Thank you,
Marty C
Rosie May

Awake (Are We)?
The Saga so far

Part 1 Journey to the Waterfall Kingdom

With the birth of a child comes his impossible destiny. An evil, dark presence hangs menacingly over the fate of two worlds. A war is coming, and no one from the Wake World is aware of the danger. The Shadow Night Lord and his dark army have the world of Sublin dangling on a thread waiting for the time when he can seize the ultimate power of destruction.

Can the One Dreamer of the Wake World harness his own dream energy and stand tall against the power of such an adversary in Sublins darkest hour, or will he be seduced by the rewards of such supremacy? Only the path he chooses can define the fate of the Worlds.

Part 2 The Rebirth of Sublin

It was inevitable that a great war was coming to the world of Sublin. A vast army led by the Metalmares was seen approaching the Waterfall Kingdom with one thought in mind: destroy and control.

The frightened and unprepared citizens led by Kustos stood paralysed on the battlefield. Weapons at the ready, they were set to fight, but were greatly outnumbered and knew it was an impossible task to protect the walls of their kingdom.

Seeing victory in his grasp, the Dark Lord appears before the battered army and confronts the One Dreamer. Is it time for Will to take on the power of the Shadow Night Lord and fulfil his destiny?

The faithful followers of The Waterfall Kingdom think their sacrifice is valid and in an effort to divert the attention of the Dark Lord and hopefully assist the Dreamer in his quest, they come up with a plan. Factions led by Lord Reginald and Lady Joan split up their resources and travel to the far reaches of Sublin to defend its shores, but at the same time, they face their darkest days.